Virtual Arcana

VIRTUAL ARCANA: BOOK 1

VIRTUAL ARCANA

KAREN AMANDA HOOPER

Virtual Arcana

First Edition

ISBN: 978-0-9961470-0-2 (hardback)
ISBN: 978-0-9961470-1-9 (ebook)

Published by Starry Sky Publishing

Cover design and interior artwork by Steve Graham
theinfinitycreative.com

Image credits: Bigstock.com; agsandrew, Atelier Sommerland, bigldesign, conrado, Estteban, mkabakov, Natalia_Rashevska, olly2, Ostill, Rolffimages

Edited by Marie Jaskulka
mariejaskulka.com

Visit author Karen Amanda Hooper at
karenamandahooper.com

Dedicated to Becca Zeno,
inspiring and unstoppable at every level.
You are a talented trump.

0: THE FOOL

Level 0.1

As I stood in the coffee shop waiting for my order, I eyed the girl standing beside me. She was reading an early 22nd-century fantasy novel. Like most interactive books from that era, the book was in bad form. Cover cracked, faded hologram images no longer active, sensors stripped: but it appeared that at some point, every aerogel page must have been dog-eared.

I smiled to myself. Nothing brought me joy like seeing a well-loved book that had survived The Crash and endured the long journey to the present.

I wanted to ask the girl so many questions: How did she come into possession of the novel? Was it her first time reading it? Was she enjoying it? But as the new girl in town, I couldn't summon the courage to speak to a stranger. Or maybe I didn't want to interrupt her while she was reading. To me, escaping reality was a sacred experience which should not be disturbed.

"Kelsey!" the barista shouted over the hiss and gurgling of the machines.

I practically leaped forward, taking my latte from her. "Many thanks."

Besides books, coffee was my other drug of choice. Harmless and oh-so-delicious, it was required for me to stay awake during morning classes—especially on my first day at a new school. I inhaled the rich, minty aroma of my peppermint latte as the exit door slid open. I was certain Caffeine Machine would be my second favorite place in our new town.

The parking lot was crowded, but I spotted my sister waiting in the second row. I squeezed between our piece of junk craft and the newer, but modest model parked beside it. A steaming cup sat on the roof of the neighboring craft. The guy in the driver's seat powered up and hovered.

I knocked on the window and he turned. His questioning eyes met mine through the pane of glass.

I pointed to the cup on his roof. "Your coffee."

"What?" he mouthed as his window lowered.

I reached up, grabbing his drink then handing it to him. "You forgot something."

He bashfully grinned while taking the cup from me, but his fingers pressed over mine during the hand-off. A spark of excitement made me tingle. The dark-haired stranger was totally my type. My preference wasn't the hot model or jock, but the much more hard to find subtle sort of attractive. Blessed with a baby face, radiating confidence with no hint of ego, he'd befriend everyone from a science geek to the prom queen. I liked the type who flew low under the drama radar like me.

"Many thanks." His voice was deeper than I expected but almost as warm as the beverages we were holding. "Losing my coffee would have started my day off horribly."

I wriggled my fingers free from his and let go. "I wouldn't wish that sort of tragedy on my worst enemy."

"Kelsey!" My sister, Keekee, shouted from her driver's seat. "Come on. We'll be late!"

I offered a quick wave and turned to open our craft door, but Mr. Smooth-voice asked, "Are you new around here?"

"Moved into town yesterday." I grimaced as the passenger door squeaked open. Between the two of us, you'd think Keekee and I could earn enough for a newer craft or at least basic repairs, but instead I blew my funds on books and coffee. She preferred clothes and enhancement candies.

"On your way to Century High?" Coffee Forgetter nodded at the high-rise school nestled in the cityscape. The sun wasn't up yet, so the skyline looked gray and ominous.

I raised my cup. "Indeed, I am. My first day swimming with the sharks. May the odds be ever in my favor."

He laughed. "Based on your quote, I assume you enjoy reading the classics."

"Guilty."

"What's your favorite novel?"

Cute *and* knew the way to a book lover's heart. "Shouldn't you ask my name before you ask about my reading preferences?"

"Your name is Kelsey." His chin jutted upward, motioning to my loudmouthed sister behind me. "Which is lovely, but only tells me that your parents, or at least one of them, preferred old-fashioned names. I'd much rather know the name of your favorite book because that will reveal volumes of information about *you.*"

A nervous but flattered chuckle caught in my throat. My first impression was correct—he was smart and perceptive. And growing more attractive with every word he spoke.

"I've never been able to choose a favorite," I admitted. "I like variety."

His hazel eyes gleamed with mischief. He set his coffee in his cup holder, reached into his pocket, and handed me a shiny card. "I'll see you around, Kelsey."

I took the card from him and glanced at the colorful artwork. "What's this?"

"That's step zero."

"Step zero?"

He lowered his voice. "Don't let anyone see it, especially at school."

His window raised, and he gripped his wheel.

"Wait." I tapped on the glass. "I don't know your name."

I was sure he heard me, but he didn't answer or look in my direction again as his craft rose into the air and glided out of the parking lot.

"Kelsey!" Keekee snapped. "Get in right now before I leave you here."

I slid into the passenger seat and sipped my drink. "Did you see that guy?"

"I caught a glimpse of him. I wasn't impressed. Definitely not worth being late on our first day."

We lifted into the air, our craft sputtering like usual. "He was the perfect mix of adorable, friendly, and intriguing."

"No boy distractions allowed," Keek reminded me. "We both need stellar grades this year so we can get accepted into a foreign college and escape this soul-sucking nation."

We merged with the traffic pulling into the school zone. As always, Keekee kept her focus on the sky in front of her. She was the most responsible person I knew—well, besides her illegal addiction to gaming, which, ironically, was the reason she had been expelled from three schools in three years. And why we were starting our senior year in the city of Elura where we knew no one.

Keek was busted (again) with a VR gaming card at the end of our junior year. The court systems were so overtaxed with offenders that it took until the end of the summer for her trial date, which included a verdict on whether she would be allowed to return to school. Mom and Dad loved our previous hometown, so they fought hard to have Keek's expulsion pardoned so we could stay, but as always, our nation's laws could not be bent.

Equatia consisted of five cities, and we had been banished from three of them. Elura was our last chance to maintain any sense of freedom. After that, the only place left to live would be HE—the hub of Equatia. The Hub was the center of our nation where *everyone* worked for the government for the rest of their lives. The only way to retire from that station was death.

I cringed at the thought and forced my brain to switch gears.

Sipping my coffee, I admired the artwork on the card the stranger had given me. One side was a black background with a golden eye staring at me from the cross of a letter *T.* On the other, a colorfully dressed jester appeared to be dancing in a spiraling, starry sky. *The Fool* was printed under his well-worn, curly-toed shoes. Above his silly hat was the number *0.*

What did step zero mean? And what was Coffee Forgetter's name? Hopefully, he went to Century High so I could have my questions answered. I sighed and tucked the card into my bag.

The sun was cresting the horizon, creating hints of orange and pink in the sky. One quick moving cloud briefly looked like a question mark, but then it stretched apart, resembling the whipped cream topping on my latte.

Sadly, my drink had a bitter aftertaste, which meant Caffeine Machine used cheap or stale beans. I hoped there was another dispenser in Elura who used higher quality ingredients or it would be a very long and depressing school year.

Sitting in our craft, staring out the window at the surrounding traffic, I was clueless that my 7 am pit stop at the coffee shop was the catalyst to a much different and infinitely more powerful addiction.

Level 0.2

I sat in my last class of the day with a caffeine-deprived headache and no sign of the cute Coffee Forgetter since the parking lot. I couldn't even ask anyone about him because I didn't know his name. Not like I was a social butterfly, but I had met a few decent people with friend potential. I heeded Coffee Forgetter's warning to not show his mystery card to anyone. He and his card were my own private secret, and that thought made me feel less alone in the crowded halls of Century High.

Our history teacher, Mrs. Linker, went through roll call then handed out EVRAs. Educational Virtual Reality Apparatuses were the worst. The oculars never sat comfortably over my eyes, and I almost always felt dizzy, nauseous, or both after a session. A virtual reality history lesson is just what I needed to aggravate my headache.

The complete opposite of me, my sister would trade her left arm—and maybe her leg—to own an EVRA and use it to play illegal video games. They were forbidden because, in no way, shape, or form was partaking in magical quests or digitally killing others considered educational. But Keekee drank the gamer poison a few years ago at a party and had been hooked ever since.

I hated that schools still used EVRAs for educational purposes, but expected VR addicts to resist the temptation to use them for personal entertainment. Punishments for VR violations were more lenient since we were under eighteen, but that would change in three months.

"Before you activate your EVRAs," the teacher drawled, "I'd like to review a few points. Pay close attention if you aim to pass Friday's quiz." A quiz the first week? I groaned along with the rest of my classmates.

Mrs. Linker looked to be in her late twenties. Her young age and her bob of unnaturally white hair had given me false hope that she'd be one of those cool eccentric teachers who didn't conform to strict educational policies. Another case of looks being deceiving.

"Make notes on the key players who paved the way for advances in space travel and exploration," she continued. "Prepare to present a strong defense on why you agree or disagree with restrictions on who is allowed to journey off this rock we call Earth, while others will never be afforded such an opportunity." She took a deep breath. "I'm sure the conversation will wander into a debate about why we should or shouldn't be allowed unrestricted travel and interaction with other nations. I'll permit it as long as you *intelligently* defend your opinion."

My brows shot up along with many others as looks of surprise emerged throughout the room. A teacher giving us permission to openly disagree with Equatia's ban on foreign travel and communication with nations other than our own? Last period just became a heck of a lot more interesting. I mentally checked a couple boxes on Mrs. Linker's score sheet: brave and controversial.

Keekee would be so jealous that I had a teacher who allowed students to express Old World belief in freedom of speech. I wondered if Mrs. Linker would also let us voice our opinions on ceaseless citizen monitoring and controlled usage of just about everything.

"Don't get all excited." Mrs. Linker waved her hands to quiet the buzz of conversations. "I'm not suggesting anyone take a stand against Equatia and its laws. All I'm striving for is those brains of yours to be activated by dignified debate and conversation, instead of daydreaming about how to score your next enhancement candy."

Giggles and snickers filled the room. I liked her and her five-seasons-ago neon-colored sweater vest. I admired her wanting to teach us through discussions instead of slapping EVRAs on our heads for an hour and letting technology supposedly educate us like most history teachers did.

I pressed balance patches behind my ears to prevent the virtual-reality-induced vertigo I despised so much. Mrs. Linker instructed us to secure our EVRAs and begin.

I placed mine on my head, pulled down the oculars, and inserted my access card. The intro tones beeped in my ears as I adjusted the volume. A blue sky flooded my vision as birds circled an ancient NASA rocket preparing to take off from its extinct location of Port Something-or-other in the no-longer-existing United States.

The narrator's crackly voice began his dissertation on astronauts of the Old World.

As the rocket roared to life and launched itself from a cloud of smoke, the picture flickered and I noticed a few pixels missing from my screen. I turned my head, but the image lagged and grew blurry. Apparently, the Elura school system received the same crappy EVRAs as my other schools. With all the so-called advancements of technology, you would think someone could design a virtual reality system that felt, oh, I don't know, like *reality*.

I slumped back into my chair and waited for the torture to end.

Fifteen minutes into the snoozefest about the first family to live in space, and what a catastrophic crime it was against the natural order of our universe, a familiar voice—outside of my EVRA—snapped me to attention and made my heart race.

"On behalf of the Elura Enforcement Division, I apologize for the interruption," the smooth, deep voice said. "You have an L-22 violator whom we must arrest."

I pushed my EVRA up my forehead, half-expecting to see Coffee Forgetter in an enforcer's uniform because the voice sounded like his, but nope, not even close. The enforcer flashing his badge was much older with graying hair and the same empty expression worn by all government drudges.

A kid sitting three rows in front of me threw back his chair, EVRA still on his head, and bolted up the aisle in my direction. Before Mrs. Linker could utter a word, the enforcer was right behind him. Another enforcer had come through the back door and also rushed the perp.

The three of them ended up beside my desk, so close I could have reached forward and touched the ghost-white hands of the violator being lasercuffed.

"I didn't do anything wrong," the kid spewed, saliva flying from his trembling lips. "I was using the access card the teacher gave me."

One enforcer took the card from the accused's EVRA with a gloved hand and slid it into an evidence bag. The other enforcer yanked the kid's wrist and scanned his govern band then his irises. He recited Equatia's reticence rights to Devlin Templeton, fourth-time offender, born the sixteenth day of 101 Post Crash. My breath hitched as I did the math. It was the sixty-fourth day of 119 PC, which meant Devlin was eighteen.

He would be convicted as an adult.

Devlin's EVRA crashed onto the floor. His terrified dilated pupils bore into me as the enforcers dragged him away. A copper-haired girl in the front row cried out his name then burst into tears.

As the classroom door slammed shut behind the enforcers and their latest victim, Mrs. Linker braced herself on her desk and bowed her head. The rest of the class was so silent I heard the teacher next door lecturing to his students about molecular structure. The crying girl lifted her head from her arms long enough to sob for air. I swallowed the lump in my throat, feeling sorry for her and the detainee who was probably her boyfriend.

Cringing, I imagined where Devlin was being taken and what might be happening to him. Or worse, what *would* happen to him. He would be sentenced to permanent reprogramming. His mind would be wiped clean of everything, except the information and orders programmed into him by the government. Most likely, Devlin would serve the rest of his life as an enforcer, helping to sentence other law violators to his same, zombie-like fate.

After the government was done with him, he'd no longer remember the crying girl in the front row. Or anyone else who knew him. He wouldn't remember anything except how to be a drudge.

I stared at the illegally used EVRA still lying on the floor near my feet.

Another Equatia citizen would become a slave because he rebelled against the system.

Level 0.3

After a tense and sad last half of class, everyone's govern bands chirped, signaling the end of our school day. I turned in my EVRA, hurried down the maze of hallways and stairs and walked through the sliding doors near the seniors' fourth-floor parking garage.

I was free.

Well, not really. No citizen of Equatia was ever truly free.

I met Keekee by our craft.

"You pilot," she said. "Today nearly killed me."

Overdramatic as usual. "I bet what happened in my last class will far outweigh any drama that happened in your day."

She held up her hand. "Tell me later. I seriously can't handle anymore until I've decompressed."

"Fine, but we're stopping at Caffeine Machine. I need a caramel latte stat." Their coffee was mediocre, but one particular patron made up for it, and I hoped I'd see him there again.

"You didn't use your second allotment at lunch?"

"They didn't have flavored coffees. I wasn't wasting my afternoon fix on stale brew that the lunch ladies probably spit in." I rubbed my temple. "But the capillaries in my brain are punishing me for that decision."

"You know I'd give you my share if I could."

It was a true tragedy that Keekee's caffeine allotments were wasted every day. She wasn't a fan of coffee, disliked the carbonation of soda, and most of her favorite teas were caffeine free.

"Have our weekly funds been deposited yet?" Keek checked her balance on her govern band then pumped her fist. "Yes. Thank the stars. I could use the restorative effects of a chocolate rod."

Mom and I had a theory that enhancement candies were created to give Equatians a false sense of liberty. Candies were the one *supposedly* mood-altering substance that the government didn't restrict, mainly because only positive flavors were allowed: calming, restorative, joyous, focus, stress-relief, etc. But Mom and I agreed that the infusions used to allegedly enhance one's mood were most likely placebos. Effective placebos—people went nuts over them—but still, a waste of funds and a deception to the taste buds.

Keekee collapsed forward, letting her forehead smash against the dashboard. "How can we have no classes together, not even lunch?"

"Mom said they'd probably separate us." I navigated our craft out of the crowded parking garage as she continued whining.

"Don't they know you're my only hope of staying out of trouble?"

"I'm sure they saw our violator reports and figured we'd get in more trouble if we were together." I winced at the awful memory from our freshman year. Enforcers hauling Keekee and me away in lasercuffs didn't exactly rank in my top ten moments of life.

When we were little, consumption monitors hadn't been embedded in our govern bands, so Keekee would order sodas but sneak them to me. Mom and Dad allowed it until bands were "upgraded" to report how much caffeine—and every other food or beverage—was consumed by each citizen. If a person went over their allotment, an enforcer showed up within minutes. Home, coffee shop, craft: there was no hiding or running from them.

When I was seven years old, my parents were fed up with me throwing temper tantrums about wanting more gingerale. My dad made an arrangement with an enforcer and allowed me to drink Keekee's soda one time, so the enforcer would show up and scare me straight. It worked.

At age fifteen, I drank my first latte and quickly became a coffee addict. The second semester of our sophomore year, Keek's rebel boyfriend swore he figured out a way to outsmart our consumption monitors. Keek ordered a coffee for me, and like a hopeful idiot, I drank it. Within five minutes, we received a stern and frightening reminder that sharing controlled substances was forbidden. Enforcers busted us at school, during lunch, and hauled us away while all of our classmates watched. That humiliating day was the last time we broke the law regarding caffeine consumption. I'd been an obedient rule follower ever since.

I shook off the bad memory as we glided into the parking lot of Caffeine Machine. The smell of roasting coffee beans made me feel better. I did need a fix, but I was also somewhat hopeful that mystery guy would be there again.

"I hate our new school," Keekee grumbled.

"You've hated every school we've ever attended."

"And for good reason." She turned toward me as if her head weighed a hundred pounds. "We were born in the wrong era, you know?"

"I know." I smoothed down her dashboard-frazzled hair. "You wish we lived in the Old World, back when virtual reality gaming was at its peak."

"I'd even settle for the archaic days when people played on television screens." She pinched my side and I squirmed. "Back when your precious books were still made with paper."

I flicked her nose because that annoyed her as much as her tickling my side annoyed me. "I don't make fun of your hobbies. Don't mock mine."

"At least yours are legal." She sat back and sighed. The weight of her guilt seemed to push her deeper into her seat. "I'm sorry about all this. I'm sorry I got caught and that we had to move again and that Mom and Dad are always disappointed. Even though it's my fault, and they should only take it out on me, you also end up suffering."

"I'm not suffering. I'm fine." I shut down the craft. From the heavy silence hanging between us, I chose my next words carefully. "But you do have to stop. Our birthday is in three months, and I don't want to see you mind-stripped and turned into a drudge."

"That will never happen."

"It will happen if they bust you after we're eighteen." My voice trembled. "They hauled a guy away today in my history class because he was using a contraband VR card. He's eighteen. He's done. His life is no longer his own, and he hadn't even graduated high school yet."

Keekee's eyes were mixed with horror and sadness. "Glitch. That sucks so bad."

I reached across the center console and held her hand. "You're my other half. I can't lose you. You have to quit—for good—before I become sisterless."

"I'm trying to quit. I swear."

"Don't try. Just stop. It's that simple."

"Really?" She glared at me with one side of her mouth turned up in a smirk. "That's like me telling you to stop reading books. We're both addicted to the escape. And who can blame us? Our nation is hell and fictional worlds give us access to heaven."

I had said it a million times, so I already knew her reply, but I tried anyway. "Books are a legal escape. You should read more."

Her mind didn't work like mine. She couldn't focus or remember anything she read. She claimed her eyes would scan the lines of text while she thought about a million different things. She'd flip through a few pages then realize she hadn't absorbed any of what she'd read.

Keek didn't repeat what I already knew. She only shook her head and said, "I wish it were that easy."

Squeezing my hand, she stared out her window. We sighed in unison, both of us yearning for the thing we couldn't have as a citizen of Equatia. Freedom.

I scanned the lot for Coffee Forgetter's craft, but he wasn't there.

"We'll have to order our stuff to go," Keekee said. "I have a punishment to endure."

When we arrived home, Mom met us in the foyer. As usual, flour and splatters of other baking ingredients decorated her apron. She tightened her polka-dot bandana that was attempting (and failing) to keep her thick brown curls tamed.

"First day verdict?" She held up one thumb while the other pointed down. Keekee and I both gave her thumbs down. "Darn. Well, it's only the first day. Give it time."

We hung our bags on the hooks by the front door then followed Mom into the kitchen so we could raid whatever food she'd been making for her catering gig.

"Bad news, lovebug," Mom said to Keekee. "I ordered the wrong series from the library. You'll have to go swap it out for the correct card."

Keekee groaned and turned to me, batting her eyelashes. "Kelsey, please, please, *please* go to the library for me. You know how much I hate that place." I waited for her offer. She always provided one even though she didn't need to. "I'll buy you a latte tomorrow morning before school."

"Deal." I happily stuck out my pinky and she shook it with hers. I loved libraries, as long as they had an Olden section with real books, which I was sure Elura Library must have because the city was the largest of the five in Equatia. We'd been so busy unpacking that I hadn't had a chance to visit yet, but I had planned on exploring it this evening. Keek paying for my latte was pure bonus.

"I already called and put the correct card on hold," Mom told me. "It's waiting at the checkout desk."

"What's the title?" I asked. "I don't want to bring home the wrong one again."

Mom went back to work with her rolling pin. "Exemplifications of the 1950s, or something along those lines."

"Sounds thrilling." Keekee popped a food ball into her mouth. I reached for one, but she grabbed my hand and shook her head. "Coconut."

I pretended to gag while Mom spoke in her authoritative voice to Keekee. "You have one week to complete your rehab sentence, and you still have two series to complete. You need to take this seriously and finish soon so it doesn't interfere with your schoolwork. The rest of us are sacrificing this week's entertainment allotments so you can use the holosplay, and you know how cranky your father gets when he can't watch his favorite shows."

Keekee's *rehabilitation* consisted of immersive programs that taught valuable lessons from the past: family appreciation, manners, respect for others and rules, etc. She had already *endured* the 1930s and 40s series. She pretended to hate them so Mom and Dad wouldn't issue any additional punishments, but Keekee confided to me that she enjoyed watching people from the Old World days.

Mom and Dad had bought a few Olden games in an attempt to legally feed Keekee's gaming appetite, but Keek said pushing pegs around a game board and exchanging ancient cash was nowhere near as exciting as VR gaming. Even Mom and Dad poked fun at how ridiculous it was that people used to carry around paper money, but I liked the idea of tangible currency. The same way I loved paper books.

I didn't enjoy reading novels electronically on my band. Even with the expanded screen, it strained my eyes. Old interactive books were a little better. At least they had aerogel pages that never faded, but many of the written details had been removed from the story because sensors provided all the physical sensations for the reader. Over time, all sensors had either stopped working or been stripped, leaving out some of the best parts of a story.

Finding rare paper editions I hadn't read yet was challenging, but that made it even more rewarding to locate a great classic like *The Girl of Fire and Thorns*. I was itching to get to the Elura library to see what treasures I could find.

"I'm off to fetch Keek's ticket to the past," I announced.

"Be careful," Mom warned. "The traffic filling the skies around here worries me, and your father still needs to fix the collision shields on your craft."

"I'll be fine." I blew kisses to her and Keekee then headed out the front door.

Traveling from our landing pad to the library's lot took me five minutes. I could walk if I wanted, which would be convenient on the evenings Keekee used our craft to go out and socialize. I preferred snuggling up with a book and hanging out with fictional friends.

The library was like something out of my dreams. Pillars three stories high framed the main entrance. Wide steps spanned across the front of the entire building. I skipped up them two at a time, dying to get inside and start exploring.

The inside was as impressive as the outside. Two higher floors surrounded the main level. Shiny wood railings of the balconies glistened as sunbeams poured through the dome skylight in the ceiling. I'd heard of places called churches in the Old World, beautiful holy buildings where people repeatedly gathered to feel uplifted. Based on that description, I deemed Elura library my church.

First things first, I walked up to the counter and set down the time series card Mom had given me to exchange. I pressed the help button and a pleasant automated voice alerted someone in the back room that assistance was needed.

A noise that sounded like metal chair legs sliding across the floor was followed by a deep clearing of a throat.

I sucked in a breath and stood up straight as Coffee Forgetter stepped into view.

Level 0.4

Running his hand through his brown hair, he sounded even sexier than he did this morning. “Well, hello again, Kelsey.”

He remembered my name. My insides stirred as he smiled at me.

“Hello again, Coffee Forgetter. Now I see why you asked about my love of books. You work here.” *At the most amazing library I’ve ever seen,* I wanted to add.

“My parents continuously preached that I should choose a job doing something I’m passionate about. It’s one of the few times I listened.”

“It’s my dream to work in a place like this,” I said. “Or in book restoration services.”

“Protect stories so they continue to be passed down to future generations?”

I wanted to tell him my goal was to ensure people always had the option to live other lives, to experience worlds different from our own, to evolve by experiencing, feeling, and learning through countless journeys of others—even if only fictional. Instead, I replied, “Something like that.”

He squinted like he was contemplating whether or not he believed me. “Okay, then answer this: Earth is about to be destroyed. You have time to grab one book before you’re whisked away to safety. Which story do you save?”

I grinned smugly. “I’d find a way to save all the good ones.”

“Ah, but there’s the rub. In such a subjective world, who determines which ones qualify as good?”

“Great question. Perhaps I’ll create a system that unbiasedly sorts out those worthy of surviving.”

His head dipped as his jaw shifted like he was trying not to smile. “Let me know if you need any help with that system.”

His flirty tone left me too giddy to think of a clever reply.

I glanced behind me at the three-story atrium. "This place looks pretty spectacular."

"Upstairs is, but you're here at the access card desk instead of in the Olden section. You strike me as the type who walks the aisles inhaling the scent of old paper, so what are you doing down here?"

Was I that transparent, or did every book-lover indulge in my same stroll-and-sniff method?

I slid the card across the counter. "I'm returning this and picking up a different brainwashing series for my delinquent sister."

"Ahh. So that makes you the good twin." His eyes twinkled in a way that made my cheeks warm.

"Supposedly."

He rapped his knuckles on the counter between us. "I already pulled the 1950s vacuum-while-wearing-pearls-and-never-swear-in-public series for the woman I'm assuming was your mother who called a while ago. Let me grab it for you."

I chuckled while bouncing on the balls of my feet. Add sense of humor to his list of attractive qualities.

He returned with a new card and scanned it before handing it to me. Seemed he was always handing me a card of some sort. However, unlike this morning, our fingers never touched, and I was more disappointed about that than I should have been.

"So," I said casually, trying to act like I hadn't been wondering about his *step zero* card all day. "The card you gave me this morning. What is it?"

His eyes flitted around, searching behind me while his lips semi-pouted as he told me to shhh. I bit my lip and glanced over my shoulder at the not-so-busy library around us.

He leaned on the counter and quietly asked, "Would you like to meet me out front in the park at 8 when I get off of work?"

Whoa. Was he asking me on a date? Or just suggesting some random meet-up that required next to no effort from him?

"From there," he continued, "I was going to suggest we could go for coffee and conversation, but we could meet at a coffee shop if you'd be more comfortable that way."

Definitely a date, or at least a decent prequel to a real one. I'd never been so glad that I hadn't used my third and last caffeine allotment of the day, but I willed my voice to sound nonchalant. "I can probably meet you at Caffeine Machine."

His eyes narrowed as if he could see all my secrets, and then his lips tugged upward, approving of what he discovered. "Am I correct to assume you're a caffeine addict?"

"Guilty."

"Good." He leaned closer, and I could smell a hint of cinnamon on his breath. "I like addicts."

Something sort of sinister tainted his words, but his expression remained warm and alluring. It reminded me of a bad boy intro scene from one of my novels—the obvious red flag waving as two characters start their unhealthy relationship. As a reader, I would have been yelling at the oblivious MC, telling her to find a guy who wasn't already being described with words like *sinister,* but the witty, polite, twinkling-eyed librarian standing in front of me hadn't demonstrated any of the other bad boy tells.

"You said you'd *probably* meet me," he reminded me. "What do I have to do to turn that into a *definitely?*"

My stomach was flip-flopping in the best way possible, but I refused to be one of those giggling girls who couldn't think or form coherent sentences because an attractive guy was flirting with them. I spoke confidently, but with a hint of flirtation. "I'll meet you only if you tell me your name."

He stood up straight, his short-sleeve shirt stretching tight against lean arm muscles. "My name is Xander."

Xander, I mentally purred as if he'd said the name of the most delicious latte in the world. Even his name sounded astute.

Stay composed, Kels, I told myself. *A guy like Xander wants a challenge, someone confident who plays it cool.*

I slid the new access card into the back pocket of my pants. Citizens were forbidden to show their legs in public, but thankfully V-neck tops were allowed, and I just happened to be wearing one. I pulled my shoulders back and slightly stuck out my chest. It was the same move executed by a slutty character in a trashy novel that I rated as tasteless. I had sunk to a new level.

Xander's focus stayed locked on my face, not even a quick flicker to check out my natural assets. "I look forward to learning more about you, Kelsey, the book-loving caffeine addict."

I grinned and stepped back to leave. I didn't notice my fingers were plastered to the counter in front of me until he slid his hands forward and our fingertips touched. It was like wires connected and sent a dizzying electrical current coursing through me.

My body-monitoring chips were probably sending alerts to a proctor. The excessive firing of neurons in my brain would surely earn me an intrusive questioning session later. I wanted to rip off my govern band so nosy proctors couldn't spy on me, but that would only send up a bigger red flag. I held up my wrist while eyeing his band. "Should we exchange contact info?"

He hesitated. "I think it would be best if we waited."

"Xander, dear!" A nasally female voice exclaimed from behind me. Startled, and confused as to why he'd ask me out but not exchange contact info, I shoved my hands in my pockets.

"But soon, I promise," Xander said before raising his focus to the patron behind me. "Hello, Mrs. Perkins. How are you this afternoon?"

He winked at me. "See you at 8:06."

"8:06?" I asked.

"My shift ends at 8. It takes me ten minutes to get to Caffeine Machine. But for you, I'll make it there in six."

I tried not to tuck my hair behind my ears and blush like a smitten schoolgirl, but I failed. In less than one day, I had developed an undeniable twitterpation with a stranger named Xander.

Nasally Mrs. Perkins glanced between us unapprovingly then asked Xander about his recommendations for a good thriller, so I headed upstairs to the Olden section.

Stepping onto the escalator, I looked at Xander again. He kept talking to the woman, but his eyes darted away from her and met mine. He didn't do the typical nervous double take. His gaze locked on me, confident and smoldering, as I rode to the third floor.

After I was out of his view, I hid behind a wall and happy-danced like a maniac. Somewhere a proctor was most definitely getting an alert that Kelsey Zellar was abnormally excited with hormones raging.

The rush supplied by the charming guy downstairs lasted less than a minute, because my attention turned to the rows and rows of books beckoning me. Xander and all his endearing qualities faded from my mind with each step I took toward the Olden section.

I walked down the first aisle, running my fingers over the spines, humming with joy and adoration for each book. My love for novels far surpassed any feelings I had ever felt for a boy. As one of my favorite Old World authors, Marie Jaskulka, once said: Guys are temporary. Fiction is forever.

Level 0.5

Returning home was a buzz kill.

I lingered by the front door when I heard Mom and Keekee going at it in the kitchen.

"I'm being realistic," Mom argued. "You have a delinquent record as high as a skyscraper. The likelihood of another nation accepting a new citizen with that kind of background is slim."

Keekee defended her dream. "Somewhere that offers more freedom won't care that I've been caught gaming or gifting coffee to my sister."

"We don't know if places like that exist."

"Mother, don't be so naive. You've heard the stories too. You know every nation is not a prison like ours."

"Stories. Exactly. Which means we don't know for sure what else is out there. What if you're accepted into a nation with laws stricter than ours?"

"Don't insult my intelligence."

I rubbed my temples, preparing to walk into the sticky web my sister and mother had spun. Keekee's eyes lit up as soon as I rounded the corner.

"Kelsey, tell Mom our plan is failsafe."

I shook my head while opening the fridge and grabbing a water pac to drink. "Nothing is failsafe when it comes to escaping Equatia."

"Look," Mom said, lifting Keekee's chin and softening her tone. "You know I love you and I'm always open to discussing improving your life and future, so we will chat more about this later. Right now I have to deliver these platters to an event."

Keekee nodded as Mom kissed the top of her head. I grabbed a couple trays of food to carry out to Mom's craft.

Mom gushed about her VIP clients and how she hoped tonight went well because these were the type of people who had events catered on a weekly basis. They could provide steady income while she built up new clientele. As much as Mom loved her catering business, we all knew she could go only so far with it.

Dad's new job landed him a salary that was fairly close to the maximum total income allotted for our household. Mom could cater two gigs a week and then our parents would make more than the government allowed a family in our financial bracket. Any additional income earned would be granted to charities. Keekee believed charity was a fake, feel-good word for government coffers, and we all believed she was right.

Keek and I loaded Mom's craft, wished her luck, and went back inside.

My headstrong sister wasted no time. "You still believe in our plan, right? You're still going with me?"

I took a deep breath. "Of course. Double trouble forever, right?"

"You do believe there are better options? Nations where we won't be told what we can eat or drink, if we're gaining too much weight, where we're allowed to travel, or how we can entertain ourselves?"

"I want to believe it."

She whined. "Kelsey."

"I love you too much to lie to you. I *want* to believe. That's all I can offer without proof."

"But you are going to apply for a foreign release with me, right?"

"I promised you I would."

Applying to continue education in a different nation was an insult to our government, and one which they didn't take lightly. We had heard of a few people who were accepted to college in different countries, but once they left Equatia, they lost their citizenship and weren't allowed to return. We'd never personally known anyone who was granted departure, but underground gospel warned that if you left for a foreign college, your family went with you—unless you never wanted to see or speak to them again.

For years, Keekee had been trying to persuade Mom and Dad to leave Equatia with us. They always considered it, always heard her out, never told her to stop dreaming of a different life, but she had never gotten them to actually agree.

I agreed last year. I pinky swore that I would apply for foreign release and venture into the unknown with blind hope that another nation might be better than ours. Friends from our last school told me I was stupid to go along with Keekee's plan because we couldn't know what went on "out there" beyond the strictly protected borders of our nation. Others swore foreign releases were a myth and those "approved" for release were secretly killed.

None of those friends had a twin, so they didn't understand my decision. I had always—and would always—do anything for my sister.

I handed her the new access card from the library. "I need to use our craft tonight."

"Fine with me." She flipped the card around her fingers like a true gamer. "I'll be watching this relic program until my eyes bleed." She turned and inserted the card into the holosplay reader on our family room wall. The hologram viewing screen shimmered to life across from us. "Wait a sec, where are you going?"

"I'm meeting someone for coffee."

"*Someone?*" Her eyebrows lifted. "A new friend from school?"

"Not exactly."

"Then who?"

I fought back a grin. "The guy from the coffee shop parking lot this morning."

"What? You saw him again?"

"He works at the library."

"Oh, glitch." She flopped into a chair. "Kels, don't you dare go falling for some guy and then bail on our plan because you think you're in love."

Love? She knew me better than that. I never let myself use the *L* word about a guy unless he was a character in a novel. "I'm not. I'll keep it light and fun."

"Two semesters. Then we're out of here. That's not enough time to figure out if he's worth staying for, but it's plenty of time to become attached and shatter your heart into pieces when we leave." She leaned forward, her eyes softening with concern. "Don't set yourself up for heartache."

"Don't worry. I'm not prone to falling in love like you." I regretted the words as soon as the pain registered on Keek's face.

She had fallen in love two years ago. She and Zane were the perfect couple. Then they were busted gaming together. His family and ours were issued relocation orders, and both parents agreed that Keekee and Zane should have no future contact with each other. We have no idea where they moved, and Keek had never been the same since.

"Wrong," Keekee said wistfully. "If you find someone, or something, that makes you deliriously happy, anyone can become an addict." Her brow creased. "I feel like a horrible person for saying this, but don't let him make you deliriously happy."

I tried to lighten the mood with sarcasm. "I'll ask Xander to make a concerted effort to make me miserable."

"Xander," she said, scrunching up her nose. "His name even sounds like trouble."

I laughed. "It does not."

"Seriously, there will be plenty of guys in your future, but first, we have to get away from this nightmare nation. Don't get hooked on this Xander guy."

"Keek, we're having coffee together, not making babies."

She leveled me with a mocking, playful glare. "I've always encouraged you to just say no to coffee."

"Impossible. Coffee is too delectable." I shrugged and raised my hands, reciting the same excuse she offered every time she was busted for playing VR games. "Without it, I feel dead inside."

"Just be sure you don't ever tell me the same thing about Xander."

Level 0.6

The glowing numbers above the roasting machines changed from 8:06 to 8:07 pm.

He was late.

The glass door slid open and two girls walked in laughing and heading straight for the display case of muffins and candies. No sign of Xander behind them.

What if he didn't show?

Who cares? He's just a guy, I thought, running my fingernail along the grooves in the table where a previous customer had carved *Peace, love, and coffee.* Granted, Xander was charming, worked at the most spectacular library I'd ever visited, made my stomach flip-flop and the rest of me do a happy dance, but he was still a real-life guy, which meant eventually all his inadequacies would surface. I'd be disappointed because, never ever had a real guy lived up to my expectations set by romance books. Unless Xander's last name was Darcy, Fraser, Mellark, or Luna, I'd find a dozen flaws and be bored of him by the end of the week.

The glass door swooshed open and Xander strode into the shop.

He slid into the seat across from me. His smooth olive-toned cheeks were tinted a shade of pink and he was short of breath. "Hi."

"You're late." I managed to keep a straight face, but he didn't.

"I'm sorry." His grin was contagious. "Please forgive me."

"Okay, but only because you're tardy by one minute. If it were two, I wouldn't be so forgiving."

"Noted for future dates." Future dates? This one had barely begun, but he was already planning more? "You look beautiful," he said sweetly. "I like your hair that way."

I tugged at one of the curls framing my now-flushed face. "Thank you."

He kept grinning, but shifted in his seat and glanced at the counter. "What would you like? I'll go order for us."

"A macadamia nut latte, please."

"Good choice. Any candies?"

I bit my bottom lip, fighting back a full-blown smile while trying to sound serious. "Are you implying I need personality enhancements?"

"Not at all." He leaned across the table and spoke quieter. "But if I make you even a fraction of how excited you make me, then I thought we could both use a confidence cream or a calming chew."

Could he speak one sentence without making me blush? "I suppose one calming chew wouldn't hurt."

"Good choice. We don't need kibz drilling us with questions about our accelerated heart rates."

"Kibz?"

"Kibitzers. The more appropriate name for proctors. It means busybody hecklers."

I laughed. "Very appropriate. Mind if I steal your word for future griping?"

That made him sort of giggle but in a manly way. "It's all yours. Lavender or vanilla?"

"Lavender, please."

He held out his hand for my govern band.

I pressed the *Request* button and reported my situation as required by law. "Temporary band removal for—" I paused, searching for the appropriate term for Xander. "A *friend* placing my coffee order." After *Granted* flashed on my screen, I disconnected the sensor from the chip embedded in my wrist and handed him my band.

"Be right back, *friend.*" He turned and walked to the counter to order while I blew out an elated breath.

The rear view of him was almost as good as the front.

The guy behind the counter greeted Xander by name and they engaged in friendly banter. Clearly, Xander was a regular.

A girl who had been sitting at a nearby table strolled up behind him and whispered in his ear. My stomach tightened, and not in a good way. She obviously knew him. Until that moment, it never occurred to me that he might have a girlfriend, or a crazy ex, or be a womanizer.

He politely leaned away from her. He had his back to me, but he must have said something about me because the flirty girl's eyes met mine—briefly. She proceeded to pout while tugging on his arm and whimpering, "Please."

Was I seriously witnessing some girl hitting on my date? Or maybe an ex trying to make me jealous? My legs bounced in place, aching to stand, march over to them, and yank Xander away from her, but I had no claim on him.

He said something that caused her to pout even more and then he turned away and took our drinks from the barista.

"We'll catch up some other time," he said over his shoulder as he returned to our table.

He sat down, slid me my coffee and govern band, and unwrapped his calming chew like being hit on by some girl while on a first date was no big deal.

I took my latte without saying thanks then slid my band on my wrist. I clicked the sensor into my chip with a little too much force. The dull buzz of electrical current shot up my arm and into my neck as my band rebooted and started monitoring every system of my body. An alert of 0 caffeine allotments flashed on the small screen along with the balance of my remaining funds, which was the exact same amount I had this afternoon. I forced out a flat, "Thanks for buying my drink."

"Don't make assumptions about me and that girl," Xander said. "I'm sorry if that little scene upset you, but it's not what it looked like. If you let me explain, you'll know more about me, and, hopefully, we'll enjoy a lovely evening together."

My tense jaw relaxed. His correct assessment of my thoughts and acknowledgment of my feelings left me momentarily speechless. No oblivious, *Everything okay?* Or, *You seem upset, but I'll pretend I don't know why.* My past boyfriends would have reacted that way, but Xander wasn't playing dumb, and he was far from oblivious.

I sipped my latte. "I assume she's an ex, or she would like to be a current girlfriend."

"As I said, and I mean this with respect, your assumptions are wrong." His eyes gleamed with that playfulness I had seen at the library. "Would you like me to explain?"

My legs started bouncing again. I'd shifted from angry and offended to feeling like a drama queen who had no right to ask a stranger so much about his personal life. "It's really none of my business."

"I'd like to make it your business if you're interested." He leaned forward. "Interested in me, that is."

I lifted my cup to my mouth, hoping to hide my grin. "I'm interested in hearing why girls tug on your arm and beg like puppy dogs. But I need to know a lot more than that to decide if I'm interested in you."

He lowered his voice again. "Do you still have the card I gave you this morning?"

I was suddenly hyperaware of it in the back pocket of my pants. I could almost feel its edges pressing against my butt. "Yes."

"Do you feel comfortable enough to take a walk with me? There's a lake less than a mile from here."

I visualized the jester on the card and its label, *The Fool.* Fitting for me if I agreed to walk to a lake, at night, with a guy I'd known less than one day. "I'm not sure."

"We won't go if you're uncomfortable. It's a choice only you can make."

"You say that like it's a crucial decision."

"It is."

"Why?"

He cradled his cup in his hands, strong-looking hands that weren't too big or too small. They appeared smooth and were probably soft to touch—or be touched by. "Because it's step zero."

His familiar words made me refocus on our conversation. "You said that this morning. How can anything be step zero?"

"Because you don't begin anything unless you take the first step. Until then we're still at zero—the place where you decide if you do or don't want to experience the journey."

"Journey? To where?"

"The possibilities are endless. But first, you have to trust me enough to talk in private."

I eyed him skeptically. "Said the villain right before he killed the naive girl."

“Ahh, Kelsey.” He reached forward like he wanted to touch my hand, but then stopped and wrapped his fingers around his cup again. “You’re not naive, and I’m not capable of killing anyone. On the contrary, I help people live. Really live.”

“Which means what?”

His voice quieted like he was revealing a coveted secret. “You told me you want to save books. I understand that, and I can relate, because I want to save people.”

“Save people. Like medically?”

He subtly shook his head. “More like magically.”

I smirked, assuming he was kidding, but his expression remained intensely serious. I wanted magic to be possible as much as the next fantasy book lover, but unfortunately we lived in the limited real world. “And how do you propose to do that?”

He extended his open, tempting hand. “Come with me and find out.”

Level 0.7

I wasn't scared, or even hesitant. Logically, I should have been, but my intuition assured me I wasn't in any danger, and who could turn down an invitation to witness magic? Whatever Xander was referring to was most likely a mind trick or illusion, but I was still intrigued, so I placed my hand in his and let him lead me out of Caffeine Machine.

He kept holding my hand and I didn't pull away. As we walked, I kept thinking how I should let go, play hard to get, not be so readily available for Xander to flirt with. But I didn't let go because something about his hand linked with mine felt so right. After all, it was only holding hands. It's not like I was letting him kiss me.

What if he did try to kiss me? I couldn't deny my physical attraction to him, but I had a rule about no kissing on the first date. My *no hussy, no fussy* method seemed especially important after I witnessed the scene with the whiney girl in Caffeine Machine.

What if Xander was a man-whore who kissed any and every girl he could? I didn't want to be that kind of girl to any guy. I wanted to be special. I wanted the effect of my kiss to leave a guy so spellbound that he never desired to kiss anyone else ever again—a connection that would trump any and all others.

I also really wanted to feel Xander's lips against mine.

He adjusted his grip so our fingers intertwined. "What are you thinking right now?"

My thoughts scrambled, trying to come up with an answer other than, *I'm wondering if you're a good kisser.* Because only a hussy would say that thirty minutes into a first date.

I glanced around, looking at the moonlit pathway we were walking along, then at the distant lights of the downtown skyline on the other side of the small lake. "I was thinking how pretty the city looks at night."

"That's what you're thinking right now. But what were you thinking about before I asked, right before you started looking around for something to pretend you were thinking about?"

I bit my lip in embarrassment. I wasn't used to guys being so perceptive and blunt. Eventually, I managed, "I can't tell you."

"Why?" He stopped and turned to face me. "You can tell me anything."

"I hardly know you." Even as I said the defensive words, I found myself involuntarily moving closer to him.

"That's how you get to know someone," he said. "By being an open book."

"I can't be an open book unless I trust the person reading me."

"And what determines why or when you trust someone?"

"I don't know. I don't have specific requirements. I guess it's just a feeling."

"A feeling?" He seemed to lean closer, but it was so slow and slight that I couldn't be sure. "So what do you *feel* right now? How do I make you feel?"

My heart hammered in my chest. The tips of my fingers tingled, wanting to reach forward and pull his head closer to mine until our lips met. *Don't be a tramp, Kelsey. You don't even know this guy. He could be a psycho murderer.*

He was definitely leaning closer. My heart pounded faster. His eyes stayed locked on mine, encouraging me to reply, and then I made the move of all hussy moves. My gaze dropped to his lips.

The corners of his mouth lifted into a smirk and he inched closer. I licked my lips, preparing myself for the kiss I knew was about to take place.

Xander ever-so-slightly turned his head at the last moment. He whispered, "It's okay to admit you feel it too."

I swallowed, trying to find my voice, which was lost somewhere beneath my screaming hormones. "Feel what?"

His breath caressed my ear. "The connection between us."

I closed my eyes, savoring the moment. Sparks of light flooded my eyelids. Good grief, was he making me see stars? He looked like such a sweet, quiet bookworm. How did he also master the art of being so suave and irresistibly sexy?

I had to be strong. I didn't act like this with guys. Even as I was convincing myself to stop, I tilted my head so his lips were even closer to my ear. Why was my body betraying me?

I needed to regain my composure. "Are you like this with all girls?"

He exhaled long and slow like he might have been offended. My ear and neck practically melted off the rest of my tingling body. "I've never been like this with anyone but you."

Player! I screamed the word at myself and forced my feet to shuffle backward. No guy said things like that to a girl he just met unless he was a player. "We hardly know each other."

His gaze darted away, searching the sky, then he looked at me again. The lust, or whatever it was, had left his eyes, but his signature sincerity was still there. "I feel like I already know you. We have a strong connection."

He told me he would explain about the flirty girl in the coffee shop, and more about the card he gave me. So far, he hadn't elaborated on either subject.

"And the girl tugging on your arm a few minutes ago," I said. "Did you ever have a *connection* with her?"

He winced. "Where's the card I gave you this morning?"

I reached into my pocket and pulled it out. "Right here."

"That's my only connection to her. That's what she wanted."

"This?" I glanced at the colorful jester again then back at Xander.

"Not that exact card," he said, "but similar."

"I don't understand."

He glanced around, and even though no one was anywhere in sight, he lowered his voice. "Have you heard of the Arcana?"

Arcana. The word was familiar. I was certain Keekee had mentioned it a time or two in her rants about religion or beliefs of the Old World. "Sort of, but I don't know much about it."

"Arcana is a secret way of life. A source of magic. That card is one of the major arcana cards of the tarot. It represents an extraordinary way to live."

I rubbed the thin, stiff plastic between my fingers. "All of that in an artsy playing card?"

"I made that, so I'll consider *artsy* a compliment." He pointed at the card gleaming in the moonlight between us. "It's a key to a different world. Many different worlds."

"I don't understand."

"Have you ever wanted to be a character in one of the novels you read? Dive into the pages and live their story? That card makes it possible."

He was preying on my weakness—my love of books—but nothing he said was making any sense. I gripped Xander's miniature work of art tighter. "It's just a card."

He pressed his hand around mine, and the card curled, cutting into my palm. Xander's touch didn't excite me this time, but it made me feel safe.

"No," he said. "It's so much more than that."

He let go and peeled open my clenched fingers. Flipping the card over, he nodded to the jester staring up at us. The spiral background slowly swirled, and the question marks changed color. I blinked several times, and the card looked normal again. Apparently, Xander really was capable of magic tricks.

"The Fool card represents a journey of infinite possibilities," Xander explained. "Only you can decide if you want to go."

"Go where?"

"Anywhere you could imagine. And places that far surpass your most imaginative dreams."

Level 0.8

If Keekee had met a guy in the morning, agreed to a first date later that day, and was climbing into his craft less than an hour into the date to be taken to a secret location in a big city where we'd only lived for two days, I would have kicked her ass for being so stupid.

Yet I was doing it because it felt *right.*

If it were possible to kick my own ass, I would have.

Like a gentleman, Xander opened the door for me, and I slid into the passenger seat. As he walked around to the pilot side of the craft, I flipped my arm over and activated the com screen on my govern band. I selected Keek from my contacts and spoke as quickly as possible.

"Safety precaution. Leaving Caffeine Machine with Xander who works at the library. Don't know his last name. If I'm not home by eleven, track me."

Xander's door opened and I pushed *Transmit.* A chime confirmed my message was sent. Xander glanced at my band but didn't ask who I had messaged. "What time do you need to be back here?"

"By 10:30."

"I promise to bring you back safely and on time."

Thanks to my peripheral vision, my attention was redirected to several novels piled up on his backseat. I practically cooed with excitement. I turned, craning my neck to read the spines, but I didn't recognize any of the titles.

"I have an extensive collection," Xander said. "You're welcome to borrow any of them whenever you'd like."

"I've never met a guy who liked Olden books, much less had a personal collection."

"This morning you said you couldn't choose a favorite book, but what's your favorite genre?"

I didn't want to admit how much I loved magical romance stories, so I shrugged and said, "It's too hard to choose one genre."

"You're a tough spine to crack, Kelsey." Xander's smile was smoldering. "Tonight will be the first page of the best story you'll ever read—your own."

I nestled into my seat, happily sighing like I was snuggling up with a classic I loved and knew by heart. "In that case, bring me back by 10:45."

He laughed, powered his craft, and we rose into the sky, flying to some mystery destination. Against all sensible reasoning, I enjoyed being swept away by Xander and his promises of magic.

He was turning me into The Fool.

Xander piloted us to the outskirts of the city to what looked like a not-so-safe neighborhood, but the reassuring glances he flashed me kept me relaxed. Or maybe the calming chew I'd eaten wasn't a fake after all.

We hovered in front of a rundown building. The street was empty and eerily quiet.

Xander tapped the screen of his band and swiped a few times. In front of us, double garage doors slid open. We glided into the building as Xander's headlights lit up the large industrial space. Abandoned construction materials were scattered amongst columns of spray-painted concrete.

"Glitch." I gripped the edges of my seat. "You *are* a psycho murderer and you brought me to an abandoned warehouse to kill me."

Xander laughed. "Far from it."

"Then why are we here?" I eyed the broken windows at the top of the exterior walls, and the curtains of cobwebs draped across the steel beams above us.

"We still have one more level to go before we reach our destination." He rotated the craft forty-five degrees. Between two graffiti-covered columns, another set of metal doors parted.

I stared, flabbergasted. "Where in the world does that go?"

"It goes beyond this world."

"What?"

Xander only grinned as we flew through the opening framed by white and blue light.

The instant we crossed the threshold, the scenery changed from an abandoned warehouse to a tunnel. Dark walls surrounding the craft were covered in glowing numbers that scrolled past us.

As we traveled faster, the numbers became a blur. There was no sound except the hum of the craft and my seat squeaking as I sat forward, watching the silent light show all around us.

"Xander, seriously, where are we going?"

"A little place called paradise."

We flew out of the glowing tunnel and into a space that was larger than the first room of the warehouse. An area that was far from abandoned. A two-story loft looked like it had been created by a gifted architect. A stairway made of shiny metal connected two levels of living space and the second floor looked as if it were floating.

Xander unlocked our doors, but I didn't move. I sat there, gaping at the scene beyond the windshield.

Several feet in front of us, on the first floor of our mysterious destination, were areas that resembled the interior of a house. An L-shaped sofa and coffee table sat on a fluffy area rug along with an antique flat-screen television. An office with several tall desks and a wall of computer screens sat to the right of a kitchen equipped with a refrigerator, microwave, and a table and chairs for four.

Xander opened his door and walked around to my side of the craft. My door rose open and he offered me his hand. "Welcome to my home."

"Your home? Do you sleep in the hammock?" I motioned to the ivory canopy draped from the ceiling of the main level, or the floor of the second level depending on how you looked at it. And I was looking at all of it with astonishment.

"Sometimes. Depends on my mood. But I do have a bedroom upstairs." He braced his arms on the frame of the craft doorway and dipped down closer to me. "And no, you can't see it. At least not on our first date."

He smirked then extended his hand to me again. I hesitantly set my hand in his and climbed out of the craft. We walked together, to the kitchen where I ran my fingers along the glass table and one of the four placemats. He even had vintage Batman and Robin salt and pepper shakers sitting on the center Lazy Susan.

"You really live here?" I asked.

"I'm not a fan of traditional spaces. This place is more me." He opened the refrigerator door to reveal an assortment of food and beverages, including a couple takeout containers. "Would you like a drink? Juice, water, soda—caffeine free, of course."

"No thanks." I meandered around, taking in details of Xander's unique home. More of his artwork hung above his eight (yes, I counted) antiquated computer screens. Four (four!) holosplay control units were embedded in the wall. I'd never heard of any household having more than one holosplay.

I peeked around a curtain hanging from the ceiling beams and saw another table of some sort. "What's that?"

"Air hockey. A game that was popular in arcades of the Old World."

I pressed my fingertips against some of the many tiny holes on its cool surface.

"You like to touch things," Xander said.

I looked up at him as my hands flew behind my back. "I'm sorry."

"No need to apologize. I just noticed you're always touching things like you need to make sure they're real."

"Habit. I've done it for as long as I can remember."

He patted the air hockey table. "Would you like to play?"

"Maybe next time."

"Next time," he repeated, sounding pleased. "Deal."

At the base of the steps, framed on either side, were two beautiful potted plants. Somehow, even though his place was hidden away in an old warehouse, Xander had made it feel like a cozy and inviting home. I lingered at the bottom of the stairs, gazing up at the engineered steel and cables, the ceiling and flooring that glowed like aerogel. I wanted to touch everything, but I didn't want Xander thinking I was OCD, so I resisted the urge.

"I've never seen any place like this before," I admitted, "but at the same time, it feels familiar."

From behind me, he replied, “Maybe you were here in another life.”

I turned around. “You believe in past lives?”

“Followers of the Arcana believe that we repeat our journey, and many variations of it, until we learn or experience whatever the universe intends for us. Whether those journeys take place in one lifetime or one hundred, no one knows for sure.” He leaned against the stairway railing. “Our nation doesn’t even want us to know what happens on other parts of our planet. They’d probably mind-strip us all if we solved the mysteries of the universe.”

I shivered and muttered, “Control freaks.”

“Agreed.” He looked to his left, and his eyes sparkled with playful mischief. “Let me show you why I invited you here.”

We walked through the kitchen and then the office area. Xander parted a set of long curtains and motioned for me to step through. An arch of concrete framed a black door with a large, ornate gold knob. He reached forward, pressing his palm against the flat part of the knob. A melodic chime echoed around us, a beautiful blue light shimmered around the doorframe, and then the door cracked open. I couldn’t see anything through the sliver of open space, only darkness.

I glanced between Xander and the cracked door, not knowing what to expect next.

“Go ahead,” he urged.

“I’m nervous.”

“About what?”

“About what might be inside.”

He stuck his hands in his pockets and widened his stance. “Do you feel that way before you open the cover of a book?”

“No, because it’s fiction. Whatever happens inside the pages can’t hurt me.”

“What’s through that door can’t hurt you either.”

“You promise?”

“I promise.”

Xander didn’t seem like the type to make false promises, so I took a deep breath and pushed the knob. The door gently swung open, and I gasped.

The room was filled with books. All four walls from top to bottom were nothing but bookshelves. The only place there weren't books was the door we had just entered through. Two tall ladders on wheels leaned against adjacent sides of the room, allowing easy access to the higher shelves.

"I told you I had an extensive personal collection," Xander said.

"This can't be real." I walked toward the center of the room and slowly spun around, gaping at the overflowing bookshelves. "Elura library didn't even have this many."

"I told you. It's paradise."

I practically danced to one side of the room and scanned titles. On the first shelf I browsed, many of my favorites sat perfectly aligned as if personally organized for me.

Xander stood behind me and touched my elbow. "Choose one."

I reached forward, my fingertips landing on *Daughter of Smoke and Bone.*

"Hmm." Xander sounded perplexed. "Perhaps start with one a little lighter."

A little lighter. I scanned the titles again and found *The Lion, the Witch and the Wardrobe.* Delighted, I pulled it from its slot. "Are we going to read it together?"

"Not exactly. Open it."

I flipped open the hardback cover, but there were no pages. No paper whatsoever. An access card was nestled securely in a plastic case. I almost dropped the fake book. "What is this?"

"It's one of your favorite stories in the form of a VR card."

I snapped the cover shut. "That's illegal. You shouldn't—"

It hit me with such force that I felt like the wind had been knocked out of me. I turned, staring at the rows of books like they might slither from their shelves and bite me. "Is every book in here a fake? Do they all contain illegal access cards?"

I snapped back around, expecting Xander to answer, but he didn't say a word. His face was expressionless. I grabbed another book from the shelf and opened it. VR card. I dropped it on the floor and grabbed another. VR card.

My knees felt like they might give out. "All of them? Every book is fake?"

"No, many of them are real."

"But a lot of them are decoys to conceal access cards!" I rocked back on my heels, feeling dizzy. "Do you know how much trouble you'd be in if anyone found about this? The government would turn you into a drudge. No questions asked."

"They won't find out."

"You don't know that. I could get in so much trouble just for being here with you. A proctor is probably being alerted of my fear and anxiety right now. What am I supposed to say if they question me?"

"You haven't done anything illegal yet."

"Yet? You expect me to? Is that why you brought me here? To be all wowed and tempted by your illegal library?" The girl in Caffeine Machine flashed to the forefront of my mind. "That girl. The card. That's why she was begging you. This is what she wanted. You're a VR dealer." My hands were trembling. "You're a criminal."

"I'm a savior."

I guffawed and stepped away from him, my back pressed against the bookshelf behind me. "Someone like you hooked my sister on VR gaming years ago, and it's done nothing but make our lives hell. I don't want any part of this."

His voice was gentle. "You don't want to visit other worlds? Have supernatural abilities? Escape to times and places where you can be free?"

"Not if it means breaking the law!"

"What if you couldn't get caught?"

"Everyone gets caught at some point."

"Not me," he insisted. "My methods are ironclad."

"That's impossible."

Xander stepped closer. "What if it was possible? I've been doing this for almost five years and never had so much as a scare or possible breach of security. None of my clients has ever been questioned, much less arrested."

"You probably tell everyone that to get them hooked. Is that your angle? Find unsuspecting girls, pretend to like them, flirt with them, then bring them here and get them addicted to VR until they barter everything of value in exchange for their next fix."

He winced and swayed like I had shoved him. "I don't have an angle. I only wanted to make you happy."

“Right. Sure.” I walked toward the door, wanting to run back to the craft and find the quickest exit out of the corrupt cave of access cards. “I want to leave. Now.”

“Okay.” He didn’t argue further like I expected. “I told you the choice is yours. I’d never try to force anything on you.”

I followed him back to the craft, and even though I hadn’t fallen for his VR offer, he still courteously opened my door. I climbed in and stared at his makeshift home/secret lair. How hadn’t he been caught in five years? I didn’t want to know.

We flew out of the glowing computer-code tunnel, through the warehouse, out into the empty alleyway, and eventually merged back into the flow of city traffic. We didn’t speak a word to each other until we landed in the parking lot of Caffeine Machine.

“I’m sorry if I upset you,” he said. “That’s the last thing I wanted.”

A small part of me felt bad for reacting so harshly, but he was a criminal who tried involving me in an activity that could ruin my life and my family’s. However, if none of his clients had ever been caught, maybe he didn’t realize the havoc it could wreak.

I tried speaking calmly and with some degree of kindness. “You have to understand, my sister is addicted to VR gaming. She’s serving a government sentence right now, and it’s not the first time she’s been caught.” I blinked and saw Devlin Templeton’s wide, terrified eyes again. “Keekee and I are almost eighteen. The consequences of messing with VR are too severe. It’s too dangerous.”

I didn’t mention that Elura was our last resort before being sentenced as resident slaves of The Hub. Some family secrets were too shameful to admit out loud.

“I understand,” Xander said. “I won’t bring it up again.”

I paused, taken aback. “Again? You want to see me again even though I didn’t buy into your VR offer?”

“I didn’t want you to buy into anything. I wanted to spend time with you. I thought you might enjoy virtually escaping into one of your favorite books. I thought wrong.” He shifted in his seat so he was facing me. “But there’s a lot more to me than VR dealing. I’d like to go on a proper date with you if you’d be willing to see me again.”

Giddiness simmered deep down in my stomach, but it never fully manifested the way it had before I discovered Xander's dark side. The words felt wrong on my tongue, but I forced them out. "I don't think that's a good idea."

Sadness swept across his hazel eyes, and then he opened his craft door and climbed out.

I almost changed my mind. I wanted to beg him to stop dealing so I could see him again and not start a relationship with someone who contributed to the very problem that kept my sister in trouble and threatened my family's future. But as my door opened, I stayed quiet.

He was only one guy. One guy who was nothing but trouble.

"If you change your mind," Xander said, "you know where to find me."

I reached into my pocket to pull out the jester card he had given me, but it was gone. I patted my other pockets, but they were empty too. "I'm sorry. Somehow, I lost your card."

"No, you didn't. You chose to reject the journey."

I didn't understand. Had he taken the card back? How was that possible without me noticing? Before I could ask, Xander said, "Goodnight, Kelsey. Thanks for spending your evening with me."

Feeling dismissed, and emotionally shook up, I muttered, "Goodnight."

I turned away and walked to my craft with my stomach in knots. As expected, another real-life guy who didn't live up to real-world expectations. So disappointing.

I climbed into my pilot seat then looked up to wave goodbye.

Xander and his craft had already disappeared.

Level 0.9

I sat in my craft watching people come and go from Caffeine Machine. I wasn't ready to go home yet. Keek would ask me a dozen questions about my time with Xander. I needed to figure out how to tell her everything without telling her *everything.* She couldn't know that Xander had VR access cards. Ever.

After I mentally rehearsed possible conversations about my date and had my ambiguous story solidly plotted, I powered up the craft and sailed out of the parking lot. I flew slower than the speed limit, still dreading the inevitable—I'd have to hide the truth from my sister.

I came to the point where I could have steered left and been home in seconds. Instead, I went right and headed for downtown. I needed more time to get my head together.

I soared upward, higher than the designated traffic patterns. For a brief moment, I relished the view of rooftops and the thrill of flying above skyscrapers. A few more feet and I'd fly higher than I'd ever been, but then I'd cross into illegal airspace, and the last thing I needed was a transportation citation. I dipped downward and merged into an empty top-wrung traffic lane.

As I aimed for a deserted path between two tall buildings, my heart screeched to a halt and so did my craft.

Keekee stood on the rooftop of a building, wearing a fluffy dress, and staring up at the sky with her arms open wide. The shock of seeing her left me and my brain frozen, but then she dropped her hands and turned away from me, walking across the flat roof toward a door.

"Keek, what the glitch are you doing?" I glided down to her. Even though it was forbidden to land on top of a building that wasn't officially designated as a landing zone, I couldn't fly away and leave her. What if she was already caught up with a VR dealer?

If I hovered close to the rooftop without actually touching down, then maybe traffic enforcers wouldn't be alerted. I lowered inches from the concrete surface and left the craft powered in stationary mode as I threw my door open and jumped out. Keekee stood with her back to me in front of a rusty door surrounded by crumbling bricks.

"Keek!" I shouted.

She didn't turn around, so I picked up my pace. As I got closer, I could see her dress more clearly. She wore a gorgeous gown with a billowy skirt and off-the-shoulder sleeves that looked like they were made from ivory rose petals. She looked out of place standing on a dirty rooftop in such beautiful attire.

"Keekee, what in creation are you wearing and why?"

She looked back at me over her bare shoulder, but then she yanked the fire-exit door open.

Light poured out so strong and bright that I shielded my eyes. I heard the loud slamming of the door, then the blinding light disappeared. But so had Keekee.

I ran forward the last couple of steps and jiggled the handle, but it was locked. I pounded on the door with both fists shouting my sister's name.

I pressed my ear against the cold steel and listened for any voices or movement on the other side, but all I heard was the whirring of my craft parked behind me. Glitch. What kind of trouble had Keek gotten herself into?

I stomped back to the craft, wanting to strangle my sister for ditching me. Here I was feeling bad that I'd have to hide information about Xander from her, while she was playing dress-up and probably getting hyper-high off some VR game that made her act like a lunatic on a city rooftop. Then, to top it all off, she evaded me like I was an enforcer.

I activated my com screen and verbally commanded, "Call Keekee."

It attempted to connect, but the all too familiar *Signal Jammed* message flashed on the screen. She had a lot of explaining to do, and a ton of lattes to buy me in exchange for my silence, or I wouldn't hesitate to tell Mom and Dad about her bizarre escapade.

Furious, I climbed in my craft and slammed the door.

I blinked several times, baffled by the scene beyond my windshield.

I wasn't hovering on the rooftop.

I was still sitting in Caffeine Machine's parking lot. Customers lounged around at outside tables, sipping drinks and chatting.

What just happened? I shook my head and glanced around my craft. Had I been daydreaming? Did I fall asleep and dream the whole Keek on a rooftop thing? It felt too real to dismiss so easily.

I powered up and flew out of the lot as fast as I legally could. I needed to get home and make sure my sister was all right.

Rushing into the house, I stumbled down the hall and into our room.

Keek sat cross-legged on her bed, dressed in shorts and a T-shirt. No puffy gown in sight. She looked up from her homework. "You're back early."

"Have you been here all night?"

"Yes. Why?" She cocked her head. "Why are you out of breath?"

I pressed my hand to my chest. My heart thumped against my palm. My breathing calmed as I realized all my worrying and rushing home had been for nothing. "I could have sworn I saw you tonight."

One of her brows arched. "Where was I? And more importantly, was I having fun?"

"Forget it. It must have been someone who looks like you."

"Uh oh. Two of us are bad enough. Elura might implode with three of us running amuck."

I flopped down on my bed across from hers. "It's been a long day. My mind must have been playing tricks on me."

"You think?" She said mockingly while leaning back against her pillows. "So how was your date?"

"Fine."

"Fine? That's it? You messaged me that you were leaving the coffee shop with Library Boy. Where'd you go?"

I almost forgot my rehearsed answer because of the doppelganger roof hallucination.

Returning to my original plan, I sighed as if bored. "We just drove around and talked."

"He certainly gets an F for effort. What a lame first date."

If she only knew what an unbelievable offer Xander had made me, she'd beg for his contact link and meet him in a dark alley within the hour to barter for a session of gaming.

I checked my band, but thankfully no alerts of a proctor session. "At least you don't have to worry about him making me deliriously happy."

She tossed a pillow at me. "True, but seeing you a tiny bit excited would have been nice."

"I was mildly entertained."

"Doesn't seem like it. You seem really, I don't know, disappointed."

"Guys are always disappointing."

She smirked. "That's because you're always comparing them to the heartthrobs in your romantic, *fictional* stories."

"No argument there."

"So you aren't going to see him again?"

"Nope. He's not my type."

"I can't say I'm not somewhat relieved." She wriggled beneath her covers. "We have to stay focused on school and college applications."

I couldn't shake the mental image of her on the rooftop, in that gown, arms open and staring at the sky. "Speaking of school, I need to sleep. Morning will arrive too soon." I fluffed my pillow and rolled over so I didn't have to look at her and keep thinking about my hallucination. "And Keek, don't forget you owe me a latte tomorrow morning."

"I know, I know." She turned off the light and I listened to her sheets rustling as she settled into bed.

A few minutes later her breathing changed to the long deep breaths that meant she was asleep. I rolled onto my back and stared at the ceiling. The rooftop scene kept replaying in my mind until I wanted to scream.

Think of something else, I told myself. *Anything else.*

I forced my brain to switch tracks, but option two wasn't much better. Looping continuously and luring me to sleep were memories of Xander's friendly smile, the warmth of his breath in my ear, and his spellbinding library of stories.

I woke up in my bed calmly, like I had been floating on clouds and they were gently lowering me back to earth.

Our bedroom was dark and quiet. I pushed the backlight button on my band to check the time. Squinting at the screen's green glow, I was relieved to see we still had a few hours of sleep until we had to get up for school. I was usually a heavy sleeper, so why was I awake at 3 am?

Leaves rustled outside our window as wind blew and whistled against the house, but it wasn't loud enough to have woken me.

I rubbed my tired eyes then flipped my pillow over, nuzzling my cheek against the cool cotton. Keekee's covers were rumpled, and she wasn't in bed, but she had a habit of predawn trips to the bathroom. Maybe she had made more noise than usual and that's what woke me.

I started to drift back to sleep until three words made my eyelids fly open.

"Open the window."

I bolted up in bed. A guy stood outside, rattling the window like he was trying to open it, then he cupped his hands on the side of his face and peered inside.

My heart thumped so loud I was sure it would wake all of Elura. I slowly pulled my covers up to my chin, hoping to . . . what—hide? Stupid idea. Fear had shut down my brain. I stayed completely still, praying he'd go away.

No such luck.

He tapped on the window. In the dark solitude of our bedroom, the sound of his fingers hitting the glass was ear-piercing.

I tried summoning my vocal cords, but barely screeched out, "Keekee."

She was the tougher one of the two of us. She'd know what to do. I needed her to come back from the bathroom before I passed out from fear, or before the intruder found a way in.

But then the lurker outside said two more words. "Xander, please."

Xander?

He looked inside again, this time with no hands hiding his face. I gasped.

Devlin Templeton?

I crawled out of bed and crept to the window. He looked even more confused than I felt. Probably not the smartest move, but I unlocked our window and slid it open.

Devlin's eyes weren't as terrified as they had been earlier in the day when enforcers hauled him away, but he still appeared scared. "Where's Xander?"

"How would I know?" How did he know I even knew Xander?

"You're in his room."

My jaw went slack. "His room? No. We live here. The Zellars. We moved in a couple days ago." What were the odds that Xander used to live in our house? We must have been talking about the same Xander. Why else would a convicted gamer be tapping on a window in the middle of the night looking for a dealer? Wait. *Convicted.*

"How did you get away from the enforcers?" I asked.

He turned pale. "What?"

"Today, in history class, they arrested you."

Devlin shook his head and stepped backward. "I'm sorry. Don't tell anyone I was here. You never saw me. Promise you won't say anything to anyone?"

Even though I barely knew him, the fear in his voice made me feel sorry for him. "I promise."

He glanced around then pulled something out of his pocket. "Here, as a thank you for keeping my secret."

He tried handing me a card.

"You don't have to give me anything," I said, my hands still clenching the bottom of my shirt.

"Take it." He stepped forward, waving it at me.

"I don't want it."

He reached behind him again. In one fast and fluid movement, he slapped the card on the windowsill then stabbed it with a knife. "Just take it!"

I leaped backward, terrified. He ran down the street and disappeared into the shadows.

Struggling to breathe as my hands trembled, I pried the knife and card free from the wood, tossed them on my bed, then closed the window and locked it.

A criminal had pulled a knife on me. Where were enforcers when you needed them? Or Keekee for that matter? My knees felt weak, so I sank onto my bed.

Beside me sat a card with the familiar gold symbol on a black background. I had said no to Xander and his illegal world of VR, but here I was again, in possession of one of his cards. A card that could get me in serious trouble and most likely ruin my sister's life.

I picked it up and flipped it over. I tried to swallow, but couldn't.

The card gripped between my fingers showed a man in a suit and top hat touching a changing sky with a wand. The knife had made a slit mark under the number *1,* and on the bottom it read: *The Magician.*

1: THE MAGICIAN

Level 1.1

The emergency alert buzzed on my band. *Safety check* flashed on the screen. I faked a grin for visual confirmation then verbally stated I was fine and had just suffered a nightmare.

After *Accepted* appeared on my backlit screen, I hid The Magician card and knife under my mattress then rushed out of the bedroom to find Keekee.

She wasn't in the bathroom, so I tiptoed down the hall to check the kitchen, but I saw the glow from our holosplay in the family room. I rounded the corner to find her asleep on the sofa. The holosplay screen was still on and two 3D characters stood motionless, smiling at each other. Above their heads, in bold white letters, was one of Equatia's public service announcements. "Help us protect you and our nation by respecting and obeying all laws."

At the bottom of the screen, smaller words stated that the series was complete and viewers should notify an administrator for the summary test. Since Keek fell asleep during the program, she'd have to watch it again or risk failing the test. Dad would be angry that she'd wasted today's entertainment allotment.

I covered my sister with a blanket and whispered, "Really could have used your help a few minutes ago. I was terrified."

She didn't budge. Probably best that she didn't know about the strange and scary window encounter with Devlin, or The Magician card. The last thing I wanted was Keekee finding out that Xander's tarot cards were linked to his VR dealings. Plus, Devlin begged me not to tell anyone about his visit. I wanted to keep that promise, even though I didn't know why. I couldn't keep Devlin a secret from Keekee forever, but I could for tonight.

I shut down the holosplay and the family room went dark. I returned to our bedroom, pulling our window shade down to prevent a repeat of the peeking-Devlin incident.

My govern band beeped, signaling the message I'd been dreading. *Proctor session required. Report to Century High Administration Office at 10:00 am.*

Glitch. My nightmare lie didn't work. I tapped the screen, sending the required acknowledgment and agreement.

How could I lie to a stuffy, intimidating proctor? Explaining my excessive levels of excitement last night would be easy. A date with a guy who made me giddy wasn't a crime, but clearly a proctor didn't believe my intense indicators of fear and panic at 3 am were the result of a nightmare.

Why did Devlin have to show up at our house? I didn't want to be linked with a convicted gamer, even if only by coincidence, or they'd monitor me and Keekee closer than ever. Plus, they could now trace me to Xander, the tarot-toting VR dealer. If they found out what he was doing, his life would be over, and I could be charged as an accomplice.

I crawled into bed and pulled the covers tight around me, wishing I had a rewind button. I'd go back in time and never speak a word to Xander. Never get myself mixed up in such a shady mess.

"I wish I never met you," I said to the image of him that appeared when I closed my eyes. Quietly, I repeated my mantra until I fell asleep. "I wish I never met you."

But no matter how many times I said it, we both knew I didn't mean it.

In the morning, I paced the kitchen, encouraging Keekee to hurry up and finish her bagel so we could leave.

"We have plenty of time to stop at Caffeine Machine," Keek said. "Don't worry, you'll get your latte."

It wasn't about my latte. With any luck, Xander would be there again and I could discuss the Devlin incident with him. Promise or not, I was freaking out. Xander was the only person who might be able to explain what was going on. Like how and why did I have a knife and The Magician card hidden under my mattress at 3 am, and why had it now vanished?

In my initial moment of panic after discovering the knife and card were gone, I asked Keek if she had taken anything from my bed. She had no idea what I was talking about. I believed her, because no matter how bad her VR habit was, or how often she got busted, she had never once lied to me about anything. She'd lie to our parents, teachers, government officials, but not me. She had always said that being real and brutally honest with me was the only thing that kept her grounded.

Logical thinking would suggest I might have dreamed the whole incident with Devlin, but the recent activity on my govern band, including my 10 am proctor meeting, proved it did happen.

Keekee took another bite of her bagel and talked with her mouth full. "Are you in a rush because of that boy?"

Avoiding her question, I pretended to search for something in my bag.

"You said he wasn't your type," she reminded me. "Last night you were bored by him, but today you're wanting to race back to Caffeine Machine so you can see him again."

"It's not like that."

"Then explain why you're so fidgety and in a rush."

Mom walked in, granting me a reprieve from answering.

"Good morning, my lovebugs," she sang. "Excited for day two of school?"

Keek groaned while I mumbled a reply of indifference.

Mom took a bite of Keek's bagel then opened the fridge. "Kelsey, did you eat breakfast?"

My stomach was in knots. How could I possibly eat? "I'm grabbing a latte on our way in."

She gave me her *you know better* look. "Coffee has no nutritional value. You don't want a health advisor issued to you. Eat something."

Health advisors had harassed Mom several times since she started her catering business. When they forbid her from making her double fudge brownies because the fat and sugar content were too high, she started referring to all health advisors as serenity squelchers.

"I'm not hungry," I told her.

She handed me one of her homemade health bars, which were by no means delicious, but were most definitely an improvement on the kind available at grocery distributors. To appease her, I took a bite.

She turned away to make her own breakfast. "When did you two start playing cards?"

I almost choked on the berries and granola I was chewing.

"Cards?" Keek flashed me an uneasy glance.

"There's a deck of cards on the nightstand between your beds. I saw them when I peeked in to make sure you were awake."

My pulse lurched into overdrive. I was certain there was no tarot card on our nightstand when we left the room. Had Devlin's card magically reappeared right out in the open? But Mom said *cards*. Plural.

Keek used her fibbing skills to save the conversation. "Oh, I found them while I was unpacking. I think maybe they were a gift from Aunt M from three birthdays ago."

Aunt M had passed away six months ago. Keek was a master at quickly coming up with answers and explanations that Mom and Dad would never be able to verify.

Mom sighed with sadness. "I miss her so much. She adored you girls since the day you were born."

"She's out of Equatia, which means she's in a much better place." Keek shoved her last piece of bagel in her mouth and stood. "We have to get going. Don't want to be late for school."

"Yes, of course." Mom wiped her misty eyes and pulled Keek in for a goodbye kiss.

"I forgot something," I told Keekee. "I'll meet you out front."

I rushed back to our room. Maybe Mom assumed she saw more than one card. The last thing I needed was her investigating more closely. How and why we had a tarot card couldn't be easily blamed on our dearly departed aunt.

Rounding the corner into our room, I halted between our beds. Sitting on the nightstand in a not-so-neat pile was a deck of what appeared to be real playing cards. I stared at the generic red-and-white pattern on the back of the cards. My breath halted, and my heart pounded in what felt like slow motion.

No one had ever given us playing cards. And they were not on the nightstand when I went to bed or when I searched every nook and cranny of our room for the missing knife and Magician card.

I flipped over the top card. Two of hearts. No jester. No magician. No golden eye symbol. Just regular old-fashioned playing cards. But where did they come from?

It would look more suspicious if I hid the cards right after Mom asked us about them, so I left them on the nightstand.

"Everything okay, lovebug?" Mom asked from the doorway.

"Yes. Fine." I kissed her cheek on my way out of our room. My voice sounded as rattled as my nerves. "Everything is fine."

If only I had the ability to lie as well as Keekee.

Level 1.2

Xander wasn't at Caffeine Machine, which was probably a good thing because I had a proctor appointment. He would have stirred up more highs and lows in my emotions, and then I'd have even more explaining to do. If my explanations to Keekee were any indication of how well I'd do with a proctor, I was doomed.

I hadn't technically lied to my sister when she asked about the playing cards. I honestly didn't know how they ended up on our nightstand. I suspected they were somehow connected to Xander, but I didn't have the slightest idea how. She wouldn't drop the subject.

"Seems odd that you were missing something this morning and then those cards mysteriously appeared. I covered for you. You have to tell me what's going on."

I sighed. "I agree it's weird, but I swear, I have no idea how they got there."

She echoed my sigh, but hers was due to frustration. "So what were you looking for under your mattress?"

"I told you I can't tell you. Not yet. But I will soon."

"Since when do we keep secrets from each other?"

"We don't. I'm not trying to keep anything from you." I fidgeted in my seat, hating that I was put in this situation. "You're safer not knowing."

She gawked at me. "Safer? Isn't it my job to be the one in trouble?"

"Let's hope no one is in trouble."

She rested her hand on top of mine. "Whatever it is, you can tell me."

"I will. As soon as I understand what's happening."

She didn't look pleased, or convinced, but she stopped interrogating me.

I suffered through my first class and half of my second before being excused for my proctor meeting.

I made my way down the eerily quiet halls to the main office and gave my name to the lady sitting behind the desk. Her graying hair was pulled into a much-too-tight bun that made her eyes slant.

"My name is Kelsey Zellar and I have an appointment with a proctor at 10."

Her lips pursed in disapproval as if I were a delinquent. I wanted to tell her to stop being so judgmental. I hadn't done anything wrong. Well, besides hang out with a VR dealer and hide the knife of a convicted felon under my mattress.

I stayed silent as she scanned my govern band, followed by my irises. Double confirmation was usually only used on criminals or if a citizen's identity was questionable, so being treated like a miscreant made me even more nervous. She curtly told me to have a seat.

My legs bounced as I traced the scrolling ridges of my chair's armrests. Soon, an Equatia employee would drill me with questions about the multiple increases in my heart rate, my surges of serotonin and endorphins, and my excessive joy that was so quickly followed by anxiety and stress, and then, at 3am, off-the-charts fear.

I had decided I would mostly tell the truth because proctors had a sixth sense when it came to detecting lies. Actually, they had the advantage of portable lie detectors and machines that monitored dozens of mental and physical factors, but it might as well have been a sixth sense because the proctors I had met with in the past rarely consulted their equipment while interviewing me. Their stone-cold stares had a way of forcing you to spill your guts no matter how messy.

The truth would be easy at first. I met a cute guy at Caffeine Machine on the way to school, ran into him again at the library. We met for coffee, went for a walk, and then drove around town while chatting. I'd admit I found Xander attractive because it would explain my roller coaster of emotions.

I hoped they wouldn't ask where we drove to, or if we made any other stops. But what if they did? If I told them about

Xander's unusual warehouse, would they investigate and bust him for his VR collection?

I traced the ridges in the armrest faster. I'd have to lie. I was terrible at it, but I had to try. I didn't want to be the reason for someone's arrest. I was certain Xander was over eighteen. He'd be mind-stripped for sure.

I wiped my sweaty palms on my pants and tried willing my heart to stop beating so fast. I was sending up more red flags by the second. Hopefully the proctor would assume my surge in nervousness was about the meeting.

The office door opened. I gripped the armrests so hard that I broke a nail, but I couldn't peel my eyes away from the person who had entered.

Standing there in a black silk suit, carrying an official government-issued debriefing case, was Xander.

"Alexander Mage, proctor. I have an appointment with one of your students." He held out his arm so the office assistant could scan his band, and then she pleasantly pointed in my direction.

"Miss Zellar has already checked in. We've issued you counseling room 3."

How could Xander—who didn't look a day over twenty max—be a proctor? Proctors were usually crotchety old people. Xander worked at the library. Proctors did not work part-time in libraries.

"Splendid," Xander said without a hint of emotion. He turned to me and motioned toward the hallway that I assumed led to counseling rooms. "Miss Zellar, shall we?"

I stood and walked down the hall, feeling Xander's gaze on the back of me with every step. Each door we passed was labeled with a large red number. We reached number three, and he pushed the door open, ushering me inside.

I sat in the smaller chair designated for the student. Xander set down his debriefing case then perched on the corner of the desk. He folded his hands, resting them on one thigh.

He stared down at me, but not in a belittling way. It was more of an anticipatory I'm-waiting-for-*you*-to-start-questioning-*me* look, which was completely backward because every citizen was taught to stay silent in the presence of government officials. Only speak if spoken to. My programming held firm as we stared at each other for at least a minute without either of us so much as shifting.

My mind raced. Xander was a proctor. He could check in on me any time he wanted. See my pulse rate, my body mass index, my food intake for the day. I closed my eyes briefly at the embarrassment of the thought that he could even know when I had my period. Proctors were not supposed to be young, charming, VR dealers. Was it a set up? Had Equatia sent a young proctor to lure me into committing a crime so they could sentence my family and me to carry out a life sentence as slaves in The Hub?

Xander's voice was gentle. "I sense you want to ask me something."

I breathed long and deep. "Did I pass?"

"Pass what?"

"Equatia's test. I proved I couldn't be tempted by VR. I didn't do anything wrong. I'm not a criminal."

"Equatia wasn't testing you. Not yet, anyway."

The room felt too small and cramped. I wiped sweat from the back of my neck. "How are you a proctor? You work at the library."

"I can be whomever I need to be."

I eyed him skeptically. "What does that mean?"

"You tell me."

"Me? You're asking me to explain any of this to you? My life has been one big ball of confusion since I met you yesterday morning."

He remained frustratingly calm and composed. "What has been confusing about it?"

"The first thing that comes to mind is your—" I searched the walls and corners of the office for cameras or monitors. I didn't see any, but I still whispered, "Your cards."

I hadn't yet mentioned Devlin or The Magician card, but it was weighing heavy on me. Not to mention the deck of playing cards appearing in our room.

Xander sat forward, causing the desk to creak. "Why are you whispering?"

"Because someone could be listening or monitoring us."

"Not at the moment, I assure you."

"How can you be certain?"

Standing, he towered over me, looking much taller than I remembered. He took off his suit jacket and loosened his shirt collar. "Because I made sure of it."

"See, those vague answers are why I'm confused. Our govern bands have visual and audio monitoring abilities. The government can see or hear us anytime it wants."

He walked behind the desk, hung his jacket on the back of the throne-like chair, and sat down. "Normally, that would be true, but as of yesterday, that can't happen to you."

I sat upright. A chill crept down my spine. "Why?"

"To avoid additional accusations of being vague, I'll be specific. Yesterday, at Caffeine Machine, while placing our order, during the few minutes you were distracted by some insignificant girl begging me for a VR card, I was ghost-bugging your band. Since then, a phantom program runs on autopilot, reporting exactly what it needs to report to maintain the illusion that your normal patterns of health and obedient behavior are continuing."

My eyes were stuck open, unable to blink. Keek had told me how dealers bugged bands so they continuously looped a few minutes of recorded readings. Most dealers restricted the looping time to a maximum of an hour because the repeated feed could be detected if an official were monitoring closely. The time restriction protected the dealer and the customer, and it meant addicts had to barter for sessions more frequently. Xander was claiming my band had been bugged for over twelve hours.

"That's impossible," I argued. "It alerted you of my flux in emotions this morning."

"True. It alerted *me*."

Was he on the other end the whole time? "I completed a safety check around 3 am."

He nodded. "I was worried about you. And by the way, your lying skills could use some improvement."

My jaw tensed and my eyes bugged. *He* was the one who viewed my visual confirmation? *He* saw my bed-head of untamed curls? How embarrassing.

"That must have been some nightmare," he said in a way that implied he knew I'd been lying.

Did he know about Devlin visiting me, looking for Xander? Telling me I was in Xander's room? "Apparently we live in your old house."

He smiled like he knew all the secrets of the universe. "Coincidence or something more?"

"You're the all-knowing Kibitzer spying on me without my consent, so you tell me."

"I'm not a Kib." He squirmed as if trying to shake off the accusation. "I'm not a real Equatia official, so you don't have to worry."

I glanced at the closed door, replaying Xander introducing himself as a proctor and having his credentials confirmed. Then I glanced at his debriefing case. "The office assistant scanned your band. She confirmed your identity."

"If I ghost-bugged yours, don't you think I can disguise my own?" Xander rolled up the cuffs of his sleeves, then cracked his knuckles. "As I told you last night, I know how to cover my tracks."

When we had said good-bye the night before, Xander told me to find him if I wanted to see him again, but then he summoned me and created an elaborate deception to see me again.

"If that's true, then why are we here?" I asked. "Why did you schedule an appointment with me here at school where we could so easily be caught?"

"We're meeting here because they'd never expect us to deceive them right under their noses. The meeting is necessary because Devlin gave you something important."

How did he know about that? I hadn't mentioned it yet. I glanced down at my govern band. "You really have been spying on me!"

"Not in the way you're assuming."

"That's still a yes." I stood and glared at him. He admitted he wasn't a government official, yet he was snooping on me using some sort of hacking skills to access my band's camera whenever he wanted? "I'll be blunt. I feel violated. I didn't peg you for this type of person."

"You didn't peg me as helpful?"

"Helpful?" My voice was louder than it should have been. "How is violating my privacy helpful?"

"Would you rather be in this room right now with a real proctor? Being asked dozens of questions about your extreme reactions to our time together? Having them find out about your visit from Devlin? Detecting you weren't being entirely truthful? And then, due to your past record, labeling you a violation risk and monitoring you and your sister much more strictly? Because that's what would have happened if I hadn't bugged your band."

"I wouldn't need my band bugged if I hadn't met you."

"You made the first move, Kelsey. *You* spoke to me."

"I didn't want you to forget your coffee! I was being polite."

He spoke too calmly. "It had nothing to do with coffee and you know it. You aren't sure how or why you know, and you certainly don't understand the details yet, but you feel it. You know we were destined to meet."

He hit a nerve. My time and interactions with Xander had felt so right yesterday. Several times I wondered why I had felt safe with him, but today was a different story.

"Circumstances have changed," Xander continued. "We don't have as much time as I thought."

A bead of sweat dripped from my neck, running down my back. My damp shirt clung to me, suffocating me. "What are you talking about?"

"You need to feel safe with me."

"Well, I don't feel safe. You tricked me into meeting you here. All morning I've been stressed out about my meeting with a proctor. Now you show up as a fraud and worry me even more. I told you I didn't want any part of your VR dealings."

"VR is your only chance of changing your fate."

"My fate?" He had reached so many levels of inappropriate I had lost count. What a clever dealer to use scare tactics to recruit new clients. I had pegged him for smart, not an evil genius. "Please leave me alone," I begged. "I don't know how your shady, corrupt lifestyle works, but I want no part of it."

He crossed his arms over his chest. "I didn't give you The Magician card. Devlin did, and for a reason. Ask yourself why you needed it, Kelsey."

"He told me to give it to you!"

"All right then. Ask yourself why you need *me*."

He had gone from charming to cocky, and I wasn't a fan of the latter. "I don't need you. I didn't ask for that card or the first one you gave me. That Devlin guy pulled a knife on me! Do you understand how scary that was for me?"

"The knife was meant for Keekee."

My heart stopped beating. I saw red.

"Not to hurt her," he backpedaled. "To help her."

How dare he? "If you're involving my sister because she'd be an easy target as a new client, then I strongly suggest you stop immediately." I braced my arms on the desk between us and spoke through clenched teeth. "If you do anything to jeopardize mine or my sister's safety, I will ruin you. You'll be arrested by enforcers so fast your head will spin, and when it finally stops, you'll be a mind-stripped drudge."

He sat back in his chair, but he didn't look angry like I expected. He looked pleased. "There she is."

I scoffed. "There who is?"

"The fighter. The fire heart. The protector. The girl in charge." He stood, placing his own hands flat on the desk, mirroring my stance. "Now that the spark has been ignited, are you ready to see the light?"

I kept my gaze locked with his. Adrenaline coursed through me, but with each breath I took to calm my anger, I realized this guy was dangerous. I had to tread lightly so he wouldn't go after Keekee. I could resist his VR offer, but Keek wouldn't be able to say no—especially if he used these same sort of scare tactics on her. I softened my tone.

"Look, I don't want to be rude or mean to you, so I will say this one more time as cordially as possible: I want no part of whatever it is you do. I promised my sister that we would leave this nation after graduation. I can't let you or anyone else jeopardize that promise. My family and our future is my first and only priority, so please, take your fake identities, your hacking skills, your VR cards, and whatever else you might have hidden up your sleeve, and use them on someone else."

Disappointment swept over his eyes, but he didn't move or reply.

"Please try to understand," I added, hoping to reason with him. "I'm not the type of girl you're looking for. Not for dating, not as a VR client, not even as a friend. You're wasting your time and energy."

He straightened, drummed his fingers on the desk, and then picked up his debriefing case and jacket. "Time and energy," he repeated in a sad sort of way. "Fine. This is where I'll leave you, but if you ever do want another date, or if you need a friend, you know where to find me."

I shook my head. "I'm sorry, but it's just not in the cards for us."

Looking down, he pursed his lips and huffed like I said something amusing. "Ah, Kelsey. You couldn't be more wrong."

He walked to the door while I let out a shaky breath. I was doing the right thing. Warning flares had been popping up around Xander ever since the library. Just because a guy was smart and attractive didn't mean he was safe. I refused to be one of those girls who dated delinquents.

"Xander?" I called as he turned the doorknob.

He paused and looked back at me over his shoulder.

I held up my wrist. "Can you please put my band back to normal?"

He walked over to me and set his case on the floor. He stood so close that I was sure he could feel my heart pounding in my chest. I teetered, almost falling into the chair behind me, but he steadied me by placing one of his hands on my hip. I could smell that same breeze of cinnamon on his breath.

"No, Kelsey Zellar. I won't change your band back to normal. Because you are not normal. You are extraordinary. And extraordinary people shouldn't be imprisoned by a tyrannical government."

He tucked one of my stray curls behind my ear. I should have backed away, or told him not to touch me, but all I could do was stand there, staring up at him and wondering why he was still being nice to me. And why, even though he proved he was deceptive and dangerous, my body was aching to press against his.

"Besides, a counselor will come into this room after I leave and have a conversation with you." He slung his jacket over one arm and picked up his case. "Afterward, you'll want to thank me for protecting you with a—what did you call it—*hacked* band? But no thanks are necessary. Regardless of how shady and corrupt you think I am, this is what I do. And helping you is never a waste of my time or energy."

His close proximity and confidence, combined with his warning about a counselor, left me speechless. Before I could find my voice, he had turned and left the office.

I stared at the open door. A bulletin board hung on the wall in the hallway with posters and fliers pinned to it. Some were swaying side to side, caught in the draft of Xander rushing past them. A sheet of bright pink paper came loose from its pin and fluttered to the ground.

I crossed the room, intending to step into the hall and pick it up, but voices stopped me at the threshold. One voice in particular. I momentarily froze as a proctor—not Alexander Mage—escorted Keekee past the doorway.

I stepped into the hall, watching the proctor march my sister further away from me. I wanted to shout out to her, but that would get us both in more trouble.

As the balding proctor guided Keek into counseling room 5, my sister turned and looked at me. Not only could I see the fear in her eyes; I could feel it.

"Miss Zellar," a man said gruffly behind me. I turned to see a stout middle-aged counselor holding a digifile, presumably mine. "I'm Counselor Kramer." He motioned to the office Xander and I had used. "Have a seat. I need to ask you a few questions."

Level 1.3

Counselor Kramer reminded me of a bull. He had a huge forehead, wide nose, and permanently flared nostrils. His boulder head lowered as he entered something into my file. I regretted wearing a red shirt because I was sure he was about to charge me with his invisible horns.

He looked up and sniffled. “You are Kelsey, sister to Keekee Zellar, correct?”

“Yes, sir.”

“Your file states that you do not share your sister’s affinity for illegal virtual reality games. Would that be an accurate assessment?”

“Yes, sir.”

“However, you do have a past charge for unauthorized caffeine consumption, provided to you by previously mentioned sister, Keekee.”

“That was my fault, not hers.”

His lips narrowed and his nostrils flared even wider. “I’d say the fault lies on both of you.”

I focused on my broken thumbnail, picking at the jagged edge. Xander was right. This meeting was making me uncomfortable. How had he known about it before I did?

“Your sister is meeting with a proctor two offices down. I’m sure you can guess why.”

My voice came out weaker than I intended. “We haven’t broken any laws. We’re focused on school and achieving good grades.”

“I’m pleased to hear that. What are your plans after graduation?”

I swallowed hard. Should I admit the truth? Would Keekee tell the truth if her proctor asked the same question? I opted for a version of the truth. “Hopefully college, sir.”

"Majoring in?"

"Library sciences with a minor in preservation and restoration."

"You want to save books?"

"In a perfect world, yes. Saving Olden books would be my dream job."

"Vastly different goal from your sister who has declared she intends to major in technology programming."

"We're very different."

His angry bull eyes narrowed into slits. "Yet physically identical."

"Even then, there are differences."

"Like what?" He practically moaned the words, licking his lips while studying me like a perverted pedophile.

I shifted in my seat and crossed my legs. "I'm a half-inch taller."

We had other differences, like on my right arm I had two moles (beauty marks are what Dad called them), but no way would I mention anything about my skin to pervy bull-faced Kramer.

I wanted to change the topic and fast. "I assume you've already met Keekee since you know about her interest in technology programming."

She decided on that major during our summer break, so I knew it wasn't in her school file.

He cleared his throat and tried switching from creepy to professional again. "We've been chatting most of the morning."

Why? I wanted to ask, but I knew better. Keek hadn't mentioned a counselor meeting, which meant it was unexpected, and now she was meeting with a proctor. Did she do something to get herself in trouble after we parted ways before our first classes?

"Your sister's poor decision skills have caused you and your family to be exiled from three of Equatia's cities. One more and you'll be assigned to The Hub."

As if we weren't well aware. We had numerous dinner discussions about it. Dad warned Keek to cut her crap before we all learned the true definition of prisoner.

"No one wants to see that happen," Counselor Kramer said. "But we still have an entire school year to survive with no incidents, and even then, given your past records, your lofty aspirations of a foreign transfer are concerning."

Glitch. Keek told him we were applying for a transfer. Judging from his cold, judgmental stare (which counselors were *not* supposed to have) it looked like the rumors were correct. Attempting to leave Equatia was frowned upon. Literally and figuratively.

"She'll never make it to graduation." The counselor's words were a slap in my face. "A big city like Elura has too many temptations. Frankly, we're surprised she hasn't already located illegal cards and been detained."

I felt sick, but I tried to speak with conviction. "She won't do it again. She understands the consequences."

"Every criminal understands the consequences, but they still cross the line. It's only a matter of time before an addict becomes too tempted and seeks out her next hit."

"She won't." As much as I wanted to believe what I was saying, I had no doubt he was right.

Counselor Kramer sighed. "We anticipated you would declare firm and unrealistic belief in her ability to resist, which is why our offer is being presented to both of you. We need you working as a team. Fully committed to one another and your parents."

Offer? Fully committed? "I don't understand."

"You girls are new at this school. New to Elura. You're fresh meat." He licked his lips again and my skin crawled. "You're attractive and naive, which makes you a magnet for criminals. But you're also desperate to keep your family safe which makes you perfectly suited to help locate those criminals."

"Locate criminals?" I repeated, as my hatred for him increased due to his not-so-subtle insult about us being naive.

"You and your sister will work undercover. You'll find VR dealers, engage them, and use their services—funded, of course, by Equatia. Your sister will be granted permission to play the very games to which she is so wickedly addicted. All of your activity will be monitored, recorded, and used to build cases and collect intel on as many virtual reality dealers as you can find in the next few months."

The sickening feeling wasn't just in my stomach anymore. It had spread throughout my whole body. "And then?"

He sneered like a rabid dog. "If you succeed, then you, your sister, and your parents will be granted foreign transfer with high recommendations from government officials."

Granted foreign transfer. Until now, Keekee's idea had been only a dream. One we weren't even sure was attainable. "Transfer to a better nation?"

He looked offended. "That depends on your definition of *better.* I'm proud to be an Equatian. I don't understand why anyone would want to leave a nation that provides such care and protection to its citizens."

Spoken like a true brainwashed employee.

"A better nation as in more freedom," I clarified. "The opportunity to travel to other parts of the world, to communicate with people other than Equatians, to earn as much income as we want."

He snickered. "To consume as much coffee as you'd like?"

Not a requirement, I thought, *but it would be a bonus.*

After entering information into my digifile, he explained, "If you and your sister agree, you will discuss the details with officers who are ranked higher than I am. This meeting is only step one. You have many more to go."

Step one. Yesterday I had been told I was at step zero of a vastly different path.

Could I do such an unthinkable thing to Xander? Pretend to be interested in him while Keek and I worked undercover to collect evidence that would get him arrested and eventually mind-stripped? I hardly knew him, but even considering it made me want to slap myself. How could we do that to anyone? VR dealers or not, they were still people.

"Our allotted time is up." He rose and tucked my file under his arm. "You and your sister can discuss the opportunity with your parents this evening and make your decision. Another meeting will be scheduled for tomorrow."

"Yes, sir." I stood too, even though my legs felt like they'd give out on me. It took a concentrated effort to make my next statement sound genuine. "Thanks for meeting with me today."

The dreadful counselor waddled around the desk and stood uncomfortably close to me. He ran his cold index finger down my arm in a manner that was grossly inappropriate. I backed away, wanting to gag. "I'm still your assigned counselor, and I'll be enthusiastically guiding you and your sister on your journeys."

What a creep. How many other students had he treated this way, or worse? If the situation were different, I'd report him without hesitation, but no school officials would believe me at this point. And even if they did, the government probably pre-approved any methods Kramer wanted to use to convince (or force) Keekee and me to help with their search for VR dealers. Had he treated Keek this way too?

I wanted to tell him he was an ugly, pathetic pervert, and he'd never touch me or my sister again, but we were in a bad enough situation already.

"Enjoy the rest of your day, Miss Zellar."

He left the office as I let out the breath I'd been holding, but his departure didn't make me feel better. I felt suffocated and claustrophobic—not only because of Kramer and the cramped office, but because of our nation's leash tightening around mine and Keekee's throats.

Level 1.4

I sat at the kitchen table, my head in my hands. “How can we do that to people?”

“How can we not do it?” Keek stood over me, her voice shrill and desperate. “You know as well as I do they aren’t really asking us to do this. They’re telling us. If we say no, we won’t get to carry on carefree until graduation and then be approved for a foreign transfer. They will make our lives hell, and the only way we’ll ever leave Equatia is by death.”

“Keekee,” Mom scorned, adjusting in her seat. “What a dreadful thing to say.”

“It’s the truth and we all know it,” she snapped.

My head hurt so much that no amount of caffeine would help. “I don’t feel right baiting people into a trap that will end with them being mind-stripped or worse.”

“It doesn’t give me a warm and fuzzy feeling either,” Keek argued, “but they are criminals. We’re not making them act illegally. They were doing this stuff long before we moved to this city.”

“The *stuff* you’re referring to are the games you love so much. How would you feel helping convict one or more of your previous dealers?”

“It would suck really hard, but thankfully I don’t know anyone here. I’m emotionally detached.”

“But you won’t stay detached,” I pointed out. “You’ll get to know them. Kramer said we have to collect a few months of evidence. You’ll be visiting them regularly, playing their games, and then you’ll be the cause of their demise. That will haunt you for the rest of your life.”

She didn’t pause for a moment of remorse. “At least I’ll be haunted in a nation where I can be free.”

"You won't be free. Neither of us will. We'll be prisoners of our own guilt, and no matter how many times we move, or how far we run, we'll never be able to escape from ourselves."

Keek sat in the chair next to me. "To appease you, let's pretend saying no is a feasible choice. Tell me what you'd tell officials, and what you predict for our future."

I glanced at Mom and Dad. Worry lines had been etched on their faces since we came home from school. Officials also met with them earlier in the day. They told them about our offer, and while our parents weren't saying much, I had a gut feeling their meetings were as scary and uncomfortable as mine.

"We say, 'No, thank you,'" I explained, "because we don't want to make your addiction worse. And then we stay on perfect behavior until graduation."

"And then?" Keek prodded.

"And then we—" Saying it out loud was pointless. Keek was right; they'd never approve a transfer if we refused to help them. But there were other options. "Then we go to college and make a future for ourselves here in Equatia."

"No!" Keek slammed her hand on the table. "I'm not staying here. You know how badly I want to leave, and this isn't just a chance. It's a guarantee."

I turned to Mom and Dad. "Is this what you want? Do you want us to hang out with criminals for the next few months?"

Dad rubbed his hand over his face. His bloodshot eyes matched Mom's. "Keekee has been sneaking around to hang out with criminals for years. At least this time it would serve a greater purpose."

I shrieked, "Dad!" at the same time Keek exclaimed, "Exactly!"

"Mom," I pleaded, hoping someone would be on my side. "You can't be okay with this."

She pointedly looked at me, then at Keekee, then at my father. She brushed some imaginary substance from each hand then sat up straight and sighed. "The thing is, lovebug, I think Keek is right. The government will make our lives hell if you say no."

My mouth hung open as I tried to find words to keep defending my argument, but Keek beat me to it.

"They will monitor us every second of every day, Kelsey. They will harass us, issue us citations for anything and everything. We'll probably have to meet with proctors, health advisors, and counselors, all day every day. Remember that stupid fitness program they issued you a few years back because your body mass index was five percent over the acceptable standard? It will be annoying crap like that except a hundred times worse. We won't be able to blink or breathe without some government official swooping in and punishing us for doing it wrong. And Kramer, don't get me started on pervy Kramer and what they might allow him to do to us."

Mom made a terrified hiccup sound, then silence fell over the kitchen. I hated that Keekee was right.

"Not to mention," Keek continued. "They clearly scared the crap out of Mom and Dad, so who knows what's in store for *them* if we don't do this."

Mom looked away, staring out the window as her chin trembled. Dad's lips turned inward as he stared at his hands folded on the table. Mom and Dad weren't telling us what to do, but their fear was apparent. Convicting VR dealers would weigh heavily on our consciences for the rest of our lives, but subjecting Mom and Dad to a tortured future would weigh infinitely heavier.

"Okay," I relented.

"Finally." Keekee sighed. "I knew you'd come to your senses."

"Are you absolutely certain you want to do this?" Mom asked me, but her voice wavered. She was doing the motherly thing by letting me decide, but she was secretly hoping I would say yes.

"Yes," I said, hating myself for it. "I'm certain."

Dad stood, took two steps toward me and wrapped me in a hug so tight I struggled to breathe.

Keek sounded relieved. "I'm not saying it will be easy, but it will be worth it in the end."

We had taken the first step in making a deal with the devil, and although it seemed the lesser evil of the two choices, I was sure we were agreeing to eternal purgatory.

That night, Keekee fell asleep smiling. I couldn't believe it.

I lay on my side, in my bed, watching her across from me as she attempted to continue our conversation, but her eyelids grew heavy and her words turned into grunts. Even as her breathing slowed, a grin stayed plastered on her face.

Equatia was granting her permission to indulge in her addiction for the next few months, and in return, her dream of a foreign transfer was coming true. Of course she was happy. Me, on the other hand—all I could think about was how many lives we would ruin.

One of those ruined lives could be Xander's. The criminal wasn't the only one who suffered when they were taken away and mind-stripped. Their family and friends suffered the loss too. My chest felt tight and I had a foul taste in my mouth. I flipped over and stared out the window. No moon or stars shone. The sky looked as gloomy as I felt.

For the good of my family, I would agree to help bring down VR dealers, but that didn't mean one of them had to be Xander. He had been nothing but nice to me. He even tried to protect me by bugging my govern band. Granted, he went about it in a sneaky way, but he deserved credit for the effort. I had to warn him.

I quietly made my way to the bathroom and shut myself in the linen closet. Activating my expanded screen, I stared at the eerie glow, wondering if Xander could see me. I didn't have his contact link, but he had secretly spied on me last night so maybe he was doing the same tonight.

"Xander, I—" I didn't know what to say. I didn't even know if he could hear me. "I need to talk to you. It's important. And urgent."

I didn't want to say too much. What if Xander's hacking skills weren't as failsafe as he believed and the kibz were monitoring me? For a solid five minutes, my screen remained blank. I minimized it and stared at the intrusive band wrapped around my wrist. If a proctor were watching, I would have received a question or alert by now.

If officials inspected my band, perhaps to improve its criminal monitoring abilities in some way, would they realize it had been tampered with? How would I explain that?

Tomorrow, Keekee and I would officially announce our decision. From that point on, our every move would be tracked, every conversation monitored. I had to see Xander again before it was too late. Not only to warn him that as of tomorrow I'd be his worst enemy, but also to insist he put my band back to normal before both of us were punished for his hacking crime.

I crept out of the closet and returned to our bedroom. I had never snuck out before, never even thought about it, because getting caught was guaranteed, but tonight my bugged band provided a window of opportunity.

As quietly as I could, I put on pants, a tunic, and shoes. I slid our window open and climbed outside. Our house was only one story so the physical act of sneaking out was easy, but I was so nervous that it felt like I might have a heart attack right there on our lawn. It's a good thing my band wasn't reporting my real responses or I would have been sending up more red alerts than a proctor could count.

I couldn't drive our craft this late at night because it was past teen curfew. The craft's system would send an alert to traffic monitors. My parents would be notified, enforcers would show up, and they'd be able to look at the craft's records and see exactly where I went. I didn't want to lead them to Xander's front door.

It was a long walk, and I'd have to dodge any patrolling enforcers, but I had to try. Devlin's terrified eyes still haunted me, and I couldn't bear the thought of Xander going through the same thing because of me.

Level 1.5

With the hood of my tunic pulled over my head, I rushed along the sidewalk for only a few minutes when it occurred to me that I wasn't sure of the exact location of Xander's warehouse. Even if I could find it, how would I get in? It's not like the abandoned building had a doorbell.

I cursed myself under my breath. Why hadn't I thought this plan through better? Spotting craft lights up ahead, I froze in place. The craft turned down my street, so I hurried back to the tall hedges I had just passed and hid.

I stood still as a statue, praying the prickly shrubs were dense enough to keep me concealed from view. The vehicle flew past me, low and slow. My pulse skipped several beats. Only patrolling enforcers piloted that way.

The craft's whirring grew quieter as it continued past my hiding place, but then my fear kicked into overdrive when headlights reflected against the windows of the house across the street. The craft was turning around and coming back.

The whirring grew louder again, then the craft slowed to a stop on the other side of the hedge.

Run, I told myself. *Do it. Run hard and fast.*

My band was bugged. They wouldn't be able to track me. They wouldn't know my identity. But my slim odds of outrunning an enforcer kept my feet rooted in some stranger's flowerbed.

Footsteps approached. I closed my eyes as if that would help.

"Come with me." The deep voice made me jump and yelp at the same time.

"Shhh." Xander pulled me around the hedges and toward the street where his craft hovered.

"Xander?" I hissed his name, my adrenaline still pumping ferociously. "You scared me to death."

He opened his craft door and practically shoved me inside before rushing around to the pilot seat and jumping in. "You're a terrible hider. I could see your bright purple tunic through the gaps in the bushes."

"You just happened to be cruising by and saw me?"

"Of course not. I came to get you before an enforcer spotted you or a busybody reported you walking the streets at this hour."

"But how did you know—" My pulse still pounded against the band hugging my wrist, answering my unfinished question. "You did get my message. You're still spying on me."

"Can you please stop calling it spying? It's such a derogative term. I'm helping you."

"I was on my way to help *you.*"

He smirked. "Help me? By telling me you're agreeing to be a fink for our crooked government?"

He was spying on me even more than I suspected.

"How much do you know?" I asked.

"I know almost everything."

"Then you know to stay away from me. And my sister. Keek doesn't know anything about what you do. I won't tell anyone anything about you, I swear."

"I'm grateful, but I already knew that too."

He had crossed the cocky line again. I didn't want to get into another argument with him. I also didn't want to get caught sneaking out past curfew and cruising around town with a VR dealer. I wanted to accomplish what I set out to do and return home.

"You have to put my band back to normal."

He glanced down at my arm but then returned his focus to piloting the empty streets. "If I do that, you'll be shackled for the rest of your life."

"Officials will know my band has been tampered with, and when they ask me by whom, what am I supposed to say?"

Xander didn't reply. He stared straight ahead while rubbing his temple. I looked up to see us gliding through the open door to his warehouse. "You brought me back to your place?"

"Wasn't this your intended destination?"

"Only because I needed to talk to you, but we could do that right here in your craft."

The second set of doors, the ones covered with graffiti, were already sliding open. Xander flew into the bright tunnel of scrolling numbers.

"Stop!" I demanded. "I don't want to go any further."

"You're already in further than you realize." He held my hand as the craft glided deeper down the tunnel. "I'm here to help you find your way out."

"Make yourself comfortable." Xander motioned to his couch while I stood next to his craft, taking in the impressive sight of his warehouse loft for the second time. "Would you like a drink?"

"That would be nice." With only five steps I had closed the distance between us. Convenient parking to say the least.

"Juice, water, or coffee?"

"I've already used my three caffeine allotments."

He stopped in his kitchen and turned to me, smiling. "I guess I didn't make it clear enough this morning. Your band is auto-reporting everything. You can drink as much coffee as you'd like."

I stepped forward, somewhat shocked. "Are you serious?"

He laughed. "I wouldn't recommend binging on ten cups or anything. You'll be bouncing off the walls, but an extra cup or two sounds appealing, doesn't it?"

I'd been out past curfew for over twenty minutes and no enforcers had hunted me down yet. Whatever Xander did to my band, it must have worked. "You're certain the government wouldn't somehow find out?"

He had already opened a cupboard and was pulling down a shiny bag. "I'm certain."

"What is that?" I rushed to his side, gaping over his shoulder as the aroma of coffee filled the air. He scooped beans into a small contraption on his counter. "This is coffee and that is a personal brewer."

My mouth watered. "You have coffee here? In your house? You can make a cup whenever you want?"

"Yup." He pushed a button on the brewer and it glowed red. The machine made a grinding sound then began gurgling as

Xander leaned against the counter and waved his hands. "Poof! Homebrewed magic."

"You could get in so much trouble if anyone found out about this."

"I wonder which they'd be more upset about, my secret coffee stash or my library of illegal access cards."

He had a point. Major criminals probably didn't care about getting busted for excess caffeine. They had much bigger crimes to worry about.

Liquid heaven began dripping into a mug. I stared, marveling at my favorite substance being privately brewed for me without a distribution employee measuring the exact amount allowed and scanning my band to record my used allotment.

Xander handed me the steaming cup. "Alakazam."

I cradled it like it was a precious treasure. "You're sure?"

"One hundred percent."

I took a sip and moaned with appreciation. "It's divine. It's so fresh and vibrant. Bold instead of bitter."

"That's how it's supposed to taste."

I eyed my band, expecting it to start beeping with an alert that an enforcer was on their way, but it remained silent. I sipped some more, each gulp tasting more delicious than the one before.

"Congratulations," Xander said. "You've successfully completed an illegal act. Isn't it liberating?"

A pang of guilt tugged at me for a second, but I washed it away with another sip of coffee. "It feels forbidden, but it tastes exquisite."

My cup was already half empty.

"I can brew you another if you'd like, but I wouldn't recommend it." He gently but playfully tapped my temple. "You're capillaries might expand so wide that they burst."

"This one cup is more than enough. Too much of a good thing leaves you unable to appreciate it."

"I agree." He pulled out a chair. "Please, sit down. In a few hours, you'll need to be back in your bed. We have a lot to discuss, and the sunrise is inching closer every moment."

We sat catty-corner from each other at his kitchen table. Over his shoulder, beyond the living room area, the hammock hung between two steel beams. How many girls had been in that hammock with him? I eyed the ceiling above us, wondering what Xander's upstairs bedroom looked like.

Then I mentally slapped myself. I had no business wondering about Xander's bedroom or his hammock.

He cleared his throat and asked, "Do you have a plan?"

I finished the last swig of my delicious coffee and peered at him over the brim of my mug. He had the most non-threatening face and such baby-smooth skin. I'd never met any of Keek's VR dealers, but I had always imagined them to be rough-looking and intimidating—maybe with a few scars from fights, or pale, skinny, and strung out from hiding away in dark sunless rooms playing VR. Xander was the opposite of all that.

"I'm not sure yet," I admitted. "But I wasn't going to turn you in. I would never do that."

"I know."

"How do you know? I didn't say any of that out loud to Keek or my parents, so no matter how closely you were spying, or *helping,* you couldn't have known that."

"I'm a good judge of character."

"We have no choice. We have to do it. They'll punish us and our parents if we don't."

"I understand and sympathize." He sat back in his chair. "But let me ask, how do you foresee this ending?"

I swallowed. "It ends with us transferring out of Equatia."

His brows rose. "You truly believe that?"

"It's part of the agreement."

"And you think the government will book you and your family one-way tickets? Let you leave their constraints, and allow you to flee to somewhere else where you and three other witnesses can tell others how Equatia controls and suppresses its citizens?"

"People have transferred in the past." Even as I spoke the words, I doubted them. I had always doubted the optimists who said it was possible.

Xander didn't agree or disagree. He just stared at me, waiting for me to speak.

"At least that's what I've heard," I added. He still didn't reply, but his eyes narrowed so I asked, "It's not true, is it?"

He shook his head.

My stomach lurched, and my next question came out timid. "Do I want to know what happened to the people who supposedly transferred?"

Slower and more somberly, he shook his head again.

"Glitch." I dropped my face into my hands. "So even if we do help them, they're never going to let us go."

"Deep down you already knew that."

I slumped deeper in my chair and groaned. "It's not fair."

"It's most certainly not."

"What do we do?"

He rocked back on two legs of his chair. "What do you *want* to do?"

"I want to get the hell out of this nation along with my family, but that's never going to happen."

"So you're giving up without even trying?"

"You said it was hopeless."

He teetered back and forth, balanced on the rear legs of his chair. "I said nothing of the sort."

His balancing act made me nervous. With each rock backward, I expected the chair to slip out from under him, leaving him to crash onto the floor. What if he hit his head and damaged his impressively intelligent brain? He had hacked my band to protect me without even knowing me. He had a hidden lair with a massive library of Olden books and VR cards. He knew much more than most when it came to dodging the iron fist of our government. He should protect himself and his brain more carefully.

I gripped my mug between my hands to keep myself from reaching forward and forcing him to stay still. "Can you help us?"

He returned all four chair legs to the floor. "I thought you'd never ask."

Level 1.6

"First," Xander said, scooting his chair so close our knees almost touched. "I have to ask you to put blind and total trust in me. If I say *jump,* you don't pause to ask which direction, you leap far and fast. If I enlighten you with information, even if you find it hard to believe, you absorb it as fact unless your instincts tell you otherwise."

"That seems contradictory. What if my instincts tell me everything you say is unbelievable?"

"That won't happen. But if by some chance it does, you always default to your instincts. Always."

He wanted me to follow any and all demands, which sort of made me want to walk away from him and never look back, but then he insisted I do what feels right even if it meant going against him, which almost convinced me he really was looking out for my best interests.

"I can't agree to any of this without details of your plan," I insisted. "Will Keekee be involved? Will my parents be at risk?"

"Yes, Keekee will be involved eventually, and your parents won't have any idea what you're doing; therefore, they won't be at risk."

"What exactly will I be doing?"

He rested his hand on my knee and a warm shiver ran through me. He smiled like he knew the effect he had on me. "You'll be learning how to override the system."

"Override the system," I repeated. A different sensation pulsed through each of my fingertips and toes. My hands involuntarily flexed.

Xander studied me with an intense look of concern.

"Like you did to my band?" I asked.

"That's one miniscule part of it."

"What's the rest? Because the government wants to monitor us. Sending fake signals that I'm calm and eating properly won't satisfy my assignment to gather incriminating evidence on dealers. They're going to demand real information and real criminals."

"I could sit here for the next four hours and explain as much as I can, but it wouldn't be nearly enough time. You'd return home in the same predicament you're in right now. Plus, you'd be confused, sleep-deprived, and a jittery mess during your family's meeting with officials. Or—" He held out his hand. "You can come with me and begin your journey to a much different ending."

I stared at his open hand. I wanted to trust him. He was my only chance of finding a way out of this nightmare. Even if I didn't understand how he'd help us, I'd be a fool not to give him the chance.

"Follow your instincts," Xander reminded me. "They'll never lead you in the wrong direction."

My instincts told me to reach out and link my hand with his, but was that true instinct, or was it desperation combined with an unhealthy attraction for a charming guy? I didn't have a solid answer, but I had no other choice. I didn't want to spend the next few months as a government slave, tracking down criminals, only to end up still trapped in Equatia, or killed for wanting to leave.

I placed my hand in his. A surge of *rightness* rushed through me. It wasn't excitement or giddiness; it was a feeling of becoming solid and strong. Like I had been found after not realizing I was lost.

My thoughts were silly and unrealistically romantic. Those truths didn't escape me as we walked together through Xander's loft and stopped in front of the door to his library.

Like Xander said, in a few hours I'd have to be back in my bed to start the first day of an indefinite future as an Equatian slave. Whatever happened between now and then, even if it was silly or unrealistically romantic, I would embrace every minute of it. My family's future and mine had turned very grim, and Xander was the only person offering me a light at the end of that dark tunnel.

He turned the gold knob, pushed open the door, and ushered me into his library.

Level 1.7

My second time in Xander's library was as spellbinding as the first.

True, I knew that some (or many) of the books were hiding illegal access cards, but still, the filled shelves left me in awe.

Xander squeezed my hand. "You're going to love this."

He let go and walked to one of the walls of shelves. He climbed a ladder and removed a book from the top of the stacks and hurried back down. Hiding the book behind him, he grinned so big I couldn't help but do the same.

"Great," I said. "We have a few hours to pull off some kind of techy miracle to outsmart the government, and you want to use the time for stories?"

He shrugged. "Answers to most of life's questions and problems can be found in fairy tales."

I eyed him skeptically. I believed that, but I'd never met anyone who agreed with me.

"Okay." I held out my hands. "Which book are we reading? Or whatever you call it. Is there a term for virtually experiencing a story?"

"Immersing."

"Ah, okay then. Which book are we immersing ourselves in first?"

"I'll show you."

He rolled a ladder along one side of the room then stopped at the last stack of shelves. He tucked the book in the front of his pants and started climbing, turning and staring down at me when he reached the seventh or eighth rung. "Start climbing or you'll miss all the fun."

I gazed up at the rows of towering books above us, shrugging off my confusion. Maybe he needed another book or access card, or he had EVRAs hidden somewhere and he needed me to help carry one down. I climbed up behind him, but when the ladder shook, I looked up to see him step onto a shelf.

I gasped. "What in the world?"

He turned and peered over the edge at me, waiting for me to catch up. I climbed faster, and when I reached the top, I stood dumbfounded. The shelf was tall enough for him to stand comfortably upright, and he had to be six foot. The book spines behind him were just as tall.

"How is this possible?" I asked.

"From down there, it's an optical illusion. The shelves look normal height." He held out his hand and helped me step off the ladder to join him.

I marveled at the book spines lined up in front of me. They were wide enough for me to hug, and some stretched taller than me. "This can't be real."

He grinned and sidestepped, stopping in front of a green Olden book decorated with silver symbols, but no title. Studying it, I realized the mark on the bottom of the spine, which in most cases was the logo of the publisher, was the eye from the symbol on his tarot cards.

"I'll allow you the honor," Xander said.

"The honor of what?"

"Opening it."

"Opening what?"

He lifted my hand then pressed it flat against the silver eyeball. "The doorway."

The eye glowed and I sucked in a shocked breath. The spine swung inward like a door. The books on either side of it framed the hidden passageway to a small and oddly plain room. I leaned forward to peek inside. The walls looked like they were made from translucent gel, and the ceiling appeared to be made of frosted glass. No furniture, no shelves: it was empty.

Backing out, I assessed Xander, the larger than life bookshelf where we were standing, the countless books around us and below us, and the secret doorway in front of me.

I stepped inside. "Where are we?"

"The immersion room."

"This is where the magic happens?" I teased.

"I'll let you be the judge of how magical it is." He drummed his fingers on the book that was still tucked in the front of his pants. The top half of the cover was showing, but it had no title. He pulled it free, his shirt lifting in the process, and I caught a glimpse of his toned abs.

Blushing, I looked around for a hidden closet or something where he might keep EVRAs or equipment, but the room really was empty. Not even a rug on the shiny white floor. "I hope your EVRA is much better quality than the kind they use in schools."

"I don't use outdated junk. The apparatus is you."

"Me?"

"The human brain is more powerful than hundreds of super computers combined. Why would you want to restrict the power of your mind by limiting it to the abilities of a technological device?"

"I doubt my brain is powerful enough to make me believe I'm living inside a book."

"I promise, if you open yourself up to the possibility, you will be astounded by how powerful you are and the realities you can experience." He opened the book and held it between us. An access card that looked like it was made of glass sat nestled in one side of the fake pages.

"If you don't use an EVRA, where do you insert the card?"

"Hold it in your hand."

I carefully removed the card from its cradle. It felt cool and smooth between my fingers. "This doesn't feel like an access card."

"It's quartz—much more powerful than the plastic cards I distribute to clients."

"I'm not getting the same type of experience as your other clients?"

"No, Kelsey." The tender way he spoke my name made my skin tingle. "This card is drastically improved over the kind they circulate in schools and libraries."

"Why am I receiving special treatment?"

"We don't have nearly enough time for me to list the reasons."

My cheeks warmed. As a twin, my whole life was spent comparing myself to my sister, wondering if Mom and Dad favored her. It shouldn't have been a contest because I loved her to pieces, but the never-ending comparisons naturally evolved.

Maybe all siblings felt that way, but the twin factor made me feel not-at-all unique. Less special. In front of me stood the smartest guy I had ever met, and he believed I was special for multiple reasons. My instincts told me he meant it, and I loved the way that made me feel. The way *he* made me feel.

"Hold your palm flat," he said. "Place the card in your hand."

I followed his directions, and we both stared down at the transparent rectangle of quartz in my hand. "Now what?"

"Read it."

"Read what?"

"Read the code etched onto the card."

I lifted it closer to my face and squinted. I could barely make out a pattern of lines and symbols on its surface. "Oh yeah, I see something."

"Keep your eyes on the code etched in the card. No matter what happens, don't look away. The room around us will glow and change colors, but do not look away from the card, or we'll have to start over."

"Okay," I agreed, keeping my focus on the quartz resting in my palm. But it was difficult. Telling me not to look at a room that would glow and change colors made me want to study the walls.

"Here we go." Xander took my free hand in his then pressed the tip of my index finger onto the card's surface.

Different colored lights flashed and streamed all around us.

"Eyes on the card," Xander reminded me. "Don't look away. Not even at me."

It was extremely difficult not to watch what was happening around us. And it was always hard not to look at him.

"You're doing great," Xander said. "Only a few more seconds."

The markings on the card started glowing, and then it became easy not to look away. Numbers and symbols scrolled throughout my field of vision. I didn't have to squint to see them because they were so clear and bright.

I was no longer aware of Xander or the strange room. I was consumed by the fascinating card coming to life in the palm of my hand.

A sound like bells chiming grew louder. Everything became blurry, so I blinked in an attempt to clear my vision, but with that one blink everything went black.

I stood in total darkness. "Xander?"

I closed my fingers, feeling for the card, but it was gone. I reached out my hands, trying to locate Xander, but I sensed he was gone too. Stepping forward, hands held out in front of me, I touched something soft, like fur. I moved my fingers up and down, stroking the silky material which moved when I pressed against it.

As my eyes adjusted to the darkness, I realized I was touching a fur coat, hanging in a closet. Another one hung beside it. Behind me was another row of coats. Why was I in a closet? The moment of confusion passed as one of my favorite childhood stories rushed into my mind and heart so intensely that I squealed with glee.

Not a closet, a magical *wardrobe.*

I excitedly pushed forward through the coats. If I was where I suspected, then a lifelong dream of mine was about to come true. I felt crunching beneath my shoes, and although the sound was foreign to me, I knew it was snow because I had read the story so many times.

Racing ahead, I searched for the light that would confirm which beloved storybook I had entered. And there it was.

One single lamppost surrounded by woods and a blanket of snow.

I sighed happily and the cold air chilled my throat and nostrils. "Unbelievable."

Behind me, framed between two trees, was the door to the wardrobe from which I had exited. Just like in the story, I could see the coats hanging inside, and beyond them, Xander's glowing immersion room.

Footsteps crunched in the snow somewhere near the forest line. I could even smell the pine trees. Xander stepped out from behind a thick tree trunk. He wore a long black coat, a red and white checkered scarf, and a black top hat. "Did I choose wisely for your first adventure?"

I rushed forward and hugged him. He was solid and real.

"This is amazing. Absolutely amazing. And you're real. You're actually here with me?"

"I'm not nearly as interesting as a faun with an umbrella, but I wanted to be here so I could see your reaction."

Snow started falling around us. I spun around, watching the glistening white specs fall from the night sky. My face was covered with bursts of cool wetness as flakes landed on me. "I never thought I'd see real snow, much less feel it."

Xander threw his head back, watching the sky too. "It's not a myth, or some extinct weather event from the past like Equatia falsely proclaims. It still snows in many parts of the world."

"Really? Not just in virtual worlds?"

"In the real world too."

"It's so beautiful." I wrapped my arms around myself and shivered. Equatia was never this cold, even during winter.

Xander took off his coat and wrapped it around me.

I couldn't contain my wonder. "Are we about to meet Lucy and Mr. Tumnus?"

"In this scenario you are Lucy, and Mr. Tumnus should be here any moment."

I happily bounced side to side. "I want to meet all of them. Every single character."

Xander smiled down at me. A snowflake landed on his dark eyelashes, causing a sparkle that made his gaze seem even more magical than usual.

Tugging on his scarf, I said, "These red and white checkers remind me of the cards that appeared on my nightstand."

His good mood fizzled. He blinked and the glistening snowflakes on his lashes evaporated. "What cards?"

"Old World playing cards. I assumed you had something to do with them."

"Playing cards," he repeated. "Not tarot cards?"

I shook my head, and the snowy forest around us blurred. The virtual scenery around me was lagging, unable to keep up with my visual perception of it. The same thing always happened when I wore EVRAs; it's what gave me vertigo and nausea. I refocused on Xander, trying to regain my balance while the virtual world around me stabilized.

Xander's tone was anxious. "We have to go."

I whined as if I were Lucy's age. "No, please, let's stay a little longer."

“We can’t. There’s someone we must see right away.”

“Who could be more interesting than the characters I’m about to meet right here?”

He was already guiding me back to the wardrobe. “Let’s just say you need to meet with your own personal Aslan instead of this fictional one.”

“We can come back at some point, right? It’s a cruel teaser to bring me here then make me leave before I’ve met any of the characters.”

“I promise we’ll come back.” He picked up his pace, and I struggled to keep up with him because of the thick snow.

“We’re leaving so abruptly because I mentioned playing cards?”

“Yes, and because you’ll need another coffee to warm you.”

“Tea,” I corrected. “Mr. Tumnus invited Lucy for tea.”

“You dislike tea.”

“True. Coffee is much better.” I paused at the wardrobe entrance, admiring the lifelike scene behind us again and wishing we didn’t have to leave. “A little change in the story won’t hurt anyone, right?”

Xander offered me his arm. “On the contrary, changes to this story are exactly what we need.”

Level 1.8

After we had walked through the wardrobe of coats and stepped into Xander's immersion room, I looked back, hoping the doorway to Narnia would still be there, but it was gone. The walls surrounding us had returned to their non-glowing, gel-like state. Even Xander's coat had vanished from around my shoulders. I wasn't cold anymore.

"That was unbelievable," I said breathlessly. "I have no words to describe how awesome and surreal that was."

"It's only a glimpse of what's possible."

"If the VR games Keek plays are anything close to that, then I understand why she's such an addict."

"Gamer technology isn't nearly as advanced or realistic as what you experienced, but it gives you an idea of why escaping reality is so appealing to the masses."

"I don't understand how they could illegalize something so fantastic and exhilarating. Obviously it's addicting, but why can't they issue allotments like they do with entertainment programs? Limit it to a couple hours per day per person, or whatever?"

"Because they're afraid and paranoid."

"Of what?"

"Losing control again. Citizens becoming overly dependent on technology like before The Crash. Or worse, citizens becoming more intelligent than the government and Equatia being overpowered. They do whatever it takes to make sure no one disrupts the controlled environment they've fought so long and diligently to protect." Xander grunted while rolling his eyes. "As if a nation so corrupt is worthy of protecting."

"You might hate Equatia more than Keekee. I didn't think that was possible."

"I know too many truths that others don't. I have valid reasons to loathe this nation and everyone involved with its creation and continuation."

"What kind of truths?"

A bittersweet grin spread across his kind face. "Seconds ago, you were ecstatic because of your escape to another world. It's too soon to contaminate your mind with reminders of Equatia's ugliness."

"I want to know."

"Not yet."

I didn't argue, because even though I said I wanted to know, I wasn't sure I meant it. I'd heard enough bad things through government alerts and scare tactics, even worse stuff via rumors. I didn't want to know how much worse Equatia could be.

"Will you at least tell me why you were spooked when I mentioned playing cards?"

Xander's stare grew concerned and icy. "Because the cards were a warning."

"A warning of what?"

"Danger."

"Playing cards are dangerous?"

"Again, I won't place that fear or burden on you right now."

The mere mention of the cards had caused palpable worry in Xander. Worry that had ruined my escape to a magical world. I eyed the closed door that led back to the library. "Can we skip coffee and scary talks about the government and immerse ourselves in another story?"

Xander smirked as he stepped toward me, standing so close I could feel his breath on my forehead. "Slow down, my little book lover. We have to take small steps or you'll become overwhelmed."

He reached up and touched the back of my neck, making my breath quiver. He was going to kiss me. No doubt about it this time. And I was more than ready.

His hands lingered beneath the back of my hair as he whispered, "Don't lose this."

"Lose what?" I asked breathlessly.

After a quiet clicking sound, Xander dropped his hands, stepped back, and turned away. "The charm."

“Charm?” I touched my neck and felt a cord of velvet with a cross made of quartz hanging against my chest. He hadn’t given me a perfect, passionate kiss. He had given me a necklace. Not at all what I was hoping for.

“I can’t explain how or why the charm is important yet,” he said, “but someone will tell you when you’re ready.”

“Ready for what? And who is this someone you’re referring to?”

“To answer that question, we need to make a pit stop at one of my favorite places.” Xander walked out of the room so I followed. We were back on the bookshelf.

He walked past three spines then stood in front of a black one with white lettering. The title read, *The Time Machine.*

I read the author’s name aloud. “H.G. Wells. I’ve always wanted to read one of his books.”

Xander traced the H and G and the letters lit up. He winked at me and pushed against the spine, cracking open another secret door.

“If you tell me this is some sort of actual time machine, I might pass out.”

He laughed. “It’s not a time machine, but I have a feeling you’re going to love it.”

Xander placed one hand on the small of my back and with the other, he pushed open the door. “Welcome to Higher Grounds.”

Through the door was a cafe. As my mouth hung half-open in astonishment, the aroma of fresh coffee pulled my feet forward.

The cafe was so different from other caffeine distributor shops I’d visited. Plush couches and chairs filled the room. Exquisite tapestries hung on the walls. I’d seen similar decor in entertainment sessions of Old World films, but never in the present.

A young barista with dreadlocks was topping a latte with whipped cream, but Xander stepping through the doorway behind me caught her attention. Her face lit up as she handed a customer his drink, then she turned toward us. “Xander! So stellar to see you.”

She hugged him and he hugged her back, but before I felt any jealousy, the girl sidestepped him and stood in front of me, grasping my biceps. “Kelsey, welcome, welcome, welcome.”

Beside me, Xander said, "Kelsey, this is Awol."

"Awol," I repeated, thinking it was a strange but unique name. "I like your hair."

She stroked one vibrant red braid that was hidden beneath the rest of her dreads. "Hey, thanks. Can I make you two a drink?"

Xander replied before I could. "We could both use an Awol Special. Extra strong."

We. He answered like we were a couple, but I didn't mind. I liked the sound of *we* on his lips.

Unlike the flirty girl at Caffeine Machine, Awol didn't give me any uneasy feelings. She stepped back behind the counter, but she was smiling and her eyes were pinballing between Xander and me. "So stoked that you two are here. *So* stoked."

Lights hung above her and the coffee bar. Each one glowed a different color through its artsy glass shade. Funky music played from speakers I couldn't visibly locate, and that worried me.

"They could get shut down for playing music publicly," I said to Xander.

He shook his head. "No one will ever shut down this place."

One of the brewing machines hissed to life as a cloud of steam danced its way to the high ceilings. That's when I noticed a second floor overlooking the main room where we stood.

"What's up there?" I asked.

Xander held my hand. "Come with me and see for yourself."

Level 1.9

"We have to take off our shoes." Xander paused at the bottom of the stairway and removed his boots.

Hesitant, I glimpsed down at my flats still on my feet. "We have to take off our shoes in a coffee shop?"

"Only if you go upstairs. She doesn't like her sacred space tainted with dirt or energy from Equatia."

"Who is *she?*" I asked, standing on one foot to remove my left shoe then switching to the other.

"You'll see."

"No." I grabbed his forearm, forcing him to stand still. "You keep giving me vague answers that don't tell me anything. I want useful information, so take your pick, either tell me who is upstairs, or explain why the playing cards are dangerous."

His tensed muscles relaxed beneath my fingers. "Fair enough. The red and white playing cards are a warning sign that an important factor has changed and needs to be corrected. The red and white coloring is symbolic of a stop sign. They showed up on your dresser, which means right then, at that point you should have stopped. You were on the wrong path."

"My path was to meet you, at the fake proctor meeting you scheduled."

He studied me, evaluating what I said. "After our meeting, did you see playing cards anywhere else?"

I replayed the rest of the day and my evening to be sure. "No. Only that one time. But then your scarf reminded me of the cards."

"Right. My scarf was a sign that we weren't where we needed to be. We stopped here so we could reassess."

"But how did the cards get on my nightstand? Who put them there?"

"They—"

"Wait!" Awol called out as she glided up behind us. "Refreshments before you go upstairs." She handed Xander and me drinks that looked as beautiful as they smelled. Served in glass mugs, the coffee, cream, and something red swirled around each other without mixing together. I held it closer to my face, studying it and trying to figure out how liquid could do such a thing.

"Taste it," she insisted, urging me to drink the concoction she was so clearly proud of, and for good reason.

I took a drink and my senses were assaulted with a new taste of something resembling coffee, marshmallow, chocolate, and maybe some sort of delicious fruit all in one. "Great stars, what am I drinking?"

Awol beamed. "The Awol Special. It's infused with fresh pomegranate."

"It's the best thing I've ever tasted." I took another sip. "Seriously. Best ever."

"I'm glad you like it. Enjoy your visit with Mary." She left us as abruptly as she arrived.

"Mary," I said to Xander. "At least Awol told me her name."

"Now both of your questions have been answered." Xander headed upstairs, his Awol Special in hand.

"Hardly," I muttered as I followed him, admiring the garnet banister with veins of sparkling gold embedded inside the handrail. True, I had answers to some of my questions, but that didn't mean I understood them.

At the top of the steps was a dim room with carpet that felt exceptionally lush on my bare feet. Gold symbols and scrolling lines decorated the black carpet. The pattern drew us forward to an arched doorway with black and white curtains concealing what was on the other side.

We paused in front of them, and I ran my fingers along the fabric. They were even softer than the carpet.

"Go ahead in," Xander said. "She's expecting you."

"But she doesn't even know me."

"She does. You've already met."

I gaped at him as I searched my mental records for anyone named Mary, but I was certain I knew no one by that name. "Is this another one of your magic tricks?"

He grinned. “I have nothing to do with the relationship you and she have.” He glanced around, then stepped closer, lifting my chin so our eyes met. The background noise of all the people and activity downstairs seemed to fade away until it felt like we were alone in our own private world. The intensity of his closeness left me tingling.

“Listen,” he said. “Whatever happens in there, don’t overthink it. Stay open and aware, but don’t analyze every detail.”

Was I about to enter another VR scenario?

“I believe in you.” His fingers caressed my cheek. “Nothing can ever change that.”

“I don’t know if I should be worried or flattered.”

“Neither. Just be yourself.”

He touched my necklace then gave me an encouraging but endearing look that made me want to ignore whatever awaited me and stay with him. But he parted the curtains, and light poured through the doorway. I shielded my eyes and reluctantly stepped inside.

When the blinding light dimmed to normal, I saw an old woman sitting on the far side of the room. A crimson cloth was draped over a table in front of her, and a ball of foggy glass sat in the center.

She stood and slightly bowed to me. “Lovely to see you, Kelsey.”

A hooded robe shadowed her face, but she lifted her chin and lowered her hood as if she knew I was studying her, trying to place her. Her hair wasn’t typical gray; it was silver. Sparkling silver.

“He’s right,” I said without realizing I had spoken out loud. “I feel like we’ve met before.”

“We have.”

“When?”

“My name is Mary Linker. Once upon a time, I was your teacher.”

My lips parted in shock as recognition washed over me. There was no once upon a time about it. “Mrs. Linker? But I saw you today in history class. You were . . .”

“Younger?”

I nodded, flabbergasted. Waving my hand, I motioned to her robe. “Is that some sort of disguise?”

"Quite the opposite. The younger version of me, as your history teacher, is a pretense."

"I don't understand."

"Look down," she said.

I did, bowing my head and looking at my feet. I gasped and stumbled backward, dropping my drink. I had been standing dead center on the same golden eye that was on Xander's tarot cards. Wanting to touch the glistening fibers of the symbol, I kneeled, not caring that my knees landed in the coffee-soaked carpet.

Awol pushed through the curtains. "Sorry to interrupt, but I brought you the cocoa you requested."

She handed the old lady version of Mrs. Linker a chocolate-filled glass then glanced down at me. "How old-fashioned and mannerly of you to kneel, but Mary is too down-to-earth for formalities."

My eyes met Mrs. Linker's as I asked, "Who are you?"

She stepped out from behind her table and walked over to me, kneeling on the floor with me as easily as if she were my age. The wrinkles around her eyes deepened ten times over as she smiled and touched my cheek with her warm hand.

"I am the High Priestess, but you may call me Mary. And you're long overdue for a card reading."

2: THE HIGH PRIESTESS

Level 2.1

I don't know how long I kneeled there, speechless and baffled, staring at the old woman in front of me, but eventually my knees ached. I rose, my joints popping as I rubbed my strained thighs. The High Priestess stood effortlessly without one creak or crack of her bones.

Awol was gone. I hadn't seen her leave the room, but I was alone with the High Priestess.

"Please pardon me for staring," I said, "but I still don't understand how you disguised yourself as my history teacher."

"That's of little importance right now." She turned, practically floating back to the table where her crystal ball sat. I couldn't see her feet under her long robes, but there was no gait in her walk; she seemed to float across the room.

She stood behind her table and rested her fingertips on the tablecloth. "How did you arrive here?"

Still recovering from the mystery of the woman in front of me and trying to feel worthy of being in the presence of someone called a High Priestess, I straightened my top and cleared my throat. "Xander brought me."

"Good. Stay close to him. He has a thorough understanding of the suits."

Suits? Did she already know about my meeting with government officials?

"Let's begin." She pulled a deck of cards from a pocket of her robe. "The clock is ticking, and you require a reading."

"I've never had a tarot reading before, ma'am."

"No need for formalities. You may call me Mary." Her expression was kind and sage. "The cards are always reading.

Absorbing, shifting, adjusting, aligning in accordance with your life, and always ready to reveal the guidance or reminders you require."

Xander said people believed in the Arcana as a secret way of life. Maybe this robed woman was some sort of leader for those who believed in the cards. "Can they tell me what will happen in the near future?"

"Your future is in your own hands."

"Again, I hope you'll excuse my manners, but if that's true then what's the purpose of a reading?"

"As I said, the cards guide. They remind. They enlighten."

"Can they tell me what to do to help my family?"

"That and much more."

So she did know about my situation. I estimated I had only a couple hours left before I'd have to return home and pretend I hadn't been out all night. Our meeting with officials was in the morning, and whatever happened during that meeting would change my life forever, and my family's life—for better or worse. I needed all the guidance I could acquire. "In that case, I'd be very grateful for a reading."

"Would you prefer to sit or stand?"

"Which is better?"

"Whichever feels natural to you."

I walked forward, closing the distance between us in two strides even though the room appeared to be huge. It should have taken me six or seven steps to reach the table. Everything about the scene seemed unnatural. She didn't move normally, the room's dimensions weren't as they appeared: more illusions like Xander's library.

We stared at each other across the table. I could have sworn she was much taller than me, but now we were the same height, or at least that's how it seemed. Her eyes were a bright, vivid green. Had they been green earlier when she kneeled in front of me? I couldn't remember.

Standing face-to-face with her felt like a challenge I wasn't equipped to handle, so I sat in the chair and looked up at her. "How do we start?"

Focus still unwavering, she replied, "Shuffle the deck."

She opened her hands in front of her. The deck of black cards with the gold tarot symbol fanned out in front of me. She hadn't touched the cards, but they moved, spreading evenly atop the tablecloth. The crystal ball was gone, but I never saw her move it.

Astonished, I asked, "How did you do that?"

"We're all capable of great feats, including you."

"I can't move things with my mind." Although, that would be really cool.

"Perhaps you're able to do much more than you believe."

Conversations with her would probably be full of mystical riddles and no real answers. Of course that's how it would be with a robed woman who seemed to have magical powers. I gathered the cards into a pile and shuffled them.

The High Priestess watched *me*—not the cards moving in my hands—without saying a word. I kept shuffling, expecting her to tell me when to stop, but after a few minutes my fingers were tired and the silence between us made me anxious. "May I stop?"

"You may do whenever feels right."

I tapped the deck against the table, forming a tight, neat pile. "Now what? Do I choose one?"

"Now, we wait."

My fingers hovered over the deck, itching to flip over the top card and see what image was on the other side. "Wait for what?"

She closed her eyes and inhaled deeply. When she exhaled, a breeze blew through the room, like wind before a storm. My hair flailed around me, yet nothing moved on the High Priestess. Her robes didn't even flutter. Neither did the tapestry that hung behind her.

"What's happening?" I muttered, a little scared, but also fascinated.

The room started morphing. I gasped as the walls turned into a night sky. The globe light hanging above us floated higher and became a gorgeous full moon. The tapestry behind her parted. Each half mutated into a tall tree—one with a white trunk, and one black, both budding with flowers whose nectarous fragrance filled the air.

Far beyond the black and white trees, a second robed woman appeared. She was the High Priestess. Same hair, same face, same peaceful aura.

"You have a twin?" I asked.

"The High Priestess card is showing itself to you by becoming real. You're here with me, but the card which represents me is manifesting as a message, so you're seeing two of me: the real me and the version of me in the Arcana."

I glanced between both versions of her, wonder tingeing my voice. "What does it mean?"

"That you're where you need to be at this moment in time, seeking a reading."

"Because you're here to give me answers?"

"Everything you need to know already exists within you. I'm here to remind you of that truth."

"But I have no idea what to do or say at our meeting with government officials."

She looked down. I followed her gaze, surprised to see the table and deck of cards still sitting between us. They seemed so out of place in the dreamlike outdoor scene.

"Should I draw another card?" I asked.

"Is that what your instincts tell you to do?"

I wasn't sure about my instincts, but my curiosity caused my fingers to itch. I flipped over the top card but accidentally grabbed two. They fanned open between my fingers, The Fool and The Magician.

I looked up to ask the High Priestess what it meant, but she was gone.

Level 2.2

Beneath my feet, the carpet turned into dewy grass. The gold lines and patterns in the carpet became sparkling dirt paths lined with shrubs and flowers. Perhaps I had transitioned into a VR scene of the High Priestess card.

I strolled along a pathway to the black and white trees, hoping to find the second High Priestess. With each step I took forward, the trees faded. By the time I stood in the spot where the white tree should have been, both had disappeared. I waved my hand in front of me, assuming they had turned invisible and I'd still be able to feel them, but my fingers swept through the empty air.

Several bursts of light flashed in my peripheral vision. I blinked them away as my hands started tingling. Staring at my fingernails, they changed from short and clean to long and dirty, over and over, until more light bursts forced me to close my eyes.

For one brief delicious moment, I felt Xander behind me. The heat of his chest pressed against my back and his strong arms embraced me. His breath warmed my ear as the scent of cinnamon coated the words he whispered. "I believe in you. Nothing can ever change that."

The combination of his touch and the sincerity in his voice nearly melted me. I turned around to ask him why he kept saying that, but he wasn't there. Even the cinnamon smell had vanished.

"The Magician," the High Priestess stated from behind me. "Equipped with a bag of otherworldly tricks."

I spun around to face her. A smaller version of her crystal ball now sat on top of a long cane made from twisted tree branches. She held the cane to one side while her other hand hovered over The Magician card I was still holding. She seemed careful not to touch it. "You must embrace the four suits and use them wisely."

“The four suits?” I studied the card closer. The Magician’s wand waved slightly, and four symbols spiraled around his hat. “What are they?”

Her free hand rose, and she lifted a finger with each word she spoke. “Cups, pentacles, swords.” She lifted her crystal ball cane. “And wands.”

Reaching behind her, she pulled out the glass mug I had dropped earlier. The swirling layers of coffee, pomegranate, and whatever else Awol had concocted looked as perfect as when she first handed it to me. I glanced behind me at the spot where I had spilled my drink all over the carpet. A pomegranate tree stood where I had kneeled only minutes ago.

The High Priestess gestured to the drink. “Cups represent your emotions. You need a firmer grasp on them given how easily you dropped this.”

“Many apologies for spilling it. Seeing the tarot symbol under my feet startled me.”

“No apologies necessary. It’s all part of the process.” She poured the coffee onto the ground, and the liquid turned into a pink babbling brook, flowing away from us until I no longer saw where the current ended. The High Priestess continued before I could utter a word. “Pentacles represent physical worlds. The talisman hanging around your neck gives you access to many of them.”

I reached for the cross of quartz Xander had given me. “This necklace is a talisman?”

“Swords,” she continued as if she didn’t hear my question. “They are your intellect, thoughts, mind power. Strengthen and sharpen them, and you can win any battle.”

“Battle? Like a physical battle?” I didn’t want to fight anyone.

“Most battles are initiated in the mind, and could, and *should,* be resolved there.”

I can imagine how blank my stare must have appeared. The more she explained, the more lost I felt.

She sighed deeply. “And finally, wands. Representing the spirit and all the magnificence it can achieve.”

“I’m grateful for the education, but this is all somewhat confusing. Can you, or the cards, tell me what to do at my meeting? Do I agree to help the government catch VR dealers?”

"Look to the cards. What are they showing you?"

I glimpsed at The Fool and The Magician cards again. "I've seen these already. Xander gave me one and the other was—" The fewer people I told about Devlin the better. "The Magician card was given to me."

"Which means they are of vital importance, so what are they revealing?"

"I don't understand."

"Look closer," she said gently. "What do they *reveal?*"

I stared at her for a moment, confused, then I studied the cards again. The jester and magician started moving. The colors of the artwork changed and rippled. Something rushed past me in my peripheral vision, snapping my attention from the cards in my hand.

The ground beneath me moved like a conveyor belt, and I swayed, trying to keep my balance. When I stopped, I was standing on the edge of a cliff.

Xander stood across from me on the other side. Far below us was a pink river. Behind me was an empty desert with nothing but dusty land. On Xander's side was a lush green landscape filled with gorgeous trees, flowers, and waterfalls. We stared at each other from the edges of our cliffs.

From behind me, the High Priestess said, "You aren't able to see the whole picture yet, and he can't tell you what's real. You must seek reality deep within you."

I didn't need to look over my shoulder to know she had vanished again. I could feel that she was no longer physically with me. It was only Xander and me, and a great divide separating us.

"Is that where you want to be?" Xander asked. He should have been shouting so I could hear him across the river roaring below us, but he spoke at a normal level and somehow I heard him fine.

I motioned to the barren land around me. "Pretty bland compared to your side. I'd rather be over there."

"I'd rather you be over here too."

"How do I get there?"

"Make the leap."

I snickered. "I'll fall."

"It's a possibility, but between the leap and the landing—" He raised his arms to his sides like they were wings. "You will soar."

I stepped closer to the edge. A piece of the cliff broke away beneath me. The drop must have been at least a hundred feet or more. The river's current was so strong there were whitecaps. "You're crazy. I'd never make it that far. I'll die on impact when I hit that river, drown to death, or have a heart attack on the way down. All three possibilities end in death."

"I told you there would come a point when I'd tell you to jump and there'd be no time to pause. You'd have to leap far and fast. The moment is here, and you're not only pausing, you're convincing yourself you won't survive."

"Because I'm not a lunatic."

"You don't trust me."

"Because I won't leap to my death? If that's what determines whether or not I trust you, you're out of luck."

"This won't work if you don't have total trust in me."

"What won't work?"

"Us."

"We won't work out because I won't leap to my death on command?" I didn't care how smart or attractive he was. No guy was worth dying for. I joked, "Is this how all of your relationships end?"

"You're in the world of Arcana, Kelsey. Nothing can physically hurt you here. Not even a swan dive off a cliff."

His words, and what they implied, seemed to ricochet between us. Everything that had happened since I entered Xander's library seemed impossible. Had he been guiding me through one virtual reality scenario after another?

"None of this is real," I muttered, more to myself than to him. My gaze rose and his narrowed eyes were studying me. "This has all been games or stories?"

"All of it has been important in helping you understand yourself and learning to trust your instincts."

"My instincts," I repeated.

Xander's voice echoed deep within me, but his lips didn't move. His words were a memory replaying in my mind. *If I enlighten you with information, even if you find it hard to believe, you absorb it as fact unless your instincts tell you otherwise.*

I had just started exploring the world of virtual reality. I didn't feel ready to do something so daring and dangerous as jump off a cliff, even if it wasn't real.

"Tell you what." Xander stepped to the edge of his side. A vine snapped free from a plant and dropped over the ledge, swinging back and forth as he spoke. "We leap together. I know you'll make it, but until you believe in yourself, I'll be there to catch you."

My hands were sweating so I wiped them on my shirt. Could I do it? Could I be brave enough to jump? Could he catch me when I fell? He was smart, but he wasn't a superhero who could fly. I scanned him from head to toe a few times. Maybe he could fly in his virtual worlds. I imagined him soaring through the air with me wrapped in his arms. I had to admit, that ride sounded like one I'd enjoy.

"Kelsey," Xander said firmly. "This is it. You either trust me or you don't." He held out his arms like he was confident I'd land in them. "If you trust me, make the leap."

I took a deep breath, debating between what my mind was telling me and the whispers from my instincts. Only one could win. Mind or instinct, mind or instinct?

Level 2.3

My mind won.

I hopped in place. “That’s as far as I’m willing to go at this point.”

Xander didn’t say anything. He froze, flashed in and out of existence like a holosplay short-circuiting, and then everything went dark. Completely black. And silent. Even the river below us stopped roaring.

“Xander?” I called out. His name echoed half a dozen times. My voice sounded slightly different each time, but then silence swallowed me again.

Until someone exhaled, long and heavy.

Bubbles of blue light rose around me. One large orb landed in front of me, glowing brighter and illuminating the darkness until I saw it was the High Priestess’s crystal ball sitting on her table between us.

The details of the room I had first entered gradually reappeared: the globe light hanging above us, the tapestry wall behind her, the black and gold carpet under my feet. Even my glass mug of swirly coffee sat on the crimson tablecloth near my right hand.

Rattled and feeling disoriented, I asked, “What just happened?”

“The cards showed you information relevant to your current point on your journey.”

“Xander and I were standing on two different cliffs, and he wanted me to leap to my death.”

Her thin silver brows rose. “Interesting interpretation.”

“I never would have made it. The distance between us was too far.”

“Your mind perceived it, so you believed it into physical reality.”

"I made the logical choice."

"Logic has no place in the Arcana. What did your instincts tell you to do?"

"I admit part of me wanted to attempt the leap." *The crazy part,* I thought to myself. "Are you saying I should have jumped?"

"I cannot tell you what to do. I can only advise you to meditate on all of your questions, and then listen closely to your truest self for the answers."

I sat down in the chair again. Semi-confident that I had made the right choice, I tried convincing her—and maybe me too—that I was right. "The fall would have been fatal."

"Sometimes one must die before they can truly live."

"I'm not ready to die. In real life or a virtual one."

"You're interpreting my statement literally. Death comes in many forms. Death of the mind, of old ways of thinking that are replaced by new; death of the emotions, when one's heart is broken and they must learn to rebuild it stronger; and death of the spirit, when one feels disintegrated, but then rises from the ashes more radiant than before. Physical death is like any other form: it serves a purpose, but it is temporary."

The creaking of my chair matched the cracking of my voice. "Temporary? I've known a few people who have died, and it wasn't temporary."

"Are you certain of that?"

Our conversation was getting too deep for me, and we hadn't made any progress about what I was supposed to do or say when Keekee and I met with officials. "I appreciate all of your sage wisdom, and these virtual fantasy worlds are fascinating, but soon I need to face reality and make a commitment to help the government catch VR dealers. I'm a lot more worried about that right now, so is it possible to do a card reading that gives me some sort of answer or direction about that issue?"

"The cards will show you what you need to know."

"But how?" I was getting frustrated. "They haven't shown me anything yet except for you, and Xander standing on a cliff. Neither of which helps me with my predicament."

"Interesting interpretation."

"You said that before." I leaned forward, searching her face for the answers she wouldn't provide. "Am I interpreting everything wrong?"

"There is no right or wrong. The cards are merely guiding, reminding, and enlightening."

"They haven't guided, reminded, or enlightened me at all yet."

"Perhaps you should revisit your reading. Meditate on what was revealed to you, and consider it more carefully."

She was even more cryptic than Xander. I crossed my arms over my chest. "You're never going to give me any kind of real explanations, are you?"

"Everything you need to know already exists within you."

"You already said that too."

Her green eyes sparkled as she opened her hands nonchalantly. "Then it must be true."

"If I already have all the answers, then why did I need to come see you? Or let you do a tarot card reading for me?"

"Because you haven't accessed the information you need. You require transcendental help, and I'm a conduit for higher power."

"Higher power? Like how some groups from the Old Word believed in Jesus and Buddha and other deities?"

"The power I connect with is universal."

We were getting nowhere. "Can you please tell me what I'm supposed to do or say when I meet with government officials in—" I wasn't sure how much time had passed. Did I still have hours, or were we down to minutes? "Whenever I meet with them?"

"You are supposed to follow your instincts."

"My instincts aren't giving me clear direction either way."

She folded her hands on top of the crystal ball between us. "Succumb to the system or override it. The choice is yours."

"Override the system?" Xander had used those same words earlier. "How do I do that?"

"Let your instincts guide you."

I shook my head. "You're investing way too much faith in my instincts."

"You're not investing enough."

Succumb to the system or override it. Succumbing probably meant helping the government with their hunt for VR dealers.

Overriding must mean finding a way to fool them, which sounded extremely dangerous considering the consequences if I got caught.

"Neither choice seems ideal," I said. "What if I decide wrong?"

My question stretched out much too long. I forced my lips closed to stop myself from involuntarily moaning the words.

The tapestry behind her sparkled until it became translucent.

A holographic image of Xander formed, but he looked different—older, tired, and sad. So different from the Xander I knew. He was facing me, but staring above my head. His eyes scrolled side to side as if he were reading invisible words on a page.

Torment tugged deep within me. A longing to help him. I didn't know why or how. I didn't even know why he looked so forlorn, but it made my heart ache.

The High Priestess sat between us, a living wall of silver hair and robes like a sheet of glass separating us. She swiped her hands high in the air.

The image of Xander dissolved, and I stared at the tapestry, blinking until I refocused on her.

Time seemed to lag. I was still finishing the question I had asked before the vision of Xander appeared. My words came out slowly, but I had no control of my voice. " . . . if I decide wrong?"

She smiled as if nothing strange had happened. "What if you decide right?"

Level 2.4

I pressed my palm to my forehead. "What just happened?"

The High Priestess asked, "What did you see?"

"For a second, it was like I was watching him on a screen."

"Watching whom?"

A sad future version of Xander, which made me incredibly sad, but I have bigger problems to worry about than a guy I hardly know. Like the future of my family. I shook my head, trying to shake off my fatigue. Mentally and physically. "I'm not sure."

"Be careful and discerning. Veils have a way of blurring reality until you can no longer trust what you see."

"Right. Useful advice." I had no idea what she meant.

The magical, morphing room was perplexing, and the High Priestess, while frustrating at times, calmed me. She felt like the wise grandmother I had never known, but I couldn't waste any more time sitting with her and talking in mystical circles that only led to more questions.

"Many thanks for your time," I said. "But I should probably get going."

She stood and bowed slightly. "We'll meet again soon."

"We will?"

"Whenever you need a reading."

A reading that provided no answers or guidance. Not exactly the best use of my time. I turned to leave and had almost reached the curtain doorway when a thought occurred to me. "What happens later?" I asked her. "When I go to school, you'll still be my history teacher, right?"

"A different version of me will be, yes."

"Will you remember me? Will you know this conversation took place between us?"

"The more important question is, will *you* remember?"

I half-chuckled. "You never give a straight answer, do you?"

"The answers are—"

I held up my hands, cutting her off. "I know, I know. The answers are within me. Nice to meet you, High Priestess. Many thanks for everything." Everything meaning absolutely nothing useful.

I parted the heavy black-and-white curtains and stepped into the area that looked down over the main part of the cafe. Steam rose from the machines. Music filled the public space as if it weren't illegal. Huge jars of enhancement lollipops sat on almost every table free for the taking, and people lounged around drinking as much coffee as they wanted. Higher Grounds also had to be a VR scenario because reality could never be so wonderful.

I scanned the crowd, searching for Xander, and found him standing in a dimly lit corner surrounded by a small group of people. He was handing out his cards. The recipients were so happy they might as well have been receiving new deluxe crafts.

Xander paused and looked up at me. His eyes locked with mine right away, not searching for me, but seeming to sense I stood there watching him from above. He said a few words to his groupies and then left them and made his way up the stairs.

"How'd it go?" he asked me.

"I'm not sure. I had a cool experience with a couple of virtual scenarios, but she never explained what they meant, or answered any of my questions directly."

Xander's brow wrinkled. "Virtual scenarios?"

"You know, a VR scene where tarot cards became real and the impossible seemed possible." I didn't want to get into details about him being there and telling me to jump off a cliff, or the sad Xander vision. That would have revealed the fact that my mind thought about him way too much.

"I see." The creases in his forehead deepened as he cocked his head to the side. "Did the High Priestess provide any answers at all?"

"She said the answers are within me, but never gave details. She's good at answering questions without actually answering them."

He leaned against the railing, studying me the same way I had studied the High Priestess every time she attempted to tell me something that made no sense. Like he was trying to figure out a puzzle, but didn't have enough pieces.

"What time is it?" I asked. "I need to get home before everyone wakes up and realizes I'm gone."

"We have plenty of time," he said, not straying from our conversation about the High Priestess. "The cards she showed you, were they my cards or from a different tarot deck?"

"Yours. Why?"

He stood up straight, a burst of excitement jolting through him. "That means you're ready."

"Ready for what?"

He guided me past the High Priestess's room and down a hallway I hadn't noticed before. We stopped in front of a stained-glass door.

"Where's that go?" I asked.

"You see it? The door?"

"Of course I see it. How could I not?"

"Stranger things have happened." He pushed on the latch-type handle, and the door swung inward, revealing a tiny room with nothing inside except a spiral staircase.

"Are you going to tell me where it leads?"

"It leads to people I've been eager for you to meet." He entered the tight stairwell room and motioned for me to go first.

I took the first step, wondering who and what awaited us at the top.

Climbing the stairs with Xander right behind me, I became well-aware that with every step we took, Xander had a prime view of my butt. I was hyperconscious of my movements, trying to sway my hips without looking too obvious, but also in a subtly-sexy-enough way to make him like what he saw. I shook my head and stopped trying so hard. When had I become such a tramp?

I reached the top landing and found a plain steel door.

"Go ahead," Xander urged from below me. "Open it."

I pushed on the metal bar and it swung open. Nothing could have prepared me for what I saw on that rooftop.

Level 2.5

Anyone else might have been initially consumed by the expansive view of what appeared to be all of Elura, but I couldn't stop staring at the floor. Or the roof. Or whatever lay stretched out in front of me in a patchwork of books.

Book covers stared up at me, like a never-ending colorful carpet, stretching farther and wider than I would have ever thought possible. While it was beautiful, it was also disturbing.

"What is this?" I asked Xander, unable to step forward. "Someone used books for flooring?"

"In a way, yes. More like they used books for paths of learning and evolving." He stepped out into the open air and directly onto an Olden cover of Lewis Carroll's *Through the Looking Glass.*

"Don't step on them!" I squealed in horror. "Some of these are ancient and priceless." I glanced up at the dark sky. "They're exposed to the elements. They'll be ruined." I took a mental inventory of a fraction of the numerous titles. They didn't look worn or weathered. "How are they not already damaged?"

Xander stood silent, watching me with an amused grin.

Over his shoulder, several yards away, under an open-air domed roof, people were gathered in small groups. They lounged on couches, chairs, in hammocks. It was similar to downstairs in the cafe. Some people were walking around, stepping on the floor of books as if they weren't priceless works of art.

"I don't understand," I grumbled, still frozen in place in the doorway. "You love books too. How can you watch them be treated this way and not do anything to stop it?"

"Look closer," Xander said. "What is unusual about these books?"

I studied them. Colorful. No fading. No rips. No stains. And more importantly, "They're too big," I noted. "They aren't real books. They're replicas?"

He hummed a confirmation.

"Oh, thank the stars," I breathed with relief. "But who did this? I mean, it's unique and wonderful, but why did they do it?"

"All will be explained in due time." He accurately read my shifting jaw and irritated breath. Why wouldn't anyone give me a straight answer? Xander held up his hands in surrender. "Due time as in tonight, I promise. But first, can I introduce you to the people I mentioned? They'll help me answer many of your questions."

"I hope they're more forthcoming than you and the High Priestess."

He smirked. "They are knowledgeable and direct. You'll like them."

I tentatively stepped out onto the floor of book covers. It still felt wrong, but knowing they weren't real, made each step a tad easier.

We passed a group of people sitting at a round table, each holding several tarot cards. Looking over one girl's shoulder, I saw the same style of Xander's artwork.

"Yours?" I asked.

"My designs, but the cards belong to the person in possession of them."

"They seem very popular."

He shrugged. "Everyone here collects them."

"Really?"

"The surprise in your voice is a bit insulting," he said playfully. "You don't like my artwork?"

"It's gorgeous. I'm just surprised so many people would be into collecting tarot cards."

We passed group after group of cardholders, but unlike downstairs, no one seemed to pay attention to Xander or me. They were all consumed by conversations about books and Old World movies.

One guy passionately defended the actions of Colonel Graff in *Ender's Game,* while the girl across from him argued that Graff was a compassionless villain.

I paused, eavesdropping on the stimulating debate. Xander stood beside me, watching me from the corner of his eye the same way I had done to him so many times.

"They're discussing stories," I said. "These are my kind of people."

"See, there's much more to the Arcana than pretty pictures on cards."

"Tarot cards, virtual reality, book lovers: they all seem to blend together here."

Xander agreed and we continued on. The furniture of the rooftop space was almost as fascinating as the people. I had lived in all the cities of Equatia except for The Hub, but I had never seen such sleek and colorful decor. The rooftop—the whole building—seemed as though it were a future place in a faraway land, far *far* from Equatia.

I stopped walking. "Can I please be let in on the big secret now?"

Without missing a step, he turned to face me. Almost as if he knew I would pause and ask a question. "What makes you think there's a big secret?"

"It hangs in the air so thick I can taste it."

He sort of smiled then licked his lips. "And how does it taste?"

I leaned slightly closer to him and lowered my voice. "Almost as good as your coffee."

He trumped my flirting by stepping so close to me that his chest almost pressed against mine. "Wait until you taste what else I can dish out."

I had never ached to kiss someone so badly. I didn't even care that we were surrounded by so many people. I tried encouraging him by slowly batting my eyelashes and tilting my head.

He whispered so sweetly. "Kelsey, I really want—"

"Xander!" A female voice shouted from behind him.

He stepped back, our moment ruined. He didn't turn around to see who called his name. His gaze stayed on me like he was silently apologizing for the interruption. "Kelsey, meet Blaze."

The kiss-destroyer stood beside Xander. I managed to pull my focus away from him, but I stiffened at the sight of her. "You."

"Me!" she said happily, pulling a yellow lollipop out of her mouth.

She was the girl who sat in the front row of my history class. The girl who bawled her eyes out. "You're Devlin's girlfriend."

Her eyebrows, which matched her copper hair, arched abnormally high. She and Xander glanced at each other, and Xander started to speak, but Blaze touched his forearm. "Devlin and I have never dated. We're good friends."

"My mistake. I assumed you were involved because of how upset you were when they arrested him."

Xander turned his back to us and stuck his hands in his pockets.

Blaze sucked on her lollipop while studying me. "It was very upsetting."

"My apologies. I didn't mean to bring it up." She didn't seem that upset, socializing on a rooftop two days after his arrest.

She reached into the pocket of her tunic and pulled out a lollipop. A round bulge in her left cheek formed as she tried talking with her mouth full. "Spirit Sucker?"

"That's what you call lollipops?"

She removed the candy from her mouth. "This flavor soothes the spirit." She pulled another one from her pocket. "Or this one strengthens."

"No thanks. I filled up on coffee a few minutes ago."

She rolled her eyes. "The Awol Special?"

"Yes, actually." Must have been a popular choice.

"Greedy goblet," Blaze mumbled. "She always strikes first."

"Greedy goblet?" Were they not friends? Awol had struck me as the type of person who couldn't possibly have enemies.

Xander rejoined the conversation. "Blaze, I was about to tell Kelsey how things work around here. It's her first time visiting Higher Grounds, so maybe you could gather a curator for each of the suits to help me explain."

"I'd be honored." Blaze spun on her heel and dashed away.

"Suits?" I asked Xander. "Is this more of the cup and swords stuff the High Priestess told me about?"

"She discussed the suits with you?"

"A little bit."

“Perfect. That confirms now is the right time for you to get to know them better.”

“The High Priestess said the suits were cups, swords, wands, and—” for some reason I couldn’t remember the last one.

“Pentacles,” he reminded me. “And that’s true. But everyone here, majors and minors, favors one of the suits.”

“Majors and minors would be?”

“Members of the Arcana. Let’s have a seat and wait for the others. They’re more experienced when it comes to explaining the system to new journeyers.”

“Am I a journeyer?”

“Technically everyone is, but you chose to take the first step, so now you’re officially in the Arcana.”

I touched the necklace Xander had given me, worrying that I had jumped into an illegal world without knowing much about it. Keekee had been lured into gaming the same way, and she became a hardcore addict. I chose to take a chance in hopes it would help my family, but what if it did the opposite? What if I made a horrible mistake? “Xander, you said I’m officially in the Arcana, but I can get out if I want, right?”

“You won’t want to.” He sounded so confident. “You might change paths, but no one has ever wanted to permanently resign.”

“But if I did, if it were necessary for safety reasons, I’m free to leave at any time, right?”

“Yes, but—” His eyes scanned my face, then lowered to my necklace. I was still thumbing the smooth quartz, but I paused when his gaze lifted and met mine. “Without the Arcana, you’ll never be free.”

Level 2.6

Xander sat beside me on a small sofa that barely fit both of us. A large, round coffee table made of a material that looked like frosted glass was the centerpiece of our sitting area. On each side of the table was another sofa or comfy-looking chair, but I was flattered that he decided to squeeze in beside me.

"Anything you want to tell me before everyone else arrives?" I asked him.

He stared at his hands in his lap, blinking fast like lots of thoughts were filling his head, but someone a couple tables over made a loud, excited whooping sound and Xander's attention shifted to the laughing group who was applauding.

"They're sure happy about something," I said.

"They're celebrating."

"Celebrating what?"

"Someone upgraded." He closed his eyes for a few seconds. Like he was cherishing the moment and didn't want to be disturbed.

I watched the loud group of four celebrating: hugging, high-fiving each other. One girl even jumped up on her chair and started dancing. People from other groups came over to congratulate them. I'd never seen people get so excited about cards, or anything for that matter.

Awol set a tray filled with mugs of coffee on the table in front of us, then she flopped down into the chair to my right. She kicked her bare feet up on the table and gazed at the night sky. "And for a delicate, fleeting moment, ours was a world of hope."

"And awakening," Xander added.

Awol sat forward, grabbing a mug and raising it toward him. "To awakening."

Xander lifted a drink from the tray and they clinked their mugs together. He handed me one and repeated the ritual.

Awol still held her mug toward us, so I tapped mine against hers too.

"Cheers. Make us proud, Kelsey," she said before sipping her coffee.

Watching her large mug hide half of her face caused a mental click inside of me. "Cups," I said. "Cups are your suit."

She lowered her drink and tossed her long dreads over her shoulders. "Correct."

Blaze strolled into our sitting area. A guy I hadn't seen before followed close behind her.

She took her lollipop out of her mouth, leaned forward, and waved her Spirit Sucker over the table. A flame sparked to life, creating a cozy fire. She sat down like it was nothing, like she hadn't just created fire with a flick of her . . ."

"Wand," I said. "Your suit is wands."

Her eyes met mine over the flame dancing between us. She smiled and stuck her lollipop back into her mouth.

I felt silly asking, but after what I had just witnessed I needed to know. "Is that lollipop some sort of magic wand?"

She waved it around her head. "Rods, sticks, spears, lollipops: anything can serve as a wand as long as the journeyer believes it has power."

The guy standing behind her stepped into our circle as if annoyed that no one had introduced him yet. "Don't fall for Blaze's trickery. There's a button on this side of the table that ignites the fire feature. She pressed it with her knee."

Blaze grinned then slugged him in the arm. "Why do you so thoroughly enjoy shattering the joy and awe caused by illusions?"

"Because illusions are poor substitutions for genuine skill." He pulled a dagger from his arm holster, swiped it through the fire, then tossed the flaming weapon high above his spiky black hair before catching it (without being burned, I might add). He blew out the flame, then stabbed the table, causing a web of cracks in the glass. "They call me Jag."

"Show off." Blaze snorted as Awol and Xander laughed.

"Charmed to meet you." Sarcasm leaked through my tone. He had damaged the beautiful table for no reason other than to stroke his own ego.

I glanced around the group of people seated around the table. Awol was cups. Blaze was wands. Jag was swords. Next to me sat Xander.

"Are you pentacles?" I asked him.

"Pentacle is my specialty suit, yes."

I looked at Awol's mug, Blaze's lollipop, Jag's dagger piercing the table, and then at Xander, empty-handed. "What's your thing?"

"My thing?"

"What represents pentacles?"

He reached into the collar of his shirt and pulled out a pendant like the one he gave me. His was a circle of quartz with subtle etchings similar to mine. "This."

"He's a master world-builder," Awol explained. "And an artist of many mediums."

"He's the best curator Higher Grounds has ever seen," Blaze added.

"Someday, he'll be a trump," Jag declared while punching Xander's knee.

"Curator and trump?" I repeated. "What does that mean?"

"Let's start at the beginning," Xander said. "Before you understand the Arcana and what we're trying to achieve here, you need to know the truth about Equatia." He cracked his knuckles. "Everyone seated comfortably?"

Awol, Blaze, and Jag all adjusted and held onto either their seat or chair arms.

"Sit back and hang on," Xander told me.

I scooted backward and held onto the arm of the sofa with my right hand, but there was nothing on my left except Xander.

He touched his necklace, and Jag's chair swung out and away from us, followed by Blaze, and then Awol. I gaped at them, but then our sofa followed.

At the sudden rush forward, my hand shot to Xander's thigh. Heat flooded my cheeks, and I quickly withdrew my hand, apologizing. "Sorry. I didn't mean to grab you like that. The sofa lurched forward, and you were the only thing I could hold onto."

He took my hand and set it back on his thigh. "Always follow your instincts. Especially when they tell you to hold onto me."

Curse my fickle heart. Why was I so attracted to him? I didn't want to be, but his touch gave me a bigger rush than the floating furniture.

Our sofa rose upward, gliding between Awol's and Jag's chairs. All the seats were aligned, facing the same way as they hovered far above the rooftop full of tarot-wielding groups who didn't even glance in our direction.

"This is amazing," I said. "I mean, nothing should shock me at this point, but this does."

Blaze nodded. "Just wait. It gets better."

The buildings below us didn't look familiar. "Exactly where are we in Elura?"

"We're not in Elura," Awol said from beside me.

Jag snickered. "We're off Equatia's grid."

"Off the grid?" I felt sick. "As in beyond our borders?"

Setting one foot outside of Equatia was forbidden. The borders were strictly protected. During community exhortations, and even in school, we were warned about people dying because they unlawfully tried to escape our nation. I didn't want to be a death statistic.

Xander's hand was still pressed over mine, his thigh muscle firm against my palm. I resisted the urge to grip him tighter as I stared over the edge of my seat.

We slowly rose higher. The round rooftop became a pool of light, and the people were dark specks swimming on its surface. My stomach dropped as my mind registered how high we were—well above the legal limit for a craft to fly.

Everyone knew about our nation's height restrictions. Crafts couldn't fly above zone 1 or they'd be ticketed. If anyone flew into zone 2, they'd be arrested. Zone 3 meant anyone, or anything, crossing the extensive height of our nation's protector beams would be disintegrated. When we stopped climbing, the tallest building seemed impossibly far below us.

My throat was tight and my hands were cold. "We must be in zone 3, which is impossible because we'd be dead."

"You're on a journey in the world of Arcana." Awol wiggled one finger at me. "You have to start believing in the so-called-impossible."

Right. I had to keep reminding myself this was a VR scenario. Everything looked and felt so real that it was easy to react as if it were reality.

"Look at it." Xander gestured to the twinkling lights below us. "From up here, you can see the entire layout."

I studied the view below us, then, as if my vision had been blurry but suddenly focused, I saw the familiar pattern from history books. Equatia was spread below us like a living map. Connecting together to form a circular border around the Hub were the four compass cities: Elura, Warna, Nertia, and Solva. Each lit up in a different color, making it easy to see the arc shape of the four outlying cities forming a ring around the glowing Hub.

"A circle within a circle," Xander recited in a steely tone. "Strongest at its core, and protected by the commitment of its citizens to remain a nation of safety." It was one of the principles every citizen was taught.

Jag held up his middle finger. "They can suck my core, because I'll never protect theirs."

I didn't know whether to glare or laugh at Jag.

Xander gently squeezed my hand. "How many people do you think are down there?"

I should have known the answer to his question, but I couldn't recall the total population of Equatia.

Jag replied before I could guess. "Almost 200,000. Most of whom aren't allowed to think outside of Equatia's brainwashed box. Do you know how many of those people are government employees?"

"I have no idea," I admitted.

"Close to 2700." Jag's voice hitched, and for the first time I sensed he might care about someone other than himself. "2700 govies for a nation with a total population of 200,000, yet they convince us that 2700 can control 200,000."

"Let's not forget that a good portion of those 2700 are drudges," Blaze said.

I was afraid to ask. "Do we know how many are drudges?"

Xander, Awol, Blaze, and Jag answered in unison. "Over 2600."

"Glitch." I hissed under my breath. I had no idea it was that many.

"Hardly anyone volunteers to work for the government," Awol explained. "They have all been convicted and programmed. That means they were guilty of not thinking how the government wanted them to. It means more than 2,600 minds used to believe in a different way from what they've been taught. And I promise you, there are many more in Equatia who keep quiet for fear of being discovered."

Xander sighed. "It's a broken system that continues by arresting people for petty crimes, and reprogramming those people to only think and do what they've been told. Train drudges to capture and develop more drudges so the government grows stronger while its citizens lose more freedom."

Jag stood on the seat of his chair. My stomach lurched, imagining what might happen if he lost his balance and fell. He stepped on the back of it then leaped onto our sofa, squatting on the armrest beside me. Not one trace of fear that he might have plummeted to his death.

"Before The Crash," Jag told me, "computers, phones, televisions, and countless other devices created a dumbed-down society where electronics did most of the thinking. Much of the human race became addicts. Their drug was technology and they became so dependent on it, from communication to managing their finances and everything in-between. It was only a matter of time before the plug was pulled. The world had to reboot or perish."

"I know all of this," I said. "Every citizen of Equatia is taught about cyberterrorism and The Crash since elementary school."

"Yes, but what they don't tell you is that Equatia's founders foresaw what would happen. They predicted the catastrophe, and they prepared for it."

"They did tell us that," I argued. "The founders created our nation to protect us from the chaos and the aftermath of what the world became. To build a new, protected nation where history would never repeat itself."

Jag laughed and stood, waving his hand at the illuminated layout below us. "Equatia's founders took over a desperate island that was falling to ruins. They created a new society, implementing laws written by a few rich, power-hungry politicians. Then they perpetuated that system for over a hundred years, deciding what advancements we should be allowed to access and which we shouldn't. Don't you think there's something wrong with that?"

Blaze snorted. "I can give you a whole list of things that are wrong with it."

Jag pulled out another, smaller knife and started polishing it with the bottom of his tunic. "Equatia's founders were guilty of what many leaders and nations did throughout much of history. They divided their nation into two classes: sheep and wolves."

Blaze pointed her lollipop at me. "And if you are a disobedient sheep, they program you to be a wolf."

Xander shifted beside me. "I speak for many when I say we refuse to be either."

"Where did you hear this stuff?" I asked. "Is this some radical uprising group or something?"

Awol smiled. "Or something."

I wanted so badly for my sister to be involved in this conversation. These were her kind of people. She'd fit right in. "Keekee has always believed nations exist that offer more freedom than Equatia."

"Your sister knows what she's talking about," Xander said. "Except you can't imagine how much freedom exists out there."

"Where?"

In one fluid movement, Jag jumped back to his own chair. He opened his hands out in front of him, in the opposite direction of the lights of Equatia. "Beyond the grid. Across the oceans. To the place where energy and information aren't controlled—they're embraced. Where the power of the human mind isn't limited by petty laws and excessive restrictions."

"Which nation is that?" I asked.

"Not one nation," Blaze answered. "The rest of the world."

Our seats pivoted, facing away from Equatia. Xander sat forward. "Beyond our borders is freedom. A very different way of life."

Awol's chair glided to a stop directly in front of me. "Kelsey, Equatia is the only dictatorship nation left after The Crash. The planet rebuilt itself stronger and healthier. Humans evolved into a more peaceful and conscious species. Out there, technology is used to help mankind, not control it. The rest of Earth has become a one-world mentality. Divided and controlled nations only exist in history books. Except for Equatia."

I stared at her, trying to stay focused on her words, but I was distracted by the rippling skin on her cheeks. Her eyes flickered with light in an unnatural way, as if miniature bulbs were turning off and on behind her pupils.

"What's wrong with you?" I asked her.

"What do you mean?" She tossed her long dreadlocks back over her shoulders, but they mutated. Every braid stretched out behind her, lengthening and darkening as they twisted and spiraled above her head. I scooted back in my chair, eager to distance myself from her creepy hair.

Xander's voice sounded far away. "Kelsey, tell us what you're seeing."

I turned to look at him, but rain started pouring down. Dipping my head, I tried covering myself with my hands, but no drops hit me. I glanced up at the sky and saw countless tiny shadows falling all around me. Some were light, some dark, and they fell at different speeds. Every time I moved my head, I saw more, but I couldn't focus on them.

"Kelsey?" Awol touched my knee.

I looked at her and shrieked, crab-crawling backward until I was perched on the back of the sofa. Her hair had turned into black wire coils that were wrapping around her and binding her arms against her sides.

Xander gripped my leg. "Close your eyes and focus on my voice. Whatever you're seeing isn't real, but my voice is. Focus on me."

I closed my eyes, but the strange shadow-rain still flooded my senses. The echoing of drops hitting tin grew louder. The strong smell of sulfur made me hold my nose. Every raindrop changed into a spark of light that glowed so brightly my eyelids flew open in search of relief.

Xander was gone.

Sitting in his place, with his revolting hand clutching my thigh, was the sickening pervert, Counselor Kramer.

"Don't touch me!" I yanked free of him, thrusting myself backward again, and toppling off the back of the sofa.

I screamed as I fell through the sky. The rooftop full of people came closer as I kicked and grabbed at empty air. I was going to die. I was sure of it. Shutting my eyes tight, the faces of everyone I loved flashed in front of me. I cried out, terrified for the moment of impact.

It never came.

My cramped eyelids fluttered open. I wasn't falling anymore. The foul smell and metallic noises were gone.

I was sitting on the sofa and we were back—safely—on the rooftop. The fire in the center of the coffee table was still burning. People still bustled around, chatting and socializing around us.

Xander was kneeling in front of me, holding my chin with his hand and repeating my name.

Awol sat behind him. She was leaning forward, watching me, concern creasing her brow, but thankfully her skin and hair were back to normal.

My throat stung, probably from all my screaming. "That was awful."

"I know," Xander said gently. "I'm sorry. It was one of their viruses. The bugger slipped past my firewalls."

"Flashers or floaters?" Jag started cleaning his fingernails with his switchblade.

I shook my head, confused by his question and how calm he seemed. "What?"

Xander's voice was delicate. "Did you see shadows or sparks of light?"

"Both," I murmured, pressing my palm to my temple. "And Awol's braids were coils of black wire."

Awol sat up straight. "Kramer. That's his modus operandi."

"You know Kramer?" I cringed. "He was there too."

Xander's jaw tightened, but his gaze remained warm and reassuring. "The government knows you fear him. All viruses are designed to feed on your fears, but they aren't real. They activated a distraction because we were educating you with the truth."

Awol grunted. "More like we were revealing their dirty not-so-little secrets."

My stomach lurched, and I gripped Xander's forearm tighter than I intended. "How would they know what we were discussing? You said I wasn't being monitored."

"You aren't being monitored by your band," he explained. "But they have other methods."

"You said I was safe."

Sorrow-filled shadows swept over his eyes. "I do everything I can, but every now and then, they find a crack in our barricade and momentarily sneak in." He held my hands. "But it's only in the VR programs. In reality, you are safe and so are the others."

"For now," Jag snipped. "But you're running out of time, Xander."

Xander's head dropped and his shoulders slumped, but he quickly regained his composure. He stood and turned, towering above Jag, who didn't look up from his fingernails. "I will make the deadline. There's still time."

"Deadline," I repeated. "Deadline for what?"

"Soon, there will be an awakening," Blaze said. "Others from outside of Equatia will help end Equatia's reign."

"Like a war?" My heart accelerated. "But that's precisely what Equatia has been trying to avoid. It's why they sequestered our nation and have no contact with others, to avoid conflict so we can live in peace."

They all glanced at each other. I had spoken like a true brainwashed citizen.

Xander ended the tense silence. "Currently, Equatia is the only nation capable of destruction. The only nation that threatens harm in a gross demonstration of power."

"The worst kind of power," Jag said. "The planet-damaging, mass-murdering kind."

I gasped. "Mass murder?"

Awol left her seat and sat beside me. "The Arcana offers people a way out before it's too late."

"The Arcana is the only way out of Equatia," Blaze said. "Besides death."

Keek and her dream of escaping filled my mind. "Are you serious about this? This isn't some made-up story to get me addicted to a virtual world?"

Xander stared down at me in such an intense way that my spine went rigid. "I swear to you, the tarot cards are the key to permanently—in *reality*—escaping Equatia and the damage it will inflict."

“Please don’t toy with me,” I begged, almost whispering. “This is too big. This would mean freedom for my sister, and my family, and me.”

“It means freedom for thousands of people. A way out before Equatia no longer exists.”

Level 2.7

Equatia no longer existing? How could that be? I closed my eyes and rubbed my temples. All the information was too much to take in so fast.

More bursts of lights and squiggly shadows consumed the space behind my eyelids. I sprung up and out of my seat. "They're back. The flashers and floater things."

Xander held my face in his hands. "Look again. Are they moving as fast as they were, or can you focus on them?"

Hesitantly, I looked closer. They were hardly moving at all. I could see the blurred edges of each shadow, and the sparks of light were dimming with each passing second. "They're slowing and the lights are burning out. What does that mean?"

"It's just aftershocks," he explained. "Nothing to be alarmed about."

"This is overwhelming for Kelsey," Awol said. "Her first visit here and she's attacked by a virus. Xander, you two should go for a walk. Kelsey looks like she needs a break."

I lowered my head, trying to hide my embarrassment, but Xander was already reaching for my hand and leading me away from the group.

We walked out from the cover of the domed roof. I stared up at the open sky dotted with stars above us, trying to imagine a world where our nation no longer existed. Would we be attacked? A natural catastrophe? How could anyone know for sure? Even the High Priestess wasn't able to predict the future.

I felt Xander's concern as he watched me and patiently waited for me to speak first. We stopped at the edge of the rooftop. I rested my hands on the chest-high concrete wall, rubbing my fingertips against the scratchy, porous surface. "You said you help people live. Really live. This is what you meant."

Placing his elbows on the wall, he and stared out at the city. "Yes."

"How did you learn about all of this?"

He smirked in an adorable, humble way. "Would it sound cliché if I said I was chosen?"

"It would sound like something from a fantasy novel, so I approve."

"Good, because I was chosen."

"By whom?"

"A brilliant soul from the outside world who strongly believes in getting as many people out of Equatia as possible before . . . the catastrophe."

"What's going to happen?"

"Equatia will destroy itself, and anyone left within in its cage."

"How?"

"That part I don't know, but I trust the source of the information, so I'm doing my part to save as many as I can."

"If all of this is true, then you won't just be a magician, you'll be a hero."

He laughed and the warming ripple effect of his happiness made me smile. "I'll never be a magician or a hero," he said. "But many thanks for the compliment."

We would have to agree to disagree. "I need to tell Keekee and my parents. I won't go without them."

"Tell Keekee first. We can't involve your parents yet."

"Why?"

"It's one of those instances where you're going to have to trust me."

"How much time is left?"

Sadness darkened his eyes. "Not enough."

"Have you helped anyone actually leave Equatia yet?"

He smiled. No, he *beamed.* "Yes. A lot. Which is why Equatia is cracking down on dealers. They've figured out there's a connection between VR and missing citizens. It's why they've initialized disruptive viruses."

My body tensed thinking about my morning meeting with officials. "They'll know I've been using VR. They sent a virus after me."

"No. I created a scrambler program to protect everyone in the Arcana. They'd never be able to identify who their virus attacked."

"You're sure?"

"One hundred percent."

I slightly relaxed, but my mind still spun with questions. "What should we do? Me and Keekee? What do we do or say at our meeting?"

He glanced out over the city again. Any trace of his happiness was gone. "In a few hours, a national alert will transmit to all govern bands stating that a campaign to crack down on VR dealers has commenced. An exorbitant amount will be added to any citizen's income, tax-free, if they provide information that leads to an arrest and conviction."

"How do you know that?"

He stood straight, his shoulders widening. "Because I'm sending out the alert."

My head jerked back. "What?"

"Once every citizen of Equatia has this information, your problem subsides. Dealers will panic and put all business on hold, knowing any of their current customers would most likely turn them in. Any new customers would most definitely be seeking VR to earn the reward. The VR business will come to a standstill, at least temporarily."

"But what if your customers turn you in?"

"You saw our people. They are so passionate and invested in the Arcana, they hardly noticed furniture flying around the rooftop. The last thing they'd ever do is jeopardize our mission and their own future."

I hoped he was right. "Why were the people on the rooftop so different from the people downstairs in the cafe? Downstairs, people swarmed you. Upstairs, they paid you no mind."

"The minors are downstairs. They're still at the beginning of training and trying to collect all the cards required to advance to the rooftop and become majors. The majors train differently. They've already earned all the cards, so they aren't begging me or anyone else for another. They've come a long way, evolved in many areas, and continue to do so each day."

"But the majors on the rooftop were trading cards. Why would they do that if they already have the whole set?"

"I had to spice it up a little when I was designing them. I created a bonus program for each of the major Arcana cards. There's a trick to accessing them, but it's really tough to figure out, and the journeyer has to experience more than one of a specific card to have a shot at accessing the bonus program." He grinned smugly. "Out of the 22 major cards, only four journeyers have accessed bonuses."

"Who were they?"

He chuckled. "Isn't it obvious?"

I only thought about it for a few moments. "Of course. Awol, Blaze, Jag, and you."

"Not me. I'm ineligible since I designed the program. That wouldn't be fair."

"So who is the fourth?"

"Devlin."

"But Devlin was arrested."

He shrugged. "Yes, well, no one's perfect."

I knew Devlin's arrest must have been a sensitive subject, so I steered away from it. "Do the four of them have a special title because of their accomplishment?"

"What special title would you suggest?"

I tried to think of something clever, but failed. "Master reader, or something."

"Nah, they like the custom names they've given themselves. Besides, belonging to a suit is more than enough for any of us. It declares our greatest strengths without creating conflicts over rank. We may be different in many areas, but we all work together and learn from each other."

My initial assumption was correct: Xander befriended all types. He probably came from a strong and loving family. "Do your parents know you're the mastermind of this Arcana revolution?"

His neck muscles flexed, and sorrow filled his eyes. "I'm no mastermind. And my parents died several years ago."

When someone trusts you with the heartbreaking fact that their parents have left this world, there is never an appropriate or adequate thing to say. "I'm so sorry."

His chin fell to his chest. "I've made peace with it."

I couldn't imagine how hard it must be to talk about such an emotional subject. I hoped he hadn't had to face that kind of loss alone. "Do you have any siblings?"

He turned to me, peering up from beneath his dark lashes. "You ask a lot of personal questions."

"I'm sorry. I just want to get to know you better."

"I can suggest a very effective way for you to get to know me better."

Please let this be our first kiss, I thought, wishing I hadn't been so stern with him at our fake proctor meeting. I wanted to erase my long tangent about how I wasn't interested in him whatsoever.

"How?" I asked, my lips aching for the magical moment of connection with his.

"I'll show you one of my favorite books."

Not what I was expecting, but surprisingly, I was exhilarated by the idea. "And by show me, do you mean we'll virtually experience it together?"

He grinned. "Now you're catching on."

"When will this virtual date take place?"

"Soon, but first you need to begin your Arcana training. The others will be anxious to show you how it works."

I glanced up at the starry sky, disappointed at the idea of having to leave the beautiful view. "So we're going back downstairs?"

"No, you'll train up here with the majors."

"But I haven't collected all the cards. Why do I get special access to the rooftop so soon?"

He slid closer, his arm brushing against my hand. "Because you're special, Kelsey. You're special to me."

As wonderful as that sounded, and as much as I wanted it to be true, I willed myself to be completely honest. "I've seen this before in my old schools. You're *the* guy. The leader. Mr. Popular. The guy all the girls want to be with, and the guy all the other guys wish they could be. I'm sure girls constantly throw themselves at you. Especially girls in the Arcana."

"This isn't high school."

"Same principles apply."

He laughed and stood taller. "You don't know as much as you think you do."

"Then educate me."

"First, girls do not throw themselves at me."

"You're being modest."

"I'm being a realist." Did he really not see his own good looks? My sister claimed she didn't think he was all that great, but I had always questioned her taste. "I'm smart. I'll admit that, but Jag is the lady's man. He's the one who has many Arcana groupies."

"Jag?" He cleaned dirt from under his fingernails in public and was way too cocky and overcompensating—flashing his silly knife any chance he could—a definite indication of insecurities. "No way. You're more sophisticated and much hotter than Jag."

Xander's brows shot up. Did I really say that out loud? I looked down, letting my hair fall around my face so he wouldn't see me blush.

"That's sweet of you to say." He brushed his knuckles against the top of my hand. It was such a subtle touch, but it sent waves of excitement throughout my entire body.

"Here's the gist of it," he continued, a slight rasp in his voice. "Since the first time I saw you, when our eyes met in the parking lot of Caffeine Machine, I knew. You were the one for me. Period. Whether or not you felt the same about me, I was yours, and I would have followed you into oblivion."

I felt like I was in one of my romance novels. I hated insta-love in books, but this was *my* story. Criteria had changed. "You sure know all the right things to say to a girl."

"I only know what to say to *you.*"

My chest and cheeks were on fire. I had rehearsed it in my head several times, but saying it out loud was totally different. "If you like me so much, and if you feel such a connection to me, why haven't you kissed me yet?"

He adjusted so he was fully facing me. "Kelsey, I want to kiss you a thousand times a day."

My words came out in a pleading whisper. "Then why haven't you?"

He tucked a curl behind my ear, like always, then pressed his forehead against mine. "Because I want you to be certain I'm the one you want forever."

Forever. The word had always seemed so fanciful. Who could ever really commit to forever? Forever meant, well, *forever,* which was a longer amount of time than the human mind could conceive. If Xander was waiting for me to promise him something so eternally permanent, we would never kiss. The thought made me feel empty.

"Xander?" Blaze called from behind us.

My breath whooshed out of me, but I stopped myself from rolling my eyes. I liked Blaze, but darn that girl and her uncanny knack for spoiling intimate moments.

"Yes, Blaze?" Xander answered without looking away from me.

"Devlin wants to speak with you."

My head snapped around, and I gaped at her. "Devlin? He's here?"

Blaze shrugged. "Part of him is."

Xander was already walking away from me. I rushed to follow him, curious to find out what part of Devlin had managed to escape the government and show up at Higher Grounds.

Level 2.8

We returned to our gathering area, but I didn't see Devlin anywhere.

Blaze set a small silver sphere on the table. A 3D hologram manifested to life above it, a stunningly lifelike hologram of Devlin Templeton.

I reached forward, my fingertips passing through the light that created his form. "Wow," I cooed, blown away by the quality of the hologram. It was far superior to the images I'd seen any holosplay produce. "He looks so real."

Devlin's hologram spoke. "I interact like I'm real too."

I jumped back, shocked by his intelligent response. "You can hear me?"

"Of course I can," Devlin said. "And everyone else for that matter." His focus shifted to Awol. "How's it going, Goblet?"

"Swimmingly," Awol replied. "Nice of you to visit us, Penhead."

Devlin was the second person to call Awol Goblet. She glanced at me and shrugged. "It's a pet-name for cups. Cups, goblets."

Nicknames seemed of little importance considering the spectacle in front of me. "But you're not real?" I asked Devlin's hologram. "Right?"

He replied, "Depends on your definition of real."

I looked at Xander, hoping he'd explain. One arm crossing his middle, the other hand bracing his chin, Xander silently watched Devlin.

"As you witnessed," Blaze said to me, "Devlin was arrested. His body and brain are being held in The Hub, sentenced to be a drudge."

"I'm a virtual form of my consciousness," Devlin's hologram explained. "Try as they may, Equatia has no power over my soul. That will always belong to me."

"But once someone is mind-stripped," I argued, "They're done. All of their knowledge and memories are erased, and the government programs them to be a drudge."

"True," Jag said, "but we have a program that can help reset them."

"Restore them," Awol corrected.

"It's a work in progress." Blaze twirled a chunk of her copper hair around one finger. "Detailed, complicated, and it requires a lot of time and work, and trial and error, but we're confident we'll succeed."

Devlin's technology-tinged voice stated confidently, "And when we do, we'll save countless mind-stripped people."

My mouth hung open, stunned by the idea of such a miracle. "How is that possible?"

"We call it Virtual Override," Xander explained. "Tapping into the consciousness and restoring the brain by using virtual journeys that resonate with the subject's soul. Their past, their loved ones, important and pivotal moments in their life."

Devlin elaborated. "The system is based on the principles we use for regular Virtual Arcana training, but instead of using fictional stories to help a person evolve, we—"

"Hang on," Xander interrupted. "Kelsey hasn't started Virtual Arcana training. No need to overwhelm her with Override when we don't even fully understand it yet."

"Agreed." Awol lifted her mug. "Baby steps, young grasshopper, baby steps."

"My apologies," Devlin said. "I assumed since she was on the rooftop she had already started her training."

"Tonight is her initiation," Xander told him. "We were in the process of briefing her."

Blaze downed the rest of her drink then stood. "And now we will happily take over while you and Devlin discuss his latest report."

Xander's brow furrowed, and he glanced at me then back at Blaze standing behind Devlin's hologram. He looked like he didn't want to leave me, which I took pleasure in, but then he conceded. "Kelsey, stay with them and learn all you can. I'll be back as soon as I'm done meeting with Devlin."

"Okay," I relented, disappointed to be separated from him, but anxious to learn more about the Arcana training.

Xander waved one hand over the table, then turned, walking away from us. Amazingly, the sphere producing Devlin's hologram floated off the table by itself and followed Xander.

Blaze giggled. "Close your mouth and let's get started. Floating holospheres are nothing compared to what you're about to experience."

We all sat down around the table again and Jag began educating me. "Tarot cards are about self-discovery. Each card represents topics that appear in everyone's life over and over again. They are reminders of what one must work on to become more versatile. The best way to learn quickly is to live a lesson in another person's shoes. It forces one to think and act outside of their own comfort zone."

"Like in books," Blaze added. "A person can live countless lives."

"Exactly," Jag agreed. "Gaining knowledge and understanding with each different experience, which is where virtual reality comes into play. Once upon a time, a wise inventor realized they could use VR to educate and train the masses. Put someone into a different world using VR and let them figure out how to survive."

"Don't make it sound so combative, Jag." Awol grinned at me. "It's so much more than that. Placing people inside of novels filled with different worlds, adventures, plots, conflicts, characters, etc., helps them become enlightened, and evolve much more quickly than if they only experience their limited reality in their own world as themselves."

Jag butted in again. "You train by experiencing different scenarios to help you develop all attributes of each suit. Some stories will enhance sword traits: physical battles, mental challenges, conflict and struggles. Other scenarios will help develop qualities of the other suits: emotions, spiritual, and whatnot. A curator helps guide you."

Awol motioned at our small gathering area. "Everyone here is a curator."

"Besides you," Jag said to me. As if that weren't obvious.

Blaze unwrapped a new lollipop. "Which means any of us will be able to help you train."

"Or help you get out of a bad situation," Jag added.

"What kind of situation?" I asked. Could the Arcana help Keekee and me with our current dilemma?

Awol must have read my mind. "Like the issue you're facing with whether or not to help Equatia find VR dealers."

"I don't understand how any of you can help with that."

They exchanged assertive glances, silently revealing how confident they were in this secret and magical system of theirs.

"Shall we crack her spine?" Jag asked.

I leaned back against my seat, protecting my spine from Jag and whatever cracking he had planned.

Awol hopped up, her dreads bouncing against her shoulders. "She should start with cups. An emotional connection is her best bet to develop her relationships and sensitivity to other's feelings."

"Oh, go write a poem or something." Blaze snorted. "Wands should be first. She needs to understand the philosophy behind it all and develop her intuition."

Jag tapped the tip of his knife against his nose. "She needs a good fight. To remind her what she's trying to save."

"No," I said firmly, surprised by my own determination. "I want to start with pentacles."

Jag groaned. "Pentacles and their *home is where the heart is* crap? I was hoping you'd be more daring."

"Pentacles it is!" Awol linked my arm with hers. "This next part is fun. You'll enjoy it. Since Xander isn't here, I'll guide you through the perusal."

Blaze threw her lollipop at Awol's bare feet. "Greedy goblet, you steal all the best moments."

Awol ignored her and asked if I was ready.

"Not in the slightest," I said. "But I suspect that doesn't matter."

She laughed. "I like your attitude. Close your eyes."

I gave one last look to our chat group. Jag saluted me while Blaze daintily waved. I closed my eyes and let Awol guide me away.

"Keep them closed until I tell you otherwise," Awol said.

It felt like she ran her fingers through my hair, but I wasn't sure. My scalp tingled and the soles of my feet warmed. It felt like we might be moving, but I wasn't taking steps forward. Her fingers brushed against the base of my neck as she lifted the charm of my necklace with her other hand. A second later the quartz dropped against my chest.

"Ready," Awol said. "You can look."

I opened my eyes and glanced around. We stood in the same place on the round rooftop, but the others were gone. Even the furniture had disappeared.

"Where'd everything go?" I asked.

"Cleared away so you can focus on your selection."

"My selection of what? A tarot card?"

"No, a book. Whichever story calls to you."

"How do I know which one is calling to me?"

"You'll feel it."

My bare feet suddenly burned like I was standing on hot coals. I jumped backward, lifting each foot until they cooled enough to stand still.

Awol turned her head and read the title of the book cover I had been standing on. "*A Game of Thrones.* Ha! I knew you weren't ready for a sword scenario."

I stood still, trying to figure out what she was talking about.

"How's that one feel?" she asked me, motioning to my feet.

Looking down, I read the title of the book where I had landed. *The Catcher in the Rye.* "I don't feel anything," I admitted. "But it's not burning me like before. Is that a good sign?"

"Complacency is never a good sign. Life is too short to spend time on a story that doesn't move you."

I stepped onto the next book cover, starting to understand the game. "So I try each of them until I feel drawn to one?"

"Exactly."

"What happened to never judging a book by its cover?"

"The person who originally said that was probably a disgruntled author who was issued a really bad cover."

I chuckled, then hopped onto the next one, feeling nothing significant. Excited by the book next to it, I planted both feet on *Wicked Lovely,* expecting to be enchanted by some sort of fairy magic. After a few seconds of watching me bounce up and down on the cover, Awol laughed. “You can’t force a story to call to you.”

I pouted and hopped in place one more time. “But I loved this book. I’ve read it three times.”

“That’s dandy, but you’re looking for the one that speaks to your soul at this moment in time. The book chooses you. You don’t choose the book.” She waved her finger. “Say goodbye to your fantasies about Seth and keep perusing.”

I strolled along the rooftop, stepping on book after book. I didn’t see an end in sight. Every time I thought I was close to the edge of the roof and expected the books would run out, more choices appeared. “I didn’t know so many stories existed.”

“The possibilities are endless.” Awol followed along behind me.

Stepping onto another cover, I wriggled uncontrollably and giggled. I spun around, expecting to see Awol tickling my side, but she was too far away to have touched me.

She nodded with a pleased grin on her face. “That’s the one.”

She walked over, tilting her head to read the title. “*The Adventures of Huckleberry Finn.* A healthy dose of pentacles and cups, with a splash of swords and a touch of wands. Makes total sense.”

“I’ve never heard of it,” I admitted.

“That’s so sad, but understandable. In the Old World, some people lost their minds and banned many great books. This was one of them.”

“Why did they ban it?”

“Doesn’t matter,” Awol said. “The story chose you. It’s time to dive in, heart and soul.”

What I didn’t know, or expect, was she meant it literally.

Level 2.9

I stood and waited. Awol watched me with an anticipatory smirk.

I stated the obvious. “Nothing is happening.”

“I don’t know what kind of books you’ve read, but usually you have to open the cover to start experiencing the story.”

“Oh. Right.” I stepped back and squatted in front of the cover. Lifting it was easier than I expected, but it swung open and there were no pages, only a hole filled with fog. I reached down into it, but felt nothing solid. “Now what?”

“Dive in.”

I stared at the fog, confused. The cover was bigger than a regular book cover, but it didn’t look safe enough for a person to jump into. Besides, we were on top of a building. Would I end up in the cafe downstairs?

“It’s like a manhole cover,” Awol explained. “Except it’s a storyhole cover. You’ve heard of wormholes, right? They’re used for time travel or journeying from one part of the universe to the other.”

“I’ve read about them in a couple sci-fi novels.”

“Similar concept. Except storyholes take you from this world into fictional ones.”

I dipped my fingers in the fog again. It didn’t feel cool or hot. It didn’t feel like anything, really. I reached in further, half-expecting to be sucked in, to start tumbling down a rabbit hole like Alice, but nothing happened.

“I’m scared,” I admitted.

Awol clasped her hands behind her back and casually circled me. “The book chose you because it has a lesson for you. It can’t hurt you—at least, not permanently. You might go through the emotions of being hurt so that you can emphasize with another person’s feelings, or suffer physical pain because the experience has to feel real in every sense, but in the end, you return back to your life as yourself. Actually, you'll be improved. More evolved, more worldly, more experienced."

"This Huck Finn is a person, correct?"

"He is."

"On these adventures of his, does anything really bad or scary happen to him?"

Awol's eyes glistened with a childlike joy. "Nothing you can't handle."

I stared into the mysterious hole, wishing I knew more about this Huck Finn character and what he did that was so terrible it made people ban his story. "I dive in? Like head first?"

She squatted beside me. "That depends. Are you a head first kind of person, or feet first?"

"I'm not sure."

"What do your instincts tell you?"

Here we were again with the instincts. I sat on the solid surface at the edge of the storyhole. Letting my legs dangle into the opening, I swung my feet even though I couldn't see them through the fog. I planted one hand on my open book cover, and the other on the closed cover beside the hole. I took a few deep breaths and looked up at Awol. "Just jump in?"

"And enjoy the journey."

One more deep breath, and then I pushed off and fell.

The fall was not the long, grand tumble down the rabbit hole like I imagined. It was more like floating inside of a cloud and never landing. Instead, a solid surface gradually formed beneath my feet, and just as slowly, but still impressively fast, a scene from a different world formed around me.

I stood in a small room with walls made from wood planks. I held a candle in my hand and set it on the rickety table in front of me. Touching my dirty right hand with my left, I realized they weren't my hands. Looking down, I glanced over my small body and tattered clothing. I was a boy.

The sensation startled me for a moment, but my own thoughts and emotions faded away as smoothly as the scene around me had formed. I was Huck Finn. Pure and simple. Familiar with my surroundings, antsy from boredom, and achingly lonely.

I continued on as Huck Finn for quite a while. I accidentally killed a spider in a candle flame and it left me feeling cursed. I snuck out of my room to meet Tom Sawyer (which took away my loneliness), and we stole a hat from a big man named Jim who talked funny. We went to the river and discussed becoming a gang of robbers with Jo Harper, Ben Rogers, and some other boys. We took a blood oath, then talked about keeping secrets and maybe killing people, and Tom made rules based on books about pirates. Tom and Ben argued a lot, but I didn't mind because I was glad to be part of something, even if it was a gang of robbers.

Suddenly, Ben and the others all froze in place, but Tom walked over to me. His physical appearance changed with each step he took: he grew taller, his hair shortened, his clothes changed into the Equatia government-issued tunic and pants. As he came closer, my awareness that I wasn't Huck became clearer.

"Devlin?" My voice sounded more like Huck's than my own.

"That's enough for now."

"Enough what?"

"Training."

Devlin waved one hand through the air. Even though he was a couple feet away from me, it felt as if a gust of wind knocked me backward.

The sound of paper pages flipping whirred through my ears as multiple scenes rewinded in front of me. I started spinning so fast the images blurred together until I was surrounded by a ring of colors.

As quickly as it started, the spinning stopped. My eyes darted from side to side, trying to steady the rest of me.

"Welcome back," Devlin said. We were on the same empty rooftop where I had left Awol. The sky was still dark and filled with stars. How long had I been gone?

Devlin handed me a glass of pink juice. "How do you feel?"

I made sure I had regained my balance before taking the drink from him and gulping it down. My book journey left me extremely thirsty. I had never tasted whatever flavor juice he had given me, but it was fruity and delicious.

Muffled noises began flooding my ears. I glanced around at the empty, book-covered ground. We appeared to be alone, and I didn't see all the majors from earlier, but I could hear them talking, laughing, and shouting like invisible ghosts.

I studied Devlin. He didn't look like a hologram, and the silver sphere that produced his image earlier was nowhere to be seen. He looked as solid as me. I poked his shoulder. "Are you real?"

"In what sense?"

"You look and feel solid, like you're a living, breathing human standing in front of me. But you were arrested, so are you an impressively realistic hologram?"

"The world doesn't define what's real. You do."

"But—"

"Look out behind you!"

I turned to see what Devlin was warning me about, but the moment I turned, everything around me blurred again.

When the tornado of colors stopped, I stood in front of Xander.

We were back in the all-white room. The one hidden in the tallest shelves of his library. The one where I had first started my journey into the world of VR. Where the real world ended, and Xander's world of make-believe began.

"Welcome back." Xander took the card from the palm of my hand and returned it to its holder in his fake book.

"Oh," I murmured, disoriented and disappointed. My heart sank to the floor. None of it was real. Higher Grounds, Awol's coffee concoction, the suits and storyholes, the secret system to escape Equatia and help mind-stripped citizens: all fiction. "It was all virtual reality?"

Xander touched my cheek. "Remember what the High Priestess told you. You are not in the world. The world is in you."

Perplexed, I leaned away from him. "She didn't say that."

He squinted and cocked his head. "What happened? Where did you go?"

They were *his* VR scenarios. Shouldn't he know where I went and what his characters said? I replied, "The rooftop."

"Rooftop?" He squinted deeper then reached for my necklace, but his beeping govern band made him stop mid-reach. "We're almost out of time. I have to get you back home." He held both of my hands in his. "Today at your meeting, agree to help them catch dealers."

"But if I do, I won't be able to contact you at all."

His face softened. "I can be with you at any moment. If you need me, just expand the screen on your band and place your hand flat against it."

"No way. I'll lead them right to you and they'll turn you into a drudge."

"Trust me, Kelsey. I know what I'm doing. It's safe to contact me that way."

I didn't want to go home yet. I didn't want to leave him. Even if I really could contact him anytime I wanted, I knew I wouldn't. I'd stay away from him to protect him. This would be the last time I saw him for a long time, and I hated that thought.

I summoned courage. "Before you take me home, can I kiss you goodbye?"

His eyes gleamed. "I won't kiss you until I'm sure it's forever."

"But *I* would be kissing *you.*"

"Then, you need to be sure *I* want *you* forever." His words were a blow to my heart. Wasn't there a mutual attraction between us? Hadn't he admitted he wanted to kiss me a thousand times a day? I shook off the memory, realizing he said that during a VR scenario, not in reality.

"Why are you making such a big deal about one kiss?"

He cupped my face in his hands. "Because *you* aren't sure about anything between us."

"Yes, I am," I said defensively, even though he was right. How could I be sure of anything when we had only known each other for a couple days?

He subtly licked his lips. "If you were sure, your left eye wouldn't be twitching like it always does when you're lying, and we would be kissing right now."

Screw it. Enough talking. It was only a kiss and I was seizing the moment. Who knew how long it would be before we saw each other again after tonight. *If* we ever saw each other again. I stood on my tiptoes, threw my arms around his neck, closed my eyes, and leaned in.

I stumbled forward, falling, but instead of landing hard on my hands like I expected, I kept falling, unable to feel or see anything solid. I didn't scream because I wasn't scared, only confused. The rabbit hole had found me after all.

As the speed of my fall increased, I closed my eyes, anticipating the moment when I'd have to land (or crash) onto something.

Xander's voice echoed from far, far above me. "It's not in the cards for us."

I opened my eyes. I wasn't falling.

I was in my bedroom, lying in bed.

Two minutes until our alarm went off and we had to get up for school. For the briefest moment, I assumed what anyone would, that it had all been a dream. Even Xander's magic library. But then I felt a card clutched in my hand.

I sat up, activating the flashlight on my band and shining it on the image. A kind-looking woman who reminded me of my mother sat in a garden holding a wand with a heart on the end that looked like a peppermint candy. I stared at the number 3 above her head and read the name in a whisper. "The Empress."

Alarms blaring on our bands made me jump. I shoved the card under my blanket and silenced my band as Keek yawned and turned hers off too.

In a tired, gruff voice, she said, "Today's the big day."

"The big day?"

"The day we change our fate and secure our future."

I groaned. That part had been real—the dismal part that I didn't want to be true. But had the rest of it actually happened? Was I still supposed to follow Xander's instructions, or had that been some much-too-hopeful version I dreamt up while I slept? My thoughts were blurring together and confusing me.

Keek climbed out of bed and walked across the hall to the bathroom. No sooner had she shut the door when my band alerted me with a message. *Stick to the plan today. I've got your back (and front). I believe in you. xX*

It was the first time Xander had ever sent me a message via my band. I read it again. Then three more times. After my brain registered that my night with Xander was real, that I was still supposed to agree to be a government fink, and that Xander would hack the system to protect me and my family, I stared at the last two letters of his message. *xX*

My first kiss from Xander was via govern band. I mentally demanded a do-over.

"Kelsey?" Mom called from the doorway.

"I'm awake." I sat up as she walked into our room and sat on the edge of my bed.

"Here." She held out her hand to give me something. "I made these special for you. I know today will be difficult and extremely stressful."

I held open my hand and she dropped two homemade candies into my palm. Red and white heart-shaped candies. I startled, yanking my hand away as they fell onto the tile floor and shattered into pieces.

"Kelsey, you're shaking like a leaf." Mom sighed and hugged me. "I'm nervous too, but it will be all right. We'll get through this as a family."

I stared, dumbfounded, at the broken candies on my floor. The same candy that I had just seen on The Empress card. I hugged my mom tight, afraid that my actions had somehow involved her.

"I couldn't sleep," she said. "So I stayed up all night making too many calming candies. Come into the kitchen and have a couple. They'll help."

"But—" I couldn't worry her even more. I had to pull myself together for her sake. "You're right. Lead me to them."

I climbed out of bed and followed her down the hall, rubbing my eyes and pushing away my worry that The Empress resembled my mother. I tried to ignore the candy connection, but when we walked into the kitchen and Mom stepped aside, I gasped.

Rows of baking sheets covered the countertops and kitchen table. Every pan contained rows and rows of red and white candies. The pattern strongly resembled the back of playing cards. The red and white cards that Xander said were a warning sign that I needed to stop and change course.

I was on the wrong path.

3: THE EMPRESS

Level 3.1

Xander told me the red and white symbolism was a warning. I was on the wrong path. Mom's candies were a flashing stop sign in our kitchen. I needed to reassess. What was I supposed to stop doing? Say no to being a fink for the government? Don't go to school?

I paced the bathroom floor, occasionally glancing at myself in the mirror, hoping my reflection might provide a magical answer like in a fairy tale. No such luck.

The only person who could help me was Xander. Could I risk contacting him? Was it safe? Was *that* action the one I wasn't supposed to take? My head hurt trying to figure out right from wrong, and what to do next.

"Kels?" Keekee shouted through the door. "You okay in there?"

"Yes, just showering."

"How fascinating, considering I don't hear any water running."

Glitch. I turned the water on full blast. "Get off my back. I'll be out in a few minutes."

She didn't say anything else, but I was sure she rolled her eyes as she walked away. I squeezed into the linen closet and shut the door. I activated my expanded screen and held my hand over it, hovering as I debated if I was about to do the right thing. Could I really contact Xander this way, or had his instructions been part of a dream? I didn't know what else to do. My band was still protected by Xander (for now), and I hoped the government wasn't secretly monitoring our bathroom.

I had to try to reach him. I pressed my hand against the screen and begged for it to work without putting him at risk.

The screen filled with colors, then Xander's face stared back at me. "Kelsey?"

"It worked."

"Did you think I was lying to you?"

I made sure the closet door was pulled tight and whispered, "I didn't know if last night was real. I woke up thinking it all might have been a dream."

"Not a dream." He squinted and moved closer to the screen. "It's so dark that I can barely see you. Where are you?"

"I'm hiding," I answered in a hushed voice, leaving out my embarrassing location. "I need your help. I woke up holding The Empress card, and the woman on it resembles my mother. She held a wand, but on the end was a heart that looked like a red-and-white candy. Then my mom came into my room, and she handed me candies that looked just like what was on the card, and then I walked into the kitchen and they were everywhere. It means stop, right? But stop what?"

"Has your mother made these candies before?"

"Well, yes, sometimes, because she's a caterer, but that's not the point. They are red and white. Tons of them. It reminded me of the playing cards, or the pattern on your scarf, and you said those were warnings to stop what I was doing."

Judging from the way his forehead lifted, my words finally registered. "Of course. Sorry, I haven't slept much. My brain must be too tired to have made the connection. What were you about to do when you saw the candies?"

"That's just it. I was waking up, about to get ready for school. Should I not go to school? I sort of have to. We have that meeting. Should I say no to helping the government bust VR dealers?"

He turned his head, staring at something to his left. "Hang on."

I watched him, wondering what he was looking at. I couldn't tell where he was in his warehouse. The wall behind him was a blank dark gray. Was that his office? I couldn't remember for certain. His eyes scrolled as if reading something beside his screen.

The water pipes of our shower started squealing. The automated voice of our home monitoring system warned that my ten-minute water allotment had one minute left. "Xander, hurry. I need an answer quick. I'm almost out of time."

"Bear with me a few more seconds."

His eyes scrolled faster, and his right arm moved like he was using one of his computers. He stopped, sat back, and leaned close to the screen. "Go back to bed."

"What?"

"Go back to bed, fall asleep, and when you wake up, things will be different."

My lips parted then closed again. What could I possibly say to that except, "Are you insane?"

The water shut off. How would I explain that my hair wasn't wet and that I hadn't showered? Keekee would know I was hiding something again. Mom probably would too. Everything felt wrong.

Xander said, "I promise, going to sleep and waking up again will work."

"How will that fix anything?"

"You have to trust me."

I pressed my hand to my forehead and exhaled. "This is crazy."

"Do it, Kelsey. Now."

"I'm contacting you again when it doesn't work, and you're going to explain your mental issues."

"I wouldn't have it any other way."

"Talk to you in a few minutes." Out of habit, I went to push the disconnect button, but it wasn't listed as an option. Instead, I minimized my screen, and it went black. I quietly crept out of the closet and cracked open the bathroom door, peeking down the hall for Keekee or Mom. Dad always left early, so I didn't need to worry about running into him, but Mom or Keek couldn't see me dry and still in my sleep attire. They'd be suspicious and ask a dozen questions I couldn't answer.

They were in the kitchen talking about today's meeting. I snuck out and tiptoed to our bedroom, glancing one last time at the baking sheets of candy on the table before I rushed into our room and locked the door.

I climbed into bed and pulled my comforter up over my head. I felt ridiculous. How could I possibly fall asleep while my heart raced and my mind whirled? I reached under my pillow and grabbed The Empress card. She looked the same as I remembered, and her wand was a definite match to Mom's candies. She and I stared at each other under the cover of my private makeshift tent. Her loving gaze helped calm me until my pulse returned to normal.

I closed my eyes. *Why me? How did I get into this mess? And more importantly, how do I get out of it?*

I tried so hard to fall asleep. And surprisingly, I did.

The blaring alarms of our govern bands startled me awake. I silenced mine as Keek yawned and turned hers off too.

Mom's face flashed behind my heavy eyelids. Something about her—something important—tugged at my tired brain, trying to surface.

In a gruff, but enthusiastic voice Keekee said, "Today's the big day."

"The big day?" Was it Mom's birthday? I rubbed my eyes, feeling disoriented and extra exhausted. Xander had returned me home less than an hour ago. My sleep-deprived brain must have been short-circuiting, because Mom's birthday was months away.

"The day we change our fate and secure our future." Keek climbed out of bed and almost skipped across the hall to the bathroom.

I groaned, hoping I'd be coherent enough to survive our meeting with officials. We had polar opposite feelings about our fink situation. Squiggly lines floated in and out of the corners of my vision. I kept blinking and rubbing them away. I definitely needed more sleep. My eyes felt even more strained than my brain.

My band alerted me with a message. *Stick to the plan today. I've got your back (and front). I believe in you. xX*

It was the first time Xander ever sent me a message via my band. I read it again. After my brain was awake and functioning enough to absorb the content of his message, I stared at the last two letters. *xX*

My first kiss from Xander was via govern band. I mentally demanded a do-over.

"Kelsey?" Mom called from the doorway.

"I'm awake." I sat up as she walked into our room and sat on the edge of my bed.

"Here." She held out her hand to give me something. "I made these special for you. I know today will be difficult and extremely stressful."

I held my hand open, and she dropped two star-shaped candies into my palm. One brown, one white. "Coffee and vanilla?"

"Your favorites."

"Thanks, Mom."

"Oh, Kelsey." She sighed and hugged me. "I'm so nervous for you girls. I hate that you're going through this."

"It will be all right." I hugged her back. "We'll get through this as a family."

"Absolutely," Keekee agreed, returning from the bathroom.

Mom let go of me and walked over to her, brushing her messy curls from her face. "I couldn't sleep, so I spent most of the night baking." She placed a couple candies in Keek's hand and kissed her forehead. "I enhanced them with calming herbs and my own special valor blend. Your father helped me flavor them. He wanted to go in late to work so he could see you off, but I insisted he be on time. He hasn't even had that position a week. I hope you girls understand."

Keek and I replied at the same time. "We do."

Keekee popped a yellow star candy into her mouth and kissed Mom's cheek. "Don't worry so much. It will all work out in the end."

Seeing my mom and sister embracing each other gave me hope that Keekee might be right about a future beyond Equatia.

With Xander's help, we might have a chance at a happy ending.

Level 3.2

Keekee and I sat side by side in counseling room 5. My knee wouldn't stop bouncing and my fingernails hurt from digging into the armrests for the past ten minutes. We had an appointment. Why were they making us wait so long?

Keek didn't seem nervous at all. She was probably internally jumping for joy because she was one step closer to legally finding her next VR fix. "I hope Kramer doesn't attend this meeting. He makes my skin crawl."

I spoke quietly, worried that the mention of his name would somehow make him appear. "I hope we never see him again."

I reached into the front pocket of my tunic for one of Mom's candies, but it was empty. I had eaten all six before 10:00 am, but I didn't feel calm, and the valor recipe wasn't working. Sighing, I stared at the ceiling, both of my knees bouncing at hyper-speed.

"Here." Keek handed me two of her candies. I gratefully took them and popped one in my mouth, grimacing at the sour lemon flavor—Keek's favorite.

"Thanks," I mumbled. "I just want this to be over already."

"It will be soon. Hang in there." She didn't tell me to calm down, or not to worry. She knew me too well and didn't waste her time telling me to do the impossible.

The door opened. Two tall, older men entered the room. Their ominous presence made the whole world seem darker, and they took up so much space I felt claustrophobic.

It will be over soon, I mentally repeated for the hundredth time this morning.

"Miss Zellar," the first official said. He had a large nose, and it twitched when he said our last name. I glanced at Keekee, wondering if he was addressing her or me. He shook Keek's hand then mine. "I'm Agent Spade. This is Agent Club."

My chin darted forward. Spade and Club? Those couldn't be their real names. Those were suits of playing cards. The connection and all the possibilities of what it might mean made me tremble.

Agent Club extended his hand toward me. He was missing his pinky. I tentatively shook his four fingers. The sensation was strange, as if I gripped the small hand of a child instead of a big, intimidating man. "No need to be fearful, Miss Zellar."

My words stumbled out of me in a halting, nervous way. "Oh, I'm fine. It's fine."

"You're shaking, but this will help." He pulled something from behind him that looked like a small plastic gun. I startled, sliding my chair backward as Keek sprang from her seat.

"Don't you dare!" she warned Agent Club. Agent Spade restrained her, but she struggled to break out of his grasp.

"Let go of her!" Before I could jump to my sister's defense, Agent Club grabbed my arm. A loud popping sound made my ears ring as heat seared my shoulder.

"You have no right to tranquilize her!" Keekee shouted.

A wave of serenity swept through me. My head bobbed side to side, but I couldn't move the rest of my body.

"It's a mild sedative," Agent Club explained. "To help her relax."

"Would you like one as well?" Agent Spade drawled.

"No, I'm not the slightest bit nervous." Keek sat down and scooted her chair closer to mine. She held my hand and reassuringly squeezed it, causing a tingling sensation to ripple up my arm. "You okay?"

I nodded. My head felt like a cloud that could drift away at any moment.

Conversations took place, but everyone's words sounded far away. I struggled to keep my eyes open. I'm not sure how much time passed, but eventually Keek shook my shoulders and forced me to look at her. Two blurry versions of her melded into one as she said, "Kelsey, you have to state that you agree to their terms."

I nodded again. At least I think I did.

"You have to say it out loud," Keekee insisted. "On the record."

My tongue felt swollen and heavy, but I forced out the words I didn't want to say. "I agree."

Sparks of light burned my closed eyelids. Something about the sensation felt familiar, maybe even important, but the flashing stopped, and I was too tired to give any further thought to the hint of a memory.

My mother's voice beckoned me awake. "It's my fault. I shouldn't have given her so many candies."

A man's deep voice replied. "We must be diligent with children, Mrs. Zellar. They aren't mature enough to understand the consequences of overindulgence."

My stomach roiled, and I almost threw up. I pried my heavy eyelids open and the sick feeling worsened. Counselor Kramer stood above me. His big bull face was even uglier than the last time I saw him.

I turned my head, hoping I hadn't imagined my mother's voice. I did not want to be alone with Kramer.

"Hey there, lovebug." Mom rubbed my arm. "How are you feeling?"

I'd never been so relieved to see her. "Where am I?"

"The school's health bay. You overdosed on calming candies."

"No." I struggled to sit up. My limbs felt like huge tree trunks. "They shot me with a sedative."

"A mild sedative," Kramer said. "It wouldn't have had much effect if you hadn't consumed a dozen enhancement candies in a very short time."

I had only eaten eight, but it was no use correcting him.

"It's my fault," Mom insisted again. "I shouldn't have let you take so many."

"It's not your fault," I argued. "They shouldn't have sedated me without asking."

Surprise and concern creased my mother's brow as she glanced at Kramer. I could read her mind as she silently urged me not to cause trouble in front of a counselor.

"I don't feel good," I admitted, holding my gurgling stomach.

"We should get you home so you can sleep it off." Mom looked at Kramer. "May she be excused for the rest of the school day?"

"I suppose I can grant her an absence due to the circumstances."

Mom helped me off the exam table, but I had to pause as the room tilted. I pressed my hand to my forehead and realized I was naked.

Well, my body wasn't naked, only my wrist, but it felt wrong and strange. Our govern bands were a part of us. Like a second skin. "Where's my band?"

Kramer answered. "It was malfunctioning. It hadn't recorded your consumption of any candies from this morning, so we've sent it to a lab in The Hub for evaluation. A new one is being programmed for you. You should have it within a few hours." Kramer stood on the other side of me and touched my elbow. He was trying to act like a nice guy by assisting me down from the table, but I wanted to run far away from him. He spoke to my mom, who stood on the other side of me. "I'll inform them that her new band should be delivered to your home."

"Many thanks," Mom said sweetly.

Kramer's rough hand started massaging my upper arm. *Massaging* me. I lurched forward to get away from him, stumbling over my own feet and landing hard on my hands and knees.

"Kelsey!" Mom squatted at my side. "Slow down and let us help you. You're still groggy."

I tried standing so we could get out of that room and away from Kramer as fast as possible, but I was so dizzy, and my hands and knees stung and ached.

Kramer stood over me like a salivating monster. "Given her condition, perhaps I should carry her to your craft."

My mom smoothed down my curls, looking at me as if she were considering letting the perv touch me.

"No," I insisted, forcing myself to stand. "I'll manage fine on my own."

Mom helped me regain my balance. I walked forward, leaning on her more than I intended, but I might have fallen over again if I hadn't.

“Thank you for the kind offer,” Mom said to Kramer. I wanted to glare at her, but I couldn’t risk turning my head and making myself dizzier.

Kramer’s toxic energy loomed behind me. “I’ll follow behind you in case you have any trouble.”

Why wouldn’t he leave us alone? The last thing I wanted was his creepy gaze staring at my backside on the long walk to the car. And if I did stumble and he tried to touch me again, I might scream.

“We’d appreciate that,” Mom said.

I gritted my teeth. *No, we wouldn’t.*

The trek out of the health bay and down the main corridor felt excruciatingly long. I fought with every step to stay steady. Kramer even followed us through the lobby and into the parking lot. Thankfully, Mom asked Kramer to open the passenger side craft door, and she assisted me as I sat down. She leaned in and reached across me, pushing the button to activate my safety restraints.

“Don’t let him touch me again,” I whispered.

She paused, looking into my eyes, then pursed her lips and inconspicuously nodded before standing and shutting my door. I breathed a sigh of relief as she thanked Kramer and said goodbye.

As Mom walked around to the pilot side of the craft, Kramer pressed his meaty, violating hand against my window and leaned down to peer in at me. “I’ll be in touch soon, Kelsey.”

I cringed and stared forward. I’d never been so eager to go home and crawl into the safety of my bed.

Level 3.3

Later, after a long and much-needed nap, I still felt tainted by Kramer. Talking things through with Mom usually made me feel better because she gave great advice, so I decided to rid myself of one of the secrets I'd been harboring. I told my mother about Kramer's inappropriateness during our first meeting. And how today he had used her blocked view as an opportunity to massage my arm.

"I know it doesn't sound *that* bad," I concluded. "But it's the feeling I get from him. Like I know he's capable of doing so much more and he's waiting for his chance."

Sitting across from me at the kitchen table, Mom looked horrified. "I have to report this."

"I already thought about that. It will only make things worse. No one will believe me over him."

"I can at least ask them to assign a new counselor to you and Keekee."

"They won't without good reason, and if he finds out we reported him, who knows what he'll do to retaliate."

Mom's eyes closed and she rubbed her brows. "I'll talk to your father and see what he says."

"Mom," I whined. "Dad will definitely file a report."

"At first he will want to, yes, but then he'll calm down and figure out what's best. He's the rational one. I'm too emotional about these things." She stood and walked around to my side of the table then touched my cheek. "We won't let anything bad happen to you."

I almost argued that she couldn't make a promise like that, but I let her have her protective parent moment. She needed to feel some small sense of security. I envied her ignorance.

My naked wrist reminded me that soon the government would be monitoring every move I made. Every waking moment, and even while I slept, I worried about what they'd find when they examined my govern band. Surely they'd figure out it had been bugged. Would they be able to tell how, and by whom? Would they question me? I had no way to contact Xander now. He had no way to protect me.

Despite my bare wrist, and the temporary (and only) window of time when my emotions and reactions weren't being monitored, I felt hopeless and trapped.

I couldn't stop imagining enforcers busting into Xander's warehouse and arresting him for trying to help a silly, stupid girl who had destroyed his noble mission because she ate too many enhancement candies.

Mom started prepping food for dinner. I offered to help, but she insisted I rest.

We were both on edge waiting for Keekee to come home from school. The second time Mom dropped her measuring cups on the floor, I cursed myself for telling her about Kramer. From now on, she would worry about him every second of every school day. As if she didn't already have enough to stress about with the VR dealer fiasco, I had added even more to her plate.

The front door opened and Keek rushed around the corner. "You all right?"

"I'm fine," I lied.

"Those bastards," she huffed. "I wanted to cut off Club's other fingers when he shot you with that thing."

Mom gasped. "Shot you?"

I glared at my sister. "An injection. It's not as bad as it sounds, Mom."

"It's the government." Keek grunted. "It's always as bad as it sounds."

"I hate this. I hate all of it." Mom returned to kneading dough with more force than before. Had she thought the sedative was a delicious tea they served and I happily drank? Maybe a pill I swallowed with no questions asked? Of course they injected me.

Keek stared at my naked wrist. "Where's your band?"

"They took it for evaluation. Claimed it was malfunctioning. A new one should be delivered soon."

"And so it begins." Keek glanced at her own band. "You realize your new one will probably be as advanced as it gets, right?

They'll be monitoring everything. Every move, every conversation."

"I'm well aware, but thanks for stating the obvious and making me feel worse about agreeing to this mission that I never wanted to do in the first place."

"It has its downsides, but wait until you experience VR for the first time. You'll understand my love for it. And don't forget, this is the first step to transferring to a country with freedom."

So optimistically oblivious.

"Keekee, did they do anything to you?" Mom asked. "Harm you in any way?"

Keek shook her head. "I was too worried about Kelsey, so I shut up and cooperated."

I snickered. "You mean you were eager to start your hunt for VR dealers so you can game legally."

Keek's head bobbed. "I suppose that's true too."

I rolled my eyes.

"Did they do anything to your band?" Mom asked Keekee.

"Not yet, but I expect they will. Nothing will surprise me at this point." Keek kicked her feet up on the chair beside her. "What's for dinner? I'm starving."

I envied my sister's attitude. I wanted to be as carefree as she seemed, but as I watched her from across our kitchen table, I knew everything was wrong on countless levels. My instincts screamed that I needed to make it right, but I didn't know how.

Dread laced every circuit of my body, and I didn't have the knowledge or skill required to rewire myself.

We were halfway through dinner when our front door alert chimed and the automated voice announced a visitor for me. "Government carrier on official business for Kelsey Zellar. Signature required."

I pushed my chair back from the dinner table. "That must be my new band."

Dad followed me to the front door. I opened it and stared at the small square box the carrier held.

"Kelsey Zellar?" The carrier asked. I couldn't peel my eyes away from the box. Inside was a band that would make me more of a prisoner than I had ever been. He cleared his throat then said, "Please sign here stating you've received the package."

I didn't move.

"Kelsey," Dad urged. "This gentleman needs you to sign his digiboard."

I blinked, snapping out of my trance. Reaching forward, I signed the screen with my fingertip.

The carrier handed me the box, and I warily placed my hands on either side, but when I tried lifting it, the box didn't move. The carrier kept a firm grip on it. I looked up at him, seeing his face for the first time.

"Jag?" I squeaked.

His eyes narrowed. "Beg your pardon?"

My focus flickered to his ID tag stating his name was James Garrison. Dad watched us, clearly confused by our strange interaction. I was confused too. Jag lifted the box closer to me. "Please, ma'am, take the package. I'm on a tight schedule."

This time I lifted the box from his hands with no resistance.

"Our apologies for delaying you," Dad told him.

"Good evening, sir." Jag slightly bowed to me. "Ma'am."

Dad closed the door and touched my shoulder. "Are you feeling unwell? You were acting strange there for a moment."

I absentmindedly shrugged, staring at the box in my hands. I opened the lid and a new govern band sat wrapped around a metallic holder.

"You should put that on right now," Dad said. "We don't want to give them any reason to harass you or make this situation more difficult."

"Right," I agreed, lifting the band out of the box. I slid it onto my wrist and its sensors hummed to life then the band tightened to fit snugly. On the screen, Equatia's flag appeared, followed by the first setup command.

I followed Dad back to the dinner table. Mom and Keek were silent until I held up my wrist. "Back in the shackles again."

Keek chuckled as Dad sighed and sat in his seat. The three of them carried on a conversation about their day, trying to take everyone's minds off the drama with the government.

I clicked through all the usual steps for booting up a new or upgraded band. It recorded my fingerprints, scanned my irises, had me acknowledge several Terms and Conditions agreements that I didn't read. (Not like I could argue with or refuse anything specified in the fine print.) After several minutes, a message declared setup was complete. The screen went dark like usual, but then it turned green. Then blue. Yellow. And finally red. I stared at it, waiting to see if it did anything else new that my old band didn't.

The screen transitioned to a beautiful shade of brown, like coffee after adding cream. Then slowly, in the bottom right corner, two white letters appeared.

xX

Those two simple letters restored my hope.

I breathed long and deep, hiding my smile with my napkin. Xander was still safe, and still with me.

Level 3.4

We finished watching one of Dad's favorite entertainment programs, an Olden feature about cowboys who rode horses and robbed trains. They had more freedom than I would know what to do with, but they also shot whomever they pleased, so I was grateful not to live in those days.

As the credits faded, Mom shut off the holosplay. "That was a much-needed escape from today's drama."

I stretched as Dad stood and carried dishes into the kitchen.

"I'm turning in for the night." Keek trudged toward the hallway. "I'm exhausted."

"Me too," I agreed.

"Me three," Dad shouted from the kitchen.

Mom flashed me a worried glance. "You girls be sure to shut your bedroom door, so we don't keep you awake while we clean up out here."

There was nothing left to clean up. Which meant Mom was going to tell Dad about Kramer, and she didn't want us to hear him if—no, *when* he reacted badly.

"Don't," I whispered to Mom. "There's no need to worry him. I already feel awful that I worried you. We can take care of ourselves."

She looked conflicted but pulled me in for a hug. "Sweet dreams, lovebug. Tomorrow will be a better day."

"Love you, Mom." I said goodnight to Dad and headed for the bathroom. I prepared for bed slowly, attempting to give Mom enough time to come to her senses and not discuss Kramer's inappropriateness with Dad.

In our bedroom, Keekee was propped up on one elbow as if waiting for me.

"Shut the door," she urged.

I hesitated, worrying the closed door would make Mom think I approved of her talking to Dad about Kramer, but Keek waved me in. "Hurry."

As soon as the door clicked shut, she started. "I think I may already have a lead."

My heart skipped. *Please don't let it be Xander.*

"A guy in my art class was whispering to a girl today about a new "scenario" he was trying to gain access to. He had to mean VR."

"You can't be sure of that."

"Not yet, but I think it's something. I'm trying to befriend them to see if I can find out more. I want those bastard officials to know I'm doing my part. The faster we give them useful information, the greater chance we have of leaving Equatia." She flopped down onto her pillow. "You have to make an effort too, whether you want to or not."

I climbed into bed, not responding.

"Kelsey," Keekee chided. "You realize how serious this is, right?"

"Yes. Deadly serious."

"I'll help you. We're in this together. Double trouble forever."

"Forever," I agreed, hating that stupid word.

She turned off the light and fell asleep within minutes. I stared at the ceiling, dreading tomorrow and wondering how or when Xander would contact me next.

No more than five minutes had passed when our bands beeped with a national alert. Kelsey stirred under her covers as I read the message on my screen: *Operation Unplug has commenced. Any citizen who provides information to enforcers regarding illegal access to satellite or Internet feeds, and/or operation of virtual reality programs, will be rewarded a bonus of 30,000 tax-free credits to their household income. The reward will be dispersed only if the information leads to an arrest and conviction. Help us protect you by obeying all laws and reporting any suspicious or unlawful activity.*

I tried to steady my breath as I pressed the acknowledge button.

Kelsey remained asleep, her band's screen glowing and blinking. It would continue to do so until she woke up, read the alert, and acknowledged that she understood. As would every govern band on every citizen's wrist.

Xander did it. He hacked Equatia's system.

Tossing and turning, I kept staring at my sister's blinking, glowing screen on her wrist. What would she say when she read the alert? Why hadn't Mom and Dad barged into our room, excited or at least shocked to receive the announcement? They must have seen them before going to bed.

Was Xander sleeping peacefully, satisfied with his work? Was he awake and worrying about what to do next? He hadn't hacked the system for me alone; he was trying to save countless people and everything the Arcana stood for, but for a brief moment, I pictured his contagious grin and imagined he *had* done it all for me. He used his brilliant mind and technological skills to protect my family and me. And that thought, that *delusion,* made me happy.

My band's screen lit up. It didn't make a sound, but a message appeared in white letters, not the usual black. White letters on a coffee-with-cream colored background like the *xX* that appeared earlier.

You awake?

I pulled my comforter over my head on the slight chance that Keek might wake up and see me messaging someone at an inappropriate hour.

Yes, I typed in reply. *Are you okay?*

Always.

What if the government was somehow monitoring us? *Is this safe?*

Communicating? Yes. No one will ever see this conversation except you and me.

Reading *you and me* made my insides tingle. I typed, *Where are you?*

In my bed.

Tingling took on a whole new meaning. I hugged a pillow to my chest, imagining what it might be like to cuddle with Xander.

He sent another message. *You still there?*

Sorry. I was thinking.

About?

I debated whether or not to be forward, but communicating electronically had a way of making me bolder. If he rejected me, I didn't have to face him. I inhaled shakily and went for it. *Thinking about what it would be like to be in your bed with you.*

My stomach fluttered as I stared at my screen, waiting in hopeful agony for his reply.

That does sound nice.

I let out the breath I'd been holding and smiled.

Another message came through. *Maybe we should try it sometime.*

I rubbed my feet together and curled into a ball, shivering happily at the thought. My fingers moved at lightning speed. *Except I'd be wanting you to kiss me, and you'd say we should wait.*

WHY would I say THAT?

My fingers flexed over the screen. He did say that. It's not like I could forget it. Had he told me that during a VR scenario, or in reality? I couldn't remember.

I sent, *Maybe I misunderstood?*

No maybe about it. You have no idea how many times I've wanted to kiss you.

A squeal of joy bubbled in my throat. He DID want to kiss me! I kicked against the sheets, unable to contain my excitement. *I wish I were there with you right now.*

Be out front in 8 minutes.

My eyes bugged. *You're coming here?*

An army of enforcers couldn't stop me.

My giddiness turned to nervousness. Could I sneak out again? The first time I was lucky and didn't get caught, but I didn't want to push it. *Not sure if that's a good idea.*

Already on my way. You're down to 7 1/2 minutes.

I grinned like I had just consumed a dozen joy-infused enhancement candies. *See you soon.*

I threw back my covers and rushed to my dresser. My hair wasn't too frazzled yet, so I tied it into a loose ponytail. I pulled a fresh tunic over my nightshirt and considered changing out of my sleep shorts and putting on pants, but the hussy in me took over. Citizens were forbidden to show their bare legs in public, but I was about to sneak out and break curfew. Might as well go for broke and show off my legs too.

I crept to the bathroom and brushed my teeth without turning on the water. The mint paste was a bit overwhelming at first, but I rubbed my gums and kept swallowing until it became tolerable. The upside was my breath would definitely be minty when Xander and I did kiss.

Great stars, I was going to kiss Xander tonight! I hopped up and down at the thought. The breeze against my bare legs made me feel free and rebellious.

With one minute to spare, I lifted the bedroom window and crawled out, then softly shut it behind me. I turned around just as Xander's craft hovered to a stop behind our parking pad.

I couldn't help it, I sprinted across the yard. Xander was already outside of the vehicle, opening the passenger door. Jittery with nerves and excitement, I jumped inside.

Xander climbed into the pilot seat, glancing at my bare legs and smiling with approval. "Your corruption has reached a new level."

I tried not to blush as I fibbed. "I didn't have time to put on pants."

"Thank the universe for that." He piloted the craft away from my house as I pretended to look out my window so he wouldn't see my huge grin. We had been so uninhibited while messaging each other, but being face to face was a different story. My shy side was back in control.

We glided down my street then out of the neighborhood. I sidled a glance at Xander, but he was focused straight ahead. As we cruised toward downtown, I fidgeted in my seat, coming to terms with the fact that our messaging may have been innocent flirting and nothing might come of it tonight.

Suddenly, Xander whipped into a dark alley and threw the craft into hover mode. My heart stopped, assuming he had spotted a patroller and hid. But that wasn't the case.

"I can't wait anymore." He leaned across the center console and cupped my face with his hand. The look in his eyes was so intense, it took my breath away.

"Wait." My fingers flew up to touch his face.

He placed his hand over mine and pressed his cheek into my palm. "I know, you need to touch me."

I did need to touch him. My stupid obsessive compulsion to touch things. He wasn't a *thing,* though, he was a person: an intelligent, intriguing, and magical person I thought about much too often in impure ways. I had ruined our passionate moment with my ridiculous quirk.

"I'm real," he said. "I'm right here with you."

My fingers ran down his strong jawline then brushed across his soft lips. His breath smelled like cinnamon. Would he taste like it too? I leaned in and his lips closed over mine. In that one moment, that one thread of time and space when our souls weaved together, I was both sanctified and ruined.

He kissed me so softly, but so fully. I floated into an alternate world of euphoria, a world where we fit together so perfectly that I didn't ever want to be apart from him. I couldn't tell where he started or I ended, but it didn't matter because together, we were complete.

He pulled back. His eyes glimmered with the same electricity coursing through me. "I told you we had a connection."

I nodded, unable to speak. I had kissed a few guys, and read countless kissing scenes in novels, but none of them compared to what I felt with Xander. And none of them ever would.

Pressing his forehead against mine, he said, "I could sit here and kiss you until the sun rises, but it's not safe."

"I know," I uttered. "You're right."

His voice was raspy, and it made my head spin with desire. "Were you serious about sharing my bed with me?"

I swallowed hard. I didn't want him to think I would have sex with him. Even if my body wasn't being monitored by the government, I wasn't ready to break that law for personal reasons. But the thought of cuddling with him? That was more than enticing; it would be a heavenly escape from reality. "Yes, sort of. I mean—"

"I'm a gentleman, Kelsey. I respect you too much to try anything." He touched my temple then his finger trailed down my cheek and ended at my lips. "Besides kissing. Now that you've initialized that connection between us, there's no turning back."

"I don't want to turn back. I'm already addicted to your kisses."

He repositioned himself in his seat and flew us out of the alley. "Good, because I want to be your exclusive dealer."

Level 3.5

We glided into his warehouse and he parked in front of the living room. As we climbed out of the craft, I didn't mean to, but I stared at the upper level where he told me his bedroom was located.

He followed my gaze then ran his hand through his hair, smiling. "Would you care for a fresh-brewed cup of coffee?"

"No, thank you."

His eyes widened. "You're turning down coffee?"

I wasn't brave enough to admit I craved him more than caffeine. "For now."

"Well, I'm flattered."

My focus wandered away from him and toward the floating stairway leading to his room. He stood directly in front of me and turned to look up the stairs too. In a theatrical voice he said, "Your stairway to heaven."

"Ha." I playfully shoved him away from me. "Remember, we'll only be sleeping. And maybe cuddling," I teased. "If you're lucky."

He stuck his hands in his pockets while restraining his smug grin. "Sleeping and cuddling. Got it. No kissing."

I pretended to reconsider. "Perhaps I'll allow a kiss or two."

"So cuddling if I'm lucky." He stepped closer and placed his hands on my hips. "And *perhaps* one or two kisses?"

I bit my bottom lip, eager to feel the rush of our chemistry again, but I played coy. "You'll have to earn them."

"Earn them how?"

"Answering some of my many questions." I needed to know him better. And I had so many questions about his VR programs that I hardly knew where to begin.

He kissed my forehead, brushing his lips back and forth ever so lightly. "I happily, and enthusiastically, accept that deal."

I rubbed his muscular forearms then each of his fingers. He lifted my chin and looked into my eyes. "I'm real. You don't have to keep touching me to make sure."

Could he read my mind too? I swallowed back my embarrassment. "But I like touching you."

"Then maybe I should reciprocate." His fingertips traced down my throat, over my shoulder then up the back of my neck. I sighed blissfully, and he leaned down and kissed me.

Thankfully, Equatia hadn't issued restrictions on daily allotments of kisses, because I had found the one addiction I couldn't resist.

His hands travelled down my sides, then he wrapped his arms around my waist and lifted me off my feet, all while never breaking our kiss. After what felt like only seconds, but was actually a couple minutes, he set me down and pulled back, grinning at me in a way that confirmed he felt the same sparks I did.

Bliss is a magical thing. I was so lost in Xander's kisses that I never realized we were moving. As impossible as it seemed, he managed to carry me upstairs without me noticing. Granted, my eyes were closed and I was hyper-focused on how amazing his lips felt and the passionate strength of his hands, but still. Impressive.

"We're upstairs," I said, glancing around his open, large, and tidy bedroom.

"That we are."

"You can deny it all you want, but I stand by my assessment that you are a magician."

His cheeks flushed a shade of pink that complimented his olive skin. "I'm glad you think so."

His bed was still made. Two blue pillows sat neatly on top of a beige coverlet. I felt the fabric, impressed by how soft it was. High quality and far above the linens issued to moderate households like mine. "That's a big bed for one person."

"You're the only person I've ever shared it with."

My eyes flew open in surprise. I still assumed Xander was a ladies' man, so it was hard for me to believe he lived alone in such a big, remarkable warehouse and never brought home any girls.

Holding my hand, he led me to his bed, sat down, and patted the mattress. "Your chariot awaits."

I smirked and crossed my arms over my chest. "It just occurred to me that I don't even know your last name. You told the school receptionist it was Mage, but I know that was incognito for magician."

Deep thought lines formed around his eyes. "How did you know that?"

I shrugged. "Pretty common knowledge."

"That's not common knowledge."

"When you read a lot of fantasy novels, many magical references become hardwired into your brain."

"Hardwired," he repeated under his breath. He seemed lost in his own thoughts so I snapped him back into reality.

"I'm still waiting to hear your last name."

"Right." He shook his head and fell backward onto the mattress. "It's Westin."

"Alexander Westin," I repeated. "It has a nice ring to it."

I crawled onto the bed and sat beside him. I wasn't comfortable enough to curl up next to him. Since meeting him, I was guilty of having hussy thoughts, and even acting like one a time or two, but I was still a goody-goody. "So, tell me."

"Tell you what?" he asked, squinting up at me like he was trying to figure me out, instead of the other way around.

"Your story."

"Which version?"

"The true version."

He rolled onto his side and propped up his head with one hand. "That one would send you running away from me."

"I bet it wouldn't."

"I assure you, it would."

Clearly he wasn't ready to open up yet. The key word being *yet.* I would crack the mystery of Xander even if it killed me. "Okay then, let's start with your favorite novel."

His eyes rolled upward as he searched his memory. "I'm like you. I can't choose one favorite."

"Then tell me one of your top-five all-time favorites."

He didn't think long at all. "*The Lost Marble Notebook of Forgotten Girl and Random Boy.*"

My jaw went slack. "You're kidding."

"I don't kid about my favorite literary masterpieces."

"I love Marie Jaskulka. I quote her stuff all the time. Her books speak to my soul."

"That's exactly why *Marble Notebook* made it into my top five."

"Do you have an access card for it?" I scrambled onto my knees, bouncing the bed and unable to control my excitement. "Can we virtually experience that story?"

"I do. And we could, but I assume you'd want to only experience the good parts."

All of Forgotten Girl's heartache tugged at my core, but so did all of her joy. "I'll take the bad with the good."

"Optimistic answer, but can I give you a rain check? I haven't been sleeping much lately." He rolled onto his back again and pressed his palms over his eyes. "I'm exhausted."

His lack of sleep was mostly my fault, and I felt horrible about that. "Rain check granted."

"Much appreciated."

I studied him, seeing him in a whole new light. A light that made him even more intriguing than before. Which I didn't think was possible. "What did you love about *Marble Notebook?*"

His hands slid up over his head and fell to rest on the pillow. "It was their story. And it was real. Harshly real at times. It showed that love isn't all sunshine and dewy raindrops glimmering in the light of rainbows. Sometimes it's dark, and messy, and leaves you feeling like—" He paused, searching for the perfect description.

I referenced one of my favorite lines. "Like your heart is a watermelon that's been cracked open."

He turned, staring at me like he related to that feeling all too well. And then—be still my fluttering, twitterpating heart—he quoted the same passage. "Sweet, sticky truth is spilling everywhere."

"Except the truth isn't always sweet."

He focused on the ceiling again. His voice deepened, but he spoke softly. "Especially when it's bittersweet truth, and it's so sticky that you can't escape it no matter how far you stretch any version of reality."

Neither of us was smiling anymore. His sadness was palpable. What had happened in his past to fill him with so much regret and heartache?

I stretched out beside him. “I wish you’d tell me some truths about you.”

He smirked and closed his eyes. “My story is so complicated that even I have trouble keeping it all straight.”

I stared at his profile. His jaw flexed every time he blinked, like he was fighting back words while trying to erase bad memories from his mind.

“Every story has dark parts.” I rested my head on the pillow beside his. “It’s a requirement so the good parts can be appreciated.”

Rolling over to face me, he brushed a curl from my face and let his fingertips linger against my temple. “I agree, but I’d rather you know the good in me first.”

“I’ve seen plenty of good in you already. Actually, I’m worried because you seem a little too perfect.”

He blushed again. “I’m far from perfect, Kelsey, but maybe I’m perfect for you.”

I chuckled and shook my head.

“What?” he asked, sounding insulted.

“It’s just so ironic. I’ve read countless books where the hero says so many swoon-worthy lines, and like most girls, I imagined myself as the female lead and thought how amazing it would be to meet a guy who said sweet things. But now—” I covered my face so I wouldn’t laugh.

Xander pulled my hands away. His expression teetered between curious and fuddled. “But now what?”

I didn’t want to hurt his feelings, so I tried to keep composed. “You’re here, and real, and delivering the same romance-novel lines, which should be a dream come true, but instead, it’s so—” I giggled and hid my face in the pillow.

“So cheesy?”

I burst out laughing. When I looked up, his cheeks were extra bright pink, but his grin was humbled and adorable.

“I’m sorry,” I managed. “I don’t know why it’s so funny.”

He shook his head as his smile grew bigger. “Unbelievable. You girls say you want us to be romantic and chivalrous, but when we are, you laugh at us and call us cheesy.”

“You said cheesy,” I corrected. “Not me.”

“You didn’t disagree.”

“I didn’t want to lie.” I laughed again and so did he.

When we both caught our breath, he said, “So I can stop acting like Mr. Darcy?”

I stroked his cheek. “Aww, Alexander Westin, you are a talented artist, and a virtual magician who saves lives, but you, nor any other man, could ever be Mr. Darcy.”

He playfully smacked my hand away. “That’s it. I’m never saying anything romantic to you ever again.”

“Thank the stars for that,” I teased.

“Ouch. Any confidence I might have maintained through this conversation has now been obliterated.” He tried turning away from me, but I grabbed his arm.

“Wait, wait. I have a suggestion that might restore some of your confidence.” I pulled myself together enough to stop smiling and be serious. “Every time you’re tempted to deliver a romantic line, stop yourself by kissing me.”

His lips parted to say something, but then he forced them shut, licked them, slowly leaned over me, and followed my suggestion.

Readers everywhere could have Mr. Darcy. My new crush was Xander Westin.

Level 3.6

My eyes sprang open at the chime of my band.

Steel beams were above me. The pillow beneath my cheek was too soft to be my own. Xander stirred beside me.

Glitch. How long had we been asleep?

My band chimed again. I lifted my wrist to see Keekee's name. Double glitch.

I sat up and hit *Accept.* My sister's face filled my screen. Her eyes doubled in size when she saw me. My hair probably looked like I'd been through a hurricane.

"Where the hell are you?" She whisper-yelled. "Mom and Dad will freak."

I was already shaking Xander awake. His warehouse had no windows. His bedside light was still on, but that did nothing to help me answer my main question. "What time is it?"

"Our alarms for school are going off in fifteen minutes. Dad just left for work. I can hear Mom in the kitchen."

My heart raced. My mouth went dry. I was so screwed.

Xander sat up and watched me with concern. "It's okay. Take a deep breath."

Keekee's eyes almost popped out of her head. "Is that a guy's voice? What in the world?"

Before I could reply, Keek disappeared. I stared at the ivory screen, trying to figure out what happened. "Keek? Keekee?"

Then I realized I was looking at her bedspread. Muffled voices were barely audible. Mom must have come into our room. Triple, quadruple, infinite glitch. The screen wobbled and then my mother's face appeared. I'd never seen her look so angry.

"Is this some sort of joke?" Her voice cracked as she tried not to yell. "This better be a joke."

"I'll be home in 10 minutes," I said meekly.

I disconnected and looked at Xander. “I’m so dead. The government won’t have the chance to arrest me because my mother will kill me first.”

He sighed and rubbed the back of his neck. “I’m sorry. I planned on setting an alarm in case we fell asleep, but I guess we both passed out before I got around to it.”

I leapt out of bed, pacing. “Come on, you have to take me home so I can be executed.”

He sat up and stretched his arms behind him, cracking his back. I couldn’t waste time thinking about how gorgeous he looked in his sheet-crumpled state. I was too busy panicking.

“Let me fix this,” he said. “It’s my fault.”

“Fix it? They can’t even know I was with you. You’ll have to drop me off a block away.”

“You’re keeping me a secret?” He leaned back against his headboard like he was in no hurry, like we actually had time to carry on a conversation. “Are you ashamed of me?”

“How can you joke at a time like this? What if a proctor is monitoring Keekee and this whole debacle? Enforcers might already be waiting at our house. My parents follow the laws. My mom will have to report me. No one can know I was with you or that I even know you. I’m trying to keep you safe.”

“That’s very considerate, but how about letting me keep you safe?” He looked deadly serious. “Let me talk to your Mom. You shouldn’t take the hit of this alone.” He stood and walked over to me then pulled me against him. “We’re in this together.”

I shook my head, but not convincingly. Part of me was comforted by the idea of Xander standing nobly by my side while I endured Mom’s wrath. But she was required to report me, and she would tell enforcers the truth. I didn’t want any of those details to include Xander. I had broken curfew laws, but I was under eighteen and would be tried as a minor. They could make up a half dozen charges for Xander, and he was an adult. Not to mention, if they dug deeper and discovered his connection to the VR world, I’d never forgive myself.

“No,” I insisted. “You told me to follow my instincts. My instincts are strongly telling me that no one can know I was with you tonight. So please, drop me off a block from my house. I have to deal with this on my own.”

"Fine," he relented. "If you're certain that's what you want."

I wished on every planet in the galaxy that he would respect my request and stay out of it.

As Xander piloted his craft down Elura's almost-empty streets, I mentally rehearsed multiple lies to tell my parents. Not one of them sounded believable. I had never done anything this bad. Not even close.

"Drop me off outside of our subdivision." I wiped my sweaty palms on my bare thighs and winced. I had to make sure no neighbors saw me in my shorts. At least the sun wasn't rising yet, maybe I could hide in shadows and behind shrubs until I made it home. Although, the thought of walking through our front door was almost as nerve-wracking as the mission of sneaking through our neighborhood unseen.

Xander cleared his throat. "If you let me talk to them I can smooth things over."

I shook my head. "No way. I don't want this to be the last time I ever see you. They can't know who you are. Neither can my sister."

"So what will you tell them?"

"I haven't decided yet. Either alien abduction or epic sleepwalking incident."

He chuckled, and I glared at him. I wasn't kidding. Those were the best two options I could come up with.

He sat up straight, and the craft slowed to a stop. "Well, decide fast or give me permission to intercede, because we have company."

I turned and stared out the windshield. Standing directly in front of us, in the middle of a street that was two blocks away from home, was my mother. Her arms were crossed over her chest. Her frown looked made of stone.

I tried to swallow, but couldn't.

"What do you want me to do?" Xander asked.

My mother stomped forward, like an enforcer about to arrest us, but with so much anger burning in her eyes that for the first time in my life, I was scared of her.

"Go," I muttered.

"Go?" Xander repeated. "Go where?"

I pushed the lever that lifted the craft several feet higher. "Anywhere."

Mom stood a few feet below us, glaring up at me.

"We are *not* running away from your mother." Xander lowered us down until I was eye level with the woman who I was certain wanted to strangle me.

I couldn't hear her, but I read her lips when she said, "Get out of that craft."

In my mind, I did what she said. I lifted my hand and tried opening the door. But in reality, I was paralyzed with fear. I couldn't part my lips to reply. I couldn't even blink.

And then Xander was beside her. I watched them through the window like a horror movie. Xander introduced himself, but Mom didn't even turn to acknowledge him. She kept her focus locked on me. I assume Xander explained that I was wearing sleeping shorts, and that's why I wasn't opening the door, because her steely glare expanded to shock. He must have suggested she get in his craft to prevent anyone seeing me, and so there wouldn't be any scene for the neighbors to witness and report, because he opened the rear door behind me. She stepped out of my field of vision. I was still frozen in place, unable to speak or turn my head.

She climbed into the backseat, and sat directly behind me. The temperature seemed to drop at least fifty degrees.

I stared straight forward as Xander walked in front of the craft, wearing a sympathetic frown.

The backseat squeaked. My mother's cold tone sent icicle daggers into my spine as she hissed in my ear. "Life as you knew it, is over."

Level 3.7

My mother directed Xander to pull around back.

"Stay right where you are, young lady," she told me. "I need to go get you pants before a neighbor sees you."

She stomped inside. I stared at our back door, waiting for Dad to storm out and drag me out of the craft. After a couple excruciating minutes of waiting, Mom returned, opened my door, and shoved a pair of pants into my lap.

"I am so ashamed of you right now. Put those on and get in the house." Her angry glare shifted to Xander. "You too. I don't know who you are, but you have a lot of questions to answer, and if you try to flee, I will report you."

Xander's voice was steady and confident. "I had no intentions of fleeing, Mrs. Zellar."

Her nostrils flared, and she cemented her gaze on me again. "You have one minute to dress and get your butt inside. One minute."

With that final command, she turned and went in the house.

"I'm so sorry." My voice cracked. My throat was so constricted with fear that I could hardly swallow. Wriggling in my seat, I pulled my pants over my shorts.

"I'm glad it happened this way," Xander said. "I didn't want you to face this alone."

"You're crazy. You haven't met my parents. We'll be lucky if we survive this."

"Your sister has been in worse trouble than this many times. You'll be fine."

"That's just it. I was their only hope of having a daughter who didn't get in trouble. I've now shattered that dream."

Xander winced then opened his door. I jumped out, rushing to make our one-minute deadline. We both hurried inside, but I struggled to breathe. My ears rang as I pushed open the back door.

Mom paced the kitchen. "Who is this boy?" Her voice grew louder. "Breaking curfew and staying out all night? Indecently going out in public! Do you know how many laws you've broken?"

I squeaked out an, "I'm sorry."

"It's so unlike you!"

Xander stepped closer and stood tall at my side. "Mrs. Zellar, please excuse my interfering, but this is my fault, not Kelsey's."

Mom spoke through clenched teeth. "I am not speaking to you right now. Move away from my daughter and wait until I address you directly."

Glitch. Mom was the nice one. If she was speaking to Xander this way, Dad would tear him to pieces.

Xander gave one nod and stepped sideways, but not even two feet. He linked his hands behind his back and stood like an enforcer on guard.

"We've only lived in this town a few days." Mom's hands flew in multiple directions as she yelled. "You hardly know him. Is this how we raised you?"

I hung my head in shame. "No, ma'am."

"How did you even pull this off? Why didn't your new band alert enforcers that you were breaking curfew? Is it broken?"

"I don't know." Blatant lie, and she probably knew it, but I refused to tell anyone about Xander meddling with my band.

"What if a neighbor saw you? If someone reports you, and they find out I knew about this and didn't follow government protocol, I will be convicted of irresponsible parenting. Didn't that even cross your mind before you put us all at risk?"

She wasn't going to report me? She was required to by law, but she wanted to protect me. My eyes welled with tears. The last thing in the world I wanted was to get my parents in trouble. I feared Keekee would get us kicked out of Elura and sentenced to life in The Hub, yet here I was putting us in a situation that could have sealed that dreaded fate.

Mom pressed her palm to her forehead. "I can't believe this is happening. How could you do this to me after all I've been through? Do you want to be an orphan? If you think I'm strict, wait until you're being parented by the government."

“Orphan? What?” I glanced at the living room then the hallway, wondering where Dad and Keekee were. Dad was always the first to start yelling when Keek got into trouble. “Where’s Dad?”

My mom looked as if I had slapped her. She shook her head and huffed then stepped so close she was within an inch from my face. “What is *wrong* with you? Have you lost your mind?”

“Stop.” Xander’s firm voice startled me. “Kelsey, are you still with me?”

I turned left to look at him and answer his ridiculous question, but when my head swiveled, my mother’s face froze and then stretched sideways. Multiple images of her appeared, piling on top of one another. I stumbled backward, gasping. “What in the world is going on?”

Xander rushed to my side. “This doesn’t make sense.”

I tried catching my breath. “You’re telling me. Why does my mom look like that?” She was frozen, and so were her blurry multiple faces. “Where are my dad and sister? Is this a VR scenario?”

“This is all wrong.” Xander cracked his knuckles and hurried into the living room, looking around frantically. “Have you been seeing flashers and floaters?”

“Flashers and what?” The term sounded familiar. Where had I heard it before?

“Never mind. I have to get you out of here.”

“Why would you do this? Why would you create such an awful VR scene?”

“I didn’t create this.” He cupped my cheek with one hand and lifted my necklace with his other. “Listen to my voice, okay? Follow my voice.”

“What do you mean? What’s going on?”

He leaned in and kissed the side of my head while lifting my necklace. Even though I was scared and confused, his touch comforted me. The warmth of his kiss made me close my eyes as he whispered, “Trust me.”

But when I opened my eyes again, it wasn’t his voice I heard—it was my sister’s.

Level 3.8

Kels, don't you dare go falling for some guy and then bail on our plan because you think you're in love.

"Keek?" I bolted upright, clutching the covers beneath me.

I was still in Xander's bed, but he was gone. Rubbing my eyes, I looked around his room while my brain slowly kicked into gear. My heart pounded so hard I could feel it in my toes, and the back of my tunic was damp. Mom's anger, getting busted for sneaking out, Xander putting me through a scary VR scenario: it was all a nightmare.

I glanced at my band. 3:48 am. I needed to get home before my dream became reality. "Xander?"

He didn't reply, so I climbed out of bed, heading for the stairs. I stopped at the top when Keekee's voice echoed through the warehouse. "You really live here?"

Xander replied, "I'm not a fan of traditional spaces. This place is more me."

Had she followed us here? I held my breath as I eavesdropped, but I couldn't silence the rushing of blood between my ears.

Bottles clanked together like Xander had opened the refrigerator door. "Would you like a drink? Juice, water, soda—caffeine free, of course."

"No thanks," Keekee answered.

They were both quiet for a few seconds. I didn't dare move. She couldn't have known I was there or she would have raced upstairs and confronted me.

"What's that?" she asked.

"Air hockey," Xander explained. "A game that was popular in arcades of the Old World." His familiar words made the hairs on my arms rise. "You like to touch things."

I stiffened as my sister said she was sorry.

They were having the same conversation we had. Almost verbatim from what I could remember.

"No need to apologize," Xander said. "I just noticed you're always touching things like you need to make sure they're real."

My jaw went slack as my sister responded with my own words. "Habit. I've done it for as long as I can remember."

"Would you like to play?"

Keek stepped into view. Her curls, identical to my own, swung against her back. "Maybe next time."

"Next time." Xander sounded much too pleased. "Deal."

At the base of the steps, framed by two potted plants, Keekee turned and looked up at me.

I gripped the metal handrail and took one shaky step toward her. "How did you find us?"

She acted as if she didn't see or hear me. "I've never seen any place like this before, but at the same time, it feels familiar."

Behind her, Xander came into view. He stood so close to her that a surge of jealousy rushed through me. That jealousy intensified when he closed his eyes and leaned close enough to smell her hair as he said, "Maybe you were here in another life."

I rushed toward them, practically falling down the steps. "Stop it!" I yelled at him. "You're using all the same lines on her that you used on me."

I tried shoving him away from her, but my hands went right through him as their conversation continued without a hitch. I stared at them, dumbfounded. "You can't hear me?"

Xander told her about the Arcana and the government, and neither of them reacted to a word I said. Backing away from them, I muttered, "What the glitch is going on?"

"They can't hear you." A technology-tinged voice said. I spun around to see Devlin sitting at Xander's kitchen table.

"Devlin? What are you doing here?"

He grinned. "Do you really want to suffer through this confusing scene all by yourself?"

I glanced at Xander again, but he was carrying on with Keekee as if I didn't exist. They walked past Devlin and me without even glancing in our direction. They continued through Xander's office and stopped in front of the curtains that concealed the door to his library. At that moment, it finally clicked.

"That's me," I mumbled in shock. "Not my sister."

"About time," Devlin said. "I was wondering how long you'd watch the rerun before tiring of the show."

I glanced back and forth between Devlin and the replay of Xander and me. "This isn't real?"

"Depends on your definition of real." His hair had grown since I'd last seen him, and stubble lined his chin. He certainly looked real—scruffy, but real.

"You said that last time we saw each other."

"I say it a lot, because it's fitting."

Xander and the other version of me walked into his library.

Devlin stood and pulled out a chair. "Have a seat so I can answer some of your questions. They must be piling up in that muddled mind of yours."

Piling up was an understatement. The deluge of questions never ended. I sat across from him.

"Well?" he asked.

"Well what?"

"Ask me anything. Start with your biggest questions, the ones that consume most of your thoughts and time."

I had at least a dozen to choose from, but I decided on the one that worried me the most. "Am I dreaming? Has all of this been one strange, multi-layered dream?"

"No."

"Not even now? This whole watching myself with Xander thing. Not a dream?"

"No," he confirmed again.

I was afraid to ask my next question, but I had to know. "Is Xander real?"

"Real as a human can be."

I sighed with relief. It would have sucked to meet the man of my dreams, but find out he existed only in my dreams.

"So this—" I motioned to everything around us. "—is virtual reality?"

"Yes."

"I thought Arcana members trained through books and living other people's stories?"

"Ninety-eight percent of the time they do."

"So why am I watching a repeat of my own life?"

"Because you need to learn from it."

"Learn what?"

"Pay attention. Analyze what happened before, during, and after. The answer will come to you because it's already within you."

"You sound like the High Priestess."

"I'll take that as a compliment."

I sat back in my chair, somewhat satisfied but still confused about many things. "But this scene, coming here for the first time, seeing the library, all of that actually happened, correct?"

He tilted his head side to side. "In a way, yes, but the details were a little different."

"Which details?"

He shrugged. "I can't give specifics because I wasn't there, or here, depending on your perspective."

"Speaking of that, where are you right now? I mean in reality. You were arrested, but you must have broken free somehow because you showed up at my bedroom window." I backtracked, mentally replaying the events of the last couple days. "And then at Higher Grounds, you were a hologram. Does this version of you even know about that?"

One side of his mouth lifted in an amused sort of smirk. "Yes."

I waited a moment for him to elaborate, but he didn't. "Are you going to answer the first part of my question?"

"Refresh my memory. What did you ask?"

"Where are you right now? The real you."

"I'm here, helping you."

"But you just said this was virtual reality."

"It is."

"So you're a hologram right now?"

"No."

I peeked under the table, checking to see if Devlin had feet. All body parts were accounted for and no holosphere was in sight.

He chuckled. "What I mean is my soul is here helping your soul."

"How is that possible?"

"Conscience, animus, metaphysics, Virtual Override." His eyebrows danced above his twinkling eyes. "*Magic.* I could explain the ins and outs, but your strong cups nature would be bored by the technical details."

"My cups nature. How do you know anything about my nature?"

He set his elbows on the table and leaned toward me. "Cups wear their hearts on their sleeves. You're very emotional. A few minutes ago, you were upset because Xander was too close to another girl." He laughed. "Even though the other girl was you. That screams cups."

My cheeks warmed. I wished Devlin hadn't witnessed me react so badly.

"But there's swords in you," he continued. "You charged down those steps ready to fight."

"I didn't want to fight. I was upset. I thought he was using the same lines on my sister."

Devlin clasped his hands together and shook his head while still smiling.

I stood and straightened my tunic. "I'm glad you find this so amusing, but it's late and I really need to get home. How do I return to reality?"

He stood too, his eyes wandering down to my bare legs.

I tugged on the bottom of my shorts, wishing I had worn pants.

He walked to the fridge and opened it, scanning the contents but shutting the door without stealing anything. "You don't want to go back to reality."

"Yes, I do."

"And what will you do when you get there?"

"Live my life instead of wasting time in some VR scenario that's a repeat of what's already happened."

"But this hasn't happened." He waved his index finger between him and me. "We've never had this conversation before."

"You mean this conversation that's getting us nowhere?"

He winked playfully. "Maybe it's the beginning of getting us everywhere."

I let out an exasperated sigh. "Do any of you Arcana people know how to carry on a conversation that isn't filled with riddles?"

"Yes, but *we* people also know the definition, and consequences, of sensory overload." He hopped up on the kitchen counter, swinging his dirty feet so they kicked the cupboard below him. “Here’s a fact you won’t like, but one you can handle. You need me.”

A bold statement coming from a guy who had been hauled away by enforcers, and judging from his appearance, was in desperate need of a shower. “*I* need *you?*”

“Yes.”

I crossed my arms over my chest. “And what do I need you for?”

“You need me to help you out of your current predicament. Xander is smart, but he has weaknesses. He can’t do what I can do.”

“He can’t invade my VR scenarios and annoy me with half-answers to my questions?”

Devlin snickered. “I’m sure he’s already done that.” He cocked his head, squinting at the beams above us. “Have you noticed he’s getting sloppy?”

“Sloppy?” I took offense on Xander’s behalf. “Look who’s talking. Have you seen how filthy you are? You’re leaving dirty footprints all over the place.”

He pointed and flexed his grimy toes like he was proud. “I’m flattered you observed that detail.”

“It’s pretty hard to miss.”

Waving one leg through the air, he asked, “Can you smell them?”

“Eww, no! Thank the stars for that.”

He laughed. “This is fun. Have you also noticed how comfortable you are with me?”

“What?”

“You’re sarcastic and playful, even when you’re annoyed with me, and dialogue flows easily between us. Why do you think that is?”

I hadn’t thought about it until he pointed it out, but he was right. Why was I so comfortable around him? I stepped backward, pressing myself against the wall. I was not attracted to Devlin. Not in the slightest. Whatever the reason for the comfort level between us, I vowed right then and there I would not become the victim of a love triangle. I hated them in books, and steered clear of them in reality as well as virtual reality.

Devlin slid off the counter, standing with his arms braced behind him. "We want the same things, Kelsey. We have the same goals, the same enemies, and we both love Xander."

My hands fell to my sides and my breath hitched. "Love Xander? I don't *love* him. I hardly know him."

"You're thinking like an Equatian. If you plan to escape our country and live in the free world, you can't be scared of love. It's a one-world mentality out there. Everyone is connected. You'll love everyone, even those you don't like, but you'll love Xander differently." He rubbed his bristly jaw. "I don't know what the word is for what the two of you share, but it exceeds love."

I had no idea what to say to that. Yes, Xander and I had a connection, and I was certain he was the best kisser in the entire universe, but love him? That was too much way too fast. I studied Devlin again, reminding myself he was a character in a VR scenario, a scenario Xander had created and controlled. Was Xander trying to brainwash me into loving him by planting Devlin to say these things? Could Xander be that manipulative?

I prodded further. "You said you love Xander too."

"Of course I do."

"Because he's the leader of the Arcana?" I assumed.

Devlin's mouth twitched into a crooked sneer. "He's not the leader."

Our conversation was interrupted by me walking out of the library. The other me.

Xander followed close behind. I looked upset and angry. Then I remembered what had happened. I had discovered the access cards in his fake books. Xander had revealed that he was a VR dealer. I demanded he take me home.

Devlin said I was supposed to learn something, so I watched them closely. Xander opened his craft door, and the other me climbed inside. She stared straight ahead, almost directly at the current me. I waved, half expecting her to wave back, but that didn't happen. A few seconds later, Xander piloted away from his loft and toward the glowing computer tunnel on the opposite side of the warehouse.

When they were out of sight, the tunnel lights dimmed until the glowing wall of numbers completely faded. I expected to see a hole, or maybe (since anything seemed possible) the tunnel opening would turn into a concrete wall like the area around it. Instead, a large, round, shiny door that looked stronger than steel slammed shut.

"Where does that door lead?" I turned to face Devlin, but stiffened when Xander stood in his place. He was leaning against the counter the exact same way Devlin had been.

"You tell me," Xander said.

I glanced at his feet. They were clean. His chin had no stubble. "How did you do that?"

Xander's brow lifted. "Do what?"

"Devlin was here. We were having a conversation."

"Right. He just flew out of here with Blaze."

"No, that was you and me. We flew out of here."

He squinted and stepped toward me. "How could you and I fly away if we're standing right here?"

I rubbed my temples. The room swayed. My tongue suddenly felt sticky, and I tried not to gag.

"Kelsey?" Xander asked gently. "Are you feeling all right?"

"My head is spinning, and I feel queasy."

Without asking permission, he lifted me into his arms and cradled me against his chest. "Come on, you've had a very trying day. You need rest."

"I need to go home."

He started up the steps. I did need to get home, but I couldn't resist resting my head in the crook of his neck. He was so warm, and he smelled so good. He set me down in his bed. "You are home. Close your eyes and get some sleep. I'll be right here beside you."

He curled up behind me and wrapped his arms around me.

The room was still spinning, but I didn't feel queasy anymore. I felt safe—until I recalled my suspicious conversation with Devlin about loving Xander.

I was exhausted, physically and mentally, but I managed to grumble, "You can't manipulate me into falling in love with you."

He squeezed me tighter and whispered against the back of my neck. "I wouldn't dream of it."

Level 3.9

You need me to help you out of your current predicament. Xander is smart, but he has weaknesses. Have you noticed he's getting sloppy?

"Devlin?" I bolted upright, clutching the covers beneath me.

I was still in Xander's bed. He was asleep beside me. Rubbing my eyes, I looked around his room while my brain slowly kicked into gear. My heart pounded, and the back of my tunic was damp. I'd been having a nightmare. Maybe about my parents? Or Devlin? Any and all details faded away with each second I was awake.

I glanced at my band. 3:48 am. We had fallen asleep, but I needed to get home. I lifted my hand to touch Xander's shoulder and nudge him awake, but he looked so peaceful. For a few seconds, I watched him, wondering what kind of dreams flooded his brilliant mind.

I caressed his cheek. His baby-soft skin was warm and smooth. "Xander?"

He barely moaned in response, but that one small sound made my heart flutter. His eyes remained closed, but he put his hand over mine, and in the sleepiest, sweetest voice said, "I'm right here, Kels."

I bit my lip, fighting back a smitten smile. "Wake up. You have to take me home."

His lashes fluttered and his fingers twitched. I couldn't help grinning down at him as his eyes opened and he licked his lips. In a groggy voice he said, "I was having the best dream. We were kissing and couldn't stop. We lasted so long that we fell asleep."

I chuckled. "That was reality."

He touched his mouth. "That explains why my lips feel swollen."

I rubbed my tender lips together. "Mine too."

Reaching up, he ran his fingers through my curls. "I know I have to take you home, but I wish you could stay."

"Me too, but we both know that's impossible."

"You'll come back soon, right?"

I mocked the same line he had messaged me earlier. "An army of enforcers couldn't stop me."

"Good." He sat up and ran his hands through his hair. "Let's get you home before any of your neighbors wake up."

"Wise idea."

"I need to use the restroom and then we can go. I'll meet you downstairs in a minute."

"Okay." I walked down the steps, running my hand along the cool metal of the handrail. Pausing at the bottom, I looked around his place again. It was still as impressive as my first visit.

Drawings were scattered on his coffee table. I meandered over, admiring the large charcoal sketches of images I assumed would be made into tarot cards. I lifted the one that looked like a different version of The Empress card. The woman no longer resembled my mother, and her candy heart wand was gone. No grass grew around her feet.

The drawing beneath it caught my attention because it was the only one in color. I picked up the picture of a man sitting in a chair. The backdrop looked like the same desert and cliff I had stood on during my High Priestess scenario, but the sky was bright blue. The man wore a top hat. In one hand, he held some sort of cane, and above his other, floated a red glowing orb.

"The Emperor," Xander said from behind me. "What do you think of him?"

"Your art is so impressive. I could never draw anything close to this."

"Many thanks, but what do you think of *him*? What kind of vibe does he give off?"

I studied his face. He was frowning and staring directly at me, as if he were real and knew more about me than I did. "He looks stern and powerful. I wouldn't want to mess with him."

Xander took the drawing from my hand. "Good. That was the goal."

"Now you'll make him into a tarot card?"

"Yes, and then—" He stopped and set the drawing back on the table. "Never mind, let's go."

"Tell me what you were about to say."

He cracked his knuckles. "Can you keep a secret?"

"I've kept *you* a secret."

"Fair enough. I was about to say that this Emperor card will have a hidden scenario embedded inside. It's a chance for another suit to excel in the Arcana."

"What will the hidden scenario be?"

"A sidestep from the journey they're on. They'll have to be brave enough to explore an uncertain path, but if they do, they'll be rewarded with a secret code."

"A code to what?"

Xander's lips pursed, like he didn't want to tell me, or maybe he didn't know if he could trust me yet.

"I won't tell a soul," I assured him. "You can't tease me with knowledge of a secret code and then not tell me what the code is for."

His smile broke free. "The code to access an AVRA session."

"An EVRA? You said they were outdated pieces of junk."

"Not an EVRA, and AVRA. Arcane Virtual Reconnaissance Ark."

I could imagine how confused I must have looked.

Xander explained. "It's a special craft designed to train and gather information in ways that far exceed what standard virtual reality can do."

"*Standard* virtual reality? I can't imagine anything exceeding the virtual scenarios you've shown me. They feel like reality."

"Wait until you've experienced the Ark."

"Will I get to experience it?"

He grinned. "You might be able to bribe me into letting you try it."

"How?"

"By spending the night with me again."

Adrenaline surged through me from my toes to my fingertips. "I'd have to sneak out again."

"You'll have to decide if it's worth the risk."

He was worth the risk, but I couldn't tell him that. I didn't want to come on too strong so soon. But it didn't hurt to flirt a little. "Is this Ark thing more magical than you?"

He rubbed the back of his neck, appearing to fight back a laugh as he blushed. "So much more. As people of Olden times used to say, it's out of this world."

"Then I guess we'll have another midnight meet-up tomorrow."

He stared at me for a few seconds, his eyes happily scanning my face. He started to say something then stopped and held my hand. He kissed my knuckles. "Let's get you home."

"No, stop doing that. What were you about to say?"

He turned, leading us to his craft. "Something cheesy and romantic. You would have hated it."

I laughed, squeezing his strong hand and almost asking him to say it anyway, but then I decided he couldn't have delivered a more perfect line.

Xander cruised past my house to make sure no lights were on. The neighbors' windows were all dark too.

"I think it's safe," I said quietly.

Neither one of us had talked much during the ride. It was like if we spoke too loudly, someone might hear us. We knew the penalty of breaking curfew, along with the other violations we'd be charged with if a patrolling enforcer spotted us. Xander had assured me he could protect us from patrollers, but I didn't want to test his belief in that theory.

He circled back and hovered just past my house. "I'd walk you to the door, but, well, that would be stupid instead of chivalrous."

I smiled. "It's the thought that counts."

"How about a proper date tomorrow evening? During respectable hours of the day."

"I'd love to," I said. "But not yet. Being a fink for the government is too new. I don't want them to suspect you of anything. Even if it's only that you're distracting me from my assignment."

"I can protect myself, Kelsey. And I can protect you."

"Still, I'd worry less if we waited."

"Okay then. See you tomorrow night at an indecent hour?"

"Definitely." I climbed out of the craft as quietly as possible and waved for Xander to go before anyone saw him. His craft glided away as I hurried to my bedroom window.

I pushed up on the glass, but it was locked. Glitch. How could it have locked itself? I peered inside, hoping Keekee might be awake, but she was a motionless lump under her covers. I couldn't wake her because that required telling her I snuck out, and then she'd demand I tell her why. Also, Keek could sleep through a hurricane, so I'd probably have to make enough noise to wake up the neighborhood.

Creeping alongside the house, I hid in the shadows until I reached the back door.

I stared at the fingerprint reader. If I used it to unlock the door, my parents would be able to see that information on our log. They'd know I entered the house from outside at 4 am. How would I explain that? Would the government be alerted by a 4 am home entry? I didn't know for sure, but I assumed they would.

"Kelsey," Xander whispered.

Snapping my head around to look behind me, I saw no one.

"Kelsey?" Xander called again, but his voice came from my wrist.

I lifted my band, and his concerned face lit up my screen.

"What are you doing?" I hissed quietly.

"Did you really think I'd drop you off in the middle of the night and fly off without ensuring you made it safely inside?"

I would have been wooed by his sweet gesture, but I was too preoccupied with fear and worry about getting caught.

"Unlock the door," Xander said. "I've temporarily disabled it from recording your entry."

"Seriously?" I wanted to leap through the screen and kiss him for being so skilled.

"Hurry, before a neighbor sees you."

I took a deep breath and placed my fingertip on the reader. The two beeps sounded startlingly loud, and so did the lock clicking open. I pushed the door inward painstakingly slow, trying to prevent the hinges from squeaking like always.

I tiptoed in, turning and shutting the door just as slowly. I flinched when the latch clicked again. I locked the door and took another deep breath. Looking out the window, where I had stood just seconds ago, I thanked the stars that I had successfully crept inside without getting caught.

Holding my finger to my lips, I warned Xander not to speak, but then I gave him a thumbs up to confirm I was inside. He nodded and then a message scrolled across the bottom of the screen. *Told you, I have your back.*

I replied with, *And my front?*

He grinned while typing a reply. *The front is my favorite part.*

I'm glad it was dark, so he couldn't see me blush. *Many thanks. See you tomorrow.*

xX was his last message before the screen faded to black.

I took off my shoes, careful not to make any noise, then tiptoed through the kitchen. I had almost reached the hallway when the living room light clicked on, nearly blinding me.

There, sitting on one end of the sofa as if he'd been waiting for hours, with a clear view of the kitchen door and every move I had made, sat my father.

He eyed my bare legs and his nostrils flared.

I no longer needed to worry about the government. My father, the stern and powerful emperor of our family, would most certainly kill me.

4: THE EMPEROR

Level 4.1

My father and I stared at each other for several silent moments. In those fear-filled seconds, so many thoughts rushed through my mind, each one jump-starting my heart and filling it with fear and dread.

He had watched me sneak in the back door far past curfew. He saw me communicate with someone on my band. My bare legs were in plain view. He was required to report my transgressions to authorities. What would happen to me? More importantly, what would happen to our family? After all my worrying that Keekee's gaming habit would cause us to live as slaves in The Hub, it turned out I would be the one to seal our fate.

"I'm so sorry," I murmured pathetically.

"Sorry?" My father's tone was arctic. "You're sorry?"

I nodded, even though we both knew sorry couldn't adequately describe how I felt, or how much worse I would feel once my punishment had been delivered.

Dad leaned forward, his eyes narrowing. "Who is he?"

I looked at my feet, trying to come up with an answer that wouldn't reveal Xander's identity.

My father yelled, "Who is he?"

I startled, wanting to run to my room and hide beneath my covers. "It was all me. No one else."

He stood. "How dare you lie to me? It's heinous enough that you have broken so many laws tonight I've lost count, and that you put our entire family in jeopardy for a boy you just met and hardly know, but now you have the audacity to lie to me on top of it all?"

Mom emerged from the hallway, followed by Keekee. "What's going on?"

I trembled and couldn't look any of them in the eye.

My father practically hissed, "Would you like to tell them, or shall I?"

Glancing up, I saw the shock and confusion on Mom's and Keekee's faces. Tears blurred my vision.

Mom's voice was filled with trepidation. "Tell us what?"

Somehow I managed to force out a reply even with the boulder of shame lodged in my throat. "I snuck out."

Mom gasped. I have no idea how Keekee reacted because I couldn't look at any of them.

"Snuck out?" Mom stuttered. "How? Where? Why? Dressed like *that*?"

"All for a boy," Dad said. "I saw him drop her off out front."

"Kelsey!" The outrage in Mom's voice sent more tears spilling down my cheeks.

Keekee walked over to me and held my hand. "The coffee shop guy?"

I flashed her a pleading look, begging her not to say another word. I had to protect Xander's identity, not just for him but for the Arcana and all the lives he was trying to save.

"What coffee shop guy?" Mom shrieked. She began pacing. "This can't be happening. We raised you better than this. You know we're already on thin ice with the government. You wouldn't do something so selfish, so dangerous. It's all a mistake, right?" She stopped and stared at me, paler than the moon. "Please, Kelsey, tell me this is a really tasteless joke."

In a strained whisper I said, "I wish it were."

Mom's hands flew to her chest.

My father wrapped his arm around her shoulder. "The longer we delay, the worse it will be, I have to report it now."

"No!" Mom and Keekee shouted in unison.

I hung my head and closed my eyes.

Dad's voice was firm, but hidden beneath his obedience was the eternal echoing of heartbreak. I had crushed him. Disappointed him in a way I could never recover from. "I have failed as a father by allowing my daughter to believe that breaking the law is okay, but I will prove by example that it is most certainly not permitted. As much as it pains me to do it, our laws are in place to protect us and they must be followed, even the ones that seem impossible to obey."

My mom ripped herself free from him.

Keekee gripped my hand tighter.

My father pressed a few buttons on his govern band.

It all seemed to happen in slow motion.

Dad's eyes locked with mine as an electronic voice spoke from his band. "What is the nature of your call?"

He swallowed hard then turned his back to me. "I need to report my daughter's criminal activities."

A sob gushed out of me as I sank to my shaking knees and waited for the enforcers.

Keekee helped me to my feet and sat beside me on the sofa. As soon as Mom and Dad were out of the room, she asked, "What were you thinking?"

"I wasn't."

In the kitchen, Dad rattled off a list of his interpretations of my crimes to the voice coming from his govern band. As bad as they sounded, I was thankful he didn't know all the crimes I had committed.

Keekee grabbed my chin and turned my face so our eyes met. "Did you hear me?"

"No," I admitted.

"I said, 'Did you really risk so much for that boy?'"

"No," I lied. But was I lying? I didn't risk so much only for Xander. I risked so much for a cause. For the hope of a future that might include freedom. Keekee wanted that more than anything. She would understand. But I couldn't tell her. Even if I had enough time to explain anything about the Arcana, it wouldn't be enough to make sense, and it would put her at risk.

Dad had stopped talking.

We were out of time.

Keekee and I knew all too well that it only took seconds for enforcers to show up. And in situations such as ours, they wouldn't knock politely.

The front door swung open. I jumped to my feet. The sound of boots stomping through the house sent shivers racing down my thighs. I wanted to run, but knew it was pointless.

"Keep all your answers short," Keekee advised as quickly as possible. "The less you say, the better."

I fought to breath as the stomping of boots grew closer. My ears were ringing and I couldn't feel my fingers.

Rounding the corner, wearing an enforcer's uniform, was Blaze.

A gush of air escaped my lungs. My cramped shoulders slightly relaxed.

Blaze did not have the blank, brainwashed expression of a government drudge. Her eyes shined as brightly as her copper ponytail. I half-expected her to pull out a lollipop and flop down on our sofa, but instead, she marched over to me and lifted my wrist then scanned my band.

"Kelsey Zellar," she stated, scanning my irises, which was easy because I couldn't stop staring at her. She gathered both of my hands in hers and lasercuffed me. "On behalf of the Elura Enforcement Division, you are being detained. Because you are a minor, this is not an arrest, but you are being taken into custody for questioning and assessment of your crimes. Do you understand?"

I nodded.

Her brows lifted. "State that you understand, Miss Zellar."

I cleared my throat, finally finding my voice. "I understand."

She led me to the front door where another enforcer spoke to my parents. "You will be updated through each step of the process."

"Yes," Dad told the woman. "Unfortunately we've been through this before with our other daughter."

The enforcer finished scanning my parents and then turned to face me. I shouldn't have been surprised to see Awol, but I had to stop myself from grinning at her. The biggest shock was that she didn't have dreads. Her straight, long hair was pulled into the same tight ponytail as Blaze's, or any other female enforcer.

My fear subsided. I didn't know how Xander pulled it off, but again, he had found a way to protect me. I was a little too eager to be led away by the two "enforcers" because I suspected they'd take me back to Xander.

Awol cocked her head and pressed one finger to her earpiece. After a few seconds of listening to instructions, she replied, "Understood." She turned to my parents. "Mr. and Mrs. Zellar, we will also be detaining Keekee Zellar for questioning."

"What?" I muttered, as all my panic and then some rushed back into me. "No. She wasn't involved." I didn't want her to know about any of this. Not Xander, or Awol and Blaze, or the Arcana. I wasn't ready, and she'd be furious when she found out I kept it a secret.

Awol ignored me as my parents glared at me for attempting to argue with whom they rightfully assumed was a real enforcer. Awol walked past me, maintaining her stern facial expression as she scanned Keekee's band and irises.

"It's fine," Keek said, lifting her other wrist to be lasercuffed. "I'd rather you not go through this alone."

"She's not involved!" I insisted. And I didn't want her to be.

"Kelsey," my father chided. "Quiet. Show them some respect before you make this situation even worse for everyone."

Blaze clutched my arm and marched me past my parents and out the front door. I'd never seen such disappointment on Mom and Dad's faces. Not even during the multiple times Keekee had been in trouble.

"Stay quiet and cooperate," were the last words Dad said to me.

Mom stared silently, clutching the collar of her robe, while a tear ran down her cheek.

Awol and Keekee followed behind us. We were assisted into the backseat of a government craft. During the brief moment when the door shut and we were alone, Keek said, "Maybe they'll take it easy on us since we agreed to spy for them."

Before I could reply, Awol and Blaze opened their doors and sat down in front of us. As the craft lifted into the air, I resisted asking Awol and Blaze if they were taking us to Xander. I didn't want Keek to know I knew them.

Keekee kept flashing me reassuring looks, but the longer we flew, the more worried I became. Her band hadn't been ghost-bugged yet. Had it? Was the government aware of what was happening? Were kibz monitoring her? Would real enforcers, or even scarier officials, follow us? Had Xander considered that possibility before hijacking my sister and me?

We passed any and all routes that would have led to Xander's warehouse. Instead, we flew toward the deserted outskirts of Elura. My hands went numb when we glided up to a border station. Officials stopped our craft, and Awol reported her name: Undercover Enforcer Amelia Lark.

Undercover. The word punched me so hard in the chest that for a moment I couldn't breathe. Awol told the guard she had been ordered to deliver two transgressors to HE.

My eyes flew open wide, and I choked on the squeak in my throat.

I turned to Keekee and whispered, "The Hub?"

Her eyes widened too. She had never been to The Hub. We didn't know anyone who had. Because once citizens crossed the border and entered the core city of our country, they never came out. Unless they were working for the government.

Keekee slid closer to me so that our shoulders touched, but my fear-induced paralysis had spread through my upper body and I couldn't feel her.

The official waved us through. Our craft flew across the border and into The Hub. Awol's cold gaze met mine in her rearview mirror. Any trace of the carefree, passionate, and friendly girl I had met at Higher Grounds was gone.

I stared at Blaze's profile, hoping, mentally begging that she'd turn and smile or wink at me—something, anything, to assure me everything was okay and that she and Awol were just really good actresses. But Blaze didn't glance in my direction, not even as she told Awol, "Two VR transgressors *and* identification of the Arcana leader. I want the reward and a promotion."

"We'll get both," Awol said. "Kramer will make certain of it."

Keekee went rigid beside me.

They knew Kramer. They were working with him. His words ricocheted through my memory. *You girls are new at this school. New to Elura. You're fresh meat.*

We were meat Kramer had used to coax Xander into a trap. We foolishly agreed to be bait. And now we'd all be caged for life.

My seat felt as if it fell out from under me. I went from scared, to light-headed, to my stomach churning as the tall skyscrapers of The Hub spun outside my window. Dark rain poured down around me.

I mumbled, “I think I’m going to pass out.”

I don’t know if anyone heard me because the world, along with my family’s future, and Xander’s, faded to black.

Level 4.2

I woke up on my side, cheek pressed against a white floor that was so shiny I could see my own reflection. I sat up, patting my chest and arms to make sure they were still there. That I was still there, or here, wherever there or here might have been.

Surrounding me were white walls that matched the floors, but the top halves reflected light (from a source I couldn't locate) like they were made of glass.

My soft tunic and pants had been replaced with drab gray, scratchy ones. My feet were bare and I shivered from the chill in the stark room. My mouth was so dry I couldn't find enough saliva to lick my lips.

"Where am I?" I asked, not expecting an answer.

But I received one from a speaker in the ceiling. A female voice said, "You're in containment. How do you feel, Kelsey?"

The emptiness in my stomach made me gag. "Not so good."

The female spoke again, but this time I recognized her as Awol, because the gentleness and compassion she displayed at Higher Grounds had returned in her voice. "Can you turn around so I can talk with you?"

I pivoted on my butt, grinding my sit bones against the floor as my hip joints popped. Every muscle in my body ached. What the hell had they done to me while I was passed out?

Awol stood on the other side of a large glass window, looking down at me. "Tell me what you're feeling."

I wouldn't tell her anything. She was a traitor. I hadn't known her long enough to be hurt by her deception to me, but I hated her for deceiving Xander and risking the whole Arcana mission. He could have saved so many people. I had believed Awol was part of that mission. Instead, she had double-crossed Xander, captured me, and fed me to the wolves. Or at least put me in a cage so the wolves could dig in whenever they wanted.

"You're dehydrated," she said. "I'm sending in a nutrient pac."

A small door slid open under her window. A circular robot no bigger than my head rolled into the room and stopped inches from my hand. A cover slid open, and inside sat a pink package of fluid.

"Drink it," she urged.

I had never been so thirsty, which made my refusal difficult to say for a couple reasons. "I'll never accept another drink from you."

She grimaced and tugged on her hair. "Let's start with your emotional state. How are you feeling?"

That didn't require much thought. "Betrayed."

"By whom?"

I snickered. And then the real worry and panic kicked in. "Where's my sister?"

Awol closed her eyes and bowed her head. My heart sank. I didn't know her well enough to accurately read her body language, but I knew her reaction meant nothing good. "Try to focus on you right now."

"Screw you. Where is she?" I tried standing, but the room tilted, and I stumbled sideways.

"Stay still," Awol commanded. "You're in no condition to move."

I didn't want to do anything she said, and I needed to find my balance, so I forced my feet to stand beneath me. The window where Awol stood watching me bounced side to side, blurring her face.

"Don't try to walk," she warned again. "You'll get sick."

I stepped forward, tripping over the robot. I tried throwing my hands out to catch myself, but I wasn't quick enough, so I face-planted onto the floor. I groaned at the pain shooting through my chin, nose, and forehead.

Awol's voice sounded urgent but caring as it came through the speaker above me. "I'm going in to help her."

"No," another female said firmly. "It's forbidden."

I rolled onto my side, searching Awol's window for the source of the other voice, which sounded like Blaze, but Awol still stood alone peering in at me with concern wrinkling her brow.

Her focus shifted upward, above my head and past me. "She won't hurt me."

"Clearly. She can barely stand." The second voice definitely belonged to Blaze. "But no one goes in. It's protocol."

I rolled onto my back, glaring at the stupid speaker embedded in the white ceiling. Then I kept rolling to face the opposite wall from Awol. And there, staring down at me from another window was Blaze.

I had never been taken into custody for questioning, but Keekee had told me about her experiences, and they did not include being trapped in a room while undercover enforcers peered in at you from windows. They were treating me like a caged animal. And no one was allowed to enter with me? I was hardly a threat to the robot, much less to two cunning and deceptive enforcers.

The old, friendly Blaze had returned too. She wasn't smiling, but her eyes glimmered with compassion as she stared down at me from her window. "Drink the nutrient pac. You're only hurting yourself by refusing it."

"What do you care?" I snapped. No further need for manners or pleasantries. I had been detained, and from the looks of my cell, they had no intentions of asking me a few questions and letting me go home.

"I care very much," Blaze said. "So please, drink it."

Anger boiled inside me as I fought the nagging itch to gulp down the liquid and soothe my dry throat. They deliver Keekee and me to the trenches of The Hub and then pretend to care about me? I was a fool for trusting them before, but I'd never trust them again. The pac probably contained some sort of truth serum and she only cared that I drink it so I'd leak information that would earn them a promotion.

I uprighted the robot, picked up the pac, and threw it at Blaze. It bounced off like the window was made of rubber instead of glass. And now that my eyes worked, the window looked like a clear, gel surface I'd never seen before.

"Why am I in here?" I asked. Xander's face flashed through my mind. Had he been detained too? Was he being kept in a room like this one? Under my breath, I muttered, "How could you betray him this way?"

Awol asked, "Betray whom, and in what way?"

I clenched my eyes shut. She knew I meant Xander, so I wasn't wasting my limited energy answering her. My last memory of him was his smiling face on the screen of my band. I reached for my band—reached for him—realizing for the first time that it was missing. My wrist was bare. My only connection to him was gone.

"I told you it wouldn't work."

I spun around and found Devlin standing in the room with me.

"You," I hissed.

"Judging from the disdain in your tone, I'm guessing you aren't happy to see me."

"You're in on it, too."

He clasped his hands in front of him. "One of these times, you *will* be excited to see me. I eagerly anticipate that moment because hatred isn't very becoming on you."

"He trusted you," I growled. Glancing at Awol and Blaze looking in from their windows, I shouted, "He trusted all of you!"

"And what about you?" Devlin stepped closer to me, dipping his head to make eye contact with me. "Who do *you* trust, Kelsey?"

"Not you, that's for sure."

His gaze shifted to Awol. "How about Awol? Do you trust her?"

"Screw her. Screw all of you."

"I see." He crossed his arms over his chest and sighed. He watched me for several moments, studying my face like he was waiting for me to say something else. After our silent stare-down went on too long, he turned to Awol and said, "Satisfied?"

"He's not awake yet," she said. "Let him decide our next step."

Fear crept up my spine. I suspected she was talking about Kramer. I didn't want him deciding anything in regards to me, or anyone else I cared about.

Devlin stuck his hand in his pocket, fiddling for something. "He trusts me to do what's best."

Blaze argued with him. "She never drank the pac. You can't do anything."

He paused, his focus drifting to the side of the room where the pink pac lay on the floor untouched. "Drink it."

"No," I deadpanned, but wanting hydration so bad it hurt.

He squinted, the gears in his mind turning until he came up with a threat that he knew I couldn't ignore. "Drink it, or I'll visit the room next door and make things much worse for Xander."

My heart seized in my chest. Xander was here? Next door? Even if Devlin was lying, he could trick Xander and lead him here the same way Awol and Blaze captured me. How could they be so cruel? I glared at Devlin. "You said you loved him."

"I do, but in cases such as this, tough love is required to accomplish our goal." He couldn't mean the mission of the Arcana. This was the opposite of what Xander wanted to achieve.

"What goal?" I asked.

"The vital goal of you drinking that nutrient pac."

I clenched my teeth. Truth serum or not, I wouldn't betray Xander. "Promise me you won't hurt Xander."

"I give you my word." He just stood there, staring down at me.

The monster couldn't even be courteous enough to get the pac and hand it to me. I rose to my feet, swaying a few times, but I made it to the stupid drink. Picking it up, I tore off the tab and raised it to my lips. "I hope karma gets you," I said. "I hope it gets all of you triple fold."

Devlin smiled as I chugged the liquid. "Now *that* sounds more like you."

"Don't act like you know me," I snapped.

"What card are we on?" Devlin called out.

Awol told him, "The Emperor."

Devlin nodded while rubbing his forehead. "Run X-4–2."

"You just said it wasn't working," Blaze argued.

He stepped closer to me and grinned. "Goodness knows I've been wrong before."

"What's X-4–2?" I wiped my wet lips, already feeling better physically, but fearing what the near future had in store for me.

“Keep asking questions, Kelsey. You’ll find the answers within you.” He turned his back to me then circled one finger high in the air, signaling to Awol.

Colors lit up the room. Streaks of red, blue, green, and yellow crept up the walls, then beams crisscrossed the floor where I stood.

“What’s going on?” I backed up, pressing myself against the wall behind me.

Devlin faced me again, but he was on the far side of the room, standing directly in front of Blaze’s window.

“Embrace the journey,” he told me.

He pulled something out of his pocket and threw it like a Frisbee. The object sailed across the room in slow motion. It had made it halfway when I saw it was a tarot card. As it came closer, I saw The Emperor sitting in his chair. The card flipped over, revealing Xander’s black and gold symbol, and then, on instinct, I reached up and caught it.

Devlin disappeared. So did Awol, Blaze, and my cage.

Level 4.3

For a moment, I stood on a rooftop, staring at a closed metal door.

Before I could gather a thought or do anything, the world shifted into a blur of colors. When it stopped, I was looking at the High Priestess. She was on a screen in front of me, squinting and asking, "Are you certain you can trust him?"

I opened my mouth to ask who she was talking about, but again, I was carried away in a blur of color and lights.

The next stop was Kramer. He stood in Xander's warehouse, with his meaty hand on the door to Xander's library.

"No!" I ran to him, determined to stop him from discovering Xander's secrets. But as my feet propelled me forward, the floor beneath me moved backward like a conveyor belt, keeping me in place.

"Stop it!" Hands gripped my shoulders, jerking me around to face the source of the man's voice.

I froze, my feet rooted in place as the conveyor belt halted. My father stood in front of me. In Xander's living room. Except he wasn't my father. Deep down, I knew that he was a replica, some VR character designed to fool me.

I shoved him away and growled, "Don't touch me."

He squinted, his eyes blazing with fury. "You think you know better, but rules exist for a reason."

"You ratted out your own child!" My hand flew to my mouth. Why did I shout that? He wasn't my father. Why was I engaging in an argument with him? "You're a fake," I said. "This conversation is meaningless."

Lines of horizontal light cut through him, starting at his torso and spreading outward to his head and feet. His voice became tinny, like he was speaking through a can. "Kramer assured me you wouldn't be hurt."

The mirage of my father faded to one spinning ball of red light. I turned toward the library, but Kramer was no longer at the door.

"Kelsey?" Xander called.

I spun in place, desperately searching for him. The kitchen was empty. He wasn't by his craft, or in his office. I stood alone in the living room. "Where are you?"

"I'm right here," he said from behind me. "Who were you talking to?"

I slowly turned to face him, afraid that the scene might blur and take me somewhere else again, or that Xander wouldn't be the real version of himself. The coffee table was between us, but he stood close enough for me to examine him in detail. He looked real. Solid and real.

His hazel eyes searched my face, then his gaze shifted to my hands. "What are you doing?"

Looking down, I saw that I held scissors in one hand and a drawing in the other. Charcoal sketches covered the coffee table, along with pieces of the one clutched in my hand.

Xander reached out and gingerly took it from me. He examined it, then raised one brow. "I assume you're not a fan of my Emperor drawing?"

"No," I replied, thoroughly confused as to why I had cut up Xander's artwork, and hating that I couldn't remember doing it. "I mean, the artwork was great, but I hate what he stands for."

I lifted the scissors, pressing the cool blades against my lips. Why did I say that? I wasn't even sure what The Emperor card represented.

Xander nodded, like he agreed. "He did look stern and powerful. I wouldn't want to mess with him." He took the scissors from my hand and grinned. "Or you."

It was all too familiar. Had this moment already happened? Had we already had this conversation about his Emperor drawing? "Is this really happening?"

He cocked his head. "What do you mean?"

"Is this real, or a VR scenario?"

"Why would you ask that?"

"Because I feel like I've been here before. I'm having déjà vu. I vaguely remember this." I motioned to his living room. "Standing in this very spot, and you and I having a conversation about the Emperor drawing."

"Interesting."

I rounded the coffee table and stood directly in front of him. "Don't dodge the question. Is this a VR scenario?"

We stared at each other for several heartbeats until he said, "Go ahead."

"Go ahead and what?"

"Touch me. Check to see if I'm real."

I flinched. Why hadn't that occurred to me in the first place? Reaching up, I caressed his baby soft cheek. I ran my hand through his silky hair. In a whisper, I confirmed, "You're real."

"Good." He pulled me tight against him. "Because virtual kisses aren't nearly as good as these." He leaned down and kissed me. Any doubt of his solidity whooshed out of me. I didn't want to stop. I never wanted to stop kissing him, but it was late and we had work to do.

I pulled away, brushing my lips over his knuckles as I stepped back to escape the bubble of euphoria he emitted. "Can we draw another one?"

"Another Emperor?"

"Yes."

I sat on the sofa, sorting through the sketches on the coffee table. "We need one for you to make into a new tarot card and program a—" I stopped mid-sentence, finding a version of a man sitting in a chair. The backdrop was a desert cliff with a bright blue sky. The man wore a top hat. In one hand, he held some sort of cane, and above his other, floated a red glowing orb. "This one will work."

Xander sat beside me. "Tell me what you were about to say."

"When?"

"Just now." He rubbed my thigh. "You said I'd have to make a new card and program something."

My knees bounced, excited by Xander's touch and my own idea. "Can you keep a secret?"

"I've kept *you* a secret."

"Fair enough." I placed my hand on top of his, grateful to have him in my life. We made a powerful team. "I was about to say that this Emperor card will have a hidden scenario embedded inside. It's a chance for another suit to excel in the Arcana."

His head jerked back, but his surprise was quickly replaced by a grin. "What will the hidden scenario be?"

"A sidestep from their current journey. They'll have to be brave enough to explore an uncertain path, but if they do, they'll be rewarded with a secret code."

"A code to what?"

He had proved that I could trust him, but I wasn't sure if I could tell him so much so soon.

"I won't tell a soul," he assured me. "You can't tease me with knowledge of a secret code and then not tell me what it's for."

I decided to take the risk. "The code to access an AVRA session."

"An EVRA? You said they were outdated pieces of junk."

"Not an EVRA, and AVRA. Arcane Virtual Reconnaissance Ark."

He looked adorably confused, so I explained, "A special craft designed to train and gather information in ways that far exceed what standard virtual reality can do."

"*Standard* virtual reality?" He rubbed his forehead. "I can't imagine anything exceeding the virtual scenarios you've shown me."

"Wait until you've experienced the Ark."

"Will I get to experience it?"

I skimmed my fingers along his forearm. "You might be able to bribe me into letting you try it."

"How?"

"By spending the night with me again."

He rubbed the back of his neck, appearing to fight back a laugh as he blushed. "I'd have to sneak out again."

In my best flirtatious tone, I said, "You'll have to decide if it's worth the risk."

He turned and stared directly into my eyes. "Is this Ark thing more magical than you?"

"So much more. As people of Olden times used to say, it's out of this world."

He stared at me for a few seconds, his eyes happily scanning my face. "Then I guess we'll have another midnight meet-up tomorrow."

I wanted to tell him everything. I wanted him to be so much a part of my world that he'd never want to leave no matter what. But I couldn't overload him. I couldn't rush such an important turning point. So instead, I linked my hand with his. "I believe in you."

Not understanding the significance of what I had just told him, he squeezed my hand and smiled. "I believe in you too."

Whether he meant it or not, I knew I would never, ever, forget that significant moment.

Level 4.4

"Miss Zellar!" a woman shouted, startling me awake.

I sat up as people around me giggled and snickered. My scalp itched from the heavy EVRA on my head, and my eyes strained at the glowing screen flashing *Lesson Concluded.*

I ripped off the EVRA and found Mrs. Linker standing in front of my desk wearing an unflattering scowl. "Did our lesson bore you to sleep?"

I shook my head, trying to answer her while also forcing my fuzzy and tired mind to clear. "I don't know what happened," I admitted. "Many apologies."

She crossed her arms over her chest. "Did you remain awake for any of the lesson?"

I rubbed my aching temples. To save my life, I couldn't remember what the lesson was about. I didn't want to get myself into more trouble, so I replied, "Not enough to comprehend it. May I stay after school and complete a do-over?"

She sighed. "You may, but do not let this become a habit. This is the one and only time I will grant you this chance."

"Many thanks," I said, avoiding eye contact with my classmates who were still chuckling and making comments under their breath.

As Mrs. Linker walked away, I rubbed my eyes, trying to relieve the headache pounding inside my skull. She was most definitely a younger version of the High Priestess, but her indifference toward me proved that VR worlds and reality were not intertwined for her like they were for me.

My gaze landed on two students sitting in the front row. A curly-haired guy sat in the seat where Blaze had cried when Devlin was arrested. I searched the room, but Blaze wasn't in class. I must have daydreamed that she was an undercover enforcer. Clearly, I wasn't trapped in a white room in the Hub. Keekee and I hadn't been detained.

I touched my govern band, wanting to contact my sister and confirm she was safe. I couldn't even remember waking up and going to school today. My brain felt fried. Sorting out dreams, VR, and reality felt like an impossible task that my aching head couldn't handle anymore.

When history class ended, students fled the room as I not-so-patiently waited for Keek to answer my band transmission. I exhaled a sigh of relief when her face appeared on the screen.

"What's up?" she asked.

"I'm staying late to make up an assignment."

She rolled her eyes. "How'd you earn yourself that opportunity?"

I glanced at Mrs. Linker sitting at her desk. She was also chatting with someone on her band and paying no attention to me. I asked quietly, "Is everything okay at home?"

She squinted. "What do you mean?"

"Are Mom and Dad upset with me for any reason?"

She tilted out of view as she opened our craft door and climbed into the pilot seat. The screen stabilized as she tucked a curl behind her ear and said, "Mom and Dad are never upset with you. You're the good child, remember?"

I shook off the very-real memory of Dad busting me for sneaking out and reporting me to enforcers. Had I dreamed all of those things when I dozed off in class? And why didn't I remember any other classes from today?

"Are you okay?" Keek asked. "You look awful, and you're acting strange."

"I'm not feeling so hot." I couldn't explain the real source of my unease, so I dismissed it with, "We just had an EVRA lesson and as usual, it gave me a headache."

"I see. Well, feel better and let me know when you're ready for me to come back and pick you up. I'm on my way to do some reconnaissance work."

I winced at her use of the word that had been used in my dream-conversation with Xander. "Reconnaissance?"

She whispered, "Is anyone around you that might hear me?"

Mrs. Linker was still chatting and laughing with someone on her band. "Just my teacher, but she's preoccupied."

"Good," Keek said, but she still spoke quietly. "I befriended one of the girls I told you about last night. We're meeting for coffee right now. I was hoping you could come and meet her, but maybe it's better this way. I can gain her trust quicker if I'm alone. I'm ninety-nine percent sure she's a VR gamer."

"Be careful," I warned.

She shrugged. "No need to worry this time around. Instead of breaking the law, I'm doing what the government asked."

"Kelsey?" Mrs. Linker called. "Are you ready?"

"Yes, ma'am," I replied. "Just letting my sister know I'm staying after class." I returned my attention to Keekee. "I have to go."

"All right. Let me know when you're finished, but try to give me at least an hour with Amelia."

"Okay, see you later."

I pressed the disconnect button and massaged my neck, dreading the impending moment when I'd have to put the crappy EVRA back on my head.

Mrs. Linker walked up the aisle and handed me an access card. "This is a different version of the lesson you missed, but it contains more action so it might keep you awake."

"Many thanks," I said, uncomforted by her confidence in the lesson because no matter what, the EVRA would make my aching head worse and my mind more muddled.

She returned to her desk as I pressed my pads behind my ears and centered the helmet on my head. The weight of it pressing against my skull made me groan. I pulled the visor over my eyes and waited for the program to begin.

Disturbingly delayed, Keekee's last words registered. She said the girl she was meeting with was named Amelia. My eyes went wide as the screen turned bright white.

Undercover enforcer Amelia Lark.

Glitch.

For a brief second, I considered ripping the EVRA off of my head and begging Mrs. Linker to let me redo the lesson tomorrow so I could stop Keekee from meeting up with Amelia, who was most likely Awol, and whom I was no longer sure we could trust.

But I was sidetracked.

Sidetracked and speechless, because Jag appeared on my EVRA's screen.

In surround sound, he said, "Welcome, young citizen of Equatia. By now, you've learned about the past problems and disasters of space travel. Today's lesson will focus on aviation within our atmosphere."

Clips of passenger jets from the Olden days played on the screen while Jag commentated. "During The Crash, the dangers of high-flying aircraft were solidified in a grave and unfortunate event. When cyberterrorists wiped out all satellite feeds to Earth, one of the most impactful results, and the one which caused countless deaths, was the failure of aircraft equipment and systems."

The jets, which had been sailing through clear blue skies, no longer glided peacefully. One video showed a plane rocking violently; another demonstrated the nose tilting up so far that the plane went completely vertical and fell out of the sky; while another spiraled out of control above countless skyscrapers.

Jag's narration continued. "The latest in GPS radar and technology had provided the world with a false sense of security. Every day, over a hundred thousand aircraft traveled at unsafe speeds, some within hundreds of feet of one another. Pilots became too reliant on automatic programs to pilot for them, and radar systems to ensure their safety. When technological systems went down worldwide, planes went down with them."

I knew what came next. I had seen lessons like these before. Planes collided in mid-air, some disintegrated or ripped apart, while others had wings sheared off. They burst into flames on the ground, or smashed into buildings or oceans. Many caused more casualties and destruction as they crashed. Onboard cameras showed close-ups of passengers panicking, crying, screaming, and praying.

Clenching my eyes shut so I didn't have to watch the horror, Jag continued spewing out heartbreaking facts like the staggering estimate of lives lost that awful day, and the wars that broke out privately and internationally. Horror like that should have never been recorded, much less replayed over and over for citizens to witness.

“As you can imagine,” Jag continued. “We would never again allow a catastrophe like this to occur.”

I didn’t want to hear more about Equatia’s mission to protect its citizens from the mistakes of the past. “How does this have anything to do with our senior history curriculum?”

I pulled off my EVRA and gasped.

The classroom was gone. I sat at a long curved desk in an unfamiliar gray room.

Mrs. Linker was life-sized on a screen in front of me. She sighed, sounding exasperated. “I agree it’s too easy to remove, but your idea seems drastic and dangerous.”

I glanced around, assuming she must be talking to someone else, but the room—filled with screens, blinking buttons, and techy gadgets—contained no one but me.

Her lashes fluttered, then she leaned so close to the screen that her green eyes looked like two tunnels of light. “You have to discuss this matter with your parents. I’m useless on this subject.”

“My parents?”

“Don’t be afraid to tell your father the truth. He’ll understand. Now, put that back on and disconnect me before our signal is detected.” She pressed her hand flat against the screen. “I’m so proud of you.”

Static wiped away her image. She was gone. The screen shut off. I was alone and confused.

What did she want me to tell my parents? How did I end up in this strange room? It couldn’t be part of the school lesson because I took off the EVRA. Looking down, I stared, dumbfounded, at my own hand.

The same hands I had used to take off my EVRA just seconds ago no longer held the bulky contraption. Instead, the necklace Xander had given me dangled from my fingers. I quickly put it back on, tucked it under the collar of my tunic, then stood and backed away from the desk.

Turning round and round, I searched for someone or something who might provide an answer. I spotted a round door on the far side of the room, so I rushed over to it. Using all of my weight to push down on the long handle, I forced it open.

Outside was a dark tunnel. A very long, very dark, and very empty tunnel.

I shouted, “What the glitch is going on?”

My voice echoed. Again, and again, and again. With each passing second of no one answering, my heart pounded faster.

I leaned out of the doorway, straining to see where it led. To my horror, it looked like there was no floor, nothing at all to walk on, and I had no idea how far I’d have to jump (or fall) before I’d hit a solid surface.

“Hello?” I called again, my fear reverberating louder this time.

Still no answer.

I backed up and shut the door, more afraid of what might lurk in the tunnel than of being alone in the mysterious room. Then it occurred to me that I didn’t have to be alone. Xander was only a call away.

Expanding the screen on my govern band, I placed my hand flat against it like Xander had instructed me to do if I ever needed him. I waited, hoping and mentally urging him to answer. Then I waited some more.

My screen remained blank.

“Xander?” I whispered. “Please answer me.”

After having no success, I pulled up my contact list and searched for Keekee’s name, but it wasn’t there. I muttered, “What the hell?”

My finger hovered over *Mom.* Even if she answered, I couldn’t explain where I was, so she’d panic and alert authorities. Same if I tried contacting Dad. I didn’t have contact information for anyone else in our city yet, and I most certainly couldn’t send out an emergency signal or multiple government divisions would be notified. None of whom I trusted.

A loud series of beeps went off behind me and a voice said, “Good, you’re still there.”

I turned to see a dark-haired, older man on the screen. He seemed very familiar, though I couldn’t place where I had seen him before.

“I’m still here,” I confirmed, moving closer to study him. I knew him. I was sure of it. But who was he?

He stroked his scruffy beard. “Mary told me about your idea.”

“My idea,” I repeated, so lost I needed a more powerful and accurate description for my state of *huh?*

“Let me show you something.” He held his hand out flat beside him. A red orb formed, glowing bright and hovering above his palm.

I stumbled backward, shocked at the familiarity of the orb from Xander’s drawing. How did it take me so long to realize it was him? I sputtered, “The Emperor.”

He continued as if he hadn’t heard me or noticed my reaction. “This allows your method to be possible, but it’s too intensive to use on everyone. You’ll have to select a trusted few as test subjects so we can see if your theory is sound, and, of course, they’ll have to agree. In the meantime, I suggest sticking to the original plan for the masses.”

“What are you talking about?” My voice cracked, so I cleared my throat and spoke louder. “I don’t understand what’s happening. I don’t even know where I am!”

He relaxed back into his chair. “Good. I’m glad we’re in agreement.”

“What? No.” I stepped closer, clenching my fists. “Didn’t you hear me? I don’t understand any of this!”

The screen flickered. His face froze and the sound distorted into an annoying, continuous beep. I pressed my hands over my ears and shut my eyes tight, trying to block it out.

“Kelsey?” Mrs. Linker’s voice didn’t just vibrate around me; it felt like it went through me. I kept my eyes shut tight. I didn’t want to see her on the screen again. I just wanted all of it to stop. In a muffled, but loud voice, she shouted, “Kelsey, relax!”

Cold hands tugged at my wrists until I finally stopped struggling. A weight lifted from my head, and a rush of air made my scalp tingle.

“Open your eyes,” she commanded.

I hesitantly cracked one lid, followed by the other.

I was sitting at my desk in history class. Mrs. Linker was crouched in front of me, her expression filled with trepidation. An EVRA lay between my rigid hands.

“Great stars!” she panted. “What happened? You were shrieking so loudly, you could have woken the dead.”

Taking several quick breaths, I patted my chest and torso. Was this real? I pressed my hands against my thighs and tried assessing what I just experienced. Was the EVRA triggering hallucinations?

Mrs. Linker stared at me like I was a mental patient.

My throat burned and my words came out scratchy. “My apologies.”

“Why were you making that sound? You seemed terrified.”

I couldn’t explain the strange gray room and her on a screen, and the tunnel to nowhere, and the man with the glowing orb. She’d have me committed. I tried recalling the lesson she had given me. Aviation.

“All those people,” I said, “dying such tragic deaths. I couldn’t watch it.”

“I see.” Her tone softened. “I know the EVRA makes it feel real, but remember, it’s not. What you watched was in the past. It wasn’t actually happening.”

“Still, it *did* happen.” I leaned back in my chair, trying to relax my tense muscles. “They *did* suffer.”

She straightened and folded her hands in front of her. “True, but their suffering wasn’t in vain. We learned from it and developed a safer present and future.”

I nodded, fighting the urge to ask her if she genuinely believed that. Were we safe under Equatia’s tight control?

“You can complete the follow-up assignment at home,” she said. “I can tell it’s been a trying day for you.”

“Many thanks.” I opened and closed my fingers, trying to ease the ache in my knuckles. After blood flowed through my hands again, I sent Keekee a message that I was ready to be picked up and would wait outside of the main lobby.

I started gathering my belongings and then the door opened.

Much to my horror, Kramer stepped inside. “Everything all right in here? I heard screaming.”

“Everything is fine,” Mrs. Linker assured him. “Bad reaction to an EVRA lesson.”

“I see.” Kramer’s pervy eyes scanned me from head to toe, then lingered on my chest. I hugged my bag to block his view and looked away from him.

Mrs. Linker hung the EVRA I’d been using in the equipment cabinet and locked it. “We’re fine, but we appreciate your concern.”

“Miss Zellar,” Kramer said. “Would you like an escort to the lobby where you can wait for your darling sister?”

My jaw tensed, not only at the thought of being alone with him, but also at his use of an affectionate name for Keekee.

“That won’t be necessary,” Mrs. Linker said. “I’m on my way out, and Kelsey and I need to discuss the lesson. I’ll escort her to the lobby.”

Thank the stars for small miracles.

Kramer didn’t look pleased, but he nodded and said farewell.

“Ready to go?” Mrs. Linker asked me.

“Yes.” I shrugged my bag over my shoulder and joined her at the door.

She paused and reached into a pocket of her sweater vest. “Here, you dropped these during our struggle to snap you out of your episode.”

She handed me a thin stack of cards. My stomach lurched when I saw the gold symbol on the shiny black background. My fingers trembled as I took them from her.

Patting my arm, she lowered her voice and said, “I’m sure you wouldn’t want to lose those.”

“Yes. I mean no, I can’t lose them.” I tried sounding calm so she’d believe the same lie Keek had told Mom. “An aunt gave them to me.”

“I once had a tarot deck of my own.”

“You did?” I asked, surprised.

“Yes, but I gave it away.”

“Why?”

“A family member needed the guidance of the cards more than I did.”

I flipped through the stack. Some of them I’d never seen before, but compared to the rest of the events, dreams, and VR scenarios of the day, a few unexplained tarot cards were child’s play. “I didn’t peg you for the mystical type.”

She grinned. “Sometimes, we all need help along our journey.”

“Did your cards ever help you?”

“Oh, yes. Many times, but eventually I realized they were only a guide.” She ushered me into the hallway and pulled the door shut behind us. "All the answers I sought were already within me."

I stood there agape at her words, all-too-similar to what she had said as the High Priestess in a VR scenario. Testing her, I said, "I think you may have told me that before."

She turned and started walking down the hallway. I followed close behind, eager to hear her response. In a wily way, she replied, "Sounds to me like you have an exceptional memory."

I clutched her arm, glancing around to make sure the hallway was empty, then I whispered, "Do you know what I'm talking about?"

She lightly tapped my temple. "The more important question is, do you?"

Level 4.5

After debating how to answer Mrs. Linker's question, I decided silence was my safest option. I walked away from her, knowing she'd follow. We still had to get downstairs and reach the lobby—plenty of time for discussion. I'd let her speak first. She could lead the rest of the conversation. I worried I may have been falling into a trap and saying too much.

I would not mention the Arcana or Xander.

"Stairs or elevator?" she asked me.

"I'm fine with either."

We descended three flights in silence. I kept sneaking side glances at her, but her focus remained straight ahead. She looked relaxed, like it didn't bother her at all that our conversation ended with neither one of us answering the other's question. As we neared the lobby, she told me, "Be sure to finish your assignment this evening. I won't grant any extensions or another do-over."

"Yes, ma'am. Thanks for allowing me this one." She turned, adjusting her bag and digging through it. "Be sure to get adequate sleep tonight. The brain tends to misfire when it doesn't have sufficient time to rest." She handed me a candy. "It's a Deep Rest candy, lavender flavored. They always knock me out when I have insomnia."

I took it because I didn't want to be rude, but I wouldn't eat it. Lack of sleep or not, I would be spending most of my night with Xander. And I did not want to be knocked out. "Many thanks."

"See you tomorrow."

She headed off for the faculty lot while I walked down the steps to Keekee waiting in our craft.

Opening the passenger side door, I could already feel her excitement pouring out of the craft.

"How'd it go?" I asked as I slid into my seat.

"Awesome. Amelia and I totally connected, and my suspicions were right. She's heavily into the VR scene."

"She came right out and told you that?"

"Not only did she tell me, but she also gave me this." She whipped out a tarot card. One of Xander's cards. My breath hitched as The Fool stared up at me. "It's like a secret invitation to their VR circle." She smacked my shoulder. "We're in."

I glanced at her band then looked around our craft, wondering if kibz or some other authorities were monitoring our conversation. I worried I'd never be able to have a private conversation with my sister ever again. Unless, of course, we somehow managed to escape Equatia, but we were light-years away from that goal.

"Come on," Keek whined. "Get excited."

I felt queasy. It was only a matter of time before she sniffed out a VR ring, but why did it have to be Xander's network? "I'm never going to be excited about what we're doing. It's scary and it feels wrong on numerous levels."

"Just wait until you experience one of your precious storybooks in virtual reality. You'll be singing a different tune."

I clenched my teeth together to stop myself from confessing that I had already been immersed in a couple stories and it didn't change my loathing of our assignment.

She sat back in her seat and piloted us into the school exit lane. "I'm assuming you won't want to go with me tonight when I meet up with Amelia again?"

"No way." I was an awful liar and a worse pretender. I couldn't see Awol and act as if we'd never met before. And the first thing on my to-do list, once I was out of earshot, was contacting Xander to tell him about Amelia/Awol and her new relationship with my sister. We also needed to discuss the very realistic dream I had about Awol and Blaze being undercover enforcers.

One of my many questions was, *if* Awol and Blaze were undercover agents, why they would befriend Keekee, who had just agreed to be a fink for the government? Wouldn't someone higher up realize they were working for the same team?

Like most events and questions from the last few days, I had no reliable answers. But I knew someone who might.

Between Mom and Keekee flitting around the house non-stop, I couldn't find any opportunity before dinner to sneak away and contact Xander.

While we ate, Keek asked Mom and Dad if she could meet up with a new friend after the dishes were done. I almost choked on my asparagus when she voluntarily announced—as if it should impress our parents—that the friend was a gamer.

Mom and Dad lectured her. Even though it's what the government wanted her to do, she still needed to be careful. Three times in less than an hour, Mom warned that, "those VR types could be dangerous."

I wanted to remind her that Keekee, her own flesh and blood, was one of "those VR types," but I kept quiet. I had too many other worries plaguing me.

"Are you going with your sister?" Dad asked me.

I pushed my plate away, hoping Mom wouldn't nag me about not finishing all of my food. "I have other plans."

Mom looked relieved that I wouldn't be joining Keek on her outing with gamers. "What other plans?"

"I'm meeting a friend at the library to do homework." It was so close to the truth that I didn't feel bad about almost-lying.

Xander was a friend who I was hoping would be working at the library tonight so I could discuss all the chaos and confusion with him. That qualified as research, and research was homework. Especially if I obtained information that would keep my family safe, because they were my home.

Level 4.6

I had Keekee drop me off at the library. Even if Xander wasn't working, I could contact him and ask him to pick me up. I wanted her to have the craft just in case she needed to quickly get away from her meeting, which I had a bad feeling about.

She waved goodbye as I turned to climb the steps outside of Elura Library. I pushed all the worries aside to savor each step into my holy grail. I stood in front of one of the sets of double doors, touching both ornate door handles at the same time.

So many answers existed inside of a library. I hoped I'd find the answers I was seeking.

I yanked open both doors and stepped inside. Closing my eyes, I inhaled, but the smell of old books was too faint. Whether Xander was working or not, I'd visit the Olden section upstairs to get my book aroma fix.

The main floor with its open atrium was beautiful as ever. I headed toward the access card desk, but kept looking up at the railings and banisters shining in the glow of the sun setting through the domed skylight.

"Careful or your neck will get stuck like that and you'll never be able to read another book." Xander's warm voice made me smile.

I turned and stepped closer to the desk he stood behind.

"Not true," I said. "I would just hold the book above my head and read it."

He smirked. "You have a solution for everything."

"Actually, I don't, but I'm hoping you might."

His brows rose, and he leaned across the desk. "I will gladly help you any way I can."

Like a magnet drawn to him, I leaned on the desk, too, and our hands touched. "I've been experiencing some weird stuff, and it's worrying me." I lowered my voice. "But we'll need to speak in private."

He hooked one of my fingers with his. "Lucky for you, my shift ends in ten minutes. Maybe you could peruse the Olden section until then."

"That's a brilliant plan." I wanted to kiss him, but knew that wouldn't be appropriate at his place of employment. Plus, I didn't want any cameras catching an intimate gesture like that. You never knew who might be watching. That thought made me unlink my finger with his. "Meet you out front in ten minutes?"

"Let's plan to meet in fifteen. Ten minutes up there won't be long enough for you."

My cheeks warmed because he was right, and I loved that he already knew me that well. I gave a flirty wave before riding the escalator to the third floor, where the musty scent of old paper made me temporarily forget about any and all of my problems.

I was swept up in the beginning of *A Wrinkle in Time.* Not because I hadn't read it before (I'd read it four times), but because it's the kind of opening that always left me completely absorbed.

The storm, the strange/suspicious/serendipitous people, the supernatural powers, the looming mystery of the tesseract: it all resonated with me. Maybe because I wanted so badly to believe in magic, and now, ever since I had met Xander, impossibilities happened in my real life instead of only in books.

At the point in the story where Meg, Calvin, and Charles Wallace reach Uriel, Mrs. Who recited one of my favorite quotes:

"When shall we three meet again,

In thunder, lightning, or in rain."

I sped through the succeeding lines of dialogue, wanting to reach the next great quote even though I knew it by heart. I read the words out loud. "*Nothing is hopeless; we must hope for everything.*"

Hugging the book to my chest, I pressed the page over my heart, willing the words to seep through and become ingrained in my soul.

Glancing down at my govern band, I realized I was already six minutes late. I snapped the book closed, sprang from my seat on the floor, and slid the masterpiece into its slot.

I hustled down the escalator and out the front door where Xander waited, sitting on the steps and staring up at the sky. Without turning around, like he had some sixth sense and knew I was standing several feet behind him, he asked, "Which one were you reading?"

I grinned and walked down the steps then sat beside him. "*A Wrinkle in Time.* Sorry I'm late."

He leaned sideways so our shoulders touched. "I thought you'd be later."

"I'm a fast reader." I allowed my weight to press against his strong arm, but it still wasn't close enough. "Can we go somewhere and talk?"

He turned his head, and the tip of his nose brushed along my jawline, sending delightful tingles down my neck. "Just talk?"

Cold from the concrete step had penetrated my pants and left my butt chilled, but the warmth radiating from Xander made up for it. Knowing we'd end up kissing at some point, but not wanting to seem too eager, I teasingly said, "Let's see how it goes."

He laughed and stood, offering me his hand. "Yes, let's."

I placed my hand in his, and he helped me to my feet, but then he pulled me tight against him. His hands kneaded up my back, making my knees weak, and then he ran his fingers through my hair. He stood one step lower than me, so our faces were level.

I whispered, "Someone might be watching."

He whispered back, "Let them watch. Ours is the best story ever told."

Level 4.7

We made small talk during the ride back to the warehouse. I stayed quiet as he opened his secret doors, and I watched with wonder as we flew down the light tunnel of scrolling numbers.

He parked in his usual spot and, as always, offered me a cup of coffee. I happily accepted. Not only because he made the best coffee in the world, but also because I wanted my brain capillaries to be expanded and ready to process any and all information that came out of this conversation.

In less than two minutes, Xander handed me a fresh, steaming mug of coffee. It still amazed me how accessible it was for him.

"So," he began. "What's weighing so heavy on your mind?"

I sipped my drink. "You can tell my thoughts are heavy?"

"As heavy as the bags forming under your eyes from sleep deprivation."

I sighed and rubbed just above my cheekbones. I had noticed my dark circles too. Not flattering at all. "I'm thinking I should go home at a reasonable hour and get a good night's sleep."

"I don't like spending my nights without you, but I agree you need more rest, so I support your plan."

He sat on his sofa, and I joined him, facing him so I could carefully watch his body language. I wanted the truth, and if I sensed him dancing around it, I'd call him out and be demanding.

"This needs to be a brutally honest conversation," I insisted.

"Uh oh." He cracked his knuckles and leaned back against the cushions. "Okay, brutal honesty. Understood."

"My dreams have been vivid. I wake up questioning what's real or not."

"That's to be expected. Your brain has been spending a lot of time in VR mode. That means new neuron pathways are forming, and that can overload your system if too many form too fast." He stroked my hair. "I know this isn't what you want to hear, but you need a break from your storybook escapes."

"But I haven't been doing a lot of them. Just those two so far."

"Two?" His eyes bugged, and he chuckled. "Denial is a sure sign of an addict."

I racked my brain, making sure I was correct. My first time was the wardrobe scenario, and then at Higher Grounds I jumped into *Huck Finn*. That was it. How did that make me an addict? "It's only been two books. I'm certain. And both were days ago."

"Days ago? So you're not counting last night at Hogwarts?"

"Hogwarts?" I shrieked. "I have never been there. I would love to virtually be a wizard and play Quidditch, but I haven't done either."

His forehead creased so deeply, his eyebrows almost disappeared. "Glitch. It's worse than I suspected."

"What?" My voice trembled. "Are you messing with me?"

"No, I'm not. You've been working through my access cards faster than anyone else in the Arcana. Last night, Jag had to escort you off the roof of Higher Grounds because you were overdosing. They said it took three suits to pull you out of a storyhole because you wouldn't leave willingly."

I laughed, but he remained serious.

I stood, shaking my head. "No, I would remember that."

"But you don't." He held my hand and pulled me back to sitting. "Unless *you* are messing with *me,* which you don't seem to be, so that means your memory is damaged."

I could hardly breathe. I pressed my hand to my forehead, wanting to heal my brain. "How do we fix it?"

"I have no simple answer for that."

"Do you have a complicated answer?"

His chest rose, then returned to normal. I could tell he was holding back. "Time. You give your brain time to readjust."

"*That* is a simple answer. Now tell me the complicated one."

"The alternative has consequences too. I'd much rather you go the safer route, which is to just give it time."

"How much time?"

He pulled my legs across his lap. "A day or two of no VR, no sensory activities whatsoever, then you should feel better."

I could wait a day or two. It's not like I was so addicted to VR that I couldn't give it up. However, I still needed to understand the craziness in my damaged brain. "I'll give it time if you explain why everything is such a mental hodgepodge for me."

"I'll try my best, but you'll have to elaborate on your definition of hodgepodge." He started rubbing my calves, and it felt so good I almost forgot what I intended to ask. Almost. "Why can't I keep track of time?"

"What do you mean?"

"For example, in my mind, last night, I snuck out to see you. We came here and made out until we fell asleep." I paused, waiting for his eyes to glisten, or, if it hadn't happened in reality, for him to make some kind of comment, but he had no reaction.

Puzzled, but not wanting to wander off track, I continued. "My mother busted me for sneaking out, and it was scary and awful, but then she froze like a VR character, and I woke up in your bed again. Like time started over. You took me home and helped me sneak into my house, but that time my father busted me and reported me to enforcers."

Xander blinked fast, listening intently, but showed no other reaction. No calf massaging, no wide eyes, nothing to hint at what he might be thinking. He'd have to react to my next bit of information.

"But in that dream, or sequence, or whatever it was, Awol and Blaze were the enforcers who arrested me. They detained Keekee too, and they took us to The Hub."

His face was still a blank slate, but he grumbled, "Go on."

I finished my play by play before I forgot what happened next. "I passed out, and I woke up alone in a white room, but Awol and Blaze were watching me through windows and talking to me through a speaker. And Devlin showed up and he—"

I rubbed my temple, trying to remember what Devlin did or said.

"And Devlin what?" Xander asked, finally showing some interest in my story.

"See, this is one of my problems. The details slip away the longer I'm awake. Half of the time I can't even tell if I'm awake, asleep, or immersed in VR."

"What happened after Devlin appeared? Did you go anywhere after that?"

"I think so." A cloud of haze drifted through my mind, almost causing me to lose my thoughts, but I pushed the veil away. "I woke up in school wearing an EVRA. I had fallen asleep during a history lesson."

"And then what?"

I tugged at a loose thread on the sofa cushion between us. What happened after that? Anything? I couldn't remember. "I think that was it. That was today during my last class."

"What was the EVRA lesson about?"

I shuddered at the image of countless passenger jets falling from the skies. "The aviation disaster during The Crash."

"That's all? Nothing seemed off about the lesson?"

"Not that I recall."

He squeezed my calves. "Think hard."

I pulled my focus away from him and glanced around his living room as I strained my brain for any other details. I ended up staring across the warehouse at the tunnel where we entered and exited. Like always, the light and scrolling numbers had faded to black, but the dark tunnel was still there.

"No, that's it," I confirmed. "I left school, went home and had dinner, and then went to the library to meet you, and here we are."

"How did you get to the library?"

Finally, a question I could answer. "I walked."

But after I said it, I questioned myself. Did I walk, or had Keek dropped me off?

"Why didn't you take your craft?" he asked.

"Because it's a short walk."

He tentatively nodded. "Okay."

"Okay, what? How do you explain any of that?"

"It's nothing to be alarmed about. Like I said earlier, your brain is trying to adjust to all the recent stimulation. It's borderline sensory overload because you're forgetting some past events, but with time they should be accessible to you again."

"What about the scary stuff with my parents?"

"Fears manifesting as nightmares. You've been worried about sneaking out, so your mind created a graphic story about getting caught."

“So they weren’t VR scenarios? You didn’t create them?”

“I would never create a scenario that would scare you like that.”

I reclined back against the arm of the sofa, relaxing a bit. “I didn’t think so, but I had to ask.”

“So we’re in agreement that you’re taking at least two days of no VR, right?”

“Yes. I don’t want to do any more damage.”

“Good.”

His hand rubbed up my leg to my thigh. I resisted the urge to pounce him and devour him with kisses because I wasn’t even certain if our make-out session had been real or imaginary. “Xander?”

“Yes?”

“The part I told you about sneaking out and us kissing until we fell asleep.” He grinned, so I continued. “That did happen, right?”

He slid my legs off of his lap then climbed over me. He braced one hand on the sofa beside my head. His lips hovered a hairsbreadth from mine. “That was very real, and very intense, which is why you haven’t forgotten it.”

“Good.” I pulled his head forward and kissed him, delighted to discover he tasted like cinnamon-flavored coffee. After a long, delicious few seconds of kissing, I drew back. Without thinking, I whispered, “I believe in you, Xander.”

His eyes widened, and he went rigid. He climbed off of me and rubbed his hand over his mouth.

“What’s wrong?” I asked, feeling abandoned and foolish on the sofa by myself.

“What did you just say?”

I sat up and tugged my tunic back in place. “I’m sorry. I didn’t realize—”

He shouted so loud it startled me. “What did you just say, Kelsey?”

Meekly, I repeated the words that sent him scurrying away from me. “I said I believe in you. You’ve said it to me several times.”

“Is that why you said it? Just because I’ve said it to you before?”

"No." I didn't understand why he was so unhinged. "It slipped out. Why was it so wrong?"

He kneeled in front of me and held my hands. "It's not wrong, but it's an indicator that I was wrong about assessing your mental state."

"What do you mean?"

He caressed the side of my head then touched my necklace. "It's time for me to show you something. Something important."

Level 4.8

Xander kept my hand tight in his as he guided me across the warehouse to the dark exit/entrance of the tunnel. He waved his fingers, and the wall blurred, then shifted sideways until a round metal door was in front of us.

"See?" I pointed at the door. "That sort of stuff makes me swear this is a VR scenario. How did you do that?"

He grinned while slightly bowing. "You claimed I was a magician, so why does it surprise you that I can perform magic?"

"Because magic isn't real. It's an illusion."

He tugged on one of the shorter curls framing my face, then his fingers trailed down my neck. His touch was so gentle and so warm, my skin crackled with longing. "The connection between us is magic, and it isn't an illusion, so that disproves your theory."

"Fair enough," I managed breathlessly. Willing myself to look past my seductive magician and his sleight of hand, I asked, "Where does the door lead?"

"I'm glad you can see it."

"Of course I see it."

He pressed on the heavy latch with both hands. Veins bulged in his forearms as he strained to accomplish the task, but a loud metal click initiated the door swinging open.

I peered inside. Only a few feet away from us was a solid wall of concrete. "It leads to a wall?"

"Look down."

I leaned forward and saw a dark tunnel. "Hello?"

My voice echoed half a dozen times.

"How deep does it go?" I asked.

"Jump in and find out."

“Jump in?” I snickered. “Jump into a bottomless dark hole? I swear, if I didn’t believe you cared about me, I would think you wanted me dead.”

“You won’t get hurt. You’ll enjoy it.”

I stepped back and motioned to the opening. “You go first.”

“Okay.” Without a moment of hesitation, he rushed inside, dropping into the darkness and out of view.

A scream lodged in my throat. My heart leaped into the black abyss with him. “Xander?”

A green and blue light illuminated the darkness. Countless rows of numbers scrolled down the walls. Xander floated in the middle with his hands held open at his sides. “Told you, it’s completely safe.”

My jaw had gone slack. “You’re . . . floating?”

“Care to join me?”

I stared, dumbfounded. It had to be VR. Or maybe he had somehow figured a way to apply the same engineering methods of hovercrafts on people. Either way, I wanted to try it, so I held my breath and stepped forward.

It was just like when I fell into the storyhole at Higher Grounds. I didn’t fall. I floated on an invisible cloud. Glowing numbers and letters continued scrolling all around us. “What do those mean?”

“That’s the boring part.” He gave a dismissive wave then held my hand. “Let’s get to the fun stuff.”

“I assumed floating was the fun stuff.”

“Nope, the best part is riding the wave.” He activated a screen on his govern band that I’d never seen before. He pressed a few buttons, then winked. “Here we go.”

The scrolling numbers around us turned to a solid bright light and we soared forward as if pulled along by an air current.

My pants and tunic rippled in the wind. My hair flew back and the breeze caressed my face. “I love this!”

“I knew you would.”

“Where are we going?”

He sped ahead of me. “The AVRA.”

I remembered him telling me it was some kind of Ark, and even though I was curious, I knew I’d see it soon enough, so I put my questions on hold and enjoyed the ride.

We rounded a corner, then swooped downward. I didn't have to steer myself or even try to keep up with Xander. We were automatically pulled along at the same comfortable speed.

I stretched my hand to my side, reaching to touch the tunnel of light around us. A crystalline mist made my fingertips tingle. I stared, trying to see if walls existed beyond the rows of scrolling numbers, but I couldn't tell, and every time I tried gliding sideways to explore, I failed. The current pulling us along kept us centered in the tunnel.

We slowed to a stop in front of another round metal door framed by yellow light. I was disappointed because our ride was much too short, but I was also fascinated that we were still hovering in the air.

Xander motioned to a small screen near the door handle. "Put your hand flat on the reader."

I did as he said, and a green light glowed around my fingers, followed by a loud clicking sound. He pushed down on a latch identical to the one back in his warehouse. He pulled the door open, and I glided inside like an astronaut traveling through a hatch in a rocket. As soon as he shut the door behind us, gravity kicked in, and we drifted downward.

My feet landed on the floor of a dimly lit, gray room with a large curved desk and a huge blank screen.

"This is the Ark?" I asked.

He nodded.

"What happens here?"

His eyes were no longer playful or excited. He seemed worried and pensive. "Remember when you asked how I became the leader of the Arcana, and I told you I was chosen?"

How could I forget? "Yes."

"That was a bending of the truth." He didn't look away from me; on the contrary, he seemed to be holding my gaze on purpose. I sensed that his sad eyes and deepening frown were a silent apology. But an apology for what?

"What's the straight truth?" I asked.

He rubbed the back of his neck, then rolled the chair out from the desk. "Sit down and I'll show you."

A sense of power came over me when I sat in the chair. Xander hadn't touched any buttons or activated the screen yet, but I could tell I was at the controls of something powerful. What was this Ark thing capable of?

"How do you feel?" he asked me.

"Excited."

He gave one satisfied nod, then rolled me closer to the desk. With one arm bracing the back of my chair, he used his other hand to press a few buttons. The large screen in front of us lit up.

Too eager to wait and see, I asked, "Will this be better than the immersion room?"

He tilted his head, and one side of his mouth lifted in a bittersweet sort of smirk. "It will be different. You'll have to decide which you think is better."

Nearly bouncing in my seat, I rubbed my hands together and told him I was ready.

Under his breath he murmured, "I hope so."

Icons floated in front of us on the screen. Xander swiped his finger through the air, and one of the icons lit up, then a band of stars spiraled like a kaleidoscope.

"Pretty," I cooed.

After what had felt like much too long, he finally grinned—even though it seemed halfhearted.

We waited, watching the stars shift and form different patterns. I drummed my fingers against the armrests, growing impatient.

He stood and stepped closer to the screen. The glow highlighted the concern in his eyes. "It shouldn't take this long."

"What's supposed to happen?"

The stars froze, then the screen turned bright blue. It started flashing, flooding the entire room with an annoyingly bright light that forced me to squint.

"Glitch," Xander huffed.

"Why is it doing that?"

A loud static sound made us both flinch, and then Devlin appeared on the screen.

The guys stared at each other, neither saying a word.

I glanced between them, wondering if Devlin could see us, and if so, why wasn't anyone saying anything? Xander cracked his knuckles. Devlin sighed and ran his hand over his buzzed hair.

Xander stood tall, his shoulders widening and making him seem inches taller than usual. In a firm voice, he said. "Devlin, abort."

He cocked his head. "I was just about to tell you the same thing."

Xander's jaw shifted as his chin lifted. "She's ready."

"She's not ready, and you know it. You also know the ramifications of what you're doing, yet you continue to make one bad move after another."

I stood and my chair rolled backward. "I'm ready for what?"

Devlin's gaze shifted to me. "You're not ready."

"For what?" I repeated.

"To use the Ark."

"Why not? Because of my memory damage?"

Devlin's eyes widened, then his focus jumped to Xander.

Xander stood at my side. "She doesn't remember the time she spent in storyholes, but she does remember dreams and VR scenarios involving important people in her life."

Devlin huffed. "Dreams and VR scenarios?" He leaned so close I could see the high-definition stubble on his chin. "She is *confused.* You're breaking so many VO protocols that your credentials should be revoked. Using the Ark at this point will cause sensory overload. Is that what you want?"

Xander didn't reply, but his shoulders slumped, and his head hung low as he looked away from Devlin and met my gaze.

"VO?" I asked. "Devlin meant VR, right?"

He shook his head and tucked my hair behind my ear. "He's right. My timing is wrong."

"What?" I stepped back and pointed at the screen. "You're letting *him* tell you what to do?"

Xander's voice was quiet and wistful. "His argument is solid. I don't want to risk your safety."

"My safety?" My hands flailed at my sides. "I don't understand what this place is or what we were about to do. I don't even know what Devlin is talking about. Stop leaving me in the dark all the time." I whipped my head around to glare at Devlin.

"Both of you do it. You speak in a secret code and it's usually about me, which entitles me to an explanation. A thorough one."

"Calm down, Kelsey," Devlin said. "When you're ready, we'll explain everything."

If this were a scene in a novel, I would have hurled the book across the room and never picked it up again. But this was real life, *my* life, and Devlin had become the meddlesome, thwarting villain.

"Don't trust him," I told Xander. "He tried convincing me that you're weak, that he was better than you."

"What?" Xander's brow furrowed. "When?"

"She's misquoting me," Devlin said from behind me.

I ignored him, wishing Xander would too. "Yesterday. I think. Or, maybe the night before. He told me you couldn't do the things that he could, and he said you were getting sloppy."

Xander glared at Devlin. "Sloppy?"

I turned around to see Devlin shrug and reply, "I'm not the only one who has made that assessment."

"We knew it was risky, but we all agreed it was a calculated gamble."

"A gamble which isn't working," Devlin argued.

"It *is* working. If you would just—" Xander halted. "Wait. You haven't been alone with Kelsey. How could you tell her I was sloppy?"

Devlin's lips parted then pursed tightly. Meddlesome, thwarting, *and* guilty.

"He was in your warehouse one night," I explained, eager to prove Devlin couldn't be trusted. Even if I didn't know why. "I was immersed in a VR repeat of the first time I visited your library. I didn't understand what I was watching. I thought Keekee had found us, but Devlin appeared and tried explaining what was happening. It quickly turned into him putting you down."

"Again," Devlin said. "Not the most accurate retelling. And consider the source."

"You've been leveling?" Xander's breath was ragged. His face flushed. "You know how dangerous that is!"

I backed away, aware that this argument had escalated to a place where my two cents would be worthless.

Devlin's flamed cheeks matched Xander's. "It was a necessary evil."

Xander lifted his fist as if he wanted to punch the screen, but he ended up slamming his hands on the desk. "No wonder her brain is damaged. Do you realize what you've done?"

"Me? You started this! It was your idea."

"It wasn't my idea! I'm following instructions."

Devlin leaned closer, his head filling the entire screen. "Instructions that even you said were a horrible idea."

"So you decided to make it worse?"

"I was attempting to fix your mistakes!"

"Damn it, Devlin, that wasn't for you to decide! Not without discussing it with me."

Shadows flickered on each side of the room. I staggered until my back pressed against a wall. The guys continued arguing while I searched for what was causing the dark streaks through the room. Every time I turned my head, another shadow moved in my peripheral vision.

"Kelsey?" Devlin called from the screen. Then quieter he said, "She sees something."

"Kels?" Xander rushed over to me. "What is it?"

"The walls," I said. "I keep seeing shadows scurry across them."

Xander's attention snapped to Devlin. "Where is he?"

Devlin's gaze shifted to the left of his screen, and his eyes scrolled rapidly. "Hang on. I'm searching."

"Who?" I asked. "Who is he searching for?"

Xander expanded the screen of his govern band, typing and swiping at what seemed like a million moves a minute. "I'm jump-driving her."

"Jump-driving?" I murmured, confused by everything they were doing and saying. They went from shouting at each other to working as a team in mere seconds.

"A wall was breached," Devlin stated, but then he grumbled under his breath, "Sneaky bastard. Where are you hiding?"

Xander gripped my shoulders. "Are you certain you saw floaters?"

"Floaters?" The word triggered a twist in my gut.

"Shadows you can't focus on." Xander was talking so fast. Too fast. "Dark movements on the edges of your vision."

"Yes, that's what I saw. What were they?"

"Are you still seeing them?"

I glanced around the room.

"Black wires," I sputtered, noticing four long cords creeping out from under the door.

"Send her home!" Devlin yelled, still working on his side of the screen.

"Tell me what's going on!" I pleaded.

Xander held my face in his hands. "You trust me, right?"

I nodded. My pulse hammered in my ears.

"Then close your eyes and listen to my voice," he said soothingly.

The wires snaked across the floor, getting closer to us. "That won't help."

"It will. Trust me and do it."

My lids fluttered closed. I pressed my hands over Xander's, terrified the serpentine wires would yank him away from me, or do something worse.

He lifted my necklace and kissed my temple. "Remember earlier, at the library, you were reading *A Wrinkle in Time*?"

Reading? He expected me to think? I was panicking!

"I said home!" Devlin yelled.

"Imagine you're still in the library," Xander continued calmly. "Sitting on the aisle floor with the book in your lap."

I pictured it in detail, even smelled the paper. But how did he know I had been sitting on the floor?

"He's there!" Devlin shouted. "In the library! Reroute her!"

My eyes flew open due to the panic in Devlin's voice, but he and Xander were transparent like ghosts, as was everything inside the Ark. Overlapping the desk and screen was a tall row of bookshelves.

I reached forward. "Xander?"

"Close your eyes," he urged. "Just a few more seconds."

But I didn't close my eyes. I couldn't look away from the scene morphing all around me. The Elura Library became more solid as the Ark, Xander, and Devlin faded away.

Movement to my left caught my attention. Black wires shot out of the escalator steps, rising into the air then collapsing. They slithered along the wooden floor. I backed away, jumping sideways to avoid one hitting my foot.

Kramer stepped off the escalator.

Glitch.

I rushed between the aisles, peeking over book spines to watch him. He walked in my direction, and I held my breath.

"Kelsey?" Xander's voice sounded so loud piercing the quiet.

I glanced down at my band. His eyes were wide, his forehead sweaty, and he looked pale and sickish. "Stay away from him! I'll get you out of there."

Looking up, I saw Kramer was only a few steps from discovering me. I bolted down the aisle and rounded the corner, pressing my back against the endcap.

A fire exit door morphed into existence several feet away then opened. Devlin leaned through it. "Come on!"

Could I trust him? Did Xander mean stay away from Kramer, or Devlin?

Kramer sang like a psychopath. "Oh, Miss Zellllarrrr? Come out, come out, wherever you are."

Devlin frantically motioned for me to run to him. Kramer was a scary perv who even Devlin seemed to fear. Devlin was just a crappy, sneaky friend who sucked at explanations. I chose the lesser of the two evils and sprinted toward the door Devlin held open.

The moment I crossed the threshold, I knew I had chosen incorrectly.

Level 4.9

I was back in the all-white room. A wave of nausea washed over me so violently that I fell to my hands and knees. I dry heaved several times, my stomach and back aching from the spasms.

I almost collapsed face first into my shiny reflection. The easy choice would have been to close my eyes so I didn't have to think about what was happening to me. None of it made sense. I was exhausted from being so confused, and scared, and now sick.

But the sound of pounding made me look up.

Keekee stood on the other side of the room, slamming her hands against the window where Awol had peered in at me during my last visit. My sister wore a bright gold, reflective jumpsuit. A puffy hood made of the same material hung low on her back like someone had tried ripping it off. It bounced with every pound of Keekee's hands.

"Let us out!" she screamed. "Someone let us out of here!"

"Keek." I tried calling to her, but my voice came out weaker than a whisper. My throat was raw, and my body overtaxed from dry heaving.

A door slid open and Awol walked in.

Keekee spun on her, advancing with fury. "You set us up! You backstabbing fink, you ruined our lives!"

I tried pushing myself up to stand so I could help her, or at the very least be by her side, but pain shot through my wrists and my arms buckled, leaving me helpless to watch from my place on the floor.

"Calm down," Awol warned.

Keek didn't verbally reply. She grabbed Awol by the hair, spun her around, and slammed her face into one of the windows. Blaze and Jag rushed into the room, both in government uniforms.

"No," I groaned. Not Jag too. They were all traitors.

Jag pulled Keekee off Awol and restrained her. Keek fought hard, thrashing and kicking even as Jag kept her hands locked behind her back.

Blaze held the same type of injector gun that Agent Spade and Club had used on me. I crawled forward, muttering "please don't." It was my final weak attempt to help, but Blaze shot Keek in the arm with a tranquilizer.

Much too slowly, I crawled across the white floor. Keek's struggle weakened until she went limp in Jag's arms. I was less than a foot away from them when she slid to the floor. Jag dropped her like a sack of garbage, and she landed on her side, facing me.

"Keek? Can you hear me?" I finally reached her. Pushing her curls off her face, I collapsed on the cold, hard floor beside her. For one fleeting moment, I thought I saw Xander's reflection. I lifted my heavy head, searching for him, but saw only the three traitors standing above us.

I pressed my forehead against my sister's.

"He'll get us out of here," I whispered. "Hang in there."

"What now?" Blaze asked above us.

Jag squatted beside me and touched the side of my head. "Separate them."

"No!" I rolled over, intending to plead my case, but a loud pop silenced me. Familiar searing pain ripped through my shoulder.

I'd been tranquilized again. I drifted away from Keekee, the white room, and consciousness.

"Miss Zellar!" a woman shouted, startling me awake. I sat up as people around me giggled. My scalp itched from the EVRA I was wearing, and my eyes strained at the glowing screen flashing *Lesson Concluded.*

I ripped the EVRA from my head and found Mrs. Linker standing in front of my desk wearing an unflattering scowl. "Did our lesson bore you to sleep?"

I shook my head, trying to answer her while also forcing my fuzzy and tired mind to clear. "I don't know what happened," I admitted. "Many apologies."

She crossed her arms over her chest. "Did you remain awake for any of the lesson?"

I massaged my aching temples. To save my life, I couldn't think what the lesson was about. I didn't want to get myself into more trouble, so I replied, "Not enough to comprehend it. May I stay after school and complete a do-over?"

She sighed. "You may, but do not let this become a habit. This is the one and only time I will grant you this chance."

"Many thanks," I said, avoiding eye contact with my classmates who were still chuckling and making comments under their breath.

As Mrs. Linker walked away, I rubbed my eyes, trying to relieve my headache. She was most definitely a younger version of the High Priestess, but clearly the VR world and reality were not intertwined for her like they were for me.

My brain felt fried. Sorting out dreams, VR, and reality felt like an impossible task that my aching head couldn't handle. The nightmare I'd just had about Blaze sedating us would never happen in real life, but I still had a nagging worry in the pit of my stomach that my sister was in danger.

I touched my govern band, wanting to contact Keekee and confirm she was safe in school like me.

Several excruciatingly long minutes later, class ended and my classmates fled the room as I not-so-patiently waited for Keek to answer my band transmission. She never did, so I sent her a message. *Contact me right away.*

I'd have to tell her I was staying late to make up an assignment, but more importantly I needed to confirm she was okay.

"Are you ready, Kelsey?" Mrs. Linker asked me.

"Almost," I replied. "Just waiting for confirmation that my family knows I'm staying to make up an assignment."

Mrs. Linker walked over to her cabinet of equipment as I drummed my fingers on my band's screen, waiting for Keek to reply.

"This is a different version of the lesson you missed," Mrs. Linker said. She stood in front of my desk, sorting through a stack of access cards. "It contains more action, so it might keep you awake."

"Many thanks," I said halfheartedly, dreading the impending moment when I'd have to put the EVRA back on my head.

She placed a card on my desk as my band chirped with a message. *Transmission failed. Signal jammed.*

I huffed under my breath. I was used to receiving those messages when we lived in other cities, when Keek hid in some seedy VR joint, but she didn't know anyone in Elura yet. She couldn't have befriended a gamer so fast. And even if she did, she should have messaged me that she'd be unavailable.

"Kelsey, you need to get started." Mrs. Linker had returned to her desk. "I have an important meeting in a little over an hour and I can't be late."

"Yes, ma'am." Trying to push my frustration with my sister out of my mind, I pressed balance patches behind my ears, then centered the helmet on my head. The weight of it made me groan. I reached for the access card Mrs. Linker had given me but froze when I saw the familiar black card with the gold Arcana symbol.

I glanced up, but she was busy typing something on her band.

Slowly, I slid the card toward me. Holding my breath, I flipped it over.

I jerked so hard my chair rammed into the desk behind me. Staring up at me was Kramer. A colorful, cartoonish portrait of him, but without a doubt, it was his big bull face. There was no number on the card. No title. It was different than the others. Maybe it wasn't one of Xander's?

"Is there a problem?" Mrs. Linker asked me.

I hesitated, clutching the card in my lap, and debating whether or not to show it to her. But it wasn't an access card, therefore I couldn't insert it into my EVRA, and without an access card, I couldn't make up the lesson.

"Yes," I replied. "I think you made a mistake. This card you gave me, it's not an access card."

Surprise and confusion washed over her. “What? I’m sure I gave you the right card.” She stood and made her way down the aisle. “Let me see it.”

I handed it to her. She looked at it briefly then shook her head. “What is this?”

“I don’t know. It looks like an artsy rendition of Counselor Kramer.”

“Who?”

“Counselor Kramer,” I repeated.

She stared blankly at me.

“My guidance counselor,” I said.

Her eyes narrowed, and she sat on the edge of the desk behind her. “Kelsey, are you feeling unwell? Do you need to visit the health bay?”

I felt disoriented and worried, and I had a massive headache, but I hated the health bay, so I lied. “I’m fine. Why?”

“Well, first of all—” She studied the card again, then shook her head. “None of the people on this card have visible faces.”

“What?” I threw my hand out. “May I see it again?”

She passed it to me, and I gasped. The card had changed.

Kramer was gone. He had been replaced by a much more elaborate scene of a hooded man standing between two large open hands. Kneeling on each palm of the hands were two girls. Below them, inside of what looked like a torn page, stood another person with two keys floating above the back of his glowing head. But Mrs. Linker was right: I couldn’t see any of the characters' faces.

The number 5 card. I murmured as I read the title aloud, “The Hierophant.”

“Secondly,” Mrs. Linker continued, “and what’s much more worrisome, is we do not have any guidance counselors at this school named Kramer.”

My head whipped up as my stomach clenched. “That’s impossible.”

“That—” She stood and nodded. “Is the truth.”

5: THE HIEROPHANT

Level 5.1

Mrs. Linker stared at me, waiting for me to make the next move in our twisted conversation. Kramer wasn't a guidance counselor? How was that possible?

He was in the health bay when Mom picked me up. Keekee and I had a meeting with him here at school. But then again, Xander posed as a proctor and met with me at school too. No one was who they pretended to be.

I rubbed my forehead, pretending to be disoriented, which wasn't far from the truth. "That's right. Kramer was my counselor at my old school," I lied. "I must have forgotten my new counselor's name."

"Ms. Balk." She squinted, still worried about me. "Perhaps we could venture down to the counseling rooms and see if she's still here. You really should meet her. She's a lovely person."

"Maybe another day," I offered, not wanting to meet anyone else any time soon. I already couldn't keep people (or anything else) straight in my muddled mind.

Patting my arm, she gently said, "You can complete the follow-up assignment at home. I can tell it's been a trying day for you."

"Many thanks."

"Gather your things and I'll escort you to the lobby."

We both packed up and I joined her at the door.

"Here." She handed me the thin stack of tarot cards. "I'm sure you wouldn't want to lose those."

"Yes. I mean no, I can't lose them." I tried sounding convincing so she'd believe the same lie Keek had told Mom. "An aunt gave them to me."

"I once had a tarot deck of my own."

I nodded, feeling like I already knew that about her. Like maybe we had discussed tarot cards before, but I was almost sure we hadn't. I was no longer entirely certain of anything.

She sighed wistfully. "But I gave my deck away."

"A family member needed the cards more than you?" I guessed.

"How'd you know?"

I had no answer that wouldn't confirm her earlier worry that I had mental issues, so I whipped up another fib. "I've been using the cards on my sister. Hoping to guide her down the right path."

Grinning, she ushered me into the hallway and pulled the door shut behind us. "Ahh, yes. Sometimes, we all need help on our journey."

I shrugged my bag onto my shoulder and kept quiet, deciding silence was my safest option. But we still had to get downstairs and reach the lobby, which was a lot of time for awkward discussion. I didn't want to accidentally say something else that might make her report me for mental instability.

"Stairs or elevator?" she asked me.

"I'm fine with either."

"Open to multiple options. That's a useful trait." She tapped her lip while looking up at the ceiling. "If you'll allow me to share some of my elderly wisdom with you?"

"Please do," I said politely.

"There is one constant I've learned about journeys. Never, is there only one path. Sometimes the journeyer travels multiple roads on their way to enlightenment, but there is no right or wrong."

I considered her logic. "What if the path leads to trouble?"

"Life is full of trouble. You learn from your experiences and plow ahead."

"What if your experiences, or *choices,*" I corrected myself, "put people you care about in danger?"

"If that happened, my best advice would be to help them find a way out." She headed toward the elevator and I followed.

"Easier said than done," I said a tad too earnestly, but our conversation about the tarot made me suspect she might know more than she let on.

"Perhaps." Distracted from our conversation, she dug through her bag. "I've left a digifile in the classroom. You can find your way from here, yes?"

Apparently, she wouldn't be the one to give me answers either. "Sure."

She pushed the down button to call the elevator then touched my shoulder. "Don't forget to finish your assignment. I won't grant any extensions or another do-over."

"Yes, ma'am. Thanks for granting me this one."

She turned and walked away as the elevator bell dinged.

The doors slid open, and my bag fell to the floor along with my jaw. Devlin and Xander stood inside.

Devlin's voice was firm as steel. "Get in."

I stood rooted in place, my eyes darting to Xander.

He held out his hand. "It's safe, I promise."

"Last time I saw you two together, you were fighting and yelling at each other. Why should I believe it's safe to voluntarily enter a small, enclosed space with both of you?"

Xander smirked and lowered his empty hand. "Fair question, and we'll answer it after we're safe from being overheard."

I glanced down the hall, but Mrs. Linker was gone. Besides me, the hallway was empty.

I crossed my arms over my chest and fixed my sights on Devlin. "I don't trust him."

Devlin snickered. "Right now, I don't trust you either."

"Yes, you do." Xander elbowed him, but kept his focus on me. "All of us are on the same team."

"The same team?" I lowered my voice in case any teachers were still in nearby classrooms. "He threw me into a scenario where Keekee and I were trapped like prisoners."

The elevator buzzed because the door had been held open so long.

Xander's band chirped too. He glanced down then flashed me a worried look that set my nerves on edge. "Unless you want another encounter with Kramer, you need to come with us."

That was all the convincing I needed. I stepped inside, and the doors slid shut behind me. "Kramer isn't a guidance counselor here."

Xander pushed the lobby button. "We know."

"Then who is he?" I asked. "And why did he pretend to be a counselor that day you pretended to be a proctor?"

Devlin shrugged. "A lot of people pretend to be someone else when they aren't happy with who they are."

I repeated my original question. "So who is Kramer, really?"

Xander's fingers danced over his band's screen as his brow furrowed with concentration. He never looked up from his task as he replied, "He's a high-ranking government official. In charge of ensuring no citizens escape Equatia."

"Well, many thanks for disclosing that bit of useful information much too late." Neither of them apologized or even had the decency to look apologetic. The whole time I had worried about leading officials to Xander, but maybe he led them to me. "Why am I on his radar? I didn't know anything about the Arcana or its mission when he first met me."

"Yes, you did," Devlin said.

"I did not," I argued.

He leaned toward me and grinned. "You didn't know that you knew, but deep down you knew."

"I didn't—" The elevator doors opened, and I stiffened. We were not stepping into the lobby of Century High as I expected. Somehow, we had traveled to Xander's warehouse. In the real world, that was impossible. "Glitch. This isn't real either."

Devlin winked at me. "That depends on your definition of real."

"Stop saying that!" I stepped out of the elevator and into the parking area in front of Xander's living room. I spun to face Devlin. "You're always saying that, and it drives me mad."

At the same time, he and Xander stepped out of a glowing tunnel (not elevator doors like I expected).

"What did you just say?" Xander asked me.

"Him." I jabbed my finger in Devlin's direction. "He drives me crazy."

"No," Xander said firmly. "You said he's *always* saying that. When has he said it before?"

Devlin stared at me, lips pinched as he tried to inconspicuously shake his head.

As if I'd keep secrets from Xander. "He said it at Higher Grounds, and in that strange VR scenario where I watched you bring me here for the first time."

Devlin's eyes glistened as he slugged Xander's shoulder. "Still want to berate me for my leveling?"

"Yes." Xander flashed him a harsh glare. "Considering the situation, it's too risky and dangerous."

"But it's working," Devlin said smugly.

"What is leveling?" I asked.

Xander checked his band. "It's not important right now."

I started to demand an answer, but Devlin beat me to the punch.

"Stop keeping so many secrets from her. She can handle it." It was one of the rare instances when I agreed with him. Devlin stepped between Xander and me, invading my personal space. I stepped back, but he braced my shoulders. "The whole point of VR is to feel real. No matter what role you're playing, or what world you're in, it's supposed to be believable. Every person, character, sound, feeling, all of it. Leveling means introducing an unnatural element to the scenario. The realization that something or someone is out of place *levels* the person experiencing the scene. Their rational mind kicks in, and they realize they're in VR."

"Like when I realized it wasn't Keekee at Xander's warehouse? It was actually me, and I was watching a memory of us."

Devlin let go of me. "Let's not discuss her right now."

Xander nudged Devlin aside. "Yes, that's a whole difference of opinion we could eternally argue. Right now, we need to focus on Kramer."

He held my hand and started to walk away, but I planted my feet and yanked him back. "Wait a second. Why would you two argue about Keekee?"

Xander sighed. I looked at Devlin who crossed his arms over his chest.

The guys exchanged glances that I couldn't interpret.

"Spill it," I demanded.

Xander stepped closer and lifted my hand to his chest. "Do you trust me?"

"You know I do, but you're not using that tactic to avoid my question this time. You two are discussing my sister. My other half. I need to know why you would argue about her, and I'm not going anywhere until you explain."

Xander's uneasy focus darted to Devlin.

He held up his hands. "Look, we knew the time would come when she'd have to find out, and considering the ticking clock looming over our heads, I'd say this seems like the ideal situation."

Xander dropped my hand and cracked his knuckles, then he looked at his band's screen and swiped it several times. A frown tugged at his lips. "Fine, but we can't tell you. We'll have to show you."

"Show me how?" I asked.

He jutted his chin toward his loft behind me. "We need to visit the library."

We walked across the warehouse and through Xander's office. He pushed open the door to his secret sanctum. All three of us stepped inside.

Even amid the tension, I breathed a sigh of joy. Being surrounded by floor-to-ceiling, overflowing bookshelves was a dream come true. Sure, many of the books were disguised cases for access cards, but the room still gave me a reader's high.

Xander walked to the side of the room and climbed two rungs of a ladder. He slid a book from its slot and hopped back down, returning to where Devlin and I waited. He handed me the book.

I read the title aloud. "*Divine Secrets of the Ya-Ya Sisterhood?*"

Xander opened it, and there sat an access card. "I have no idea what the original story was about, but it's a good cover for the answer you're looking for."

I eyed him and the card skeptically. "The answer to why you and Devlin would argue about my sister is on an access card?"

He nodded.

"How is that possible?" I asked.

"Remember when Devlin said people pretend to be someone else when they aren't happy with who they are?"

"Yes, but we were talking about Kramer."

"Well, sometimes, to understand another person, you have to put yourself in their shoes."

"Wait." Devlin grabbed the book from my hands. "Which scenario is this?"

Xander snatched it back. "It's the one Kelsey needs to see to understand our connection to Keekee."

"Connection?" I repeated. "Have you two ever met her?"

Devlin ran his hand over his bristly chin. "Kelsey, remember what you said when we arrived at the warehouse. This isn't real, so this conversation, and details of any scenario you're immersed in, can change according to the creator."

How had I forgotten that what we were experiencing wasn't reality? Why did I keep forgetting that when it seemed vitally important? "But it feels so real. It always does."

"It's supposed to," Xander said. "That's the whole point."

"But—" I stopped myself, worried that if I reminded Xander he told me I needed a break from VR, he wouldn't give me answers about Keekee. I changed my question. "If this is VR, where am I right now? The real me."

"In an immersion room," Xander said.

Devlin nodded, confirming Xander's answer.

Trying to figure out how long I had been immersed, I recalled the first time I visited Xander's hidden room at the top of the bookshelves. Swirling colors of light had transported me into the wardrobe, but I remembered returning from that trip. Plus, that had been days ago. Had there been other times I went into the immersion room? Fuzzy broken memories of conversations between Xander and me flashed through my mind. All of them took place in his immersion room.

Xander suspected my brain was damaged from too much VR, but I remembered pieces, which were enough for me to feel safe enough to do one more scenario so I could find out how Keekee was involved.

"So even though I'm already in the immersion room and in *this* VR scenario—" I pulled the access card from its holder in the book. "You're putting me into another one where I'll learn something about my sister?"

"Yes."

"Isn't that more leveling?"

Devlin replied. "A scenario within a scenario isn't leveling. It's called stacking."

I shook my head. I would probably never understand the VR masters and all their confusing terms and vague explanations.

Stacking seemed like a lot of extra work. "And you can't just tell me this mysterious information?"

Xander spoke so gently it worried me. "It will be easier to understand this way."

My primary concern was my sister, and if stacking myself in another scenario would give me answers, then I was eager to jump in. I walked over to the ladder that led to the illusory top shelf of life-size books, one of which was a hidden door to the immersion room.

I motioned to the ladder. "After you, gentlemen."

Xander began climbing.

Devlin grabbed a rung then whispered to me, "When the time comes, choose me. It's the only path that can save anyone."

A shiver shook through me, and a blur of darkness in my peripheral vision made me turn my head. Other than the three of us, the library was empty and the door was still shut, but I could have sworn a shadow floated across the room. Before I could refocus and respond to Devlin's backstabbing comment, he had climbed up and away from me.

Determined to gain some clarity, I tucked the access card into my pocket and climbed toward the room that would provide answers. As soon as this scenario ended, I'd be sure to tell Xander about Devlin's latest betrayal.

When I reached the top, the book spine door was already open. I stepped into the stark white immersion room and froze in place.

"What's wrong?" Xander asked me.

"This feels really familiar." *And not in a good way,* I wanted to add, but the suspicious way Devlin watched me made me keep that last part to myself.

"You have been here quite a few times," Xander reminded me.

I nodded, pretending I remembered those times, and ignoring the tight knot in my chest. I pulled the card from my pocket and held it in my hand. “Just focus on it and don’t look away, right?”

“Right.” Xander stood in front of me and pushed my hair behind my ear then caressed the side of my face. “See you soon.”

Level 5.2

Beautiful beams of colored light. That's all I remembered about my dream. Colorful, bright rays that blurred every time my body shook.

"Wake up," Keekee said, shoving my shoulder a few more times.

I rolled over in bed, groaning. "Stop shaking me."

"It's the only way I could get you to wake up. Your alarm didn't faze you."

As I rubbed my aching eyes, my sister came into view. She looked well-rested. The sunlight pouring through our window lit up her face like a holosplay character. I pulled my pillow over my throbbing head. "I'm sick."

"Sick?" Keekee grabbed my wrist and pressed a few commands on my band to check my vitals. "Nope, your temperature and blood pressure are perfectly normal. Mom and Dad will never buy it."

"I don't need a fever to be sick."

"Maybe not, but you need a fever if you have any hope of getting out of a community exhortation."

My head throbbed harder. The last thing I wanted to do on a day off from school was suffer through an exhortation of stuffy government advisors preaching about Equatia laws and citizen obedience.

She walked to our dresser and returned with two enhancement candies. "Take these. Energy and mental clarity."

Recalling my alleged overdose on Mom's calming candies, I pushed her hand away. "I don't want those."

She shrugged and unwrapped one then popped it into her mouth. “Go shower. You know how Dad hates being late. I’ll contact M and provide an update.”

My bed might as well have tilted on its side. The whole world seemed to shift, throwing me and all my thoughts off balance. I sat up. “What?”

Keekee’s face blurred too. It wasn’t a sensation like the bed/world tilt; her face actually blurred, leaving a trail of duplicate images as she moved. “What do you mean, *what*?”

“You said you’d contact M and provide an update.”

Her face transitioned back to normal. “Right.”

“Who is M?”

Her brow crinkled. “What did you two do last night? You’re acting exceptionally strange.”

“You two?” I repeated. “Who are you referring to?”

She stared at me, the concerned creases around her mouth deepening. She couldn’t know about Xander. I didn’t tell her I was still seeing him. Did I? I ran my fingers through my rat’s nest of curls, trying to focus my thoughts. Was I with Xander last night? Why couldn’t I remember going to bed, or anything that happened yesterday?

My sister’s voice snapped me back into our bewildering conversation. “You experimented again, didn’t you?” Her lip twitched like it always did right before she accused me of betraying her. “You promised. We agreed we’d do this together.”

Was she referring to our fink mission? “We *are* doing this together.”

“Then tell me what happened last night.”

My lips parted. I wanted to give her an honest answer, but I couldn’t even remember last night, much less did I have any recollection of what had happened.

“I knew it!” she hissed. “Your silence says it all.”

Really? I wished my silence said it all to *me* because I was baffled by our entire conversation.

“Keek,” I began, hoping a rational explanation would magically form on its own. “I *want* to tell you what happened last night, but I can’t remember anything I did.”

"Was Jag there?" Keekee snapped. I sat up straight. She knew Jag? "Of course he was." She paced the room. "You wouldn't have tried it without all four suits."

My eyes bugged. How did she know about the suits? A flicker of knowledge tugged at the back of my brain. The echo of a recent conversation where Keek said, *Amelia and I totally connected, and my suspicions were right. She's heavily into the VR scene.*

How long ago was that meeting? Had they already become friends? Did Awol take her to Higher Grounds and show her around? Introduce her to Jag and the others?

Our bedroom door opened, and Mom stuck her head inside. "Morning! You girls—" Her smile drooped when she saw me. "Kelsey, why are you still in bed? We're leaving in twenty minutes, and both of you need to eat breakfast."

I scooted out of bed. "I'm sorry. I'll be ready in time."

Keekee glared at me then shouldered past Mom and out of the room.

"What's wrong with your sister?" Mom asked me.

Finally, a question I could answer truthfully. "I don't know."

She sighed. "None of us enjoys exhortations, but the alert said this one is Code Red Imperative."

The severity of her words vibrated through me like a shockwave. I almost had to sit down again, but I managed to stay on my feet. Only one other time had Equatia declared an exhortation Code Red Imperative, and that was years ago, to announce a security breach by an outside nation. Why hadn't Keekee mentioned today was a Code Red?

I touched my band. More importantly, why hadn't I remembered something so significant? I must have received the alert. Every citizen of Equatia received exhortation notices.

I looked up to find Mom still staring at me. "Code Reds are pretty upsetting," I said, trying to ease her worries. "Maybe that's why Keek is rattled."

Mom rubbed her arms. "It has me rattled too, but we knew this day was near." She lowered her voice. "It's what we've been preparing for, right?"

My heart skipped a beat. *Preparing* for. My mind raced, trying to make sense of what Mom just said. And what Keek had said earlier. I was at a total loss. Nothing made sense.

“Get dressed and come eat some breakfast.” She turned and walked down the hall.

I stood in place for a few moments, disoriented and desperately wanting answers to all of my questions. Shaking my head, I walked over to our closet. I stood in front of the double doors, but when I touched the metal doorknobs, a jolt of electricity shot through my fingertips so hard my hands flew to my chest.

“Ow,” I grumbled, flexing my fingers to ease the painful tingling. I touched the wall beside the closet in an attempt to ground my energy so I wouldn’t get zapped again. Hesitantly, I touched the closet handles and made shock-free contact. I opened the doors, and then my hands fell to my sides. I swayed on my feet.

“What the glitch?” I whispered.

In front of me, in *my* closet, hung government-issued pants and tunics too big to fit me. Not to mention, there wasn’t one feminine color in the entire wardrobe.

Behind me, I felt Keekee walk into the room and look over my shoulder. I couldn’t stop staring at the strange clothes in my closet. “Are you seeing what I’m seeing?”

“Not exactly.” The deep-voiced reply forced me to turn around.

It wasn’t my sister standing behind me. It was Devlin.

He grinned. “Well, isn’t this awkward?”

“Are you insane?” I took a step back. The clothes in the closet brushed against my shoulders and bare legs. I tugged at my nightshirt, trying to cover myself. “What are you doing here?”

Devlin stepped forward. He didn’t even need to touch me. His forbidden presence forced me deeper into the closet.

He pulled the doors closed, and I held my breath. I didn’t know which I feared more: him breaking into our house with not-so-friendly intentions, or imagining my parents discovering him and reporting us to enforcers.

The closet was so dark I could see only the outline of Devlin’s face inches away from mine. He didn’t even bother whispering. “I told you Xander was getting sloppy.”

His band lit up and he swiped his finger across the screen, attention fully focused on his task.

Instinctively, I touched his chin. His stubble didn't feel rough. It didn't feel like anything.

"I didn't have time to program tactile details," Devlin said, not averting his focus from his screen. "Just bear with me."

"This isn't real. It's a VR scenario."

"More like a poor substitution for one."

I grabbed one of the tunics, rubbing the material between my fingers. "But I can feel this shirt. I felt these clothes brush against the back of me a few seconds ago."

"Xander always programs tactiles for you, but like I said, I didn't have time."

"Time for what?"

Devlin lowered his wrist along with the glowing screen between us. His face was a shadowed silhouette. "To design a proper override of Xander's virused program."

My chest tightened. A virus couldn't be good. "This scenario is virused?"

"Of course it is." Devlin parted the clothes. The hangers screeched across the bar so loudly it made me flinch. "How else do you explain the male attire in your closet?"

Before I could reply, a rectangle of light formed on the back wall, illuminating the cramped space. The light grew taller and wider until it formed a glowing doorway.

Devlin motioned toward it. "Ready to discover the information you *really* need to know?"

I eyed the doorway, squinting to see if numbers really scrolled through it, or if I had imagined them. My attention shifted back to Devlin. "Answers are in there?"

"Yes."

I had been in a whirlwind of confusion for days. Had it been days? I couldn't keep track of time anymore. All I knew was I wanted—no, I *needed* useful information before my brain spontaneously combusted from an overload of unanswered questions. But could I trust Devlin?

"I don't trust you," I admitted.

"Your trust isn't my concern right now. I'm here to deliver some much-needed brutal honesty. Now, go through that doorway so I don't have to shove you."

I tensed, wanting to warn him not to lay one finger on me, but then I realized he couldn't. At least, not in reality. This was VR, and nothing he did or said was real. Venturing through his light-filled doorway to seek answers couldn't hurt me, and neither could he.

I stepped into the light and kept walking. I closed my eyes for only a second—one brief blink to adjust my vision. But with that one blink, and one final step forward, I discovered I was wrong.

Devlin had the power to hurt me in ways worse than I ever could have imagined.

Level 5.3

I was back in the all-white room, suffocating in a puffy gold jumpsuit. Waves of nausea rolled through my stomach.

I heard dry heaving behind me, so I turned around. Xander was on his hands and knees. Sweat dripped from his pale face onto the floor.

"No," I pleaded. How did Xander end up in this awful place with me? He was sick and needed treatment.

Frantic, I glanced at all four windows, searching for help, but they were all empty. I ran over to one and pounded on the glass with all my might.

"Let us out!" I screamed. "Someone let us out of here!"

I kept pounding, the hood attached to my suit bounced against my back.

A door slid open and Awol walked in. Darkness clouded my vision. I advanced with fury. "You set us up! You backstabbing fink, you ruined our lives!"

"Calm down," Awol said.

I grabbed her by the hair, spun her around, and slammed her face into one of the windows. Blaze and Jag rushed into the room, both in government uniforms.

"No," Xander groaned from too far away.

Jag pulled me off Awol and restrained me. I thrashed and kicked even as Jag kept my hands locked behind my back. Xander was so weak. I had to get him out of here.

Blaze approached me with an injector gun. I bucked and squirmed even harder.

Xander crawled toward me, muttering, "Please don't," just as Blaze shot me in the arm with a tranquilizer.

The dose was strong. It hit me like a craft at lightning speed. Xander still fought to reach me, but everything transitioned to ultra-slow motion. I went limp, unable to feel my face or limbs. Jag let me slide onto the floor. I landed on my side so I could still see Xander as he finally reached me.

"Kels?" My name stretched from his lips like the softest of enhancement candies. "Can you hear me?"

He pushed my curls from my face, then collapsed onto the floor beside me. His fingers were ice-cold, and his face was pale. My heart and soul ached at seeing him so sick. He lifted his head, searching, or maybe he was just disoriented, but then he pressed his clammy forehead against mine.

"He'll get us out of here," he whispered to me. "Hang in there."

Blaze's voice was muffled above me. "What now?"

Jag squatted beside us and touched Xander's head. "Separate them."

"No!" Xander groaned, trying to roll over.

Shhhh. I mentally pleaded with him. *You're right. He'll get us out of here. We'll get you healed.*

But I knew Xander couldn't hear me. The loud pop of the tranquilizer gun silenced his efforts to keep us together. His lids grew heavy as he tried to stare into my eyes. My vision blurred as I made one more mental declaration. *I believe in us.*

I woke up in Xander's hammock.

He sat beside me, bracing my shoulders. "Kels, breathe. It was only a nightmare."

I sucked in a breath, willing my heart to stop thrumming so fast. I was clenching the hammock netting on either side of me. After another breath, I loosened my death grip. A soft, tranquil song played from a vintage (and illegal) music pod on a nearby shelf.

Xander tucked a stray curl behind my ear and caressed the side of my face. "Must have been a bad one."

I attempted to sit up, but the hammock buckled and swayed.

“Just relax,” Xander said, steadying both of us. “Give yourself a few minutes to recover.” I reclined back again and tried to relax. He held my hand, rubbing his thumb over my wrist. “Do you remember any details?”

“It’s fading too fast,” I admitted. “I think it might have been about my family, but I’m not sure.”

“It’s okay. You’re here, safe and sound.”

I had a nagging suspicion I was forgetting something important. “Where’s Devlin?”

“Running amuck somewhere with Jag.”

“Blaze and Awol?”

He grinned confidently. “Recruiting. And before you ask, yes, the Ark is secure.”

The Ark? Why would he assume I’d ask about that? My instincts were whispering that something wasn’t right. I was overlooking something, but what?

“You’ve had a tough day.” Xander repositioned himself, then stretched out beside me. The hammock tilted too far to his side so I scooted over, and he followed. He wrapped his arms around me, and I cuddled against him, resting my head on his chest. “Tomorrow will be even tougher, but we’ll get through it.”

Tomorrow. What was happening tomorrow? What happened today for that matter? I didn’t ask Xander those questions because he was already too worried about the supposed damage to my brain from excess VR.

“I believe in you.” He kissed the top of my head. “I believe in us.”

“I’ll believe in you until my last breath.”

His chest rose and fell against my cheek. “That’s not enough.”

I lifted my head and looked at him. Playfully, I said, “I thought that was a very generous declaration of my commitment.”

But the look in his eyes wasn’t playful. He was serious and solemn. “Never stop believing in us. That’s the deal. Whether it’s you or me taking a final breath, we believe, and we keep believing—fiercely—that we’ll be together again.”

His words went down smooth as coffee, warming my heart and soul. He held my gaze, urging me to respond, but what could I possibly say to top that, or even equal it? I leaned in to kiss him, but he stopped me by touching my lips.

He whispered, “Tomorrow will change our lives in ways we can’t imagine.”

I’m not sure why, but I replied with, “I hope so.”

And then he kissed me.

He was wrong; the change wasn’t starting tomorrow. It began that moment. Or maybe everything had changed the moment we first met. But in that hammock, with the power of that kiss, I felt time, space, and the entire universe rewiring itself so that Xander and I were bound together. Our fates were intertwining as blissfully as our bodies. And for the first time in my life, I believed in forever.

Level 5.4

"Welcome back," Xander said, jolting me from the magical moment of our kiss.

I felt his lips disconnect from mine before I opened my eyes.

We weren't curled up in the hammock. My feet were planted firmly on the floor. As much as I didn't want to exit our cozy make-out scene, it had ended.

My lids fluttered open.

We were in his immersion room.

He stood in front of me, watching me with concern. I glanced to my right where Devlin stood, leaning against the white wall. I looked down to see an access card resting in my open hand.

My gaze lifted to meet Xander's again. I rubbed my lips together, wishing I could dive back into the kissing scenario. My body still tingled from his touch.

"How'd it go?" Xander asked.

I dropped my hand to my side, gripping the access card and the memory of our amazing conversation and kiss. "It was the best immersion I've experienced so far."

"And your question was answered?"

"My question?"

"About your sister."

I stared at him, trying to figure out what he was talking about. My thoughts and memories were cinched so tight, I couldn't access an answer. I didn't want him worrying about the VR damage to my brain again, so I fibbed.

"Yes." He didn't need to know I was referring to him and me when I finished with, "it was beyond satisfying."

Devlin cleared his throat and walked over to us. "Are we finished with this frivolous detour, because we should be focused on the impending problem of Kramer."

Kramer. His name made me shiver. "What about him?"

"He's a threat," Devlin said. "He found a way to breach our firewalls, so we need to protect you."

I held my band to my chest. "What do you mean? Like, he can monitor me again?"

Devlin's tone was grim. "He can do more than monitor."

"Stop scaring her." Xander stepped between Devlin and me. "Just like before, it will be easier for you to understand through VR, but this scenario won't be a happy one, and Devlin and I have a major difference in opinion on whose point of view you should experience."

Devlin stared at me, pointedly, over Xander's shoulder. "So we're letting you choose."

Xander turned slightly, motioning to Devlin behind him. "You can learn through my scenarios, or his."

"*But,*" Devlin interjected, "before you make your choice, you have to hear the truth about our qualifications."

"What qualifications?" I asked.

"First," Devlin began, "there's an important fact you need to know. You've witnessed Xander and I argue a few times. That's normal. It doesn't make us enemies. Don't choose him just because you two are *involved.*"

I looked at Xander, waiting for his side of the story, but Devlin grabbed my attention again when he flashed a cocky grin followed by a verbal bomb drop. "We're brothers."

My mouth hung open, and my eyes bounced between them. "Brothers?"

Devlin nodded. "I'm two years older and a lot wiser."

"Wiser is up for debate," Xander said.

I studied them. They both had dark hair, but Devlin's was always cut so short, sometimes buzzed. Devlin was paler, and he always needed a shave, where Xander had baby smooth, olive skin. But looking closer, I could see resemblances: the same strong jaw, almost identical noses, similar builds, and they interacted so comfortably with each other. "How the glitch did I miss that?"

Devlin's arrest replayed in my mind. "Wait. When they arrested you, they said your name was Devlin Templeton." I pointed an accusatory finger at Xander. "You told me your last name was Westin."

Devlin chuckled. "Templeton is a private joke between a few of the suits."

"It was a fake name to protect his real identity," Xander explained.

"A fake name with hidden meaning." Devlin declared proudly, "Our real last name is Westin."

"But the government scanned your irises and band," I argued. "How could you fool them?"

"Which brings us to our next fact." Devlin stood tall. "I'm the mastermind behind a lot of our security."

Xander snickered. "That's quite the exaggeration. Just because you know how to program and override doesn't qualify you as a mastermind."

"And build firewalls. Don't forget that impressive skill."

"Still." Xander shook his head. "Not the mastermind."

"At the present moment, I understand the system better than anyone else, so I'm sticking with my title."

I watched them argue, realizing how obvious it was that they were brothers. Devlin had made several comments that made me question his loyalty to the Arcana and Xander, but now I saw it as common sibling rivalry. My doubts about Devlin disintegrated. "Can you two finish your bickering so we can get back to this Kramer issue?"

"Ohhh." Devlin grinned at me, looking impressed. "Your spunky side is showing. I like it."

"Don't try to flatter me." I stood by Xander's side. "I'm still choosing Xander's way."

Devlin's smile vanished as Xander wrapped his arm around my waist. He quietly told me, "Wise choice."

"Hang on," Devlin argued. "You don't fully understand the options."

"I understand enough to know that I'd choose Xander's way no matter what. Even you told me that Xander knows me too well. He programs scenarios with the details I value most."

Devlin raked his fingers over his chin while Xander's grip tightened around my hand.

"When did he say that?" Xander asked me.

I glanced at Devlin, trying to remember when that conversation took place. "I'm not sure, but he said it."

Xander looked at his brother, but Devlin only shrugged. "Sounds like something I'd say, but I don't recall."

"Whatever. The clock is ticking. Let's go to the Ark."

Excitement surged through me. "I'm experiencing your lesson in the Ark?"

"I think it would be most productive that way." He ushered me to the door of the immersion room and motioned me through. I stepped out onto the life-size bookshelf and Devlin joined me, followed by Xander. I climbed down the ladder first, but when I reached the bottom, the guys were still at the top, talking in hushed voices. I rolled my eyes and scanned book titles while I waited for them to finish their argument.

Eventually, Devlin came down the ladder. He glared at me, but I ignored him and watched Xander descend and join us. Devlin stepped behind him, and before I understood what was happening, a loud pop echoed through the library.

I gasped, rushing closer as Xander spun to face Devlin.

Devlin twirled a tranquilizer gun in his hand. "Sorry, X. You two left me no choice."

Level 5.5

Xander pressed his palm to his temple as his eyes went glassy. "That's impossible. It wouldn't work."

Devlin tucked the gun in his pants and caught Xander as he toppled forward. "My methods always work. I'm sorry you forgot that important fact."

I shoved Devlin and shouted, "What did you do?" I couldn't believe what I had witnessed. Xander's eyes were shut, and he was limp in Devlin's arms. "You tranquilized your own brother!"

Devlin dragged Xander to a bookshelf. With one hand, he grabbed a thick paperback and set it on the floor, then he delicately laid down Xander and rested his head on top of the book. "He'll be fine."

"What the glitch is wrong with you?" I punched him in the chest. Hard.

He rubbed the spot where I hit him and glowered. "Don't make me shoot you too. That will defeat the purpose of everyone's efforts."

I kneeled beside Xander, holding his hand.

"I told you to choose me." Devlin stood over me. "My scenarios are what you need. His have been compromised. You didn't listen, so this is the consequence."

I didn't care about scenarios anymore. I only cared about reality. If he thought I'd willingly go anywhere with him after what he did to Xander, he was mistaken. "I'm not leaving him."

"You have to. Blaze and Awol will take care of him."

"Blaze and Awol?" I couldn't even remember the last time I saw them.

"Don't worry," Awol said from behind me. I spun around to see her and Blaze standing in the doorway. "He's in reliable hands."

"You're unhinged. All of you." I glared at all three of them, feeling so protective of Xander that the adrenaline surge made my teeth ache. "I'm not going anywhere with Devlin, and I'm not leaving Xander." I jabbed a finger in Devlin's direction. "And if you attempt to come near me with that gun, I will break your hands."

He smiled, and I resisted the urge to kick in his teeth.

"You were right," Blaze said. "Her swords side is more than adequate."

"Shut up!" I barked. I was fed up with all the secrets and deceit, and everyone speaking in riddles. I just wanted Xander to wake up so we could get away from them—away from everything, except each other.

Devlin stepped closer, and I stood, fists clenched at my sides.

"Try it," I warned. "If you come any closer, or attempt to take me away from him, I will claw out your eyes. I'm done being jerked around and controlled."

"Save all that anger and determination. You're going to need it."

I cemented my teeth together, refusing to ask him what he meant. I had asked enough questions, and no one ever gave me answers with any substance.

"Ready?" Devlin calmly asked me.

"No," I snarled.

"I'm warning you, this one will hurt." He rocked back and forth, taunting me. "Ready or not, here we go."

Every muscle in my body coiled, ready to spring on him if he moved forward even an inch. But he didn't move. The ground beneath me did. A circular hole opened up, fog rose around me, and I was sucked down, out of the library, and into darkness. Alone.

Gradually, my feet found a surface to stand on again, but I couldn't see anything. I strained my eyes, trying to find a clue that would tell me where I had gone. Had I traveled through another storyhole? Would Tom Sawyer or some other character show up to greet me?

A lock clicked, then a sliver of light appeared several feet in front of me. A door opened.

"Miss Zellar." His voice alone knocked the wind out of me.

I shuffled backward, needing to get away from him, but Kramer kept strutting toward me. My back pressed against the wall. I couldn't peel my focus from Kramer's bullish face, but now I could also see the small, gray room. The walls and floor were made of some sort of metal.

"Welcome to The Hub." Kramer grinned at me so sinisterly it kicked my heart into overdrive. "You were so close. You could have been out of Equatia forever. I didn't think you were so stupid."

I swallowed hard. I didn't know how I ended up in a room with him, but it was obvious he knew I was a traitor to my assignment.

He touched my neck and I held my breath. "Such a waste."

His hand traveled down my throat, then he ripped my collar, tearing the fabric as I cringed and fought back a whimper. My eyes were clenched shut. I didn't want to look at him. I wanted to pretend my worst fears weren't about to come true.

"There's what I need," he cooed. His stubby, disgusting fingers reached into my cleavage. His hand lingered on my chest. He was practically panting, and his breath smelled like rotten eggs. He touched one of my breasts, and I jerked away, but he yanked me back toward him. He squeezed me so hard that I yelped. With his other hand, he gripped me by the hair, forcing my face closer to his. "You can't win this fight, so don't bother trying."

I head-butted him. Our foreheads cracked loudly, and he let go, stumbling backward and cursing at me. I clutched my ripped tunic, but realized I was wearing a puffy suit. Only the gold fabric was torn. My V-neck tunic beneath it was still intact.

I ran for the door, but Kramer grabbed me and threw me down.

He wrestled me onto my back, and tried securing my arms as I swung wildly at him and kicked like a madwoman. I screamed at the top of my lungs for help. Kramer swore and grunted as my fists connected several times. I kneed him in the groin right before he straddled me and pinned my arms on either side of my head.

"You little bitch." He squeaked out in a strained voice. Sweat beaded on his wrinkled forehead, and his hair was splayed in every direction. I kept screaming for help.

His grip tightened around my wrists, then he slammed my arms against the floor several times. "Scream all you want. No one can hear you. And even if they could, they can't save you."

I bucked, thrashed, tried spitting on him. I fought and screamed until my throat was raw and my muscles shook. His weight crushed my lower half, and my legs were going numb. His grip on my wrists never loosened. If anything, it only strengthened.

He panted heavily, nearly out of breath. "Are you finished, you little brat?"

I didn't answer. Terrifying thoughts of what he was about to do made me gag and spit up on myself. Saliva dripped down the side of my face as Kramer leaned closer, his entire weight on top of me.

He pressed his nose against my neck and inhaled. "So that's what your fear smells like. Mmmm. Delicious."

Tears burned my eyes, but I refused to cry.

"Did your little Westin boy ever have you in this position?" He pushed his pelvis against mine, and nausea rolled through me like a tidal wave. "How many laws did you break for him? Was sex before marriage one of them?"

I grunted and squirmed again, unable to give up. I had to keep trying to get him off of me. I wouldn't stop until one of us was dead.

"I hate you," I hissed. I kept repeating it, discovering the mantra boosted my strength. We fought another round, and when Kramer pushed up to readjust himself, I seized the opportunity. Jerking my leg up with all my strength, I kneed him in the groin again.

A whoosh of air rushed out of him as he collapsed forward. I tried squirming out from under him, but he was too heavy. He sat up then slapped me so hard I thought my cheekbone shattered.

"This is no longer fun." He let go of one of my wrists and clawed at my chest again. But this time, it was quick, and there was a sharp tug on the back of my neck. Kramer had ripped off my necklace. He held it up for me to see. "This is much more valuable to me than your tainted body."

He stood warily, holding the crotch of his pants and grimacing. I sat up, scurrying backwards on my hands, my feet barely keeping up. Was he actually giving in? Had I somehow avoided being raped by the monster? I was certain that was his intention, but maybe my knee hits to his groin rendered his equipment inoperable.

He smoothed down his hair and wiped his brow, sneering at me. "I'm tempted to leave this memory for you. Perhaps I'll give it a different ending where I win. Wouldn't that be a nice slice of hell for you to relive over and over?"

I didn't fully understand what he meant, but I understood enough to make me shudder.

Kramer raised my necklace to his lips and kissed the quartz cross. "Finally, I have you. Now, I'll have all three of you." He chuckled in a menacing way. "Oh, the pleasure I'll have messing with your minds. Controlling you like my puppets."

What the glitch was he talking about?

Kramer contacted someone on his band and spoke into it. "We're done in here." He turned and limped toward the door. "I had one of them long ago. Did they tell you that?"

I didn't mean to reply. I didn't want to give him the satisfaction of me being interested in anything he said, but the word slipped from my lips. "What?"

"One of the Westin boys. It was so many years ago that I don't even remember which one. They looked so different back then."

Sickness unfurled deep within me. He couldn't mean what I think he meant.

Kramer smiled like a true psychotic pervert. "So young and innocent. I think he enjoyed it, but not as much as I did. He didn't put up a fight like you, but why would he? He was taught to respect and obey government officials. Just as you should have."

I sat there, shocked and horrified. It couldn't be true.

Kramer opened the door. I couldn't see who was on the other side, but he told them, "She's long overdue. Mind-strip her."

Level 5.6

For several strangled breaths, I sat in the same spot on the floor, paralyzed by Kramer's command: *Mind-strip her.*

I was about to become a drudge.

Fight, I told myself. *Get up and fight until you break out of here, or die trying.*

My body ached. I was exhausted and most likely suffering from shock, but I'd survive another hardcore battle with whomever walked in and attempted to strip away my life, memories, and free will. I'd win. My future depended on it.

Using the wall to brace myself, I managed to stand on my shaky legs, but my determination to fight drained out of me the second Devlin stepped into the room.

My chin dropped to my chest. I slumped against the wall, choking back a sob. "This can't be real."

Devlin closed the door then walked over to me and lifted my chin. "I wish with all my heart and soul that it wasn't."

My jaw trembled and tears pooled in my eyes. "You're really going to mind-strip me? That's why you brought me here?"

His voice soft and kind. "I would never do such a heinous thing to you. Or anyone for that matter." He continued with hatred filling his words. "Except maybe Kramer. Him, I'd do a lot worse than mind-strip."

"Then why are you here?" I clutched his wrist, desperate for it to be over. "Please tell me this isn't real. Tell me it's a cruel, ugly, terrible joke of a scenario."

"I can't tell you that."

"But Kramer just said he . . ." I couldn't say it out loud. The mental image of Kramer assaulting Xander or Devlin in such an intimate manner made me look away. "He said he did something unthinkable to you or Xander."

Devlin's arm quivered, and he tried pulling free, but I kept a gentle grip on him. I wanted him to know he could trust me.

His words were gravel grinding into my heart. "Unfortunately, that's true."

The pain and shame in his eyes revealed that he was the victim. I hated myself for being relieved that it hadn't been Xander. I hated Kramer a million times more for taking something so precious from an innocent person. And I hated Equatia for allowing one of its own officials to get away with such a deplorable crime.

A tear rolled down the side of my face. "How old were you?"

"Eleven."

A gasp lodged in my throat. I released my grip and gently held his hand in both of mine. "I'm so sorry."

His eyes were glassy, and his jaw tensed. "I survived. You will too."

"Survive what?"

"Kramer. Equatia. All of it."

"Not if they mind-strip me."

Devlin pulled his hand from mine and stepped back. "Do you know why I love VR so much?"

I shook my head.

"It's an escape," he said. "You have no idea how desperately I needed to escape my own thoughts and feelings after Kramer . . . did what he did to me. I've been escaping since I was eleven. *Eleven.*" His tone was so seething it left singe marks on my soul.

"I'm sorry, Devlin. "

"All those influential years that most kids spend developing friendships, having their first crush, first dates, and learning about the changes in their body and hormones. I spent all those years hiding and feeling ashamed. For the longest time, I didn't trust anyone except my family."

I couldn't think of anything appropriate to say. Nothing I said would comfort him. Nothing could change what had happened to him.

"Then, finally, I met someone I learned to trust. She was a VR addict like me. We loved fantasy worlds so much we designed programs for each other." Joy gleamed in his dark eyes as he talked about her. "Her name was Zane. She was beautiful inside and out. My first and only girlfriend."

I let the silence linger. I didn't want to ruin his bittersweet reminiscing.

He turned away and clasped his hands behind his head then sighed. "I miss her every day."

"What happened to her?"

He kept his back to me. "It doesn't matter. She's gone."

"I'm so sorry," I offered again, wishing I could heal his emotional scars.

He turned around and flashed me a fake grin. "Losing her forced me to improve my skills. I became a better programmer and designed tighter security methods. Hacking into systems became second nature to me."

My heart hurt for him. But I couldn't ignore the fact that we were locked in a weird metal room together. A room in which Kramer had attacked me and then ordered me to be mind-stripped. How did I go from that to standing around having a heart-to-heart about Devlin's past?

"What happens to us now?" I asked.

Devlin widened his stance and stuck his hands in his pockets. "Do you remember being at Higher Grounds when Jag explained how tarot cards and the Arcana worked?"

I thought back to my first night on the rooftop, sitting around the fire-pit table with Jag, Blaze, Awol, Xander, and at one point, a hologram of Devlin. "Yes."

"What did Jag tell you about using VR to educate and train the masses?"

I stared at the floor, trying to recall Jag's long winded rants. "He talked a lot that night. I can't remember everything he said."

"Think hard, Kelsey. Why do we use VR to educate and train the masses?"

I rubbed my temple. I knew the answer to this. I paid attention that night. Learning about the Arcana felt like such a privilege. I couldn't have forgotten the rules and explanations I had learned. I closed my eyes, picturing Jag on the edge of his seat, preaching passionately. And then his words came to me. I recited them out loud. "Put someone into a different world using VR and let them figure out how to survive."

"Yes. And what did they teach you about curators?"

"Curators," I repeated quietly, remembering that conversation more easily. "They said they were all curators and could help me out of a bad situation."

"Correct. So choose one of them to help you out of this dreadful situation."

I glanced around the room. "Why can't you help me? You're already here."

"I'm swords. I've done my part. You need a different suit."

"I don't understand."

"Yes, you do. The answers are deep within you. All you have to do is follow your instincts."

"No." I stepped closer to him, lifting my chin so we were eye to eye. "Don't come in here and pretend to bond emotionally with me over a traumatic event in your past and then go back to dodging my questions and jerking me around."

"I'm trying to help you."

"Then tell me who I need to get me out of here!"

"Ask the cards for guidance."

Anger boiled inside of me. "I'm asking *you* for guidance."

"I'm not the one they are about to mind-strip. Only you can figure out what and who you need." The lock to the door clicked open. Devlin backed away from me. "They're coming Kelsey. You better hurry."

My heart nearly leaped out of my chest. "No, don't leave me here."

The door opened, and I turned, watching wide-eyed as four male drudges marched inside and shut the door behind them. I reached to my side for Devlin, but he had vanished.

One of the drudges crept forward holding a high-tech wand. "This can be easy or difficult. The choice is yours."

"Please don't do this," I begged, knowing it was hopeless. Drudges had been mind-stripped and reprogrammed by the government. They were devoid of most human emotions.

None of them replied. The other three surrounded me as the one who had spoken activated a sphere of colored light on the end of his wand. I couldn't stop staring at the light. Even as one of the drudges secured my hands behind my back, I didn't move or blink.

That quickly, and that easily, my mind-stripping process had begun.

Level 5.7

I always imagined mind-stripping to be excruciating. They removed all your memories, any feelings or emotions that might make you vulnerable or unpredictable, basically erasing the essence of what makes you human. That had to be painful, right?

Except it wasn't. Physically, there were tingles. Slight buzzing sensations in my scalp, my sinuses, behind my eyes, but nothing more. Mentally, I was in a trance. I didn't even think about my family. I wasn't scared, or sad. I was *nothing.*

I lay on the floor, motionless as the drudges moved around me, poking, prodding, scanning, and waving tools around me. Using a small, sharp blade, one drudge made an incision behind my right ear. I felt no pain whatsoever. I didn't even flinch. With a large pair of tweezers, he parted my flesh and removed a tiny white and silver chip.

Astonished, I muttered, "What the glitch?"

And then I separated from myself. Literally.

A second version of me formed. A version that was the opposite of nothing. A version that was so mentally and physically aware of what was happening to me that I thought I would burst. My heart pumped harder than ever, my pulse beat so fast I could feel it in my fingertips. One drudge waved something over my eyes, and my lungs screamed in pain. I didn't know whether to breathe in or out, so a frantic combination of the two forced my chest to seize.

Fight, I commanded myself. *Get up and fight.*

I scrambled to standing, screaming and swinging at the drudges as the room spun.

I stumbled forward, planting my feet to stop myself from collapsing back onto the ground. Shaking my head to clear my blurry vision, I slowly turned around.

The drudges hadn't even noticed me. They still flitted around doing their work.

Working on *me.*

Looking down at myself, I patted my chest and arms. I felt solid, and I was hyper-aware of every raging emotion and physical sensation in my body, so I had to be real. But the version of me sprawled out on the floor being mind-stripped looked real too.

"Hey," I called quietly, half-afraid the drudges would hear me and throw me onto the floor. But none of them responded, so I shouted, "Can you hear me?"

Not one reaction. I rushed forward, determined to knock one of them down. I wanted to stop them from mind-stripping me. Instead, I ran right through the guy. I even stepped on myself. Not exactly *on* myself, my feet passed through my legs and torso as if I were a ghost.

I stepped away, circling the drudges. Even though I knew they'd pass through me, I still moved aside every time one of them almost bumped into me. I helplessly watched them mind-strip the other me, the me who wasn't putting up one ounce of fight. I was disgusted with myself, until I remembered being in that position moments ago and feeling nothing, being able to do nothing. Sympathy for my other self seeped into me.

Eventually, the drudges finished their job. They packed up their equipment and marched out of the room as calmly as they entered.

My other self just laid on the floor, staring at the ceiling.

I walked over and gazed down at her—at me. "I don't understand this. It's a VR scenario, right?"

She didn't blink. I didn't expect her to answer, but we were the only two bodies in the room, and talking to her made me feel less alone. I glanced around, hoping Devlin might have returned to give me answers or whisk me away to the next scenario.

Before he disappeared, he had wanted me to remember what Jag said. *Put someone into a different world using VR, and let them figure out how to survive.*

That meant this was a VR test so I would learn how to survive. He had said I needed a curator to help me out of the situation. But which one? He was swords, and he couldn't help me, so neither could Jag. Xander was pentacles. As much as I wanted Xander to appear and whisk me away, my instincts told me that's not who I needed. I closed my eyes, picturing Blaze and Awol.

Awol's dreadlocks and facial features became vividly clear, almost as if I were looking at a CGI version of her. She held up a tarot card, and I flinched at the sight of it. *The Devil.* She held up another, sliding it between her fingers so it sat beside the ominous card. It said *The Tower,* and the image was detailed, but she didn't give me enough time to study it before revealing two more cards, upside down, in her other hand. I tilted my head so I could read *The Star* and *The Moon.*

I blinked and found myself still standing in the strange metal room, the other version of me on the floor at my feet. Awol was gone.

I closed my eyes again, expecting to see her and the cards, but no matter how hard I tried, I couldn't visualize her.

"Awol," I called, searching the private darkness of my clenched-shut eyelids. "I need your help."

At first, the music was so faint I thought I'd imagined it, but the volume gradually increased, along with the murmurs of conversations behind me and the hissing of brewing machines. The aroma of coffee comforted me before I even opened my eyes.

"Kelsey, welcome, welcome, welcome." Awol stood on the other side of the counter from where I sat. She poured pink cream into a glass mug, preparing one of her famous concoctions.

Higher Grounds was still perfect. The people, the smell, the music, the rich fabrics and colorful decor. I sighed happily. "Is Xander here?"

She smirked and one of her brows rose. "This isn't the time for romance. You came here to see me, and for an important reason. So concentrate."

"You know I'm here to see you?"

“Of course.” She topped the coffee she was making with whipped cream, then shaved pieces of fresh chocolate on top of that. My mouth watered as she finished it by placing two raspberries on the rim of the glass. She wiped her hands on her apron, then set the masterpiece in front of me. “Do you remember where you came from?”

“Yes, I was—” I blanked. My lips were parted as I stared at the bottles and pitchers behind Awol. Where had I just been? With Devlin? No. With Keekee? I shook my head. “This is weird. Suddenly, I can’t remember.”

She motioned to the drink between us. “Drink up.”

I wrapped my hands around the warm mug and took a sip. The whipped cream tickled the tip of my nose, but the flavor was delicious. “You make the best drinks I’ve ever tasted.”

She bowed with flair. “Many thanks.”

I sipped again and again, unable to get enough of the decadent drink.

Awol watched me, grinning as she wiped down the counter and machines. “How are you feeling?”

“Good.”

“How’s everything going with your mission?”

“My mission?” Hazy hints of the government swept through my mind, but Awol was probably referring to the Arcana. “You mean my training?”

“Sure, we’ll start there. How’s training going?”

“Pretty well, I think.”

“Which scenarios have you recently completed?”

I tried remembering the last card I received, or the most recent storyhole I experienced. I scanned Awol’s red and black outfit. I remembered seeing her as a CGI character. She had showed me four tarot cards. I listed them as each one popped into my mind. “The Devil, The Tower, The Star, and The Moon.”

Awol’s eyes widened as her head bobbed forward. “Really? All four of those at once?”

“Two were right-side up, the other two were upside down.”

“I see.” She fiddled with the ends of her braids. “Who gave them to you?”

“No one gave them to me, but you showed them to me.”

Awol inhaled deeply and leaned on the counter in front of me but didn't say anything.

"What does that mean?" I asked.

"It means you're ready for the emotional part of your journey, which is the most important part." She swung her braids behind her shoulders. "But I'm biased. If Blaze were here, she'd tell you the spiritual part is most important."

"But Blaze isn't here."

"Right. You chose me this time, so I'll help you through this."

This time? I tried remembering another time I might have chosen one of them and came up with nothing. However, I was woefully aware that my mind wasn't working as well as it should. I refocused on what Awol had said and asked her, "Help me through what?"

"The emotional impact of The Devil and Tower, and then the next wave of different emotions caused by The Star and Moon."

I fought back a tired sigh. "I don't understand a word you're saying."

She placed her hand on top of mine. "I know, but you will. You chose to conquer your emotions this time. That means you're ready for an awakening. And when that storm hits, I'll help you survive it."

"Survive what?"

"The truth."

My heart clenched, warning me I was venturing into dangerous territory.

"Come on," she said, untying her apron and hanging it on a wall peg behind her. "We're going to the rooftop."

I downed the rest of my drink as she walked out from behind the counter. I stood, and she linked my arm with hers, guiding me toward the stairway.

"Why the rooftop?"

She paused at the bottom of the steps and faced me. Her eyes were warm and caring, but I also detected a hint of worry. "Because sometimes, fantasy is the only way to survive reality."

Level 5.8

We climbed the steps, cruised through the second floor with its lush black and gold carpet, passed the curtained reading room, and then Awol opened a door that led to a spiral staircase.

"You first," she insisted.

I stepped carefully, placing my foot on each narrow platform and holding onto the rail that wound its way to the top.

"Do you know what's up here?" Awol asked from not too far behind me.

"Journeyers," I answered. And how could I forget the most impressive part? "And storyholes."

"Good."

I pushed the door open and stepped onto the rooftop made of book covers. Awol joined me. Same as my last visit, groups of people sat around holding tarot cards and passionately discussing stories, journeys, and characters. I searched every gathering area, every group, every face, but didn't see Xander anywhere.

"Ready to peruse?" Awol asked me.

"Sure," I said, excited at the idea of diving into another story. "Same as before, right?"

"Same as before, but with a different outcome." She turned toward an expansive area where no people were gathered. Only book covers stretched out in front of us. "Go ahead. Find the one you need."

I randomly stepped onto a classical romance, but felt nothing, so I kept moving. Winding side to side, I waited to feel a pull or sensation that would assure me I had found the one. After a few minutes, I glanced back at Awol. "Do you know which one it might be?"

She grinned. “I’m hopeful, but I can’t interfere.”

I continued stepping from one cover to the next. Throwing my head back, I looked up at the stars shining in the evening sky. Quietly, I asked, “Please guide me.”

I closed my eyes, basking in the starlight. Envious that the stars were far, far away from Equatia, free to shine however and whenever they wished. A flash of a man’s face made me rock backward. I had seen him before. Maybe many times. I felt a connection to him. The Emperor? I kept moving, but I shut my eyes, letting my other senses guide me.

I sidestepped to my right and my entire body jerked from the powerful current that rushed through me. I dropped to a crouch, needing to touch the cover.

Bridge to Tarotbeatequatia.

I smirked at the silly, not-so-subtle title. My gaze lifted to meet Awol’s. Even though I never saw or heard her move, she stood directly over me.

“Really?” I asked. “Tarot beat Equatia? Someone couldn’t have thought of a better title?”

She grinned, her eyes glimmering with even more positivity than usual. “It’s one of my all-time favorites.”

“Is this the one you hoped would choose me?”

“It’s the one we’ve all been hoping for.”

I scooted back and opened the large cover. Inside, a foggy storyhole awaited me. I took a deep breath. “Ready or not.”

“Here you go.” She pumped her fist in the air.

I laughed at her, swung my feet over the edge, and jumped in.

After falling through darkness, a solid surface formed under my feet. Bursts of light flashed in my peripheral vision. I blinked them away and shook my tingling hands. Staring at my fingernails, I watched them change from short and clean to long and dirty, over and over, until more bursts of light forced me to close my eyes.

The ground beneath me moved like a conveyor belt, and I swayed, trying to keep my balance. When I stopped, I was standing on the edge of a cliff. Xander stood across from me on the other side like a gallant and breathtaking mirage.

My fingers flexed uncontrollably, aching to touch him.

Far below us was a pink river. Behind me was a field with sprouting plants and crops that looked like they were struggling to thrive.

On Xander's side was a lush green landscape filled with gorgeous trees, flowers, and waterfalls. We stared at each other from the edges of our cliffs.

From above me, Awol's voice echoed, "You aren't able to see the whole picture yet, and he can't tell you what's real, but you'll know it when you feel it."

I looked up at the sky as if I might see Awol peering down at us from a storyhole in the clouds, but Xander and I were alone.

"Is that where you want to be?" Xander asked from across the great divide separating us. He should have been shouting so I could hear him across the river roaring below, but he spoke at a normal level and somehow I heard him fine.

"How do I get there?"

"Make the leap."

I stepped closer to the edge. A piece of the cliff broke away beneath me. The drop must have been at least a hundred feet. The river's current was so strong there were whitecaps. "What if I can't make it that far?"

"I told you there would come a point when I'd tell you to jump. A time when you'd have to leap far and fast. That moment is here, and it's critical to your survival."

His words, and what they implied, ricocheted between us. Everything that had happened since I met Xander seemed impossible, some of it terrifying, some of it magical and amazing, some real and some VR, but through it all, I trusted him. I trusted him with my safety, my mind, and my emotions.

He stepped to the edge of his side. A vine snapped free from a plant and dropped over the ledge, swinging back and forth. It triggered a memory.

"I've been here before," I said. "I remember being here and having this conversation."

"I'm proud and impressed."

"I'm right, right? I'm not crazy? We've done this already?"

"Yes, a few times."

"Of course. This isn't real." My confident gaze met his narrowing eyes. "It's another one of your programs."

"Yes, but it's important in helping you understand yourself and learning the truth."

"The truth about what?"

"Everything." Xander's voice resonated deep within me, but his lips didn't move. His words were a memory replaying in my mind. *If I enlighten you with information, even if you find it hard to believe, you absorb it as fact unless your instincts tell you otherwise.*

I believed I could jump and make it to the other side, but even if I didn't, I trusted Xander would catch me if I fell. "I trust you."

He held out his arms like he was confident I'd land in them. "Then make the leap."

Taking a few steps back so I could get a running start, I breathed deep, ignoring the doubtful whispers in the back of my mind. My mind could be my tricked and fooled, but my instincts would never lead me wrong.

My eyes locked with Xander's.

He waved his fingers, motioning for me to jump to him. "I believe in you."

I ran forward. The dirt and gravel crunched and shifted with every step of my bare feet. I crouched midstride and pushed as hard as I could off the edge. My face tilted toward the sky, my back arched as my hands flew out at my sides like wings, and for several precious, breathtaking seconds, I soared.

The wind rushed through my hair. My pulse hammered between my ears. I inhaled the sweet scent of flowers and fresh air.

And much too soon, I landed. My knees buckled from the hard impact, but Xander caught and steadied me.

"You did it." He hugged me tight against his chest.

"I did it!" I gasped, adrenaline pumping through me so hard I trembled. "I made it."

"I knew you would." He lifted my chin and kissed me so sweetly that my knees went weak again.

Awol's voice echoed behind me. "Here comes the hard part."

My eyes flew open, and I pulled away from Xander. "Why did she say that?"

"Why did who say what?"

Dark clouds rolled through the sky impossibly fast.

"Kelsey?" Awol called. "Are you still with me?"

I spun in place, searching for her. I thought I spotted her darting behind a tree, but then multiple shadowy figures blurred around me. And I knew.

He had found us.

"Alexander Westin!" Kramer boomed from behind me.

His voice sent chills down my spine and through my toes, anchoring me to the ground with fear. I didn't turn around right away. I didn't want him to really be there.

I looked at Xander. Hatred filled his eyes, his nostrils flared, and his jaw tensed so hard it could have been made of stone. "Kramer's here."

I grabbed Xander's hand and turned, knowing we could face him together.

Level 5.9

Kramer skulked on the other side of the divide, almost in the same spot where I stood moments ago.

His dreadful voice vibrated across the valley. "Where is her chip?"

"How would I know? You stripped her."

"Not the original. I want its cleverly manufactured twin."

"What is he talking about?" I whispered to Xander.

They silently glared at each other for the longest time. They were both coiled and rigid, like at any moment, one or both of them might spring across the gap and attack.

Xander spoke first, but he didn't answer me. He addressed Kramer. "Do you want to explain it to her, or should I?"

"Equatia law mandates citizens must remain unaware of the protocol for their own protection. Give me her other chip, and in exchange I'll guarantee you and your brother a transfer from our nation."

"As long as those chips exist, you and this abysmal country won't ever free anyone." Xander lurched forward. "Humans are not for you to control!"

"Equatia citizens are protected by their government."

"Equatia citizens are *imprisoned* by their government!"

"I don't have time for this insubordination! Turn yourself in and surrender her chip or you will be charged with mutiny."

Xander chuckled. "You can't charge me with anything if you can't find me. The big bad wolf has lost some of the sheep." His grip tightened on my hand. His muscles flexed so hard, I flexed my own. "It's because we're not sheep anymore, Kramer. We've become lions. Lions trump wolves."

Kramer's eyes flared with rage. "You can't begin to fathom the ways we can destroy you."

"Keep hunting, Kramer." Xander sounded so threatening, it made my insides ripple with pride. "But don't be surprised when *you* become the hunted."

Black cords sprouted from Kramer's feet, spiraling into the air and stretching across the gap. My heart plummeted into the river below us.

"Let's go." Xander tugged my hand and we started running.

We dashed toward the line of lush trees. He was fast, but I kept up. "Where are we going?"

"Someplace he can't find us."

Xander darted left, and we ended up behind a towering, thick tree. He pressed his hand against the bark and a doorway of light formed. He ushered me inside, following right behind me. We stood at the bottom of a spiral staircase, similar to the one at Higher Grounds, but these steps were made of wood.

Xander sealed the door shut behind us as I started climbing.

"Where does this lead?" I asked, unable to see the top.

"I'm not sure yet."

His answer made me nervous, but I kept moving.

Below me, Devlin asked, "Where are you?"

I stopped and looked down, seeing Xander's band glowing with Devlin's face on the screen. Xander said, "X-17–4. Unfinished tree gateway."

"Seventeen?" Devlin sounded shocked. "You cycled the cards way too fast."

Xander nearly ran into the back of me. His eyes met mine, and he genuinely smiled. "She was ready. She made the jump."

Devlin spoke quickly. "I'm programming a patch at the top of the stairway. Hurry. I haven't located the breach."

Xander nudged me forward so I climbed the stairs again.

Xander told Devlin, "Jump-drive us to X-18–4."

"You said it still had bugs."

"I worked on them. It will suffice for now."

Somewhat out of breath and seeing no end to our climb, I asked, "Please tell me what's going on. What chips was Kramer talking about? And what are you and Devlin doing?"

"I'll explain when we get out of this stairway."

I halted in place, needing to rest and catch my breath, but more importantly, needing a straight answer. "Tell me now, or I'm not taking another step."

He looked irritated, but he glanced down the stairs and then explained. "Quick summary. Every child born in Equatia is kept from their parents for three days. Do you know why?"

"Observation," I answered. "We receive immunizations."

"No. More lies. It's because they insert a chip into every citizen. The chip is behind your ear every second of every day, and it's always recording. If and when the government needs to know your thoughts, or what you've done, they have access."

I touched my ear, horrified by the thought of such an intrusive procedure, and an even more intrusive existence. "Why does he want my chip?"

"Because you have valuable information he needs."

Black cords slithered up the handrail far below us.

"He's close," I said, hurrying up the steps again as Xander followed.

"Devlin and I were coordinating a plan to get you and me away from Kramer." Blue light illuminated the stairway several steps above us. "And there's our exit, so let's go."

I climbed two more steps. Four more and I'd be standing in the doorway of light. The black cords crept closer. "My chip is still in me, right?"

"No, he has it."

I turned and gaped at him, momentarily frozen with disbelief.

Xander lifted me off my feet, carrying me the last two steps. "But we designed another chip that overrides it."

Before I could reply, black cords wrapped around Xander's torso and neck. His face blurred, forming multiple versions of him overlapping each other.

Every version of him spoke at the same time. "I was wrong, Kelsey. It's not in the cards for us."

"No!"

He was yanked backward, but I held onto him.

Together, we fell down the dark stairway, toppling over each other as our bodies slammed against the walls and railings, breaking almost every wooden step on our way down. And possibly all of our bones.

When we finally stopped, I was a crumpled heap of aching bones and muscles. I gasped for breath, clutching my stomach and chest as I rolled onto my back. I reached all around me, feeling for Xander, but only felt the metal floor beneath me.

I was no longer in the stairway.

A door opened several feet away, and dim light poured into the dark room.

“No, please no,” I begged, trying to deny the familiar sickness washing over me. I didn’t want to be back in the metal room as Kramer’s prisoner. But I was.

“Miss Zellar.” His voice alone knocked the wind out of me.

I sat up and shuffled backward, but Kramer kept strutting toward me. My back pressed into the wall behind me.

“Welcome to the new and improved version of this memorable encounter.” Kramer grinned, kicking my heart into overdrive. “You were so close. They thought they could hide you forever. I didn’t think they were that stupid.”

I swallowed hard. I didn’t know how I ended up with him, but it was obvious I was about to battle for my life again.

“Such a waste.” He touched my neck, and I held my breath. “Go ahead, try to fight me off this time.”

His hand traveled down my throat, then he ripped my collar, tearing the fabric deep and wide, exposing my bra. I tried lifting my arms to hit him, but I couldn’t. I couldn’t even make a finger or toe wiggle.

His eyes glistened with sick excitement. “Looks like I’m the one in control this time.”

I was about to relive the nightmare, but now I was paralyzed. I tried head-butting him, spitting on him, anything, but I was completely immobile. This time he’d succeed with his mission.

His stubby, disgusting fingers traced the edge of my bra. His hands lingered on my chest. He was panting as he pressed his body against me and squeezed my breasts. “You can’t win this time. Try to enjoy it as much as I will.”

I tried screaming, but failed. I wanted to knee him, break his nose, anything to get him off of me. His filthy hands rubbed down the front of me, and he finished ripping what was left of my tunic.

He tossed it aside while eyeing my exposed upper body and licking his lips. “My pretty young puppet. I’m going to be generous and give you your voice back so you can scream. It will make this so much more enjoyable.”

And then, like a magic button had been switched on, I felt my vocal chords.

I screamed at the top of my lungs, hoping someone would hear me and burst into the room to save me.

“Scream all you want. No one can hear you.” He yanked down my pants.

“No!” I begged. “Don’t do this!”

He spun me around and shoved the side of my face against the wall.

I screamed so loud my throat should have been raw, but I kept shrieking, yelling for help, begging him to stop.

He kicked my feet wider apart, then pinned my arms behind my back and pressed his vile lips against my ear. “If it helps, you can pretend I’m your precious Westin boy, but bigger and better.”

My worst nightmare was about to come true, and I could do nothing except scream.

His weight crushed against my back, and his grip on my wrists tightened. “Save this one so you can relive it over and over.”

Bright lights flashed all around me.

My screaming faded. A faint voice called my name from somewhere far away. The wall Kramer had me pinned against disappeared and I fell forward, landing hard on a floor.

Another light flashed so brightly, it burned my eyes. I clenched my lids tight as surges of icy cold rushed through my limbs.

Above me, Awol’s voice grew louder. She kept shouting, “Abort!”

“I’ve got her!” Devlin said frantically from somewhere beside me. “She’s back.”

Another voice, maybe Blaze, asked, “What the hell happened?”

With every inch of my body tense and aching, I pushed myself up onto my shaking hands and knees. The floor beneath me was shiny white and rocking like a seesaw. I threw up pure liquid.

"Everyone shut up!" Devlin commanded in a hushed tone. "Dim the lights."

I backed up, not wanting to crawl through my own vomit, but my arms gave out, and I face-planted onto the floor.

"Kelsey, stop moving," Devlin said quietly. "Stay still."

I couldn't stay still. In my mind, I was still fleeing from Kramer. He would find me any second if I didn't keep moving.

"You're suffering from AWS," Devlin said. "Alternate World Syndrome. You have to rest."

More spasms ripped through my stomach and chest, forcing me to curl into a ball.

Devlin crouched by my side. His tone was gentle and caring. "I'm so sorry. I'll never let that happen again."

A circular robot rolled toward me, stopping in front of my face. I rolled away from it, letting my back sink against the hard floor as I struggled to breathe. The room was dimly lit, but I could still see the white ceiling with a speaker in the center.

Tears pooled, blurring my vision. I blinked them away, but every time my lids closed, Kramer's face haunted me.

Kramer hadn't raped me. I knew that as true and deep as my hatred for him. But I remembered the first time—the real time—I fought off Kramer, when he told me what he had done to Devlin.

As I lay there, sick and in shock, looking up at Devlin, I saw the depth of his emotional scars reflected in his glassy eyes. I heard the anguish in his voice as he said, "I wouldn't have wished that scenario on my worst enemy."

A sob escaped my throat and tears rolled down the side of my face. I cried for Devlin, and for me. Because I remembered not only Kramer's sick confession, but also what happened afterward—when he ordered drudges to mind-strip me.

My voice shook. "It really happened."

"No," Devlin tried assuring me. "He hacked into your mind and programmed it to feel real, but I swear, he didn't—"

"Not that," I said, struggling to keep it together. He may not have physically raped me, but he violated me in a way just as bad, maybe worse. The words were hard to say. "I was mind-stripped."

Devlin's sadness was tangible. I felt it radiate off him and into me. "But you remember it," he said tenderly. "That's the first step to recovery."

I expected him to comfort me. To hold my hand, assure me it would be okay, anything to help me cope with the brutal realization I was trying to process. Then I realized it wasn't his comfort I craved. It was Xander's.

Why wasn't he by my side instead of Devlin? A fire-breathing dragon clawed its way up my throat, warning me not to ask, but I pushed it back into its cave and croaked out, "Where is he?"

Devlin's shoulders slumped forward. He looked up at someone behind me—probably Awol—and circled his finger in the air.

"The Lovers," he said somberly. "Run D-6–5."

Awol's voice crackled through the speaker. "Are you sure she doesn't need replenishment first?"

Devlin reached toward my face, but his fingers hovered in place, never actually touching me. "What she needs is Xander. Run it. Now."

Streaks of colored light filled the room, and then dozens of tarot cards fell from above. One landed in the palm of my open hand. I didn't need to look to know it was The Lovers card. I felt its power instantly connect me to Xander.

"Thank you," I whispered to Devlin. "We believe in you."

Just before I closed my eyes, he smiled in a way that soothed my soul. "Don't forget that fact."

6: THE LOVERS

Level 6.1

Devlin had ordered me into a VR program, and I didn't argue. In fact, his words drifted through me like a lullaby lulling me into a dream I'd been begging to experience. *What she needs is Xander.*

Eyes closed, I was almost fully immersed. The colored lights filling the immersion room were fading, transitioning me to my desired location. Xander. But somewhere in between, I was surprised to hear Jag say, "Xander's getting worse. He needs help."

Me, I thought. *He needs me.*

My eyes flew open. Devlin stood above me but stared straight ahead. He was transparent, and fading much too fast. My fingers clawed at the shiny white floor I was lying on, trying to stay connected to reality. I called out, "Devlin!"

He looked down at me, appearing shocked, but I couldn't be sure because what was left of his ghostly form vanished.

Darkness cloaked the room in the time it took me to sit up.

Physically, I clutched the blanket covering me. Figuratively, I clutched onto any and all details of what had just happened. The room was too dark to see anything, but the plush mattress and soft, luxurious linens revealed I was in Xander's bed. Alone.

Where was he?

Deep down, some part of me whispered an answer I didn't want to hear. He was getting worse. He needed me, but I couldn't reach him. "Why?" I asked aloud. "Where is he?"

I pounded my palm against my temple. *Think, Kelsey. Where is he?*

I hated myself for not knowing. I needed to remember. Bone-chilling flashes of Kramer attacking me surged through me. I stiffened at the realization that it had actually happened. My hand flew to my chest as I thought about Devlin and what he had endured.

My whole world was caving in on my head (or maybe inside of it) and all I could think was how much I hated Kramer for mind-stripping me.

A delayed gasp lodged in my throat. I had been mind-stripped.

Truth, I told myself. Harsh, unfortunate, and unthinkable, but me being mind-stripped was most definitely real.

So much of my confusion finally made sense. Or at least the lack of it making sense now had a logical explanation. My life, all my memories, my ability to think and act for myself, had all been ripped away from me.

"But I remember," I whispered.

Devlin's words flooded me with hope. *That's the first step to recovery.*

"Recovery." My consciousness was a fragile glass box that could be shattered at any moment. I needed to build walls to protect it.

My eyes had adjusted to the darkness. I was in the warehouse bedroom, and I could sense Xander nearby. I threw off the covers and scurried out of bed, toward the stairs. The main floor was dimly lit. As I tiptoed down each step, I saw the only light on was over the kitchen stove. I cleared the last step and checked the couch, but it was empty. I turned, intending to search Xander's office or library, but I relaxed when I saw him in his thinking place.

I crept toward the hammock and studied his sleeping face. He looked so tranquil. I didn't want to wake him, but I couldn't resist touching him. My fingers trailed down his forearm, and I happily sighed at the solidity of him. He stirred and opened his eyes, then he reached up and brushed his knuckles against my cheek.

I didn't give him a chance to speak.

"I want this to be real. This," I said. "Right here with you. Please tell me this moment is reality, and I can stay here with you forever."

His sleepy voice was gruff. "Kelsey—"

"Tell me." I climbed into the hammock beside him. "Tell me being here with you, feeling happy and unafraid, assure me that it's real and won't ever end."

His Adam's apple bobbed, and he looked away for a long moment then met my gaze again. He brushed my hair behind my ear. "You and me, our connection to each other, that's always real."

I kissed him, desperately wanting to convince myself he hadn't told me a twisted version of the truth. I touched his face, grinning at the feel of his baby-smooth skin against my fingertips. "Not fiction," I said. "We aren't fiction. This isn't a game. You're not a character in some VR scenario."

His lips twitched and he glanced at the ceiling. "What if the universe is one massive console, and we're all players in a never-ending game?"

"That would be beyond cruel."

He adjusted so he could look me in the eye. "Why would it be cruel?"

"Why would a universal game creator, or whatever, put us through that?"

"What if we put ourselves through it? Maybe we chose this existence."

I shook my head. "Choose to exist with monsters like Kramer? Never. No one would choose that."

"Countless people have chosen much worse."

I scoffed. "Worse than Kramer? No, you can't convince me of that."

"Think about gamers. They have many games to choose from. They play what appeals to them, whether it's a mysterious world of witches and wizards, hopping along a path of magical mushrooms and riding rainbows, or stalking a battlefield while being sprayed by dozens of bullets. The options are endless, but they aren't all fun. Yet many choose to endanger themselves when they become a character in a game."

"Right. A game. Not reality."

"What if that's the same concept as our universe and life, except on a much larger scale? The place we all came from, and the place we all return to when we die—just like in games—isn't the true end. It's the place where we reflect on how well we played. We sort through all the other possible games, all the possible scenarios of existence, and we choose our next adventure. And maybe replay a favorite because we didn't get it right on our first try, or our hundredth. Maybe we never even make it past the first level, but we enjoy the challenge, or the addiction, so we keep playing until we grow bored and move onto another choice. Another game. Another existence."

"Wow." I ran my finger across his forehead. "Your mind is magnificently twisted."

"So is yours."

I kissed his chin then expanded on his theory. "Let's say you're right, and the universe is one big never-ending game. Would you keep choosing me as your teammate?"

His smile grew bigger. "Without a doubt."

"Even if you had to keep stalking a battlefield and taking dozens of bullets for me?"

"Child's play. I'd endure much worse than that to be with you."

I laughed. "Well, if we do get to choose, let's agree on the magical mushroom and rainbow slide option. It sounds much more fun."

"I agree wholeheartedly."

We grinned at each other for several seconds, gazing into each other's eyes like the cheesiest of characters in a romance novel.

His next words shocked me. "Let's pledge ourselves to each other."

"What, like marriage?"

"No. I hate Equatia and their idea of what a marriage should be. We'll make our own pledge. No government involved."

"I don't know whether I love that idea because it's rebelling against the system, or because I love you so glitching much."

His cheeks turned an adorable shade of pink. "Please do it for the latter."

I hoped Mom and Dad would approve. They had to. He meant the world to me. "Okay."

"Okay? Is that your official answer?"

"I'm not sure. Did you officially ask me?"

"I don't know how to ask since we haven't given it a name."

"Let's call it—" I closed my eyes, searching for the perfect name. "Joined."

"We're *joined?*" Xander's face bunched up. "Sounds like we've been accepted into a pretentious club. How about . . ." He thought, but not long enough because the best he came up with was, ". . . united?"

It was my turn to make a sour face. "United was the name of a major airline during The Crash. We all know how that ended. Feels like a bad omen."

"Good point."

I reflected back on our relationship and everything we had been through together: how important the Arcana was to both of us, how VR played such an important role in our lives and our future. Then, I thought about the first time Xander kissed me, and how our bond felt so hardwired and unbreakable. "I've got it!"

His brows lifted, waiting for me to declare a proper and worthy title. "So, spill it. What shall we label our commitment to each other?"

I grinned so big my cheeks hurt. I held his hand, entwining my fingers with his. "Linked."

"Perfect." He squeezed my hand and pulled me closer to him. "Kelsey Zellar, will you link with me until one of us breathes a final breath?"

I shook my head. "That's not long enough. It has to be forever."

"Deal."

To solidify the deal, we kissed. Long and passionately. I felt relieved to be committed to my one and only. Exes and book boyfriends were now history. My present and future were, and always would be, Alexander Westin.

I snuggled up against him and rested my head on his chest. *Save this one to memory,* I thought. *It's a happy one.*

I squeezed Xander's arm and pushed myself up so I could look at him. We swayed gently. "Why do I need to save this? Why did I just think that?"

He squinted, shaking his head. "Think what?"

I leaned farther away from him, confused by my own thoughts. *Linked, linked, linked.*

Bright lights flooded the warehouse, and I leaned too far back, falling out of the hammock and landing flat on my back.

Level 6.2

Xander's deep, sexy voice coaxed me awake. "Kels, are you sleeping?"

A night sky filled with twinkling stars formed a canopy above me. I was on the rooftop of Higher Grounds. I remembered sprawling out and wishing for the safety of my family, but I must have dozed off.

Xander sat beside me and ran his fingers through my hair. "I like watching you sleep out here, bathing in the possibilities of the future."

"*Our* future." I lifted my head and rested it on his thigh. He was always so warm and comfortable. Custom-made for me.

"Did you have any dreams?"

"Yes, about our linking day and the dress I'll wear." My scalp tingled as his fingers worked their usual magic.

"You're wearing a dress?" He sounded surprised but delighted.

"An Olden gown with a billowy skirt and off-the-shoulder sleeves made from ivory rose petals."

His thigh muscle tightened against the back of my neck. "I see. So I guess that means we aren't getting linked until we're out of Equatia?"

I rolled over and sat up on my knees. "It doesn't mean that. We don't have to wait."

"You have access to an Olden dress like that?"

"Well, no, but I could probably make one."

He licked his lips then bit the bottom one, suppressing a smile. "And where will you find the material for a billowy skirt and rose petal sleeves?"

I narrowed my eyes. "You're a real dream stealer, you know that?"

He laughed, then stood and held out his hand. "Come on. I want to show you something."

I placed my hand in his, and he pulled me to my feet. "What is it?"

"You'll see."

We strolled along the rooftop of book covers. I wondered where we were going, but then he stopped and turned to face me. My insides danced with anticipation. I felt lightheaded, like I had gorged on a dozen joy enhancement candies.

He didn't say anything, so when I couldn't take any more of the excitement rippling through me, I asked, "Well? What are you showing me?"

Still holding my hands, he stepped back and motioned to the space between us.

I looked down and saw that I stood on a sparkling book cover. Craning my neck to read the title, I squealed with glee. I dropped to my knees and traced the glowing infinity symbol. "*Circles within Circles*," I read aloud. "*The Kindrily's Book of Inner Secrets*."

I wanted to pick it up and hug it to my chest, but I knew I couldn't. But because I couldn't, that meant. . . I gingerly lifted the corner of the cover and peeked inside. My hand flew to my mouth. "It's a storyhole!"

"Slightly altered and brilliantly disguised, but yes."

I stroked the cover again in disbelief. "But the author never wrote this book. She and the family agreed the world should continue believing they were fictional."

"Just because a book wasn't published doesn't mean it wasn't written." He shrugged. "Okay, truth be told, M helped me with most of the details."

I stared at him agape. Then I looked at the cover again. My instincts were gnawing at me to dive inside. Xander had given me the perfect gift at a time when I needed it the most. I grabbed his hand and pulled him down to me. He kneeled, and I threw my arms around him, devouring him with kisses. Between kisses I managed, "I have to go."

“I know.” He brushed his lips lightly across my forehead. “Enjoy the journey.”

I kissed him again, opened the cover, and dove in headfirst.

I landed on the back deck of the Luna house, gazing out at the red rocks of Sedona. The warm Arizona sun shone down on my face. I savored the moment, but didn’t dare close my eyes for fear it would vanish.

“Well, well,” said a familiar, suave voice from behind me. “Fancy seeing you here.”

I hugged myself, inhaled the fresh desert air, and turned around. “Hello, Nathaniel.”

He opened his arms wide, and I rushed forward and hugged him. His words were music to my soul. “The stars have been waiting for you.”

“Where are they?” I asked. But he didn’t need to answer because I looked up and saw them standing in the living room, staring at me—smiling at me—on the other side of the windows.

Save this one. It will guide you home. The words hovered outside of me, spoken by someone I couldn’t see. I turned to Nathaniel. “Did you hear that?”

He handed me two cards. His green eyes were intense, but kind. “She said there will come a time when they will have to guide and enlighten you.”

The cards had a black background, but instead of the gold tarot emblem, they had silver infinity symbols. I flipped them over, curious to see what was on the other side. I touched the two faces staring back at me. “She’s certain?”

“Has she ever been wrong?”

The sun rose rapidly above the desert. It shined so radiantly against the tall glass windows that when I turned to face the house, the reflection blinded me. I lifted my arm to cover my eyes, but I stumbled backward, landing on my butt with a hard thud.

I groaned and rubbed my hips. Everything ached. My legs, arms, hands, even my hair and teeth. I opened my eyes and saw the shiny white floor between my knees. I hated the stupid white room. I hated feeling so sick. I hated being out of control.

Blaze squatted in front of me, pushing my shoulders so I sat up with my back against the wall. "There, there," she said, wiping my cheeks. "Tears are a good sign."

I had no idea what she was talking about. I wasn't crying. But the damp streaks Blaze's thumbs left behind indicated I was wrong.

"Do you remember where you were?" Devlin asked me.

Lifting my throbbing head, I sighed at the sight of him standing above me. "Please send me back."

"Send you back where?"

"To them." I hugged my knees to my chest as every joint cracked.

"Tell me what you remember before it fades away."

Floaters invaded my vision. I turned left, but the squiggly shadow-worms moved to my right. I mumbled, "Not again."

"Uh oh." Blaze followed my gaze to the ceiling.

One of Kramer's black cords hung from the speaker, creeping downward and swaying above us like a snake in a tree. Another one slithered across the floor behind Devlin. My tongue and lips weighed a hundred times their usual weight, but I forced out, "Keep them away from me."

"Who?" Devlin asked. "Keep who away?"

I was too tired to respond. Too drained to fight. Resting my head on top of my knees, I closed my heavy eyelids.

"Kelsey?" Devlin called my name so loud it made me flinch. "Stay awake. Talk to me."

Exhaustion prevented me from speaking, but in my mind, I assured him that I understood. *The Kindrily restored a member's memory after it had been erased. I get it. Proof that I can recover even after being mind-stripped.*

"Kelsey?" Blaze called louder, but no matter how hard I tried, I couldn't find enough energy to stay awake.

I collapsed to the floor, wishing for happy dreams. Or happy VR scenarios. I couldn't tell the difference anymore.

Level 6.3

The alarm on my band wouldn't shut up.

I threw my arm over my head, whacking my wrist against my nightstand. I buried my face in my pillow and smacked my band several more times. Unfortunately, it continued to beep. I lifted my head to turn it off, but startled at what I saw.

Across from me, stretched out on his side in my sister's bed, was Devlin.

He winked. "Rise and shine."

In a domino effect of spastic moves, I clutched my covers to my chest, sat up, and scooted back against the wall. "What are you doing in my room?"

"Poignant question, Kelsey. But you tell me, what am *I* doing in *your* room?"

I stared at him, realizing my pulse wasn't racing like it should have been. I should have been terrified of getting caught with a guy in the house. Plus, Keekee was missing and I didn't hear her in the bathroom or bustling around the kitchen. I didn't even hear my band alarm anymore, but I never pushed the off button.

"This isn't real," I said.

He sat up. "Your mind is strengthening. You're detecting the differences between reality and VR."

"Good, I passed," I said with no enthusiasm at all. "Now take me back to reality."

"You're not ready for reality yet."

"Yes, I am."

He leaned forward, resting his elbows on his knees. "I assure you, every aspect of you is being monitored and assessed: physical, emotional, spiritual, and mental. You are improving in leaps and bounds, but you're not ready for reality. It will crush you and set us back in ways we can't afford."

"I know what happened. I understand now. I was mind-stripped. You and Xander have been trying to help me remember my past by putting me into VR scenarios. I get it."

"That's an extraordinary stride of progress, but there's a lot more to it."

"Like what?"

"When did you last see me? Before right now, what was our last interaction?"

I blanked. Frustrated with myself, I tossed out a guess. "At the warehouse."

"Wrong. Let me give you a refresher. Do you remember being in a white room and feeling wretched? Vomiting, the world spinning, feeling as if all your organs would explode? It's called Alternate World Sickness. I put you back into VR before the worst of it hit you."

I did sort of remember, but "sort of" didn't sound convincing. "I can handle it."

"No, you can't. Not at full force. You've been under for way too long. You didn't even get a glimpse of what could have happened."

"It's my mind, my body, and my soul. You don't get to control me."

"Really? Because I have been controlling you. So has Xander. Even Awol, Blaze, and Jag have taken turns at the controls. And do you know why? Because we had to. Because it's the only way for you to survive."

Controls. Survive. The words seemed to float in the space between us.

Devlin stood and moved to the edge of my bed. "I can't imagine how you must feel. I'm sure it must seem impossibly hard, but you have to trust me. We've brought you this far. Trust us to take you the rest of the way."

"I can't keep living like this. Jumping from one VR scene to the next, never sure of what's real or synthetic. I need answers. I need reality."

"We've been giving you answers, slowly but safely."

I glanced around the room then gazed out the window. "Why are you here instead of Xander?"

He frowned. "You really know how to make me feel appreciated."

"Dev, I'm serious. Something feels off. I want to know what it is and why."

He sighed and rubbed his chin. "Xander is resting. We take turns. This isn't exactly a one-man job."

A bad feeling plagued me. I was missing something, and Devlin wasn't exactly forthcoming with answers.

"This doesn't feel quite like VR," I said. "It feels like you and I are in the present and having a real-time conversation." A conversation Devlin was tiptoeing around.

"Very good. This is interactive VR. It's more complex than the scenarios sideloaded from your memory."

Everything he said felt foreign and familiar at the same time. Like I was trying to recall a language I hadn't spoken in years. Not that Equatia permitted us to learn any languages other than our own.

"So this—" I waved my finger between us. "This isn't a memory. This conversation is new?"

"Correct. Most of the events and conversations you've been experiencing already took place. You're virtually reliving them. Rebooting them to your memory, so to speak. But this one is new. Your conscious self is communicating with mine."

The name for the process escaped my lips in a whisper. "Virtual Override."

Devlin grinned, his eyes gleaming. "Yes, and it's finally working."

"Finally?" I asked. "How long has this been going on?"

"Let's just say we've had to rerun a few scenarios, sometimes alternate versions, to get them to stick."

"Alternate versions?"

Devlin held his hands up and shrugged. "If at first you don't succeed, try a different formula."

"Have you been altering my memories?"

"Only some of them."

"You had no right to do that."

"Actually, I did. And I still do. You authorized it."

“Me? I would never let you control my mind.”

He smirked. “You would, and you did. You authorized Xander to as well.”

“You’re insane!”

“Hey, mentally connecting us was your idea.”

I stood and threw my pillow on the bed. “You’re lying. Or you’re manipulating me. I don’t understand how or why yet, but I’m not listening to any more of this.”

“How about we come back to that accusation after I explain linking?”

“Linking?” I stiffened. “You mean like . . .”

He leaned back and crossed his ankles as if he didn’t have a care in the world. “Like the name you and Xander gave to committing to each other? No.” He chuckled. “At least you better hope it isn’t the same thing because you’re also *linked* to *me*.”

“What?” I gaped at him.

“Easy. Don’t get your circuits in a fritz. Xander and I aren’t love triangle types.”

“Neither am I,” I said defensively.

“Are we going to continue this pointless stroll around your mental block, or may I continue educating you on subjects that matter?”

I crossed my arms over my chest and hoped I wasn’t blushing. “Continue.”

“*Linking*—not the makeshift married kind, but the other definition—means your memory chip is linked with someone else’s. In this case, you linked the three of us: you, Xander, and me. But again—” He waved his hand across his throat in a slashing motion. “*Not* in a love triangle way, in a three minds are better than one strategy.”

I shook my head, refusing to believe such a preposterous lie.

“You trusted us, Kelsey. We knew the odds of one or more of us getting mind-stripped were extremely high. We needed to be linked as a safety tether.”

“Why are you saying this?”

He groaned. “Glitch, I really thought you had progressed further than this, but you’re reverting back into denial and anger.”

"Uhh, you think? You're sitting in my bedroom, uninvited I might add, trying to convince me that I gave you open access to control my brain."

He stood and stuck his hand in his pocket. "Let's try it your way. You swear you're ready for a glimpse of reality, and the clock is ticking, so we don't have much to lose. I'll give you a small dose of what you claim you can handle, and we'll see how it goes."

"What exactly does that mean?"

"It means I'm stacking you." He pulled out a deck of tarot cards and fanned them in front of me. "What do you see?"

Most of the cards were blurry colors. I couldn't even read the titles, but then my eyes honed in on two cards sitting side by side. They were crystal clear. I read their names. "The Chariot and Strength."

"Xander might kill me for this, but here we go."

We transported to a room that reminded me of the Ark. A large screen hung above a curved, white desk. I was drawn to the center, where an indent allowed me to stand close enough to touch the blank screen.

"Is this the Ark?" I asked Devlin.

He pressed a button on the console near my right hip.

Countless pixels lit up on the screen then dissolved to reveal a window. On the other side of the glasslike surface was a white room, and lying on the floor was Keekee. I threw my hands against the window, shouting my sister's name.

Devlin squeezed my shoulder. "Stop. She can't hear you."

"Why is she in there?"

He only stared at me.

"Let me in there," I insisted. "I need to make sure she's okay."

"See," he said gently, "you aren't ready for reality. Your perceptions are still haywire."

"That's my sister." I shoved his chest then turned back to the desk with all the buttons, switches, and monitors, pressing everything I could. "How do I get in? You can't keep me from her."

"I can't keep you from *her?*" He held my elbow, forcing me to look at him. "Or keep you from *you?*"

I froze, my hand still pushing a button that I couldn't feel. I stared at the unconscious body in the middle of the floor. *Me?*

I couldn't act shocked. I had to stay calm. Devlin needed to know I could handle anything he threw at me. "Me," I said. "That's me. Now I remember."

A red light illuminated a window to my right. On the other side of the glass, Awol stared back at me. The window to my left lit up yellow and Blaze waved. Directly across from me, bathed in blue, was Jag. Together, our four curved windows formed a circle around the room.

It was so familiar. I kept blinking, trying to force answers into my mind. I wanted to figure it out on my own. I wanted to impress Devlin, make him believe that I understood it without him explaining. But all I could focus on was the fact that Devlin and I were standing in the fourth, and final, windowed room.

My eyes scanned the circle again.

Awol. Cups.

Blaze. Wands.

Jag. Swords.

Xander. Pentacles.

"Where is Xander?" I asked Devlin.

"I'll take you to him."

"The real Xander, not a VR scenario of him."

"I'm giving you what you need."

My fists balled at my sides. "Give me the truth."

The lights above us flickered, then Devlin morphed into Xander. Shocked, I stepped backward and fell into a chair that started spinning so fast the room blurred into a cloud of green.

Level 6.4

"Whoa, easy, Kels." Xander slowed my spinning chair to a stop.

When my brain finally caught up with my eyes, I saw we were in the office of his warehouse. I glanced at all the blank computer screens, then focused on Xander. Touching his face confirmed my suspicion. He was an imitation.

"Devlin said he'd give me what I need, so why am I here?"

Xander smoothed down my hair and caressed my cheek. "Because I need to talk to you about something important."

"This isn't even real. You're not really here."

"I don't know how to respond to that."

"Where is the real you?"

"I don't know how to respond to that."

"See, you're not even here mentally. You're responding like a robot with limited answers." He didn't know what to say because we were in one of Devlin's scenarios. Devlin hadn't predicted me remembering it was more VR.

I spun my chair, turning my back to the inadequate version of Xander and shouted, "Xander! Where are you?"

The library door opened and a second Xander stepped through it. "Kels?"

I looked behind me. The first Xander was frozen mid-reach. The one coming out of the library looked authentically worried.

"Don't come near me unless you're real," I warned. My voice shook. "I mean it. I can't handle much more of this."

He walked toward me. Correction, he strutted toward me, so confident that he was real and I was his. He leaned down, grabbed my hand and pressed it against his face. Warm and smooth. "I'm real."

I sighed with relief then kissed him. I ran my hands through his silky hair, another confirmation that he was real.

Our kiss was interrupted too soon by Devlin fake-coughing behind me.

Xander broke free long enough to say, "Go away, Devlin."

"I would happily take a break from you two if I didn't think you'd waste the majority of our time making out."

I pulled away from Xander and practically barked at Devlin. "What we do is none of your business."

Devlin yanked my chair around to face him. "Yes, it is. My brother is my highest order of business, and as frustrating as you are at this moment, you're still ranked right up there beside him."

Xander wedged his way between us. "Dev, just give us a little private time, please?"

"Denied. I know what you're doing. You've stopped strategizing. You're not even running your reversal programs anymore."

"That's my choice."

"You're giving up."

"I'm not giving up, I just—" Xander's shoulders slumped forward. "I'm exhausted, and I want her to remember the good times we shared."

"She's finally making substantial progress."

I stood and Xander reached behind him, moving me so I stood by his side. He wrapped one arm around my waist and kissed the top of my head. "Of course she is. I never doubted that she would."

My focus bounced between them. "I'm trying to keep quiet because sometimes just listening to you two argue gives me more answers than when I ask direct questions, but this conversation is worrying me."

Devlin ignored me. "No matter what happens, she would remember the good times you shared. I'd make sure of that."

"And what if you don't survive either?" Xander asked.

Devlin's eyes widened. "I knew it. You're losing faith in the plan."

"It's not that." Xander breathed deeply then pressed his hand to his forehead. "I'm losing track of it all. You were right. I'm getting sloppy." He looked down at me. "We're not excluding you from this conversation on purpose. It's probably best that you hear this."

"That would be great if I understood what you were talking about," I said. "But I'm fairly lost. And the things I am assuming, I don't want to be true."

Xander's attention darted to Devlin. "Lately, we've been disagreeing about the best way to perform Virtual Override on you."

"There's more than one way?"

"It's like reading a book from multiple points of view," Xander explained. "One of them is bound to resonate with you more than the others. We've had to try different scenarios to trigger your memory, sometimes multiple versions." He sat down and cracked his knuckles. "In most cases, we stuck to how everything actually happened, but in other cases, we sprinkled in some fiction."

"Not *we*," Devlin said. "I wanted to follow the original script."

"It's working, so I don't regret my decision."

"What parts have been fiction?" I asked.

Devlin waved his hand. "It doesn't matter because so far you don't retain any of it long-term."

"It matters to me," I huffed. "It's my past and I want the authentic version."

"Tell us what you remember," Xander said. "We'll tell you if it's genuine or altered."

I thought hard, mostly recalling moments with Xander. I wanted those to be real. I wasn't ready to hear that they weren't, so I tried choosing a scenario that didn't include him. One that felt important and sparked questions.

Flashes of Kramer assaulting me made my heart race. "Kramer. Please tell me he's fiction."

Xander rubbed the back of his neck. "We wish, but unfortunately, he's real."

Devlin stared at the ground. Fairly certain Devlin's history with Kramer was also true, I felt guilty for bringing up his name, but answers might help me move past my fear of him.

"Those creepy floaters and black wires seem to be connected with him." I shivered. "They are fiction, right?"

Xander squeezed me before letting go and sitting on the edge of the desk. "Those are indicators of when he's hacking into your brain chip, trying to mess with your mind or issue you commands."

Devlin added, "But he never gets far because we override his system."

I was grateful, but perplexed. "How?"

They exchanged apprehensive glances, but Xander nodded so Devlin explained. "Kramer controls your Equatia brain chip—the one implanted in you since birth. He also has your decoy chip, which he assumed was your backup device."

I reached for my necklace, but it was gone.

Xander noticed and interjected with, "Yes. You led him to believe the decoys were in our necklaces."

Devlin continued. "Kramer doesn't know there's a third chip, a true backup device. And he can't ever figure it out because *that* is how we keep him from controlling you. It's how we keep him from controlling all of us."

The information resonated with me. All of it.

I rubbed my forehead and The Emperor card came to mind—the man who looked like my father.

"What about The Emperor?" I asked. "I had a conversation with him in the Ark. He held a red orb like the one on the tarot card. He talked to me, but didn't react to my questions. Was that real?"

Xander squinted so deeply I could barely see his eyes. Devlin stared at me speechless, which was such a rare event that his silence scared me.

"Real or fiction?" I pressed.

Xander blinked a few times then asked Devlin, "One of yours?"

Devlin shook his head.

Xander walked over to me. "Do you remember any other details of what the Emperor said?"

Details were there, lingering below the surface. I just needed to pull them free. "He said my method would work. That I needed test subjects."

Devlin made an elated guffawing sound and clasped his hands behind his head.

Xander smiled and placed his hands on my cheeks then kissed my temple.

"What?" I asked. "Do you know what that meant?"

"It was a memory." Xander braced my shoulders. "A real memory. One we didn't program or control."

"That's good, right?"

"That's amazing!"

"Not just amazing," Devlin added. "It means you're starting to recover on your own."

"So who was the Emperor?" I asked. "Why did I remember him?"

Xander bounced on the balls of his feet. "We can tell you, but it will have a much stronger impact if we show you through another memory."

"That will improve my chances of the information staying with me, right?"

"Yes."

"Then show me."

"Already uploading." Devlin held The Emperor card in front of me while Xander swiped his band's screen.

For the first time (that I could remember) I was excited, and prepared, to jump into a different scenario.

Xander stood leaning over me, wiping his brow. "I can't believe I'm doing this."

I was lying flat on a desk. A red orb floated in front of my face, glowing and radiating warmth against my cheek.

"You ready?" Xander asked me.

He held the orb in one gloved hand while his other hand massaged my head where my temple met my hairline.

Insertion, I thought. *It's not going to hurt. My parents tested it. It's completely safe.*

I folded my hands together and tried to relax. "I'm ready."

My father's voice filled the command room of the Ark. "All right, Xander, place the orb against the insertion point and let the light warm her skin."

Xander did as he was instructed. I flinched when the heat first touched me, but then it became soothing. Xander's worried eyes locked on mine.

"I'm okay," I assured him.

"Next," Dad said, "Locate the slight indentation along her hairline, just above her cheekbone."

Xander's fingers gently pressed against my temple. "No disrespect, sir." He glanced at my father on the screen. "But it doesn't seem like there's enough room."

Dad's voice was calm and confident. "I assure you, there's room. The chip is micro-thin and will rest just below the skin. We're not inserting it into her skull."

A slight grin tugged at my lips as Xander swallowed hard. He whispered to me, "Let's just stick with the necklaces. You don't need a third one."

"We know what we're doing." I squeezed his arm reassuringly then folded my hands on top of my stomach again. "Go ahead, Dad. Next step."

"Now, you're ready for the chip, Xander. Be careful not to touch the chip with anything except the forceps in the kit."

"Yes, sir." Xander moved slowly and carefully. His glistening brow furrowed with intense concentration.

"The Hexis Sphere will remain connected to her until you pull it off, so I suggest using both hands to insert the chip. Pull the skin taut, and be sure to position the chip so the incision runs with the hairline. The mark it leaves on the skin is barely visible, but her hair will hide any trace of it."

Xander rubbed his lips together and held his breath as he moved the chip toward my head. He had a death grip on the forceps and they were slightly shaking.

I whispered, "Don't be nervous. It won't hurt."

"You don't know that."

"My parents wouldn't lie to me."

"All right," Dad said, leaning closer and filling most of the screen. "Gently slide it beneath her skin, like sliding a notecard into an envelope. You'll be surprised how easily it penetrates the skin."

I held my breath. Xander flashed me one last look that silently asked, *Are you sure about this?*

"Do it," I said.

His fingers stretched my skin tight. A slight tingle made me blink, then after a couple short tugs, Xander lifted his fingers.

"You can remove the Hexis now," Dad told him.

The warm red light vanished as Xander asked, "Kels, are you okay?"

I sat up and lightly stroked my temple. "I'm fine. Is it in?"

"It's in."

My skin itched a little, but other than that, I wouldn't have known another memory chip had just been inserted into me.

"Well done, Xander." Dad sounded proud of him, and that made me happy. "Easier than you expected?"

The tension melted from Xander's rigid muscles. "Much easier. It was like sliding a straw into liquid."

"I told you, the Hexis Sphere is a reliable, non-invasive surgical tool. Kelsey's idea was brilliant." He smiled proudly at me and I beamed. He lifted his hand and started to say something, but then froze.

"Dad?" The screen went black.

Xander stepped behind me and placed his hands on my shoulders. "Coming from someone as exceptionally intelligent as your gifted father, that was a huge compliment."

I turned to face him. He wasn't sweating anymore. He wasn't even wearing the same tunic. The red orb was nowhere to be found. All of the supplies Xander used for my insertion had vanished. "That was a real memory of my real father."

"Do you remember him?"

"I do, vaguely." I touched my temple to see if I could feel the chip beneath my skin, but it felt normal. "I remember a different Dad too. More strict."

"I substituted mine in a few recent scenarios. It was easier to program my dad in scenes because I knew him better. Plus—" Xander rubbed the back of his neck. "Your dad has never stepped foot in Equatia. I wanted to keep it that way. In reality and VR."

Thoughts jumbled in my mind. I struggled to sort through what I had recently learned, possibly remembered, and the new information Xander and Devlin had given me. I was on the verge of a big breakthrough, an important realization, but I couldn't quite grasp it. "I feel like I almost know the answer to what I'm about to ask, but how is it possible that my father never stepped foot in Equatia?"

"You aren't able to see the whole picture yet, and I can't tell you what's real, but I can show you."

This was as close as I had been to piecing together my puzzle of confusion. I didn't want to lose momentum, or knowledge, by transitioning to yet another scenario alone. "Devlin appeared in a scene once. I was watching you and me the first time I visited your warehouse. But Devlin was there talking to me. This me. Not the me we were watching."

I knew what I meant, and it still sounded confusing. "Does that make sense?"

"His conscious self was communicating with yours while you were both stacked in a scenario."

"Yes! I think. Can you do that too? Can this you, who knows what we've been discussing, watch the next memory with this me, so I don't forget our conversation?"

He grinned. "Are you asking me to accompany you while you stroll down memory lane?"

"I am."

"I'd be honored." He offered me his arm, and I linked mine in his.

I was certain that whatever we were about to experience was important. His hand arched high and wide, and the room swayed, but I held on tight.

By the time I found my footing, the lighting in the Ark had changed, but Xander's arm was still hooked around mine. I hung onto him with my free hand and squeezed tight. I needed to make sure the real him stayed by my side.

He turned us around to face the opposite direction, and I gasped.

A second version of him and I were standing steps away. Xander wore an Olden suit, and I was in my billowy, Olden, beautiful dress.

"It's my dress!" I exclaimed. "The dress of my dreams. How is she—I mean, how am I wearing that?"

"I made it," Xander whispered in my ear. "With the assistance of Awol and your mother, but stay quiet or you'll miss a good part."

Seeing us dressed like characters in an old romance novel *was* the good part. How could it get better than that?

Beside us, the screen activated. At first, all I could see was the front of a man's suit filling the frame, but then he backed up and a whole group of people stood behind him dressed in what I assumed was their best attire. They looked so elegant.

The other me squealed and waved, ecstatic to see everyone on the screen.

"We're all here," the man in front said. It was my dad. My real father. I had no doubt about that anymore. Especially when he said, "I can't believe I'm giving my little girl away long distance."

"Don't worry, Dad," the dressed-up me told him. "We'll have a second ceremony with you guys as soon as we're out of Equatia."

I whispered to present-time Xander. "My dad is the Emperor."

He hummed a *mmm hmm* in reply as an older woman moved to the front of the crowd.

"The High Priestess!" I tugged Xander's arm and he patted mine. "Shhh, just watch and take it all in."

The other me held the other Xander's hand while she introduced the radiant elderly woman. "Xander, this is Mary."

"Nice to finally meet you, Mary." Dressed-up Xander grinned and he looked so adorable. "So you're the one who started the memory curse?"

She laughed. "Everything happens for a reason. Look how far we've come since then."

Dressed-up me fluffed her skirt. "Mary is regarded as a powerful luminary in my family, so she'll be the one linking us."

Xander bowed. "Many thanks for being our linker, Mary. It means the world to us."

"Kelsey swears you're her soul mate, and she has never taken that subject lightly, so if she declares it to be true, then it must be."

"I'm a lucky man." Both Xanders said it at the same time. The Xander next to me looked down at me with a loving gaze.

"Yes, you are," Dad told the Xander standing in front of the screen. "And don't forget it."

"I won't, Mr. Carson. I vow to take exceptional care of your daughter."

People were still talking when the happy scene faded. The screen went dark and everyone disappeared from the room.

"No," I murmured. "Come back." I stepped toward them, my voice hitching. "Please?"

Xander wrapped his arms around me and kissed my forehead.

I let my weight sink against him. "That one was so real it hurt."

"I'm sorry. I didn't mean to upset you. I hoped it would give you some clarity about where you came from."

"It did." I stared at the blank screen again, still imagining their smiling faces. "I do remember them, and I miss them so much."

I missed them because I hadn't been with them for a long time. Too long. I didn't remember how long exactly, but the homesickness hit me hard. Had they really approved of me linking with a guy they had never met in person?

A thought occurred to me. I asked Xander, "How long have we been together?"

"A little over two years."

"Two *years?*"

"Time flies when you find your soul mate."

He let go of me, but still held my hand. He guided me to the chair. "Sit down. I have another one that I've always thought was pretty significant. It's from the beginning of our relationship."

I sat down but kept a firm grip on his hand. "You're coming with me again, right?"

"This one will be more effective if you experience it as it actually happened."

"But—"

"Trust me, Kels. It's more intimate that way."

The way he said *intimate* sent delightful quivers through me, so I agreed and let go of his hand. He tapped on his band's screen then flashed me a winsome grin.

A whirlwind of colors spun around me like I was inside of a tornado. I felt weightless, like I might have been flying, but when the spinning stopped, I was still sitting in my chair in the exact same spot in the Ark.

Xander sat in another chair several feet to my right. His hair was slightly longer, and his tunic color had changed again. Most noticeably, my palms were sweaty and my heart was lodged in my throat.

I rolled my neck and shook off a momentary rush of dizziness. My nerves were making me fidgety. I shuffled through my tarot deck until I found the Strength card. I silently begged it to transfer me some courage.

How was I supposed to start such an important conversation?

Level 6.5

I inconspicuously watched Xander again. He was deep in thought, working on a new card scenario. He'd write VR code, then switch to sketching a new tarot card. When he focused on a detail, the tip of his tongue would peek out between his lips. It took all of my willpower not to rush over and jump in his lap.

I promised myself I would not act like a lovesick hussy while we were working, but great stars, he made keeping that promise extremely difficult.

I tried focusing on my work. I didn't need to have *the talk* with him. Sure, I had obsessively rehearsed it dozens of different ways in my mind and I swore today would be the day I'd tell him, but the moment had arrived, and I couldn't dislodge my courage from my constricting throat.

Xander glanced up and caught me watching him. I looked away and pretended to write code.

"Everything okay?" he asked. "You seem stressed."

"Fine. Everything's fine." I fiddled with my hair. "I'm fine."

He chuckled. "Well, since you said it three times, it must be true."

I tried glaring at him, but it probably looked more like a flirty smirk.

He rolled his chair closer. "Tell me what's on your mind."

This was my chance. All I had to do was open my mouth and start the story I had practiced over and over. My lips parted, I took a deep breath, and then I lost my nerve again. "I'm just tired."

"We can take a break. Do you want some coffee?"

I shook my head and tapped my knuckles on the desk. This conversation had to take place. It was now or never. “No coffee. I lied. I’m not tired. I’m nervous.”

“Nervous? About what?”

I forcefully swallowed my heart down my throat and back into my chest. “Do you remember the first time I told you that I believed in you?”

“About a week ago, when you first told me I might get to experience this.” He motioned to the command controls around us.

“Right. Do you understand what it means?”

“You letting me in here and teaching me how the Ark works? It means a lot.”

I fiddled with my hair again because I didn’t know what else to do with my hands. “I don’t mean the Ark. I mean my saying I believe in you.”

“Oh.” He scanned the room, then cracked his knuckles. “I can tell it has significance for you.”

Significance. He had no clue what an understatement that was.

He suddenly looked nervous too, like he suspected I had set him up to pass a test he didn’t study for. His next words sounded more like a question. “I believe in you too?”

“Stop saying that.”

“But—”

I cut him off. “That’s why I brought it up. I need you to understand what it means because it’s not fair that you don’t know what it means yet you say it back to me.” I couldn’t tell if he thought I was crazy. We’d soon find out. “I haven’t told you much about my family because they’re . . . complicated. I mean, they’re amazing, but they have some unfortunate parts in their history.”

“I think most families do.”

“Not like mine. Mine is a bit extraordinary.”

His eyebrows arched as he leaned forward.

I took that as my cue to continue. “A long, *long* time ago, one of my great aunts forgot who she was. She didn’t remember the people who loved her.”

“She was mind-stripped?”

“Sort of. But not like how it’s done here in Equatia.”

His pencil bounced between his fingers. “She had amnesia?”

"A form of amnesia, yes. No hope of ever remembering who she had once been."

"That's very sad."

"It was downright tragic, but before she forgot everything, she believed nothing was impossible, and so did the rest of the family, including her soul mate."

He flinched at the term *soul mate*—typical guy—but I forced myself to continue. "Long story short, it should have been impossible for her to restore her memory, but the people who loved her refused to accept that. They never gave up. And eventually, she remembered."

"She recovered from the amnesia?"

"Yes," I said. "Full recovery."

"That's awesome."

"I agree. But do you understand why she recovered?"

"Because her family and—" He fidgeted and swallowed before saying, "*soul mate* loved her so much."

"Close, but not quite." I rolled my chair closer and our knees touched. "They did love her, and love is extremely powerful, but that wasn't enough. They *believed* in her. They believed she would remember again. They believed she could do the impossible. Even when all the signs said it was hopeless, they never stopped believing in her."

His knee bounced, but he didn't break eye contact with me.

"Love is common," I continued. "It happens every day everywhere, which is great. Beyond Equatia's borders, love is what unites the rest of the world. It's as essential as water and breathing, but belief is something different. Where I come from, especially in my family, if you believe in someone, it's highly regarded. It's cherished. Belief is more powerful than love."

He blinked several times, set his pencil on the desk, and leaned forward. "And you truly feel that you believe in me?"

I held his hand, lacing my fingers with his. "Since the first time I saw you, when our eyes met in the parking lot of Caffeine Machine, I knew you were the one for me. Whether or not you felt the same, I was yours, and I would have followed you into oblivion."

He smiled. "You just stole my lines."

Warmth started at my cheeks and spread to my toes. "What can I say? It was very quote-worthy and summed up my feelings perfectly."

He bit his bottom lip while studying my face. "So you shared your family story with me because you want me to understand how significant it is when you tell me you believe in me, but you don't want me to say it back anymore unless I understand its connotation and truly mean it?"

"Exactly."

He pulled my hand so my chair rolled even closer to him. His knees sandwiched mine as he held my face in his hands. "Kelsey Zellar, I believe in you. Nothing can ever change that."

He kissed me, holding me so tightly I felt invincible. I was on top of the world. It was the moment I loved reading about in novels, except now I was living it. I didn't want to ever turn the page.

And the page didn't turn.

It was ripped out.

Xander slumped against me. His whole body went limp as if all of his bones had disintegrated. I caught him, but his dead weight rolled my chair backward, and when I tried righting him, the chair toppled out from under me and we both fell to the floor.

"Xander?" I rolled him over and patted his cheek. I grabbed his wrist and attempted to initiate a health scan on his band, but the interface was nothing I'd ever seen before. The tarot eye and other symbols like a chalice and star-coin blinked on the screen, but I had no idea how to navigate his band.

"Wake up." I delicately parted his closed eyelids, but instead of pupils, I saw scrolling *0*s and *1*s. I jerked back. "What the glitch?"

A burst of light formed across from me. It flickered a few more times before a hologram version of Devlin appeared. He looked at Xander, turned away, then punched the air as he bellowed, "I told him this would happen!"

"What happened?" I shrieked. "I don't understand. One second we were kissing and then he just passed out."

Devlin crouched beside us as he swiped commands on his band. "His system couldn't keep up anymore."

I studied Xander's peaceful face. Too peaceful. "What are you telling me? You're not implying that he's . . ." I couldn't say it. Just thinking about it crushed my windpipe.

"He's not dead. He's exhausted," Devlin said curtly. "This is VR, but even in reality, he's out cold. He won't be waking up any time soon."

I exhaled with relief then caressed his face. His smooth skin felt real. Everything we had just shared felt genuine. But was it? *Yes,* my instincts whispered. *It was real.*

Glimmers of a discussion I had with Xander before reliving this memory gave me the confidence to trust my intuition. He had been showing me the truth. He had been helping me remember people and events that were important to me.

"You should rest," Devlin grunted.

"Rest? I can't leave him like this."

"You're long overdue for several hours of undisturbed sleep and so is he. I'll look after him."

"And where do you suggest I go?" I didn't know where to rest. I didn't even know how to contact my family. Meeting Devlin's harsh gaze, I admitted, "I don't have a home."

His eyes softened. "Yes, you do. Home is where people love you. And you have a surplus of that as long as you're with us."

He entered another command into his band. The lights dimmed until the room was so dark I couldn't see him. I felt around for Xander, but he was gone too.

Devlin's voice was quiet and gentle when he said, "Try not to dream. It will only make you more disoriented."

Level 6.6

For the first time in what felt like ages, I slept. As in actual, real-life sleep, not waking up in my bed—or a VR scenario—with no idea how I got there.

The clues started when I was jostled awake. I was in the white room, but the lights were dim. Jag lifted me then set me down on a lumpy cot mattress. He covered me with a stiff blanket from the Ark's emergency kit.

Exhausted as I was, three important clues registered in my tired brain and signaled my *reality* alert.

1.) Jag was in the room with me, not Devlin.

2.) Jag smelled like bad body odor which no one would ever program in a VR scenario. Jag usually doused himself in musky cologne that made my nose itch.

3.) I remembered packing the emergency kit, which is how I knew where the blanket came from.

Cling to the facts. My eyes drifted shut, but I mentally repeated my thoughts so I wouldn't forget. *Jag in the room. Body odor. Emergency blanket. Reality.*

"I know you can hear me," Jag said quietly. "And I know you think I preach too much, but consider something while you rest. Think about how our crafts work. The seat and mirrors automatically adjust to fit our height and weight, accident shields activate when we fly too close to another craft. If we fly too fast, the speed controls take over so we slow down. Why are all of those precautions in place?"

His speech exhausted me and gave me a headache.

"To protect you," he continued. "So, wouldn't it make sense that if there are systems outside of you, there are also systems inside of you?" Mental, physical, emotional, and spiritual safety nets to protect your entire being?"

He was scolding me just like Devlin had. Too much too soon. *I know, Jag. I've heard it all before.* I swallowed and barely murmured a reply. "I'll slow down."

He leaned closer. "No. Don't slow down. That's what I'm trying to tell you. You're equipped with built-in safety shields. Fly fast and hard. Even if you crash, you'll bounce back. Fight to reach the finish line."

He pulled the blanket up to my chin and tucked the sides around my shoulders. "Get some rest, Kelsey. You've come a long way. I'll be cheering you on until the very end."

Brush your teeth, I wanted to tell him, but I had already drifted to sleep.

I dreamed that I stood in front of the Ark's screen, which displayed a deck of tarot cards. With a wave of my hand, the black and gold cards spread from left to right.

I flicked my finger and one flipped over, revealing Xander as The Magician. I selected another and it was my mother as The Empress, followed by Dad as The Emperor. I pushed one card to the top of the screen before turning it over to reveal Mary as the High Priestess. As if that weren't a given.

Tilting my head and slowly raising the corner of a card, I saw part of the robed figure I knew was Kramer as The Hierophant, reversed. I let the card fall face down then slid it off screen. He wasn't worthy of being in my reading.

From a smaller screen to my left, Mary chided, "Setting a card aside doesn't make it any less part of the reading."

"I respectfully disagree."

I turned over the next card, expecting to see The Lovers, but instead it was The Hermit. The cloaked girl guided herself through a dark tunnel using her own lantern.

"Inner guidance," Mary said. "A time spent seeking answers within yourself. Especially your unconsciousness."

"But it doesn't make sense," I argued. "I asked what *will* happen. I can't help others if I'm focused on myself."

"You won't be able to help anyone if you don't help yourself first."

"But why would I need help?"

"Ask the cards."

I flipped the next one. The Death card made me smile.

Mary chuckled. "Only a deep understanding of the tarot would evoke that reaction when revealing the Death card."

I recited one of the meanings she taught me. "It's not the end. It's a new beginning."

"Very true. Possibly a resurrection."

"Change is on the horizon." I drummed my fingers on the desk, debating whether or not to ask what would happen after the change. "It means we'll succeed at the mission. That's all I need to know."

"You aren't considering the whole spread. Don't be biased with your interpretation."

I didn't look at her. I pretended to study the cards.

But she knew me too well. "Kelsey, you must reveal the eighth card."

"I have all the information I need."

"You most certainly do not. The reading is pointless without the eighth card." Her tone was stern. "Don't avoid the truth, even if it's painful. Fate and truth are two powers you should never fear. Listen to every internal whisper—every gut instinct. No matter how farfetched or impossible it sounds, listen close. Then act with belief and love."

I had taught Xander that same important lesson.

My focus darted to The Magician card. The figure staring back at me had changed to Devlin. Xander was the significator of the reading, but clearly Devlin's future would be affected too.

"I don't need the eighth," I insisted.

"It links the other cards together. Divination is pointless if you don't embrace the process."

To appease her, I flipped over another card. I sucked in a breath. *The Hanged Man.* Reversed.

I sank back into my chair, staring at the silhouette of a man hanging from a rope between two cliffs. Martyrdom, loss of faith, sacrifice. "It has to be wrong."

My intuition was shouting certainties I didn't want to hear. I shook my head as Mary spoke. "It most definitely suggests a grim period, but that could mean many things. Loss of time, suspension, inability to move—"

I slammed the card facedown because the shadowed figure's features became Xander. "I can change it. There's still time."

I rolled my chair sideways and opened one of the new programs I had been working on. "When the time comes, he won't lose faith or sacrifice himself. I'll make sure of it."

Mary sighed. "No one could ever deny that you are part of our family. Your will may prove to be stronger than mine."

I intended to thank her for the kind words, but I was already honed in on my task. Starting with the Ace of Cups, I sorted through the minor arcana cards, making sure I utilized any and all of the suits we might need to survive.

"You're a trump," Mary reminded me. "You've mastered the ability to change the outcome of a spread, but let me remind you that changing outcomes always has repercussions."

"That's what I'm counting on."

I had gotten Xander into this mess. I had to ensure he had a safe way out.

Level 6.7

Hanged Man. Trump. Reality. Safety nets.

I woke up in the dimly lit white room. I was curled in a ball on the thin mattress, still covered with the emergency blanket. Devlin sat against a nearby wall, knees drawn to his chest, head resting on top of his arms. Not far above him was a window to an illuminated room where Blaze stood watching me.

"Hi, Kelsey," she said through the speaker.

I swallowed and forced out a dry-throated, "Hi."

Devlin lifted his head and scurried over to me. "How are you feeling?"

"Dehydrated."

The circular robot rolled into the room. My mouth, dry as it was, somehow managed to salivate at the thought of the nutrient pac zipping toward me. I sat up, my arms shaking as I tried supporting my weight. Why was I so weak?

The robot's cover slid open and I was surprised to see a yellow pac inside.

I cleared my throat. "Where's the pink one?"

"You're in wands mode," Devlin explained. "That requires a different formula."

I stared at him for a moment while sifting through the chatter in my head until I found something useful. Wands, cups, swords, and pentacles. Blaze's suit was wands. I glanced at her window again, but she was occupied, swiping her fingers through the air.

"Right," I managed. "Blaze's turn to fix me."

Devlin's head jerked back. "What makes you say that?"

"I remember a lot, Dev." I lifted the pac. Thanks to my weak and trembling fingers, it took a few tries to tear off the tab, but then I gulped down the drink. "Probably more than I should at this point."

His eyes narrowed, but the twitch of his lips meant he was fighting back a grin. He called over his shoulder, "Blaze? When's the last time you ran a fragmentation scan?"

"Running one right now," she said. "It's only on cluster one, but it's looking strong."

She tapped on her window, and I looked up at her. She waved a lollipop over her head. "I told you we should have started with wands!"

I tried returning her smile, but even my cheek muscles were too sore to move effectively.

Devlin ran his hand over his beard. "Kelsey, this is a major breakthrough."

I focused on the coarse, dark hairs that framed his mouth as he continued speaking. Every word he said sounded muffled. I kept nodding because I didn't want him to think I wasn't listening. I wanted to hear him, but my ears weren't working.

Apparently, I must have nodded too much because Devlin shouted, "Blaze, she's seizing!"

As Blaze ran into the room and reclined me back onto the cot, I tried telling her I was fine, that I was only agreeing with Devlin. But my tongue lodged in my throat—gagging me—and then my vision short-circuited.

I hated admitting it, but Devlin was right. I had a seizure.

Devlin shook my shoulder. "Kelsey? Wake up."

I was hunched over the kitchen table in Xander's warehouse. Well, not *me*, but the past version of me I was watching.

"This is a memory, right?"

Devlin and the other me didn't react to my voice or presence whatsoever. It was like watching an entertainment program on a holosplay.

Devlin shook Memory Me again. "Where's my brother?"

Memory Me sat up, looking half-asleep and smoothing down her hair. "What time is it?"

"It's almost 9 am. Xander never came home last night. Our mother is a worried wreck."

"Did you tell her where he was?"

"Of course not, but if I don't contact her with an update soon she said she'll be forced to report him missing. Do you have any idea how much trouble that will cause us?"

"He just left. He's probably home by now." Memory Me picked up her mug and attempted to take a sip, but discovered it was empty. "I was drinking coffee, but I must have dozed off. We were up all night."

Devlin's brows rose.

"Working," my doppelganger said. "Don't look at me like that."

Devlin chuckled and lifted his band then contacted his mom. I rushed to his side so I could see what she looked like, but she didn't answer.

"Transmission failed. She's probably still yelling at Xander." Devlin lowered his arm. "What was so important that you two needed to work all night?"

I tried touching the side of Devlin's face, but my hand went through him. He didn't react to me at all.

Memory Me groaned and stood to make herself another cup of coffee. "We were strategizing about my recent interpretation of a card reading."

"Which was?"

Coffee filled the mug. It smelled delicious, and I envied Memory Me for getting to drink it. She, on the other hand, looked miserable. "Most likely, I'll be mind-stripped."

Devlin swayed back, but the counter caught him and he steadied himself. "That would never happen. We're too careful. We have safety nets everywhere."

Memory Me hugged her steaming mug to her chest and shrugged. "It's a family curse. We're always challenged with memory issues, and the cards revealed it will happen to me too. But my family took that into account when I trained for this mission. We developed a way to restore my mind in case the worst happens."

"That's impossible."

"You're from Equatia. You think many things are impossible." She sat down at the table again. "I don't need you to believe in it, *yet*. But I do need you to help me with some of the programming."

"Why me? You and Xander work so well together. All night, apparently."

"You're swords. I need your mental strength. Besides, Xander won't approve of one of the new methods I'm developing."

"Uh oh." Devlin hopped up on the counter. "Why? What is it?"

"Key moments that will trigger every aspect of my being, but experienced from his point of view."

"I don't understand."

"We'll switch roles."

Devlin smirked. "As much as I'd enjoy giving my brother grief for playing the role of a girl, Xander will never agree to it."

"No, not like that. I mean *he* will be the one who recruits me. I'll be introduced to the Arcana the same way I introduced him."

"What will that accomplish?"

"I'll be forced to journey through the tarot cards just like the minors do. The system works for teaching, guiding, and enlightening the psyche."

"But you're already enlightened."

"I won't be if I'm mind-stripped. At least not consciously, but, like all humans, I will be enlightened on an unconscious level. I'll require help accessing it so I can regenerate my brain map. The cards will help me, but I'll need you and Xander to control the cards."

"We aren't tarot experts."

"Not yet, but you will be soon."

"How?"

She sipped her coffee and grinned. "I'm going to link you to my knowledge base, and then teach you everything you need to know to be a trump."

I waited for Devlin to respond. Several seconds passed before I realized he was frozen. So was Memory Me. The whole scene had paused.

I turned and found Xander leaning against the hammock post.

"How long have you been here?" I asked.

"Since around the time Devlin hopped up on the counter," he admitted. "You always hated that, by the way—Devlin kicking the cabinet doors."

"I did?"

Xander pushed off the wall and walked toward me. "That scene was a lot to take in. What do you think about what you heard?"

"Was it really my idea to switch roles?"

"Yes. I wasn't a big supporter."

"Did you ever go through with it?"

"Here and there, but only if we were desperate."

"This is fascinating." I surveyed the paused forms of Devlin and me again. "Borderline unbelievable, but still fascinating. Do you have more scenes like this? More that will show me things I've forgotten?"

He held out his hand. "I have a lot of them."

I placed my hand in his and he pulled me close. He kissed me quickly but sweetly then tucked my head under his chin and hugged me.

I pressed my cheek against his chest, inhaling the comforting scent of him. "You smell so good. That means you're real, right?"

"Shh." He held me tighter. "Close your eyes and don't let go."

When his arms finally loosened, we were standing next to the perimeter wall on the rooftop of Higher Grounds. I stared up at the open sky dotted with stars above us, trying to save the prior scene to memory so it wouldn't fade.

Devlin. Switching roles. Teaching. Xander.

"Does this moment feel familiar yet?" Xander asked me.

I glanced around then rested my hands on the chest-high concrete wall, rubbing my fingertips against the scratchy, porous surface. The texture of it took me back to an important conversation. "Yes, this is where we discussed—"

Devlin shouted behind us. "Xander, no! She's not ready for this yet."

"I disagree," Xander said calmly, watching me with admiration, as if I could do anything and everything.

Devlin practically skidded to a stop between us, but his ferocity was directed at Xander. "She just had a seizure. You're giving her too much too fast."

Xander sidestepped Devlin. "You had a seizure?"

"I—" Did I have a seizure? I couldn't be sure, but Xander's seemed freaked out, so I denied it for his sake. "I don't recall that."

He glared at Devlin. "You're lying so I won't do this."

"I'm not lying," Devlin insisted. "Too many neural pathways are forming too fast and it's wreaking havoc on her brain."

"That wouldn't cause a seizure. It could have been sleep deprivation or nutrient imbalances. Neuron stimulation is what we want. Developing pathways are strengthening her memory."

"It's too risky. Both of you need to slow down."

Xander straightened. He looked away, but then lunged at his brother. They were so close their noses almost touched. "This isn't about her safety. You want *me* to slow down and you're using her condition as a ploy to get me to agree."

Devlin's head dropped, and then he tugged at his chin like he wanted to pull off his own flesh. "Kramer is hacking through every firewall I build. I don't know how much longer I can keep him away."

My insides tangled. I had never wished death on anyone except Kramer.

After a long deflation of his chest, Xander said, "I'll stop him."

Devlin sounded so tired. "You can't. You're compromised, and so is your judgement."

"Xander?" I tugged the back of his tunic. "What does he mean you're compromised?"

"I'm fine." His intense gaze stayed locked on Devlin. "I'm doing it my way. It's the right thing to do. I feel it. She always told us to follow our instincts, so that's what I'm doing."

They silently stared at each other for so long that I thought maybe it was another frozen scene, but then as if in a duel, they both whipped up their hands at the same time. They typed and swiped their bands faster than I'd ever seen either of them move.

Lines of light sliced through Devlin. He flickered in and out of existence as his broken voice shouted, "Xander, don't!"

Then he vanished and Xander lowered his arm.

"What the fritz just happened?" I asked.

"I didn't hurt anything except his ego. I know you much better than he does. I know what's best for you."

They had been battling to control me. The quickest one administered which scenario I experienced next. Had they been doing this the entire time? "Maybe *I* know what's best for me. Did either of you ever stop to think about that?"

"Yes." He tucked a curl behind my ear. The simple but familiar gesture calmed me. "Which is exactly why I'm doing this the way you wanted."

"Me? I wanted this?"

"The conversation we were having before Devlin interrupted, what was it about?"

I glanced out at the city then back at Xander. "It was my first time up here with you. When you told me how you became part of the Arcana."

He brushed his knuckles against my hand. "Which version do you remember?"

"You told me you were chosen."

He leaned on the wall, staring out at the city lights. "The fictional one."

"I don't understand. What's the real one?"

He inhaled deeply, then his face blurred, creating multiple versions of himself. I reached out to touch them, but they merged back together into one solid form. I felt as if the same disorienting process had happened to me.

What he said next made me lower my hand.

"You said you help people live. Really live." He turned and motioned to the majors socializing under the dome far behind us. "This is what you meant."

I rested my elbows on the wall beside his and stared out at the nation filled with people I so passionately wanted to free. "Yes."

"How did you learn about all of this?" he asked me.

"Would it sound cliché if I said I was chosen?"

"It would sound like something from a fantasy novel, so I approve."

I suppressed a grin. "Good because I was chosen."

His chin lowered, and he smirked in an adorable, humble way. "By whom?"

I gazed up at an extremely bright star. "A brilliant soul from the outside world who strongly believes in getting as many people out of Equatia as possible before . . . the catastrophe."

"What's going to happen?"

My heart ached at the thought of the impending tragedy. "Equatia will destroy itself, and anyone left within its cage."

"How?"

"That part I don't know, but I trust my source, so I'm doing my part to save as many as I can."

He leaned closer, his eyes gleaming between his dark lashes. "If all of this is true, then you won't just be a magician. You'll be a hero."

I laughed. "I'll never be a magician or a hero, but thanks for the compliment."

A few quiet breaths passed before he said, "I need to tell Devlin and my parents. I won't go without them."

"Tell Devlin first. We can't involve your parents yet."

"Why?"

"It's one of those instances where you're going to have to trust me."

He stared at the majors, a new understanding causing a worried frown. "How much time is left?"

Sadness rippled through me. "Not enough."

I splintered into two, maybe even three or four, versions of myself. I turned my head and my vision lagged, creating tracers. The dizziness made me nauseated.

Xander squeezed my arms, grounding me back into the present. I felt like one solid person again.

The sick feeling subsided until he said, "All of this, it was you. You recruited me."

"What? No. That's impossible."

He held my face in his hands. "You were the genius behind everything you've thought was mine. They mind-stripped you, but you had prepared for it. You created a memory retraining program so you could restore yourself. You designed multiple programs to trigger every suit of your being: cups, wands, swords, and pentacles."

I didn't know what to say. All I could do was stare at him as his claims ricocheted through my psyche.

"You've been calling me your magician," he continued. "But it was you, Kelsey. You were the magician. This was all your idea, your doing, your magic. *You* are the trump."

At first I just stuttered incoherently, but then I managed to find my voice. "I would have no idea how to pull off something like this."

"Maybe not right now, but you used to. Before they mind-stripped you."

I shook my head, but he nodded insistently.

"Didn't parts feel a little too familiar?" he asked. "Wasn't our connection stronger than it should have been upon first meeting me? Your feelings grew too intensely, too quickly? It's because you were reliving programs created from real-life experiences and memories that had already happened. We already knew each other."

Something had always felt off, and now I was beginning to understand. "But why like this? Why didn't I experience it the way it really happened?"

"We tried that. It didn't work. Per your directions, we changed your point of view to see if we'd get better results. In the latest version, you played the recruit. The mission of the Arcana had to impact you in a new way."

"You told me you only switched roles when you were desperate."

"We were desperate."

I rewound my mental clip until I reached the day I met Xander. "You never gave me The Fool card?"

"No. *I* was new to town. Because of Devlin's VR addiction, our family was issued relocation to Elura. You recruited me. You worked at the library. *You* taught *me* about the Arcana. You made me a believer."

Part of me was dumfounded, but the other part wondered how I didn't already figure it out on my own.

He held my hand and pressed it against his chest. "Does anything I'm saying ring true?"

"Sort of."

"Good." He smiled. "Then it's working."

"How can you be sure?"

"Because the last time we tried telling you the truth, you adamantly said no. And the time before that you violently defended that it was all one big lie of a story that we tried brainwashing you with."

"What? I was violent? With you?"

"Not me." He smirked. "But you broke Awol's nose."

I gasped. "I did?"

I felt awful and ashamed. She had always been so good to me. I'd have to apologize as soon as I saw her again. "Why didn't you guys ditch me? I was damaged government goods."

"The key word being *goods.* We weren't just trying to restore your memories. We were also deprogramming the lies Kramer and his kibz loaded into you." He tucked a curl behind my ear. "I could never ditch you. I believe in you. Nothing can ever change that. Whether you love me, forget me, deny I exist, or lead me into oblivion, I won't ever give up on you."

How could I ever do anything except love him? "You're talking like I might revert back to not remembering any of this."

"Because it's a possibility. On a couple occasions you made progress, but the knowledge didn't stick. That's why we repeat important scenarios over and over, hoping if we do it enough, those memories will become a permanent part of your brain map again."

"I don't want to forget this. What can I do to help it last?"

"We have to keep doing what's been working—letting you relive the important moments."

"I agree. But this time, I want the real program. I want to experience the past the way it truly happened. No adjustments. Is there a program like that?"

He pulled an access card from his pocket.

I took the card from him and held it in the palm of my hand. "It's like you know me better than I know myself."

"Currently, I do." He stepped back. "Ready or not."

"No. This time, I'm ready."

Level 6.8

Dad leaned too close to the screen as usual. "Stick to the plan. The decoy chips are more powerful than Equatia's originals."

"Listen, lovebug," Mom said tenderly from beside him. "Something has occurred that requires a change of plans."

"Not now," Dad grunted.

"She needs to know." Mom shouldered him aside. "We don't keep secrets from each other."

"What happened?" I asked.

Mom pressed her hands together in her signature prayer position. My stomach flipped because it meant the news was serious. "Nathaniel passed away."

My heart sank to my feet and crashed through the Ark's floor. "No."

She rocked forward like she momentarily forgot she couldn't hug me. "He went peacefully, but obviously this changes the plan."

Nathaniel wasn't just family, he was the exemplar by which I set my standards for all guys. Besides the personal grief, the realization that we no longer had a safe carrier rumbled through me like an earthquake. "How will you send me supplies?"

"That's just it. We won't be able to send you more."

"Until I figure out a new solution," Dad added optimistically. "I will transport them myself if needed."

"No," I insisted. "It's too dangerous. Officials know the borders have been penetrated. They just don't know how yet. They're on high alert."

"We know." Mom sighed. "They've globally broadcasted unbelievable threats. The whole world is on edge."

Equatia was the only nation in decades that had threatened war. My head fell into my hands. This couldn't be happening.

Dad tried sounding undaunted. "We continue with those already in the system, but the liberation may have to happen sooner than originally scheduled."

"But so many citizens aren't prepared yet," I argued. Panicking, I did the math. "If it were to happen today, we'd only save about twenty percent of the population."

Worry lines etched the somber truth around Mom's frown. "We will save every soul we possibly can. I promise."

Dad wrapped his arm around her while trying to comfort me with his ardent gaze. "Until I figure out a better solution, level up the Arcana training."

"And how am I supposed to get more cards?"

"You'll need help creating new ones," he said. "But don't risk crossing Elura's borders. Stay in your assigned location."

My eyes bugged. "You want me to trust a stranger to help me design cards?"

"The universe knows what it's doing," Mom said. "It will send you whatever, or whomever, you need."

"Remember," Dad warned me, "no more contacting us through your band. Equatia has upgraded their monitoring systems. Only use the Ark's secure signal."

"Understood." I couldn't believe Nathaniel had passed away. I felt like a heartless, self-centered brat for not asking sooner. "How's Mary holding up?"

"She's strong as ever," Mom assured me. "She's no stranger to the loss of loved ones."

"Still," I said. "It must be heartbreaking."

"She knows they'll be together soon."

My pulse quickened. "Please tell her I said not too soon. I need her help more than ever."

"She knows that. She won't desert you."

"We'll talk again soon, lovebug." Mom pressed her hand flat against the screen and so did Dad. "We believe in you."

I pressed my hands to theirs. "I believe in you too."

The screen went black. I rolled my chair away from the desk. "Glitch."

I wasn't the only manumitter hiding within Equatia's walls, training its citizens for the biggest prison break the world has ever seen, but at the moment, sitting alone in the Ark, I sure felt like it.

I needed fresh air and coffee. I need to people-watch so I could remind myself of all the innocents we were trying to save.

Twenty minutes later, I sat in the pilot seat of my craft, in the parking lot of Caffeine Machine. I stared at the ominous city skyline stretched out in front of me, imagining what it might look like on liberation day.

Mom was confident the universe would send me the help I needed, and she was rarely wrong, but when? And what would that help be?

I pulled M's tarot cards from my bag and shuffled the deck.

"What's in the cards?" I asked her, sensing her watching over me. "Who can you send to help?"

I selected four cards, one to represent each of the four suits, and laid them face down on the passenger seat. "Guide and enlighten me."

I flipped them over one at a time: *The Fool, The Magician, The Lovers, The World.*

"Well," I muttered. "If that isn't a full circle reading then I don't know what is."

I was interrupted by someone knocking on my window.

I looked left. Standing between my craft and another was a dark-haired guy with kind hazel eyes and a steaming cup clutched in his hand. He pointed at the roof of my craft. "Your coffee."

I lowered my window, and even though I had heard him, I asked again because his voice was inviting. "What?"

He reached up, grabbed my drink, and gave it to me. His fingers pressed over mine during the hand-off.

In ultra-slow motion a spark of excitement made me tingle because the guy smiling at me was totally my type. My type wasn't the hot model or jock, but the much more hard to find subtle sort of attractive, radiating intelligence and confidence with no hint of ego.

Time seemed to return to normal speed as I realized we were both still holding my latte. He bashfully grinned and said, "You forgot something."

"Many thanks," I said, trying not to blush. "Losing my coffee would have started my day off horribly."

He wriggled his fingers free from mine and let go. "I wouldn't wish that sort of tragedy on my worst enemy."

"Xander!" Another dark-haired guy shouted from the driver's seat. "Come on. We'll be late!"

He offered a quick wave and turned to go, but I asked, "Are you new around here?"

"Moved into town yesterday." He grimaced as his passenger door squeaked open.

"On your way to Century High?"

He raised his cup. "Indeed, I am. My first day swimming with the sharks. May the odds be ever in my favor."

I laughed. "Based on your quote, I assume you enjoy reading the classics."

"Guilty."

"What's your favorite novel?"

One side of his mouth turned upward. "Shouldn't you ask my name before you ask about my reading preferences?"

"Your name is Xander." I motioned to his brother behind him. "Which is probably short for Alexander, and that tells me that your parents, or at least one of them, prefers old-fashioned names. I'd much rather know the name of your favorite book because that will reveal volumes of information about *you.*"

"I've never been able to choose a favorite." His eyes gleamed with mischief. "I like variety."

I set the coffee in my cup holder and picked up The Fool card from my passenger seat. I handed it to him. "I'll see you around, Xander."

He took the card from me and glanced at the colorful artwork. "What's this?"

Little did he know he had just met a trump who could introduce him to a new world of infinite possibilities.

I silently thanked the universe for sending such an attractive new minor to be the help I needed. "That's step zero."

I struggled to sit up, dizzy, but determined. I patted my chest and arms, an old habit for confirming I had exited VR. Ignoring the urge to throw up, I pushed myself to my feet.

Devlin was gone. Good. He'd try to talk me out of what I was about to do.

Glancing at the four windows surrounding me, I saw only one was occupied.

Awol's eyes were wide, watching my every move. Her voice came over the speaker. "Kelsey, stay still. You need time to adjust."

Alternate World Sickness was awful, but I pushed through. I stumbled, but kept walking toward her. "Run KK-22–1."

My bare feet squeaking against the floor was the only sound for a long moment.

Awol's stunned voice came through again. "Kelsey?"

Licking my cracked lips, I forced a smile. The room tilted, and I swayed but kept myself upright. "I'm back. At least for the moment."

The color drained from her face as we stared at each other through the window. I pressed my hand flat against the glass. "Run my program before I forget how much I need my own help."

"But Xander and Devlin said—"

"They are suits and so are you." Exhaustion made it difficult to speak, but I managed to sound assertive. "I am the trump. Don't make me remind you that I outrank all of you."

She nodded and tossed her braids behind her shoulders. Reaching into a supply cabinet in her control room she asked, "Do you want to rehydrate first?"

My hand slid down the window. Physically, I was weak, but I couldn't risk losing my moment of mental clarity. I turned and faced the lonely immersion room. "Run it."

Beams of colors danced over the white walls. I pressed my fingers to my temple, feeling the edges of my secret tiny chip. And thanking the stars that it had worked.

Level 6.9

I stood in the center of the library and slowly spun in a circle. My library. My warehouse. My fortress.

The secret door on the top shelf opened. Keekee peered over the edge at me then climbed down the ladder.

"Keek?" *No.* I stopped myself. I couldn't fall back into my old thinking patterns.

She stood in front of me. Not she. Me. A duplicate version of myself.

"Well, you're here," she said. "Which means you're in a big bind."

"Can I talk to you?" I asked.

She didn't reply, just continued with her script. My script. "Xander and Devlin are talented, and you trust them with your life, but you've never been good at giving up total control. Besides, the cards revealed they could be compromised, and if you're here looking for me then that has already happened." She tapped her temple. "You need to be your own hero."

"How do I do that?"

"You're probably asking how do you do that." She strutted over to a bookshelf. "When you were a child, you read an ancient version of Little Red Riding Hood where she was eaten by the wolf. No one came to save her. The wolf got away with deception and murder. Great stars, how you hated that story." She ran her fingers along the spines with her head tilted. "Then you read another version, where the wolf still ate her, but a huntsman cut open the wolf's belly and saved Red." She stopped scanning titles and glanced up at the ceiling. "Mom and Aunt M tried making you feel better by explaining that it represented rebirth. But you never cared for that version either." She slid a book from its place on the shelf and held it in front of her. "So you wrote your own version."

"I did?"

She smiled in a way that was so confident, it bordered on wicked. I envied her, but she was me. Had I really been so sure of myself at some point? "This situation, this mess, it can turn out just like the story you wrote."

"How?"

"Tame the wolf. Be your own hunter. Save yourself. Create a happy ending."

I tried opening the cover, but my fingers moved through it. I glared at her. She didn't even take the time to thoroughly design a quality VR scenario? "So how do I do that?"

She hugged the book to her chest. "You have a few advantages over Red: your proverbial grandmother can always watch over you; your parents are exceptionally gifted and they prepared you well; you have family and friends that would risk everything for you; and, the best part, all those people I just mentioned believe in you to the stars and back. You can do this, Kelsey. I believe in you. Which means you believe in yourself."

My eyes sprang open.

I scanned the immersion room and saw the suits, my friends, watching me from their windows. Awol, Blaze, and Jag. Devlin stood in the room with me.

Worry and dread coursed through every part of my being because Xander wasn't present. I sat up, clutching my head in an attempt to make the room stop spinning. "Where is Xander?"

Devlin replied, "He's resting."

"Don't lie to me. Where is he?"

"I'm not lying. He is resting. And he desperately needs it. So do you."

"Stop telling me that." I pushed myself up to stand, but I stumbled sideways until I fell against Blaze's window.

"Careful, Kelsey," she said through the speaker. "Take it easy."

Devlin approached me. "I applaud your efforts, but why won't you listen to me?"

I licked my dry lips. "I know where I am. I just watched a message I left for myself before I was mind-stripped."

Devlin's eyes nearly doubled in size.

"I'm recovering," I continued. Everyone was staring at me. I pressed the back of my hand to my lips in an attempt to stop myself from throwing up, then glared at my bewildered audience. "Why hasn't anyone sent in a nutrient pac?"

Awol, Blaze, and Jag all startled, scrambling to send in help. Their delivery doors opened almost simultaneously as three bots rolled toward me. Blaze's reached me first. I looked at Devlin, hoping he'd hand it to me so I didn't have to move and make myself sicker. But like a selfish prick, he just stood there.

I bent down and grabbed the pac, dry-heaving as I stood up. My hands shook, but I ripped off the tab on my first try and chugged the drink.

Devlin watched me with his arms crossed over his chest.

"When did you become so unchivalrous?" I asked him. Weakly, I threw the empty pac at him, but it sailed right through his torso and hit the floor.

"Of course." I sighed and let my head fall back against the window behind me. He never touched me. He never touched anything. Not in any of my memories of the immersion room. Because he couldn't. "You're a hologram."

He smirked. "I'm still me. Try as they may, Equatia has no control of my soul."

"Where are you?" I asked, fearing his answer. "Where's your body?"

"You don't remember that part?"

"I'm recovering, Dev, but it's not an instant fix. I can't remember everything." Feeling slightly less sick, I slid down the wall and grabbed another nutrient pac from Jag's bot. I sipped the blue liquid, savoring the moisture in my mouth. "Tell me."

"You know me better than that. If you want to know my story, you'll have to live it."

I took another swig, exhausted by the thought of another scenario.

"Kelsey?" Awol's voice hummed through the ceiling speaker. "Drink some of my pac. You need emotional nourishment."

She was right. And her formula did taste best. I set down Jag's pac and reached for Awol's bot. The pomegranate drink was sweet, but having consumed three of the four suit flavors, it made me painfully aware of the one I was missing. Pentacles. Xander's.

My focus locked on Devlin. "You have to tell me where he is. As the trump of this mission, I demand it."

He looked away then gruffly said, "It's a whole other complicated story."

"I gave you an order."

Devlin bowed his head. "But I made a promise to my brother. I'm sorry, but that *trumps* my loyalty to you."

I pushed myself to stand up straight and purposefully made eye contact with each of the other suits. "Are any of you going to tell me where he is?"

Awol answered somberly, "We all made the same promise."

Jag's voice came through the speaker. "We can't tell you, but he never said we couldn't show you."

Devlin's head snapped around to look at Jag, but Jag kept his eyes on me. A sly grin spread across his face.

I circled my finger in the air. "Jag, Awol, Blaze, load me with everything I need to know. Devlin, we're doing this with or without you."

"It's too much," he warned, but this time with minimal conviction. "The emotional damage alone could revert you back to empty."

"You've been saying that a lot lately, yet here I am overriding an impossible mind-strip procedure. That makes me right, and you wrong."

Jag proudly shouted, "Did you hear that? That's all swords, ladies and gents!"

"No," Blaze corrected. "That's her fiery spirit resurfacing. Thanks to wands."

"Wrong," Awol sang. "That's her deep love for Xander. Cups at its finest."

"Maybe you're all right," Devlin said. "But Xander triggered her sense of home, and that's the breakthrough that worked. I think we owe this leap forward to pentacles."

I finished the rest of Awol's drink then stood tall. I squared off, facing Devlin. "And as trump, I'm ordering you to do whatever it takes to keep Kramer and his floaters out of my system until this is over."

"How will we know when it's over?"

"When I destroy Kramer, bring Xander home, and complete my mission."

Devlin lowered his gaze. "Fair warning, one of those is impossible, and the other two would be miracles."

I leaned forward, whispering into his hologram ear. "Where I come from, miracles are common, and nothing is impossible."

I motioned to Awol, Blaze, and Jag. "Run every version of every card until I figure out how to give all of us the happily-ever-afters we deserve."

ACKNOWLEDGEMENTS

To the “suits” in my everyday life: Mom, Dad, and John. Thanks for supporting me and my addiction to creating storyholes.

Becca Zeno, thanks for having the conversation with me that started the idea for *Virtual Arcana*, and for being such an inspiration in so many ways.

Steve Graham, you worked wonders with the cards, artwork, and covers (original and new). Thanks for making my virtual visions a reality.

Marie Jaskulka, you are a stellar editor and a cherished friend. Hurry up and release another book so I can mention it in *Virtual Override*.

Megan McBride, thanks for still reading my stuff after all these years, and for motivating me at our writing retreats. When is our next one?

Natalie Bahm, your vital critiques from all of my previous books were a ghost program running in the background of this story. Thank you.

To the “majors” who supported *Virtual Arcan*a in its experimental serial stage. In no particular order—I love you all: Amy Bosica, Sarah Quick, Marianne Robles, Jennifer Madero, Jessica Nicole, Lollita Sampson, Marianna Krasnoshtein, Veray Carter, Yara Reca-Vargas, Katarina Ortmann, Susan Schleicher, Elien Maurien, Tania Radcliffe, Christina Petersen, Jenna DeTrapani, Carly Mojica, and Beth Leneberg...you gals kept me going with your feedback and encouragement. Thank you for believing in me.

Finally, as always, thank *you,* reader. I appreciate you more than you know.

OTHER BOOKS BY KAREN

The Kindrily Series
(Reincarnation, soul mates, & supernatural powers.)

#1- *Grasping at Eternity*

#2- *Taking Back Forever*

#3- *Fighting for Infinity*

The Sea Monster Memoirs
(Merfolk, selkies, sirens, gorgons, & mythology.)

#1- *Tangled Tides*

#2- *Dangerous Depths*

#3- *Sacred Seas*

ABOUT THE AUTHOR

Karen was born and bred in Baltimore, frolicked and froze in Colorado for a couple of years, and is currently sunning and splashing around Florida with her two beloved rescue dogs. She's addicted to coffee, chocolate, and complicated happily-ever-afters. She is a co-founder of the teen-focused blog, YA Confidential, and a proud member of The Indelibles.

Sign up for Karen's newsletter to receive updates on new releases and to be entered in exclusive contests, including signed books.

www.KarenAmandaHooper.com

www.ingramcontent.com/pod-product-compliance
Lightning Source LLC
Chambersburg PA
CBHW030420310726
48979CB00009B/1549/J
9780996147002